A VIOLENT LIFE

A JIMMY BLUE NOVEL

IAN W. SAINSBURY

For Murray and MH
Thanks for getting me started. And the great chats. And for the whisky.
Could have done without the haggis, though.

NOTE

A Violent Life is set four years before the events of Winter Falls, and Jimmy Blue's revenge on the criminals who executed Tom Lewis's parents when he was a child.

CHAPTER ONE

BAVARIA, Germany

He sprints across the clearing barefoot in the darkness, holding his breath. He doesn't take a direct route, instead swerving left and right, using the shadows of the towering spruce that dot the exposed space. The Germans call these areas *schacten;* clearings in the forest sea. The watery metaphor seems apt as the freezing, boggy water squelches between his toes.

The natural beauty of his surroundings isn't entirely lost on him. At some level, the immense forests, the untouched Bavarian mountains, and the animals and birds that call them home still have the power to stun him. He has run alongside silent barn owls, heard woodpeckers type their life stories on a thousand trees, watched a lynx mother carry one of her young across a stream in its mouth while black kites circled high above.

The *schacten's* cold, ethereal grandeur bears witness to the most dangerous few seconds of his mission.

Because he holds his breath during the explosive lunge across the clearing, he hears the sound that doesn't fit before seeing the movement. He knows it means danger. Immediate danger. Small animals move in the undergrowth, but they do so with a burst of scurrying prompted by his arrival. The other sound is uncommon, less hurried. It starts half a second after he breaks cover. Something pushes leaves and twigs aside as it tracks his motion. A gun barrel.

He drops and rolls, registering the smack of the shot on the bark of a tree five yards away. Two enemies remain. It's possible they are both here, but unlikely. The final approach to the lodge offers some choice spots for an enemy to pick him off, and Anton will surely wait there.

Putting a tree between himself and the shooter, he stops, evaluates the options. Makes a decision. Instead of seeking cover, he sprints directly towards the shooter's position.

When he reaches the tree that shields him from his enemy, he climbs it in seconds, making the canopy and disappearing into the darkness of the evergreen's dense branches. He doesn't register the pine needles piercing skin as his cold, sap-covered toes find grip in the gnarled bark.

He lets out his breath slowly, evenly, and silently.

Below, his enemy is keen to press a perceived advantage, just as he'd hoped. He recognises Marcus, dark features smeared with mud to stop the skin reflecting as he moves. Marcus holds his gun ready as he nears the tree, knowing his quarry might be hiding behind it. Marcus is a clever and dangerous opponent. But not as clever or dangerous as the man watching him from the branches above.

Marcus scoops up a handful of stones and lobs them to his right. At the exact moment they hit the ground, the armed man dodges left fast, willing to sacrifice silence for surprise.

Now. Jimmy Blue doesn't jump. He drops from the branches, and Marcus doesn't know anything is wrong until a patch of dark sky gets darker still. He reacts, but there is nothing he can do to prevent the heavier man landing on him, his weight bringing them both crashing to the ground.

The pinned enemy tries to dislodge Blue by rolling. He is a talented and athletic fighter, but the weight discrepancy is too great, and his shoulder hangs awkwardly, dislocated by the impact with the tree roots.

Jimmy Blue brings his hand to his enemy's throat. Marcus slumps in defeat.

"You won't make it. No one ever has."

Blue smiles. "Someone has to be the first."

The clouds part long enough for the stars to give the scene some light. In one swift, decisive motion, he draws his hand across Marcus's throat. A dark line appears.

There's a metallic click behind him.

No.

Only one person could have got that close without him being aware. He shouldn't have allowed himself to be guided by his assumptions. Blue had been so sure the final challenge would come back at the lodge.

He turns and looks into the barrel of a gun. "Maybe," says Anton, his face an impassive mask. "But not tonight."

The barrel dips and fires. At point-blank range, even a pellet from an air pistol stings when fired into a bulletproof vest.

Anton holsters his weapon.

"You lose."

Jimmy re-caps the pen he used to draw the line on Marcus's throat and accepts the hand the older man offers, pulling himself to his feet.

He doesn't offer Marcus the same courtesy.

CHAPTER TWO

DESPITE THE STUDENTS not reaching their sleeping mats until two a.m., they are back in the exercise yard at six.

Routines, claims Anton, are important. Minds and bodies respond well to timetabled training. In the specialist workplace where his students hope to find employment, periods of inactivity are common. Some use those periods to relax, take vacations, or pursue romantic trysts. Time enough for that when you retire, suggests Anton, before reminding them that, statistically, only two of the nine students present will live long enough to claim a pension.

Anton is not blessed with a sunny disposition. He is the best trainer of warriors in Europe. He won't call them soldiers, agents, or spies, although that's what most of them are. His concept of the warrior, which he never explains fully to his students, informs everything he says and does. At sixty-one years old, no student has ever bettered him in physical combat, and the rumours suggest he has killed at least twenty people with his bare hands.

If he wants to call his programme the warrior school, no one is going to argue.

As always, Anton leads the exercises. They are similar to t'ai chi, and stem from the same ancient root, but the movements depart from anything traditional after the first six postures. The yard falls silent as the participants commit mind and body to each pose. It is winter, and the space is dark, lit only by weak lamplight. The cold would be noticeable in wool sweaters and overcoats, but the students, five men and four women, exercise in their underwear. No one shivers.

The final twenty-five minutes are a series of flowing movements requiring strength, flexibility, patience, and—beyond all—an ability to transcend or ignore pain.

To an observer, this might be a course designed for masochists. The first fall, onto the left shoulder, might seem accidental until repeated for the right. On both occasions, the master's and students' heads hit the cold dirt floor of the yard with a smack.

The same hypothetical observer would look on with concern, then fascination, as the warriors continue cycling through the movements, a sheen of sweat prickling their cold skin. The routine repeats every two and a half minutes, with no break. It might be the toughest interval training imaginable, were it not for the lack of intervals.

Only a handful of the candidates who attend Anton's school each year make it through the winter.

Twenty-one arrived in late November. It's February now. Next week, the nine who made it return to the countries, agencies, or corporations that sent them.

Only one arrived without a sponsor. A few years older than the rest, the man Anton calls Decretas showed up with no identification, one change of clothes, and the name of the school's most successful graduate on his lips.

Anton names his students after characters in Shakespeare plays. This year, it's *Antony and Cleopatra*. Decretas is a minor character, one of Antony's officers. Almost nothing is known about him. It suits this bald stranger well.

When the morning's exercises conclude, Anton observes Decretas during the ten-minute period of standing meditation. The big man's shaved head shines with sweat, and the scars above his left eye redden. The scars are old, probably gained in childhood. His body is large and well-muscled, but his speed in combat belies the disadvantages of his substantial frame. In seventeen years on the mountain, teaching the very best, Decretas is the only student who came close to defeating him. On that occasion, three days earlier, Anton hid his astonishment, but now he relives the moment when his jab to the ribs missed its target, and he walked into a cupped-hand blow that would have finished him had he not twisted his head away.

Anton realises he is indulging in reverie when he should allow his thoughts to appear and disappear unhindered by his attention. He looks at Decretas. The green eyes are open and staring straight at him.

———

After the session, Anton holds back three students. After the others have filed out, they sit, legs crossed in half lotus: silent. As the yard becomes still, he examines his own motivations for what he is about to do.

Scarus, Octavia, and Pompey are the best of this year's crop. Or they would be, if not for Decretas. The taciturn Britisher is head and shoulders above the rest. This has never happened before. And it's a problem.

Those who make it this far arrive convinced of their talent and their strength. They are already the elite. Surviving the Bavarian winter with Anton confirms their position as apex predators.

But, in the mountains, they are nothing. It is Anton's job to remind them of this. All of them learn the hard way during training, when offered the opportunity to test their skills against the teacher in unarmed combat. By the time these bouts take place, Anton has studied each student. Not so he can exploit their weaknesses. No. He studies them to decide how best to humiliate them.

Some need to be taken down quickly, brutally, their egos crushed by the ease in which this man—old enough to be their grandfather—sidesteps their attack and, with one punch, renders them defenceless. The most aggressive among them sometimes warrant a long, drawn-out humiliation, allowing them an opportunity to exhaust every move in their repertoires; frustration and rage building as the old man dances away from their kicks, rides their punches, or contrives not to be where they think he should be.

Anton left Decretas's bout for last. It is hard to humiliate a man who gives so little away. It isn't as if the other students are sociable. They avoid each other outside meals and training because they know they might find a fellow student in the cross hairs of their sniper rifle one day. But, compared to Decretas, they are gregarious party animals.

And, although Decretas did not end his bout with Anton unhurt, he certainly left it without humility. He returned to his quarters as confident in his abilities as when he left them. It was Anton who lay awake that night, profoundly shaken.

Afterwards, Anton made some calls—the first time he has ever resorted to such a measure—but they shed little light on the scarred man's provenance. He may not even be British. His accent, on the few occasions when he opens his mouth, suggests he comes from London, but it could be a smokescreen. He paid in gold; he is a dutiful student, and a previous graduate sent him, but Anton is still uncomfortable. His discomfort surprises and dismays him a little, for it betrays a shortcoming in his own mental fortitude. He should be able to live with the mystery, not probe it in search of clues.

The man's origin aside, there is still the problem of his hubris. Decretas keeps his manner deferential. But no one can display such dominance without becoming arrogant.

If Decretas leaves the warrior school without defeat, Anton will have failed him. At least, this is what the teacher tells himself when he gives Scarus, Octavia, and Pompey their instructions.

CHAPTER THREE

JIMMY BLUE KNOWS THE SIGNS; the unconscious tells, the tiny movements of the face, the tension in the body. Octavia is good at hiding her intentions, but she's not perfect.

"Pigpen," she says, standing in his doorway. None of the rooms have doors.

It's late afternoon; already dark outside. Blue is lying on the bed, eyes half-closed. Anton works his students hard and often springs surprises when they are off duty. A thirty-mile hike, a ten-mile run, free climbing an escarpment in the freezing rain. Best to take your rest when you can.

He nods, swivels his body, and puts on his boots. Octavia is her usual unsmiling self. She has an ability to give herself entirely to whatever she is doing that Jimmy admires. No one talks about where they are from, or why they are here, but he trusts his gut, which tells him Octavia is a prodigy of the Institute, Israel's secret service. Mossad. She is ruthless in training bouts, exploiting her flexibility to deliver flowing attacks of such ferocity and speed that they're often over within the first half minute.

He follows her down the long corridor. Octavia lifts the heavy-duty torch from its hook, shoulders open the door, and leads the way outside to the pen. It's dark and cold. A light rain patters on the gravel drive.

Anton's warrior school is based in an old farmhouse. There are three outbuildings. One, a big barn, houses the vehicles. A second is a wood store. Students who arrive during the summer spend their afternoons chopping wood and stacking the logs inside. The third building is the pigpen. If it ever did house animals, no evidence of their presence remains. It's a small barn, its wooden double doors kept closed and barred. Students enter using a side door. Inside, the bare concrete floor is lit by six bulbs hanging at intervals from the high roof.

Whatever purpose the pigpen might once have served, its only purpose now is as a student arena. Anton pointed it out on the tour he gave when they first arrived. "My jurisdiction ends on this side of that door. If you need to prove something to yourself or anyone else, invite your opponent to the pigpen. One-on-one only. No death matches. Only I may kill students." No one thought he was joking.

"Wait." Blue calls out to Octavia before she reaches the door. She stops. "Why me?" he says.

Jimmy Blue and Octavia have not argued. In fact, he suspects she approves of his silent focus because it mirrors her own approach to training. No one comes to Anton's school to forge friendships, but human beings are social animals, and young men and women thrown together for months form bonds, gravitate into groups, tribes. Other than Blue, Octavia is the only student who resists, remaining aloof, keeping her own counsel.

"It is my right."

Factually correct. Any student can challenge another, and no challenge can be refused. But Octavia is hiding something. He looks at her in the light cast from the torch. She holds his gaze, doesn't look away for a few seconds. Too long. A liar wouldn't look away, overcompensating by being direct.

She doesn't lie well. Mossad will have to work on that.

Jimmy considers what waits for him, now that he knows he's being set up. The empty bed he saw was Pompey's, a squat Slovakian who excels at wrestling. Of his fellow students, Pompey and Octavia are the best fighters along with Scarus, a Russian with the wiry build of a mountain climber; an intelligent opponent who employs mixed martial arts to win his bouts.

Anton is behind this, Blue realises. The teacher's ritual humiliation of his student didn't go to plan when they fought. This is his solution. In which case, Scarus is likely to be present as well. Three-on-one. As close to a guarantee of success as possible. Even with Jimmy's skills, he isn't superhuman. Under most circumstances, if he enters the pigpen, he knows this is a fight he will lose.

Refusing a challenge means expulsion from the school. This isn't a problem. He is ready to move on. But he wants something from Anton first.

If he hopes to prevail, he needs to change the circumstances in order to alter the outcome. No weapons are allowed inside. This might be another rule they've chosen to break, but he doubts it. Three against one should be a massacre. No weapons necessary.

Blue visualises the pigpen. No light spills from the cracks in the wood, so anyone inside waits in darkness. The light switch is on the wall, shoulder height, two feet from the door. His opponents think they have surprise on their side, but they know he will be quick to react when he sees them. Their best plan is to hit him hard and fast. The door opens inward, blocking any approach from the left. And the torch will illuminate anyone directly in front. The right, then. Pompey, crouching, ready to bring Blue to the ground, using his lower centre of gravity to his advantage. Yes. Then Octavia would turn on the lights and they would have him.

There's a spade leaning against the wall outside.

"After you," says Octavia, twisting the door handle and pushing the door open with her foot. It swings inward as Jimmy steps forward.

When he's alongside Octavia, he puts his hand out for the torch. "It might qualify as a weapon. Don't want to break the rules, do we?"

She nods, but doesn't give it to him. Instead, she turns it off and tosses it to one side. The sudden darkness means she only registers as an outline against the greater darkness inside.

"Go on," she says, but Blue is already moving, giving her vision no time to adjust. He sidesteps, puts his hands on her shoulder and back, and pushes, hard. She flies through the open doorway, loses her footing and falls, curling into a roll. As she rolls, Blue grabs the spade, steps inside with it swinging, and registers the satisfying shock that travels down the handle when the mud-encrusted flat of the blade meets human flesh. A grunt of shock, then someone backs away out of range. Jimmy doesn't follow, instead reaching out to the light switch on the wall. He finds it, hoists the spade up, and sends the blade into the wall above, severing the electric cables.

He pivots and uses the spade to slam the door closed. Then he stands with his back against it, and waits, listening.

The darkness is absolute. He grins.

———

The fight lasts forty-seven seconds. During it, Blue notes he has mastered restraint.

He walks into the pigpen. Four paces. Slow. Silent. He listens. The darkness speaks to him, unfolds, offers its secrets. Wooden rafters creak, stretching or contracting in the cold.

His understanding of darkness comes before conscious thought. He is home.

The three opponents are as clear as if they were waving glow sticks, screaming "I'm over here."

Scarus is the most obvious. He is five feet to Blue's left, and six feet above, perched in the rafters. The trio's plan becomes obvious. Pompey's attack from the right was intended to knock Blue off balance, sending him towards the waiting Scarus, who would drop on him. A flurry of kicks from Octavia, while Pompey pinned Blue down, leaving Scarus to employ some of the more vicious martial arts moves.

Their plan is already in tatters, and Jimmy is a master at improvisation. All three of his opponents react to the new situation. There's no coordination. In the dark, they have lost their ability to communicate non-verbally, and to speak would be to reveal their positions. They fear him. They are right to. But they think they have the advantage. They are focusing on the numbers. Three of them, one of him. Yes. One of him, filled with the darkness that came before light, life, and civilisation. He is Jimmy Blue.

He could kill them all.

Restraint.

Patience.

Scarus has a cold and cannot prevent the rattle of phlegm as he breathes. Pompey is quieter, but a scuff of feet signals he's on the move. Octavia is smarter. She came out of her roll twelve feet from the door. She is keeping her breaths slow, and she's listening.

Octavia is the one who fights with the most intelligence. He needs to deal with her first.

Blue walks directly towards the Israeli, his footsteps accelerating. He does not try to conceal the sound. He wants her to know he's coming. It's a direct attack, leaving her with few options. She can evade, roll to one side. She can use Blue's momentum, sending him over her with a double-footed lift. Or she can try to end this now with a roundhouse kick. She plumps for the middle option, as Blue assumed she would. He's nearly double her weight, so turning that advantage against him is the smart play.

The moment after he hears her shift position, dropping to the floor, he stops dead. Octavia's legs are curled, ready to power themselves into his stomach, and it's too late to change her mind. She's committed, at the mercy of gravity. When she hears him stop, she stays in her tuck and tries to roll out of reach.

Octavia's ankle is where Blue expects it to be. She grunts and twists away when he grabs it, but her balance is off. Before she can defend herself, he brings his booted foot down on the back of her knee, sending it into the concrete floor. The angle is unfortunate, and the knee breaks messily, the surrounding tendons stretching then snapping.

Octavia's brain, on receiving the bad news from her right leg, opts to shut down. She slumps, unconscious.

Pompey responds fast. Jimmy's attack has revealed his position, and the wrestler wants to get in close. He closes in on the spot where his enemy should be standing. His momentary confusion at finding no one there doesn't last long. Blue drops onto him, his jump perfectly timed. His elbow, braced across his chest, hits Pompey's neck, driving his face into the floor.

The crunch and snap of crushed cartilage is followed by a laboured, wet gargle as the man tries to breathe. Jimmy rolls Pompey onto his side to prevent him choking on blood and broken teeth.

Only Scarus remains. Blue can't hear him over the sound of Pompey's gasping, liquid wheezes.

Scarus probably believes Blue doesn't know he's there. Perhaps he thinks he can salvage this disaster, bring down Jimmy Blue, gain the respect of his teacher and the fear of his fellow students.

Or, speculates Blue as he walks towards the door, perhaps not. He hears no movement in the rafters. At the doorway, Blue pauses. Scarus is close. He listens to him breathe, a wavering quality to each exhalation. Scarus is afraid.

Blue leaves the pigpen and pulls the door closed. Waits.

It's a full two minutes before Scarus finds the courage to go for help. When the door opens, Jimmy's punch snaps his head sideways with such force that it tears tendons in his neck that have only just healed from a car crash six months earlier.

Blue prods the unconscious man with his boot. Picks up the torch from the frozen ground. Heads for the shower block. Before undressing, he sighs and returns to the main building.

Outside the dining hall, he leans on a button marked *Medic* until Franz, one of Anton's staff, appears.

The old German looks at Jimmy in mute inquiry. Blue jerks a thumb towards the outbuildings.

"Pigpen. Three of them."

Franz looks doubtful, but something in the other man's face makes him swallow his questions. Instead, he takes out his phone.

"Bring the van. And three stretchers."

CHAPTER FOUR

"ENTER."

Anton does not look up when the student walks in, but notes the tension in his own body. He recognises the stride pattern of the footsteps.

Anton forces his jaw and shoulders to relax, knowing the man standing three feet from his desk will notice any deviation from the norm.

Custom dictates that a student never speaks first. His visitor ignores the custom.

"I am leaving today."

It is one of the longer sentences Anton has heard from the British warrior. The old German keeps his eyes on his notes and reaches across the mahogany desk to top up an earthenware cup with black tea. He does not offer any to his student. Neither does he offer him a seat. The only chair in Anton's office is his own. The respectful distance between teacher and student is significant; the routines of his school designed to reinforce its importance. Those who come to him are strong-minded to the point of sociopathy. They all display levels of determination and inner strength well above average. It is an easily exploited weakness. But not with this man.

He puts down his pen and looks up. Decretas has not wiped the blood from his hands, leaving it to dry on his knuckles.

"If you leave now, you will not graduate."

"I have learned all I can from you."

In anyone else, this would be an example of the innate sense of superiority Anton strives to extinguish in his students. There is always someone better, someone stronger. Always. This grain of humility gives the warrior an advantage over opponents who lack it.

In Decretas, the sense of superiority is not arrogance. It is a matter of fact. Both men know it.

Anton brushes imaginary dirt from his forearm. Poise is everything.

"Have you forgotten that I defeated you in our bout?"

"I have not. You won. But your victory owed nothing to your fighting skills."

"No?" Anton keeps his tone colourless, wondering where this conversation is heading.

"No. Your advantage is not physical."

Decretas leaves that statement hanging. Anton bites.

"Then my advantage is mental?"

Decretas is still smiling. "No. I would not say that."

Fascinating. Anton experiences a frisson of unease. The student has observed the teacher as closely as the teacher observed the student. He thinks back to the test two nights ago. He had confronted Decretas in the clearing rather than the lodge, the first time he had broken his routine in twenty years. Why? The answer is obvious, albeit unpalatable. He feared this student might succeed where no one else ever had. And he almost did, despite the extra precautions.

Every student must break. No exceptions. Which is why he arranged last night's beating. And yet this man prevailed against three of the best.

Anton is afraid of him. Dismayed by this knowledge, he keeps his face impassive. "Then what *would* you say, Decretas?"

That smile is unnerving. It lends the student's features a strange cast, difficult to analyse. It reminds Anton of something, but he's not sure what. Then he has it. In his early twenties, Anton disturbed a brown bear shepherding her cubs across a stream. The animal eyed him for the longest three seconds of his life, before trotting back to her family.

Decretas has the same manner. The confidence of a natural predator. The student speaks again, and Anton senses the student-teacher dynamic shift.

"I need another teacher. The one that taught you how to become... absent?"

"Absent?" Anton's skin prickles, but he shows nothing.

"I cannot find a better word. The gap between thought and action, between decision and implementation. You sometimes avoid this. In our bout, near the end, there was no thought, only action."

"Correct action," mutters Anton. The bigger man nods.

Anton stands up. "I am your teacher. You quit, I dismiss you, or you graduate."

"There is nothing else I can learn here."

Although it sounds like an insult, Anton knows it is not. It is a fact, stated without malice.

"I cannot teach you what you ask."

"Tell me who can."

Anton looks the younger man in the eye. No one has ever asked this question. Then again, no one has ever guessed the reason for Anton's undefeated record in unarmed combat.

Decretas, he thinks, would make a poor student for his old teacher. This young man wants to learn what cannot be taught, and, despite a self-mastery unusual for his years, there is also rage, and a bleak, implacable hatred. Anton does not want to help him. But he made a promise. If a potential student emerges, he has to send them.

"She will not accept you as a student. Too much ego. Too little humility. She will reject you."

"I'll risk it. And I'm a fast learner."

"I agree. But it won't help you."

The two men face each other. Outside, a rain shower soaks the yard.

Anton writes a name and address on a fresh sheet of paper and hands it to Decretas.

The bald man looks down.

"California?"

CHAPTER FIVE

Santa Barbara, California, USA

The property is a bungalow, clinker brick walls studded with arroyo boulders. Most bungalows belong in communities; this one looks like it fell out with its neighbours and moved out of town.

From the rental car, Jimmy Blue scans the surroundings with binoculars. Sees a wind turbine, a solar panel array, and a generator against the north wall. The landscape west of the town is flat and dusty. No strawberry farms here like the ones Blue spotted from the coast road.

He swigs coffee from a disposable cup. Ten in the morning, and the temperature in mid-April is a comfortable sixty-five Fahrenheit. The weather reports on the drive from Los Angeles gave the temperature in Fahrenheit. The absence of centigrade remind him he's in a foreign land. Tom Lewis spent a good chunk of his teens holed up in institutions watching television, so he is familiar with the mannerisms, language and habits of the USA. It's as if he lived here in a previous life.

Daylight is Tom's domain. Blue remains an outsider here, an

intruder. At night, Jimmy can be anyone he likes. But now, even in the weak sunlight that warms his left arm as it rests on the open window, he is uncomfortable.

Tom has been close to the surface. Sometimes, Blue lets him emerge for an hour or two, blinking as he stares around a cheap motel room. He'll remember it in dreams. After childhood and adolescence in the driving seat, Tom gave it up with no complaint six years ago. He craved rest, and Blue needed freedom to plan. To prepare. To train body and mind for revenge. To be ready to face those who killed his family, moving among them like the Angel of Death.

This is the final stage. He wants what this woman can teach him, and—despite what Anton said—he believes he can learn it. In all his research, he found no reference to the technique the German used in the Bavarian mountains. Perhaps because it wasn't so much a technique as a state of mind. Anton's references to it were elliptical and evasive.

Soon, he promises himself. Soon, Tom can come back, and Blue can complete his plans cocooned in darkness.

Soon, he will return to London, resume his previous life, take up the old routines, hand over his days to Tom. But only until the night he has planned ever since Tom Lewis first became Jimmy Blue. He will avenge his parents.

He guns the engine and takes the single track leading from the road to the bungalow.

———

Blue knows it's best to assume nothing when encountering a novel situation or a new person. Assumptions help marketers and salespeople, but are of little use to him. When Blue meets a stranger, he needs to assess them for potential danger, look for weaknesses. He does it unconsciously. Assumptions get in the way.

The door opens to reveal a woman standing a shade over five feet tall, white hair shaved so close he can see the veins on her scalp. Lots of weaknesses. Not much danger.

She wears cotton trousers with a drawstring belt and a faded yellow T-shirt that says Oakland University, 1986. Her figure is slight, her expression—as she examines Blue over the top of round, wire-framed glasses—one of mild interest. Her age is hard to guess. She wears no make-up or jewellery, not even a watch. Her pale grey eyes are clear, the surrounding skin lined. Her small hands are folded in front of her. Sixty? Jimmy Blue looks at her neck. Older?

"Shoes off," is the tiny woman's opening statement. "I've made tea. I don't have milk. Follow me."

With that, she turns her back and walks away, her steps silent on the tiled floor. She is barefoot. Jimmy unlaces his boots and leaves them at the door, following her down a passage into a bright kitchen at the far end.

A large wooden table dominates the space. Other than the teapot and cups already laid out, steam curling from the pot's spout, the room is spartan. There's an oven, a fridge, and a sink; dishes stacked on a shelf. No pictures, no photographs, no hand-stitched homily suggesting there's no place like home.

The two cups on the table don't match, and neither match the teapot. The bungalow and land can't have come cheap, so this lack of concern about clothes and home comforts tells him something about his host.

He sits, and she joins him. "I don't have any sugar. There's honey in the pantry if you have a sweet tooth."

Blue puts a hand up to stop her pouring the tea. "If you're expecting someone, it's not me. I'm looking for a woman called Kai."

She fills his cup first, then her own, using a metal strainer. The leaves captured there are brackish and pungent, smelling of smoke and herbs.

"Drink your tea. I wasn't expecting anyone in particular. Just knew someone was coming, so I made a full pot."

He does as he is told and relaxes back into his customary stillness. She studies him. Her gaze is frank, and she takes her time. He lets her do it, sipping the rich brew. Her gaze lingers when she gets to his bandana, although they're not unusual in California. If she thinks her examination will embarrass him, she is mistaken.

"London?" she says. He nods.

"Long way to come. What's your name?"

"Tom," he answers. It's the truth, but it always feels like a lie in Jimmy Blue's mouth, a misshapen word.

"Tom," she repeats. "Is it really?"

She goes back to scrutinising him. When she is done, she places her teacup on the table. Then she does something unexpected, and he knows she is the teacher he needs.

Kai becomes silent and still. Not quiet; silent. Not unmoving; still.

Blue understands the silence and stillness of the predator. It is his natural state. This is different. This is the silence of stone, the stillness of deep water.

For years, Jimmy Blue has rigorously developed his senses. Most people over-rely on vision. Their bias is unconscious, but it is there, and it hands him an advantage. If his eyes tell him no one waits in the shadows but he hears faint, regular breathing and smells ten-hour-old deodorant, he can act on that information.

What this woman is doing shouldn't be possible. His brain claims a small woman in a yellow T-shirt sits opposite, but every one of his senses denies she's there. Her breathing is so slow, even sitting four feet away in a room with no competing sounds other than his own breath and heartbeat, he cannot detect it. He can neither taste nor smell soap or perfume. As if the human being who poured tea was replaced by a hologram.

In the end, he can't resist. He reaches over and touches one of her folded hands. She bursts out laughing.

"Good," she says. "You can pay attention. You're not here to sell me insurance. Where did you hear the name Kai, and what do you want?"

CHAPTER SIX

THEY TALK in the backyard while Kai waters the raised beds, and Jimmy pulls weeds. Or, rather, Blue talks, which is a novel experience. Unlike Tom, he has no problem speaking fluently. He has flirted, joked, entertained, negotiated, and threatened. But he has always been in character while doing it. When he puts on a wig, adds facial hair, changes his eye colour or wears glasses, he is playing a role. No method actor could do it better. For however long it takes, he becomes the persona he has created.

But talking about himself is different. Uncomfortable.

"You're the first one Anton's ever sent to me," she says. "So what are you? A European super-soldier? A spy? An agent in training for the British Secret Service? Freedom fighter? Jihadist?"

She stops watering for a moment and looks at him.

"Holy shit. What are you doing?"

She takes the plants he has collected from his hand and pushes them up to his nose.

"Smell like weeds to you?"

He inhales a pungent odour reminiscent of aniseed.

"Thai basil. Change of plan. You water, I weed."

She hands him the metal can. "City boys, you're all the same.

Keep talking. If you're not working for someone else, are you free-lance? An assassin?"

"No."

"No. Go back. You just condemned three plants to death."

He waters, she weeds. They make their way down the first bed and onto the next. They're both barefoot, walking on matting. Blue pinches a leaf and rubs it between his fingers, brings it up to his nostrils. He knows their flowery, bright fragrance. Coriander. Cilantro, they call it over here.

She stops weeding because he's stopped talking.

"You want my help, talk to me. You lie, I'll know, and you can go home."

He believes her. He tells her the truth. "I was shot in the head when I was twelve, my parents executed in front of me. Their killers burned down my house. I escaped by crawling through an upstairs window."

Kai keeps weeding, poking callused finger tips into the wet soil, teasing out the offending plants with a rapid economy of movement, her hand scooping underneath to lift the roots.

When he stops talking, she waves a dirty hand at him without turning from her task. "Yes? And? Go on."

His reaction to the lack of sympathy, the absence of a wrinkled brow indicating concern, is one of relief. When people find out about Tom's parents' deaths, they respond with pity, condescension, or fear. Kai is so patently unimpressed by the brutal attack that put him on his path that Blue smiles in disbelief.

He fills the can at the standing tap, then waters the next row, drenching the dry soil as Kai had done.

He talks.

Beginning with the moment he became self-aware as Tom Lewis lay in a coma, he gives her an accurate account of how he sought out the knowledge that would enable him to avenge his parents, and himself, on those who had taken everything. He told her about Robert Winter, the human trafficker, and about those who had helped him find and execute his family.

He omits the fact that, in effect, he and Tom are two people.

The old woman listens as she works, not interrupting. By the time he's done, they are back in the kitchen, where boiling water drips through coffee grounds into a jug beneath.

"Black okay?"

He nods, and she pours. She uses the same two cups after rinsing them.

She studies him again. Her gaze is neither kind nor unkind. She does not judge, she does not condone.

"Revenge is a fool's game," she says.

He sticks to his newfound transparency.

"Then I'm a fool."

"Yes. You are." She looks away from him, eyes unfocused. "But you're in good company."

"Then you'll help me?"

She drains what's left in her cup.

"I will not. I'm done with revenge. Thank you for your help in the yard."

She stands without another word, walks out of the kitchen, waits next to his boots. When he joins her, she opens the front door. He knows he's telegraphing his frustration, but he doesn't conceal it.

He looks at her, a tiny old woman. What could she teach him, anyway?

Kai eyes him.

"A warning. You're not as good as you think you are. Too much ego. Wrapped up in rage rather than ambition or lust. But it's there. You're standing in your own way."

"Then teach me."

"You won't be able to learn what I have to teach."

"Try me."

"I will not. Walk away from your dream of revenge. It will destroy you."

He could answer, tell her his very existence is woven into the idea of revenge. That he doesn't know where the revenge stops and he begins anymore. But she said she won't teach him, and he's bored with the Zen bullshit already.

She's still looking at him like she can read minds.

"How would you rate your unarmed combat skills?"

He remembers the sticky heat of Bangkok two years earlier, the way his body never recovered before being pushed to its limits, again and again. And, in Bavaria, the look on Anton's face when he caught him with a punch.

"World-class."

"Then you could defend yourself if I attacked you?"

Blue stops himself smiling. Kai is remarkable. He could learn much from her. But she's not a physical threat.

"Good. Then I'll attack you."

She waits. After a few seconds, she raises an eyebrow. A little embarrassed, Jimmy Blue adopts a fighting stance, feet wide, hands raised. Performing these actions allows the darkness at his heart to rise. He reminds himself of who he is. What he is capable of. He will go back to London and take his revenge. He doesn't need this old woman's help.

Smack.

He steps back in shock, bringing a hand to his face where Kai struck him. His feet are still in a fighting stance, his hands up. She watches him impassively. He stares back, reviewing what's happened. It wasn't the speed of her strike that shocked him. Blue has defeated faster opponents. No. This is something new. An attack with no signals, no tells. His mind and body had recognised no threat, despite her verbal announcement of her intention.

"Hmm." Her voice is unemotional. She is unsurprised by the ease with which she bypassed his defences. "You think you're pretty special, right? Quite the fighter?"

Jimmy thinks of Anton, and of his encounter with the three students in the pigpen.

"I know how to fight."

"How did I hit you just now?"

He wonders if it's a trick question.

25

She doesn't wait for an answer.

"The hand moved faster than the eye?" Her head is on one side, the grey eyes unblinking. She reminds him of a pigeon. She tuts.

"Come with me."

———

Kai leads him out to the front yard. She stops walking a couple of yards from his rental car's front tyre and faces him.

"I gave up teaching a long time ago."

As Kai speaks, she traces a circle in the dirt with her foot. The area she marks out is about the size of a sumo ring.

"But I promised Anton I would teach any student I thought was ready to learn."

Once the circle is complete, she walks back to its far edge and beckons him in.

"I owe Anton a debt I can never repay. For him, I will give you a chance."

She doesn't prepare, instead leaving her hands at her side, her body relaxed. She looks at ease.

"Four ways to win," she says. "Pin your opponent for three seconds and it's over. Say you yield and it's over."

When she says nothing further, Blue assumes he's supposed to ask the obvious. "And the other two?"

"Unconsciousness or death. Let's avoid those, shall we?"

Jimmy Blue moves forward. He is six foot three and built like a heavyweight boxer. If he fell on her, he'd crush every bone in her body. The laws of physics are unbendable. Plus, she's old, he's young; she's frail, he's two hundred and twenty pounds. If she punches him, he doubts he'll feel it. If he punches her, her tiny head might come clean off her shoulders.

Still, he reminds himself as he shifts his weight in readiness, Tom Lewis knows all about being underestimated. Blue should avoid making the same mistake.

Without warning, he rushes her. It's a technique that's served him well in the past. His bulk means opponents often make incorrect assumptions about his speed. An un-telegraphed explosion of movement leaves little time to defend, and can end a fight before it's even started. He doesn't intend to hurt the old woman, just to wrap his massive arms around her, immobilising her until she yields.

But she's not there. He allowed her little time to respond, but she used that time wisely. Kai reacts to his onslaught with an astonishing economy of movement, ducking, leaning, sidestepping to her right. Her left sleeve brushes against his shoulder as his arms close on the space she occupied a fraction of a second before.

Okay. The slap wasn't a fluke. The old woman is fast. And she's reading his intentions as clearly as if he had laid them out in bullet points before stepping into the ring.

He could jab with his elbow, catch her in the side of her head, but he is afraid of injuring her. Instead, he opts for a sweeping motion, turning as he does so, intending to knock her from her feet.

Again, she isn't where she ought to be. Her body folds at the waist and she scuttles backwards like an obsequious server leaving a table in a fancy restaurant.

Jimmy sways off-balance for a moment. Before he can adjust to the situation, Kai steps forward, sweeps a straight leg under his pivoting foot, and sends him sprawling onto the dirt.

He rolls as he lands, and is back on his feet within a second, looking for her follow-up. It doesn't come. Kai has returned to her original position in the circle, hands by her side, relaxed. Untroubled.

"Blockage where there should be flow. Disharmony. Wrong action. You cannot hope to win this way."

Blue faces her, nods. She's wrong. Her speed and flexibility is beyond doubt, and she can think as fast as she acts. But the moment he catches her, it's all over. It's a matter of time.

He rushes her again—this time with a plan. He feints left, switches his weight to the right, lashes out with an open palm. Kai, instead of dodging to avoid his feint, moves into it.

She ends up behind him. Instead of tripping him, she smacks his behind as if he were a misbehaving toddler. He swings back to face her. Kai shakes her head.

"You are holding back. Scared of hurting me, I imagine. Very well. Either show me what you can do, or I will hurt you."

Her eyes are on him again. Blue returns to his fighting stance opposite the infuriating woman. No more headlong rushes. He will prevail eventually. She didn't mention a time limit. He'll wear her down.

Kai watches his preparation. When he moves forward, she backs up, edging along the perimeter of the circle.

"Brute force, however expertly applied, can only be a blunt and limited instrument. There is more to you than this. Show me."

He keeps following, trying to get closer. Her footwork is that of a boxer's now; changing direction, weaving, always out of range.

"Why are you holding back, Tom?" The way she says the name is off. It's as if she knows it doesn't fit. "There's no way Anton would have sent someone so obvious. You're asleep. Wake up. Show me. Or go home. Go back and take your revenge on the mean men who killed your family. You figure you're stronger than your mom and dad? Smarter? I don't think so. They were weak. Not only did they get themselves killed, they couldn't even protect their little kid. Now look at you. I'm old enough to be your grandmother and I'm kicking your ass. You're weak and you're pathetic."

Although he knows what she's trying to do, a little of the darkness shifts within him, uncoils. She flashes him a look, eyes narrowing.

"Yes. That. Show me."

She moves, and he tries to follow, but it's like chasing smoke. There's a searing pain between the lowest two ribs on his left side and he gasps and flinches away, tracing the area with his right hand, convinced he'll find the hilt of a knife. There's nothing, and the pain lessens with every breath, retreating in waves.

"I could have crippled you," says Kai from behind him. "Stop holding back. Last warning."

The last two words come from his right. Blue wheels to find her, but Kai is already moving. This time, he sees her hand jab into his hip. His left leg loses all sensation, and he falls, dragging himself away. She's back where she started, watching him.

Pins and needles signify the return of feeling in his leg, and he stands.

"It would have been kinder if the guys who killed your parents had finished the job," she says. "Three graves in some London cemetery. Better than wasting your life. I'm done with you."

Jimmy Blue lets the darkness come. The veneer of humanity disappears, and he lets Kai see him as he is.

If he expected terror, he is disappointed. The old woman's eyes widen a fraction. For the first time, she brings her hands up into a defensive posture. And she smiles at him.

"That's better," she murmurs.

Kai doesn't speak for the next two minutes. The usual late morning soundtrack of the Santa Barbara countryside has been disrupted. No insects hum and scuttle in the dirt. No birds sing. There is only the sound of breathing and steady footsteps alternating with sudden flurries of activity. The occasional grunt as a punch or kick finds its target; but never fully, as both fighters are too fast, and too experienced to allow a blow to land. They dance, they weave, their movements ranging from the manic—a frenetic modern piece of choreography—to a static tableau, during which they eye each other, waiting.

The end of the fight follows a brief exchange of blows when Jimmy breaks through Kai's defences long enough to land a significant punch, a left jab to her stomach. She responds before his fist hits her, falling backwards, her right hand exploiting the gap in his defences.

Kai took his punch so she could get in close. She pinches his neck.

When Kai dances back out of range, she is wheezing. Even with little power behind it, his punch has hurt her. Blue, consumed by the darkness now, steps forward to exploit his advantage. The signal from his brain to his legs never gets past the cluster of nerves Kai pinched seconds earlier. His upper body moves, but his legs stay where they are, and he topples forward. The signals to his arms intended to break his fall are similarly blocked, and he falls onto his face.

Blue can't move. He watches Kai's feet leave the circle. Seconds later, he hears the front door of the bungalow open and close. A minute later, the sound repeats. She calls out to him from the porch.

"Humans kill each other for many reasons. Revenge is one of the poorest. You have chosen a dark, lonely path. I hope you change your mind."

He grunts, coughs, and tries again. "I will not."

"Then I suspect you might not live long enough to regret your decision."

By the time he can sit up, the door is closed, and she's gone.

CHAPTER SEVEN

AT THE MOTEL, Jimmy Blue arranges for the rental car to be picked up, leaving his keys in reception.

He closes the curtains on the sun and stands in the darkened room, toes spreading on the thin carpet, broad shoulders opening and relaxing. Within a minute, he becomes still, but some of the usual comfort has dissipated since he witnessed another human being achieve a silence so profound that she all but vanished.

He reviews the events of the morning, looking for angles of approach he didn't try. Considers the new situation: Kai knows who he is, what happened to him when he was twelve, and what he plans to do about it. He's not worried she might betray him. Whatever her past holds, she has changed. The only time she gets her hands dirty now is in her garden.

He didn't lie to her this morning, not really. But he introduced himself as Tom Lewis, not Jimmy Blue. No reason she should know about the part of him he protects. There is no Boy without Tom, no Tom without Blue. And yet he revealed more of himself than he intended during their fight.

He sits at the desk, flips open the laptop, and connects to the hotel Wi-Fi, using a virtual private network to connect to a second VPN, then entering a string of passwords to access the encrypted file he'd studied before meeting Kai. He clicks on it.

The information he's gathered on the woman now known as Kai is thin, patchy, and unreliable. It comes from dozens of sources, some of which contradict each other. He knows the name she was born with: Elizabeth Murchen. She's sixty-eight years old. In college— Penn, not Oakland—she was sporty, with average grades, graduating with a degree in history. During the Vietnam conflict, she joined protests, waved placards, and made love rather than war.

Her anti-war activities continued after Penn until, aged twenty-six, she vanished. No records, no driving licence, no employment history, no marriage listed under the name Elizabeth Murchen. From her twenty-sixth year until her forty-seventh, the information is a mishmash of hearsay, rumours, and an occasional sighting. A complex and confusing picture lacking coherence. How did an idealistic young anti-war protestor end up waging it on behalf of her country? Because that is what the information reveals.

Blue clicks on a photograph. Hanoi, 1970, a squad of US soldiers moving out. There is no mistaking the tiny woman watching them board the chopper, her body toned and muscled, a coldness in her eyes.

The following decades are even less well-documented, but the lack of data adds credence to the more speculative reports about Kai on file.

Elizabeth Murchen disappeared, but soon afterwards, within the sealed records of America's clandestine government organisations, references appeared to an operative known as 47L.

In Africa, the anti-American advisor of a ruler fell downstairs and broke his neck.

In 1973, a Chilean politician who warned of a coup threatening their fragile democracy took his own life.

Other recorded deaths are less ambiguous. Military leaders with their throats slit, car bombs obliterating political opponents of American puppet governments in far-flung countries.

It all adds up to an interesting picture, especially when cross-checked against details in eyewitness statements.

Only two mention a woman. The rest—and it took a search algorithm designed by a hacker more talented than Jimmy a full day to find them—refer to a child. Sometimes a girl, sometimes a boy. Occasionally spotted with a family group, sometimes playing with other children. Some reports mention a lost child brought into the house to be looked after.

Even at close to seventy, Kai could disguise herself as a boy. It's a brilliant ploy. If only half of the kills attributed to her are her work, she was undoubtedly one of the most prolific enforcers of US foreign policy ever set loose in the field.

Until the day she wasn't.

She vanished. For good this time. A black ops soldier knows how to cover her traces, and Murchen was among the very best.

This, after all, is the woman who taught Anton. After six years of training, Jimmy Blue's failure to defeat the German in Bavaria is galling, but being refused access to the techniques that gave Anton his advantage is worse.

Blue stretches, paces the tiny room. He considers his options. He could confront Kai with his knowledge of her past. With what aim, though? Blackmail? Two reasons to avoid that. First, she disappeared once, so she can do it again. Second, he doesn't want to do it. It isn't right. Blue isn't used to notions of right or wrong dictating his actions, but there is no avoiding his discomfort. Kai was honest, frank, and direct this morning. In return, he had been the same. No hiding, no lying, no manipulation. Just the plain truth, except concerning his complicated sense of self. No. He will not blackmail her.

Decision made, he accepts he has failed. His trip to California is a bust. He won't give up his revenge. Without it, he is nothing.

He has no immediate plans after his stay at the Santa Barbara motel. He could go back to London, but, despite his angry decision back at the bungalow to go home, he knows he's not ready. Not quite.

He has other options. He uncovered evidence of a group of fighters in Japan who live by the samurai code, working as a team of assassins. Their results are impressive, their skills in combat advanced. Their speciality is blades, from the samurai sword to a penknife. He could fly to Tokyo, offer his services, study their methods. But, under their samurai ideals, they answer to their shogun, doing his bidding without question. Blue won't answer to anyone.

If not Japan, then where?

For the first time since leaving London, he is unsure. He needs to regroup, to rethink. He craves the darkness.

Blue lies on the bed, head aching. He was unprepared for failure; didn't plan for it. Tom exists moment to moment with no thought for the future. That's no way to live. Blue is goal-driven, even a goal as short-term as who to punch next.

Time to reassess, discard any unattainable goals, and refocus on what waits for him in London. He can do that in the shadows. Tom can have a few days in the California sun.

The darkness calls. He embraces it.

CHAPTER EIGHT

TOM OPENS his eyes in a darkened room, a fan moving warm air around above him. He doesn't move for a few minutes, getting used to the light, to the sound of unfamiliar birdsong and, further off, passing traffic; to the smell of unfamiliar fabric conditioner on stretched sheets.

He spreads his palms onto the bed's cool smoothness. Looks to his left. A door with a security chain, peephole at head height. A diagram of the building showing fire exits.

Tom has been in this situation before. He's not scared. Not really. It usually lasts two or three days before Blue returns and Tom sleeps again. Jimmy Blue has been busy for years now, taking control. Soon everything will be right again. Blue will make things better.

Waking up was only scary once. Tom had been drinking milk-shake in a cafe when an angry man sat at his table. He was big, with a black beard, and he jabbed his finger in the air like conducting an orchestra. He asked questions in a foreign language. When Tom didn't answer, the man got angrier, left the cafe, and made a call outside. Tom went to the bathroom. Inside, he found an open window leading to an alleyway. He took a step towards it, then Jimmy

Blue was there, so fast it was like flicking a switch. Tom fell asleep instantly.

The next time he woke up, he was on a plane. The bearded man had gone. He closed his eyes again.

Tom sits up. The bedside lamp hums when he turns it on. The plug socket has two holes, not three. He's not in London.

Where, then?

It's been a long time since he saw a black cab or a red bus. Years since he carried bricks on London building sites for men in hard hats called Dave, Steve, or Barry.

Tom finds clothes draped over the back of the chair. Underwear, a short-sleeved cotton shirt, and a pair of light brown trousers. There's a pair of trainers under the chair.

Tom stares because his brain wants to use different words, and this confuses him. When he first looks at the trainers, the word sneakers comes into his mind. Now, holding up the trousers, part of him wants to call them pants. He knows from his television-based education that, in America, trousers are pants and trainers are sneakers. He thinks about this for a while. Trainers, he decides, is a better word than sneakers. He doesn't want to sneak anywhere, although he concedes Jimmy Blue may have done this while wearing them. But most people wear them for exercise. They train in their trainers. He is happy with that name. The trousers present more of a problem. The word sounds right to him, but what about underpants? That word only makes sense if they are being worn under pants. So it's the best word after all. He frowns as he pulls the pants on and buttons them up. The mix of two different vocabularies disconcerts him. Is he allowed to call trousers pants, but trainers trainers? Maybe there's someone he can ask. Perhaps not. He remembers a therapist he saw in his teens telling him not to overthink. He thinks he might be over-thinking now.

Tom puts on the shirt and buttons it, completing his outfit with a baseball cap hanging on a hook. At the door, he remembers to slide out the plastic key card. He steps out into an unfamiliar world.

———

Outside, it's sunny but not too hot. The motel is on the outskirts of a small town, so Tom starts walking. His stomach growls. Time to find something to eat.

Tom likes to eat in familiar places, with limited menus, where he knows how much money he is likely to spend. He is happiest keeping human interaction to a minimum. It's not that he doesn't like other people, but they often confuse him. At worst, they scare him. They ask questions and are impatient when he can't answer them. Occasionally, Tom has left food on a shop counter and fled, unable to follow what the cashier is saying. Away from home, he often relies on the predictable and comforting familiarity of a vending machine. Best of all are supermarkets where he can pay with a card. Tom has memorised the pattern of numbers he needs to press on the keypads to pay for his purchases, and he doesn't have to speak to anybody.

There must be supermarkets here, but Tom doesn't see any on his stroll. There are lots of smaller establishments, coffee shops, and cafés, but the cheerful greetings and easy conversations between customers and staff at the counters put him off. He keeps moving. At a crossroads, he stops to watch the stream of cars driving on the wrong side of the road; drivers sitting on the wrong side of the car. His head aches and he looks away. Needing to cross, he presses the button, but there's no picture of a green or red man to help him. He waits through one complete cycle, staring at the words that appear. He is almost certain he should cross when the green word appears, but he doesn't know what it says, and doesn't want to risk it. Luckily, a group of teenagers cross and he follows them. They look back at him and giggle. He feels big, clumsy, and stupid, but he's used to feeling this way. He doesn't mind the curious looks, sidelong glances, and the knowing smiles. So long as they leave him alone.

Wherever he is, it's not a big town, and he soon finds himself in its bustling centre. At one end of the street, the ocean sparkles beyond a stretch of sand. People throw frisbees and play volleyball. A dog barks and dashes away from the incoming tide.

In the other direction, more shops, more restaurants, more cars.

Tom heads towards the water. On the boardwalk, the aromas from rows of food stalls make his mouth water. He puts his hand in his trouser—pants'—pocket and pulls out a slim wallet. Inside is a bank card, a printed card he doesn't recognise, a third card with a photograph of him, and some banknotes. He hopes it will be enough.

Nearer the ocean, the wind picks up, and Tom pulls the brim of the baseball cap tighter over his head as he walks between the rows of food stalls, smelling grilled shrimp, jerk chicken, clam chowder, seared steaks, and a dozen dishes he doesn't recognise.

He sees a woman turn away from a stall, a foil-wrapped burrito in her hand. Tom likes Mexican food. There are two people waiting in line. He stands behind them.

Birds squabble over scraps of food, or sit on waves, bobbing on the glittery water a hundred yards from the shore. He wonders if this is an ocean or a sea, and what the difference is.

"Help you?"

Tom swings round and looks at the questioner; tanned, hair bleached blonde, in her forties, smiling. Tom forms the word. "Mm. Mm. Burrito."

"Sure. Chicken? Pulled pork? Shrimp? Tofu? Mild or spicy? How hungry are you, hun? Side of refried beans? Chips and salsa? How about a drink?"

Tom blinks three times. The woman is still smiling, but she spoke too fast, and although he tries hard to remember her words, they slip away and he flounders. His mouth opens and closes again. He licks his lips.

"Mm." He thinks she said shrimp, and shrimp means prawns. At least, he thinks so. He likes prawns. He gets the word ready, holds it in his mind. But before he can speak, another voice interrupts.

"Come on, bud, decision time. Hurry it up, will ya? I'm growing a beard here."

Tom looks behind him to see the same teenagers who had crossed the road earlier. Their spokesman looks fourteen or fifteen. There are three boys, and two girls. The first boy grins. Tom knows that expression well. It does not upset or hurt him. Then the smirk becomes a sneer. Tom's neck prickles with sweat and he flushes. This is what he wanted to avoid. He should have found a supermarket, but it's too late now. Panicked, he turns back to the counter and forgets what he wants, staring at the woman, whose smile falters.

"You okay, hun?"

Tom is okay. He just needs a little time and a little quiet to think. He will remember what to say if everyone gives him space. But that seems unlikely. Another voice pipes up from behind.

"Chicken, pork, shrimp, tofu, mild, spicy, beans, chips, drink. Sour cream? Chilli sauce? Jalapeños? It's easy, man. You can do it. We believe in you." Giggles greet this witticism.

Tom swivels his head to acknowledge them without having to look at the teenagers. Then it happens. A sudden gust of wind tugs at his cap, and before he can reach up to stop it, it's off his head and skimming along the boardwalk. Dismayed, Tom is unsure what to do. He takes a step towards the cap, which has snagged against a bench. Looks back at the stallholder.

The first teenager whistles and points. "Hey, what the hell happened to you? Someone drop you when you were a baby? Hit you with a hammer, maybe?"

Tom brings a hand up to touch his scar, tracing the familiar wreckage of hard tissue under his big fingers, touching without feeling. He often finds his fingers returning to the scars when he's alone. Thick cardboard skin. However hard he scratches, it never hurts, as if anaesthetised. He sometimes touches the place where the bullet entered with something like awe. It defines him. It marks the beginning of his life. Everything before it is dreamlike, insubstantial.

Not everyone laughs. One boy shuffles awkwardly, and the taller girl looks away. But they are smiling. The leader, dark-haired, tall for his age, studies Tom's shaved head. His eyes widen with a sudden idea.

"Someone shoot you?" Tom flinches at the words, not seeing the teenagers, but Marty Nicholson bursting into his bedroom, a gun in his hand, raising it to point straight at him. The flash of the muzzle and his head snapping backwards at the impact.

He stumbles away, eyes fixed on the baseball cap, determined to retrieve it and leave. The teenagers follow. They keep their distance, wary of the size of the stranger, but the leader keeps up his monologue.

"That's it, isn't it? Someone shot you, right? Man, you shouldn't cover it up like this. How many people get shot in the head and live to tell the tale, right? You are one lucky son of a bitch, my dude. Come on, we want to hear about it. Tell us what happened. You some big-time gangster or what? Special forces? Marines? Navy seal? What? Come on, man."

Tom reaches the cap, bending down to retrieve it then clutching it between his fingers, kneading it like dough. When the teenagers catch up, he doesn't remember who they are. He looks around and everything is unfamiliar. The sun, the blue sky, the immense body of water stretching out to the horizon, the people, the stalls, the thousand strange smells, the boards under his feet. It's all wrong. Even the clothes he's wearing are wrong. They are not his work clothes. He's never seen them before.

He lifts his gaze from the giggling teenagers, scanning his surroundings for something familiar, something to anchor him. His head thumps and he is sweating. He turns in a slow circle but sees nothing that can help, no one he knows.

He sees her. The white, close-cropped hair, the round glasses, pale skin, mismatched clothes. He knows her but does not remember where from. The teenagers stand between him and the woman. He shuffles straight through them, and they scramble to get out of his way. The leader loses his sneer and looks afraid. They scatter, but Tom ignores them, heading towards the familiar woman.

She turns before he gets close and takes in the exposed scars on his head.

"What didn't you tell me?" is her opening gambit. Tom stops walking and shakes his head. He doesn't understand what she means.

She stays silent for a few seconds, her eyes on his. Then she speaks again.

"What's changed? Who are you?"

She looks on intently. Tom doesn't know what she wants. He looks away, but it's a mistake.

The teenagers have followed. The boldest points his fingers at Tom as if holding a gun. "They tried to execute you, right? Gang-style. Boom."

He mimes firing a gun and the world spins. Tom looks around him for Jimmy Blue, but there's no sign. Just the sun, the boardwalk, the food stalls, the sea, the teenagers, and the strange old woman.

The cap falls from Tom's fingers, but he carries on kneading the air, not noticing. He focuses on the woman's face. Her mouth is moving, but every sound has blurred into white noise. He stumbles, and pinpricks of light appear in his field of vision, a thousand lost fireflies. As he falls, he wonders if the small woman knows why trainers are called sneakers.

The wooden boards are sun-baked and smell of vinegar. Tom closes his eyes and everything vanishes.

CHAPTER NINE

TOM WAKES up fully dressed in an unfamiliar bed. It's the second time it's happened today, and this causes a flutter of panic in his chest. He's looking up at a plain white ceiling, a white paper lampshade hanging above his head. No fan, but the air is cool. He turns right and looks through a window at pink shreds of clouds. In the distance, dark hills rise from the flatlands. Closer, cultivated herbs make miniature forests in raised beds. Tom pictures a watering can and the scent of aniseed, but the memory slips away when he pursues it.

The bed is draped with a patchwork quilt, its stitched octagons alternating navy blue and sea green. Tom pushes himself up on the pillows, a grunt of surprise escaping him when he sees he is not alone. Someone is sitting at the foot of the bed on a plain wooden chair, a lamp switched on and angled low at her lap. She's sewing.

It's the woman from the food stalls, the one he thought he recognised. Her fingers move quickly, light flashing from the needle as it darts back and forth through a pair of jeans.

"My grandmother's generation liked to make-do and mend." She doesn't glance up as she speaks, her pale grey eyes, behind the glasses, focused on her work.

"There is much to commend in that mantra, but it soured many women of her generation, leading them to criticise their daughters when they didn't follow their advice. Human beings are a contrary species, don't you think? Every generation wants the best for their children, an easier life than their own. But if their wish is granted, they criticise their children for enjoying the life they prayed for. They shake their heads when they eat out, or buy a new outfit when there's a perfectly good dress in the closet. Are you feeling better?"

With a start, Tom realises she'd aimed this question at him. There is something soothing about this woman's way of speaking, the rhythm of the words punctuated by the click of the needle on the thimble. He wasn't really paying attention to the meaning of her words. He recognises the tone, though, and nods.

"Mm. Thank you."

The small woman pauses her work and gives him an appraising look. Tom instinctively looks away, anywhere else, his gaze moving around the spartan room. A low table in one corner and a clothes rail with empty hangers. One chair. When he risks a glance, she is still staring. He looks away a second time, then fights to overcome his usual embarrassment and nerves. There is no challenge, no judgment. She simply sees him. When she smiles at Tom, he returns it.

"You remember what happened?"

He nods again. The sounds, the smells, the laughs of the teenagers, the way he froze and stammered at the food stall. The panic when the cap blew away, the flashback to being shot. Her face above him, then nothing more.

"How about this morning? When you drove out here."

Tom fishes his memory for anything that might help. This is not an alien sensation. It happens when he sees someone Blue has met. In the past, Tom has avoided any contact with those individuals. This is different. There is no threat here. He isn't sure why Blue sought out this woman, but he is certain she means him no harm. He shrugs, shaking his head.

"Interesting," she says. "All done." She replaces needle, thread, and thimble in a cloth bag looped around her shoulder, then folds the jeans and stands up. When she opens the door, Tom sees a hallway beyond. Seconds later, a delicious aroma wafts into the bedroom and he swallows. He is still hungry. Ravenous, in fact.

"You think you're up to getting out of bed on your own?"

In answer, Tom sits up and swings his legs over the side, bare feet on the floorboards. He looks for his trainers, but can't see them. He stands. No fireflies, no dizziness.

"Good," says the woman. She points. "Bathroom. Wash up, then follow the smell of curry. We'll talk when you've eaten. Remind me. What's your name?"

He tells her and she smiles.

"Yes," she says. "Tom. This time I believe you."

She walks the length of the hall and disappears into the kitchen. Her footsteps are silent. She doesn't need sneakers, that's for sure.

The bathroom is as plain as the bedroom. No moisturisers, no creams, no perfumes. A bar of soap and a thin towel. Tom splashes water on his face then walks to the kitchen.

————

The curry is one of the best Tom has ever tasted. There's no meat, but he doesn't miss it. The flavours are intense, and it's all he can do to stop himself shovelling it into his face as fast as possible. Instead of rice, the small woman brings over hot flatbreads from the oven, salt crystals glittering among the coriander leaves on their surface. Although he doesn't ask, she refills his bowl from a large saucepan and waits for him to finish. He mops up the last of the sauce with the bread. Only then does he notice how little she's eaten herself.

She tops up his glass of water from a jug with mint leaves and lemon slices. Tom drains it while she opens a drawer. She puts his wallet on the table.

"According to your ID, your name is Tom Kincaid and you're from Ireland."

Tom knows he has to be careful with names. His own surname, Lewis, can put him in danger. The police gave him his first pretend name, Tom Brown, but Jimmy Blue chooses names now.

"That's bullshit, though."

He doesn't react. She doesn't seem surprised by the fake name.

"Your medical insurance card is interesting. I checked. It's the best money can buy. They ran out of precious metals for names, so yours is platinum plus. Top sports people have this insurance. Senators, showbiz lawyers, movie stars. And you: a guy who pitched up in Santa Barbara with one change of clothes and forty-seven bucks in his wallet."

She pushes it across the table. Tom puts it back in his pocket.

"While you were asleep, I did some digging. Called in a couple of favours from someone good at finding information. If the President of the United States picks his nose in bed one morning, this guy can tell you the colour, consistency, and diameter of the booger."

The woman gives him that direct look again. "But you? Nothing. I spoke to Anton. You came to him with a reference from the Bangkok Librarian. She's never recommended anyone before. I asked my contact to dig deeper into your past. Guess what turned up?"

Questions like this confuse Tom.

"Nada," she says. "Nothing. No records, no history. A ghost. Your record makes me look like a show-off desperate to get noticed. You came from nowhere, but Anton says you proved more than competent with every weapon he threw at you. Sometimes literally. Tea?"

Tom, struggling to keep up, knows the correct answer to that last question. He's British. "Mm. P-p-please."

She boils the kettle; a heavy cast iron item on the stove. Tea, when she pours it, turns out to be a strong, bitter brew with no milk or biscuits. Tom hides his disappointment.

They drink in silence for a few minutes.

"So, Tom. I've spoken more in the last ten minutes than I have in the last three years. I'm not a talker. You're not exactly an orator yourself, are you?"

The word was unfamiliar. "I, mm, I, mm, mm, don't talk much."

She points at the scar tissue on his scalp. Tom hasn't even thought about the fact that he's bareheaded. He can't remember when he's been this close to someone without a cap or bandana to cover his scars.

"And this. An old bullet wound?"

He nods. This is nothing like this afternoon with the teenagers. He is safe here. The sense of calm in her presence goes bone-deep.

"You came to see me this morning. And yet that wasn't you."

Tom dares not answer. Despite his inclination to trust this woman, he can't give up the secret that defines his existence.

"It's okay. Don't be afraid. The other man burned with rage. Such darkness. But you... you're like the first snowfall of winter before anyone walks on it. The other Tom asked me to teach him, but I refused. You have not asked. I will help you, Tom Kincaid."

Tom searches the corners of the room. Jimmy Blue is nowhere close.

"And do you know why? Why I will teach you, but not him?"

"N-no."

"Because he is past learning anything worth knowing. I won't direct others along the path that nearly destroyed me. But maybe—maybe—you can learn the way of things. If there's a chance, I must teach you. I can do nothing else. Understand?"

Of course he didn't.

"Good. I go to bed an hour after sunset. I advise you to do the same. First lesson at five tomorrow morning. I'll leave you to wash the dishes. Good night."

CHAPTER TEN

TOM HAS WORKED early morning shifts carrying bricks or cleaning offices for years, so getting up at dawn is no problem. The red-rimmed hills define the skyline as the sun rises.

He can smell porridge. He hates porridge.

It smells worse in the kitchen.

"Help yourself to oatmeal, Tom."

Tom spoons an unappetising ladleful of porridge into a chipped bowl. There is no other food on offer. He adds a big spoonful of honey to sweeten the foul gloop. Hot water drips through a coffee filter into the pot on the side. The small woman watches him, smiling.

"I didn't tell you my name. Yours is fake. Mine, too. But I chose mine to replace a name I outgrew. I'm Kai."

Tom sits at the table and spoons warm porridge into his mouth. He eats when he can, storing the energy his body needs, even if it looks and tastes like something from the smelly end of a baby.

Kai pours the coffee, and they drink in silence. It doesn't take away the taste of the porridge.

"I swung by the motel while you were sleeping," says Kai. "Picked up your things. Hope you don't mind." She opens a cupboard and brings out Tom's backpack, hands it to him. He looks inside. One change of clothes, one laptop. One phone, switched off.

"I volunteer at a thrift store a few days a month." Kai produces a well-worn pair of hiking boots. "One perk is unboxing everything before we price it up. I don't see too many boots in a size twelve, but I remembered we had these. You're gonna need them today."

Finishing his coffee, Tom pulls the boots over his bare feet to check the size. They fit.

"Meet you on the back porch in ten minutes." Her voice comes from a room at the end of the hall. Tom jerks his head up in surprise, looking around the small kitchen. He hadn't seen or heard her move. It's like a magic trick.

Forty minutes later, they are at the foot of the hills Tom saw from his window. At first, he thinks they are heading for the summit. That's what people do. They climb hills to reach the top. Not Kai. Halfway up, she changes route, taking a path which meanders along the side of the hillside, around rocks and across streams so small they are barely a trickle.

After three or four hours, they pause and Kai hands Tom a flat-bread, a hunk of cheese, and an apple from her shoulder bag. He eats gratefully. He stretches his legs after the mixed terrain and gradients they've tackled. Kai seems unaffected. She is as sure-footed as a mountain goat and hasn't broken a sweat. They dip tin cups into a nearby stream and drink cold, fresh water.

Kai unbuttons her pants. Tom looks on, reminding himself that *pants* makes more sense as a word for the garment in question. Then he catches himself staring and looks away, blushing, as Kai squats and urinates on the ground. She registers his discomfort but does not comment on it, completing her task before straightening up and fixing her clothes.

"You need to go too?" Yes, he does. Especially now. He looks for a tree to stand behind. Tom starts off down the slope, putting some distance between him and his companion.

"Far enough." He stops walking. "You have to be able to go where you stand, Tom. Without embarrassment."

He pauses, unzips. Stands there. Waits.

"Where does the embarrassment come from? Why is it okay to share putting food and liquid into one end of your body, but not disposing of what you don't need? We all do it. Go on."

Tom tries to obey, looking out across the California landscape towards the distant ocean. He hones in on the nearby sound of the stream splashing over rocks to help him relax. But the thought of Kai watching—and he knows she's watching—stops anything happening.

"This is your first lesson, Tom. You need to pee. Your bladder is full. What is stopping you?"

It's a valid question.

"What's stopping you, Tom? Answer me."

"Mm." Tom experiences a tiny surge of happiness because not only does he understand the question, he knows the answer. "Mm it's, mm, my mind."

"Good. Why does your mind prevent you from doing something you need to do? Aren't you in control of your mind? Or do your thoughts, memories, beliefs, superstitions, and suppositions control you? This shows you who's in charge, Tom. What stops you peeing is a mountain of accumulated thoughts and beliefs. They build up over a lifetime, convincing you they are real. But your true self is beyond all that. See yourself as you are, not who your thoughts, beliefs, and memories conspire to insist you are. Start by peeing in front of me."

Some of what Kai says makes sense to Tom, and he hopes it will become clearer when he has time to think about it. But she says that his thoughts are deceiving him. So should he think or not? While he's considering this paradox, he relaxes and a stream of urine hits the dry earth in front of him. He laughs in surprise.

When he turns around, Kai is already picking a fresh path alongside the stream towards a rock-strewn passage ahead. Tom zips up and follows. He looks at the shoulder bag she carries and wants to offer to take it. She is tiny, old. He is young and strong. But he can't say the words. She has a different strength. How can someone so physically unassuming be so powerful? He walks on in silence.

CHAPTER ELEVEN

THE SECOND MORNING begins like the first, with disgusting porridge and hot coffee. After Tom washes the crockery, Kai reappears in the kitchen with a large pot of white paint and an old duffel bag bulging with brushes, rollers, and cloths.

"Home improvement today."

Tom follows her outside to a small building Kai describes as the barn, although it's more of a big shed. No larger than a double garage, it's brick-built with a wooden roof. The reference to barns becomes more tenuous when Tom sees the door, solid metal, flush to the brick. He's never seen a door quite like it, as it has no handle. How does Kai get in and out? He doesn't ask. Twenty-four hours with Kai tells him she prefers to keep conversation to a minimum. This suits Tom very well.

The barn hasn't been painted for some time. Old, grey flakes of paint peel off the brickwork.

"Prep first." Kai hands Tom a stiff brush with a long handle, takes one herself, and shows him how to brush the accumulated dust and dirt from the cracked walls. A wooden ladder stands against the bungalow. Tom fetches it for the couple of feet he can't reach.

They both work up a light sweat as they labour in silence. Before most people are awake, they finish the cleaning. A glass of water each, and they return to their tasks.

Kai levers open two gallon paint pots with a flathead screwdriver. Tom takes one and carries it to the back wall. Kai watches him begin at the bottom, the tired brickwork brightening as he passes bristles of paint back and forth.

"Today, we paint," she says. "Don't anticipate what's next. Don't think about what you've already done. It's repetitive, and many people would describe it as boring. Most folk listen to music, or the radio, talk to each other or themselves. Don't do that. Keep your mind on what you are doing, whatever the temptation, whatever the distractions."

"Mr, mm, m-Mr Miyagi," says Tom, smiling. He can't remember the name of the film, but he pictures a teenager learning martial arts from an old man who makes him paint a wall and wash his car. "W-w-wax on, wax off."

Kai's expression is blank. There's no television in the bungalow. Maybe she doesn't like films.

When she leaves, Tom nods in satisfaction. For other people, her directions may be difficult to follow, but he has spent his adult life performing tasks that offer little in the way of mental stimulation. He assumes this will be easy. He is wrong.

It's not just difficult, it's impossible. Less than ten minutes after he began, he jumps at a sharp sound. When he swings around, Kai is standing right behind him. He didn't hear or see her approach. The sound was her hands clapping together six inches from his ear. With a guilty start, Tom realises he had been drifting, not focusing. He wasn't thinking about anything in particular, but his attention had moved away from the paintbrush and the wall.

"Paint," she commands.

He looks back at the bricks. He doesn't notice Kai leave, but the regular scrape of her paintbrush begins again on the wall at right angles to his own.

Tom concentrates on the wooden handle of the brush in his hand, its polished smoothness broken up by old, dried blobs of paint. His wrist aches, as do his shoulders when he bends down to the paint pot. He is glad of the sun cream Kai offered, as the heat prickles the back of his neck. And, under his white T-shirt, drops of sweat slide from between his shoulder blades to the base of his spine.

Tom tips the brush back into the paint, swivels back to the wall and watches the white line appear, covering the faded colour. He hasn't seen many painted brick houses in London, but he remembers similar bright houses from holidays when he was small. Somewhere Mediterranean, perhaps, walking down a dusty path, holding his father's hand, the turquoise sea to their right, a pack of stray dogs following in the hope of scraps. He rarely experiences such a clear memory.

He almost drops the brush this time when Kai claps. She gives a sharp shake of her head, points at the wall.

The rest of the day, other than breaks for drinks or food, follows the same pattern. Tom doesn't keep count, but by the time Kai asks him to pack up, he is convinced she's clapped in his ear a thousand times. He imagines she must have done very little painting herself, since she spent most of her time making him jump, but when he looks at her work, she has accomplished far more than he has.

Kai catches Tom staring at the incongruous door, wondering what's inside.

"We make choices that define us," she says, not looking at Tom. "I made a choice a long time ago. Now, every day, I make it again. I see a similar choice in your life, Tom. Only you can make it."

She looks at the building in front of her as if seeing straight through the walls into its interior. "The barn reminds me of the choice I made. It reminds me that, although my life belongs in this moment, my past had consequences for others. There are countless moments I cannot change where I resisted the flow. Rather than doing what needed to be done, I did what I thought needed doing. Or, worse still, what others told me to do. Let's eat."

The barn stands thirty yards south of the bungalow, but Kai crosses half that distance before Tom notices she's moved. It's not just that she moves silently, it's something more. He packs up his paint, pushes the lid into place.

For the first time today, he remembers Jimmy Blue. Blue rarely withdraws so completely. His absence does not scare Tom. He likes Kai. He wants to learn, and even though he doesn't understand what she is teaching him, he's okay with that.

Tom trudges back to the house for a shower.

CHAPTER TWELVE

ON THE THIRD day of his stay, Kai leads him out to her battered Honda, and drives him into town.

The thrift store is on a run-down street, standing in a row of tired-looking buildings. One neighbour is an army surplus store, the other a pawnbroker's.

Kai opens a metal shutter at the back with a set of keys. Inside, a flickering fluorescent light reveals a large space, concrete-floored, lined with shelves. The shelves hold donated items sorted into categories. Toys, books, CDs, DVDs, VHS tapes. Clothes rails, like the one in Tom's bedroom, hold jackets, coats, sweaters, T-shirts, blouses and shirts. There's a plastic tub full of old telephones, cords wrapped around them, and another with dusty electronic items. Video recorders, turntables, tape players, even an eight-track, with a selection of country music cartridges. One shelf displays primitive games consoles not yet old enough to be collectible. In the centre of the room, cardboard boxes full of junk wait alongside two large bin liners, clothes spilling out. Kai upends the first bag, empties its contents onto the floor.

"Alma will be here later to open up the store. She'll bring more donations for us to sort through. Enough to keep us busy until lunch, then we'll head home. Start with the clothes. Sort them into colours and materials."

She points at big canvas sacks hanging on the back of a door leading to the shop beyond. "Once you've separated them, fill up those bags. There's a laundromat on the corner."

Tom picks up the first item of clothing: a black leather jacket, in excellent condition apart from a long rip and series of tiny tears along the right sleeve. He pictures a biker losing control, falling on his right side, the jacket taking the brunt of the damage, saving his arm from lacerations. But the rips aren't too bad. Why not repair it? Why give it away? Tom pictures the biker again, sliding across the road. This time he sees an oncoming truck, bearing down on the stricken figure. A hospital bed. A grieving family. A tearful girlfriend clearing out her lover's belongings and taking them to the thrift store.

Clap.

Kai doesn't need to say anything. "No different from the painting. Pick up the next item of clothing, check the material, make a dark pile and a light pile. You might find this tougher than yesterday. Everything you pick up tells you a story. But keep returning your attention to what you are doing. I'll be here to help."

Tom knows what she means by help. Sure enough, sudden claps punctuate the rest of the morning, echoing in the windowless space. Kai can always tell when his attention has wandered. And she's right, it is harder than painting the barn. It's difficult not to attach stories to the unused baby clothes, a shiny tuxedo with a nineteen seventy-four wedding service tucked into an inside pocket; two identical sunflower dresses folded in tissue paper.

Occasionally, he looks across at Kai. She moves efficiently, sorting an assortment of items without hesitation, unloading a large box of books, checking titles and author names before shelving them. She divides toys into those beyond repair and those which need a little care and cleaning up. At first, he thinks she's not interested in the items, but several stolen glances during the morning convince him he's wrong. She *is* interested. More than interested: absorbed. For the few moments she holds each fresh object, it's all that matters to her.

Kai's interest is completely captured by a cloth bag of wooden bricks, a folder of gardening magazines, the fixed gaze of a plastic doll's head. But once she's found a home for each item, she moves on to the next. Twice, she catches him looking, and Tom expects her hands to smack together, but it doesn't happen. She simply waits for him to return to what he's doing.

When Tom gets to the laundromat, there's only one other customer; a large black woman in her sixties who keeps up a constant stream of songs as she loads clothes into a row of machines. Tom, unable to read the instructions, tries to copy what she's doing without making it too obvious. When her singing stops, he knows she's noticed. He fumbles for an apology, his throat drying and the words failing to come, but she laughs. It's not an unkind laugh.

"Need help? Here." Without waiting for an answer, she taps one of the industrial machines. "You got quarters?" She points out a metal drawer. It has space for coins. Tom doesn't have any. He pulls out the five dollar bill Kai gave him. The woman indicates another machine hanging on the wall. "Get your change there."

The machine sucks the banknote in and spits coins into an opening. Tom scoops out the quarters. The coins slide into the washer drawer with a click. Tom empties his bag of clothes into the cavernous drum. He picks up the box of detergent he brought. Seeing his hesitation, the woman slides open a second drawer with practised fingers.

"Fill it up to the line."

Tom does so and slides the drawer closed. The woman shuts the washer and points at a button. Tom presses it. Nothing happens. The woman winks at Tom, starts singing again, accompanied by a little dance. When she gets to the chorus, she smacks her substantial hip into the side of the machine, and it whirls into life, the big drum turning slowly at first as water pours in, then faster until it fills with foamy water. She laughs and returns to her own washing.

Ten minutes later, she laughs even harder when Tom loads a second machine, and completes a dance of his own before smacking it with his hip.

The two of them sit on a bench in the middle of the laundromat, facing opposite directions, watching the clothes twitch and foam. The woman sings, Tom listens. Kai was specific in her instructions for this part of his day. Sit in the laundromat until the clothes are washed, transfer them to the dryer, then come back to the store. The wash cycle would take forty-five minutes. During that time, he needs to listen to everything happening around him, keeping his attention on the sounds, rather than any thoughts.

For a few minutes, Tom thinks he is making progress. On their walk in the hills, Kai said everybody lives in a prison built, maintained, and patrolled by their own thoughts. But the prison is an illusion. Freeing yourself might take a single instant, or years of practice. For some, freedom would never come. Yesterday, painting the barn, Tom failed to stay in the moment. This morning, he failed again, never able to stay aware of what he was doing. But now, in the laundromat, Tom thinks he might be getting there. He watches the clothes in the machine wrestle in the soapy water, and he listens to the woman sing, the machines providing her backing track.

He only realises he has failed again when his companion nudges him. "That's you done. You need a hand with the dryer?"

The washing machine is inert, a red light flashing and a regular beeping emitting from it. Tom has been staring at it, but he hasn't been paying attention. He'd been in a fugue state between sleep and waking, where half-formed wisps of thought skim by before vanishing. The woman might have sung the whole time, but he can't remember a single tune.

Tom accepts her offer of help, loads the dryer and, once the clothes are turning, returns to the store. Kai notes his expression and laughs. "None of this is easy. Simple, but not easy. And no one wants to do the work."

CHAPTER THIRTEEN

FIVE WEEKS PASS before Kai moves on to a new lesson. They follow the same routine. Three times a week, they hike in the hills. Never following the same route twice, Tom gets used to the meandering paths Kai takes. He even likes the lack of planning, and takes pleasure in the different trees, plants, birds, insects, and animals they encounter. Sometimes a mountain cat or a small rodent crosses their path. As the weeks go by, this becomes more common. These meetings delight Tom, but Kai doesn't acknowledge them. She registers each encounter with the same detachment that she notices the dry earth under their feet, the rocky trails, the burbling of the stream, the contrails of the distant aircraft in the deep blue sky. As his ability to keep his attention on what is present deepens, Tom experiences a hint of that detachment.

This new state emerges when painting the barn, repairing the roof, chopping logs, sorting donations in the store, or watching the laundry turn in the industrial washing machines. Jimmy Blue would have the vocabulary to describe the experience, but Tom does not. It doesn't trouble him. He is aware of his connection to his immediate environment, and he observes this without clinging, seeing without judging. The fact he can articulate none of this is not a problem.

He continues to be untroubled by Blue's absence; in fact, he welcomes it. He's not complete—can't be, not without Jimmy Blue—but he is more comfortable in his own skin than ever before. The idea of Blue never again appearing in the shadows, no longer protecting him, or calling him, doesn't terrify him now.

One day, on a walk which takes them higher than usual, Kai surprises him by suggesting they stay for sunset. In her shoulder bag, she has bread, a few peppers, aubergines—which she calls eggplants—onions, and a pot of home-made seasoning mixed with oil. She unfolds her clasp knife, brushes dirt from a flat boulder, and cuts up vegetables.

"Plenty of dry branches nearby, Tom. Would you collect enough for a fire?"

He returns with an armful of wood suitable for burning. Kai has finished preparing the vegetables, covering them with spice mix and pushing them onto wooden skewers. She has filled up her water bottle from the stream. Tom fills his while she arranges the wood. By the time he's done, thin curls of smoke rise from the kindling, and moments later the first flame licks at the branches. The setting sun casts long shadows across the hillside, and everything takes on a warm hue. Once the fire is burning well, Kai hands two skewers to Tom. She holds her skewers over the flames and Tom does the same, turning the food as it blackens and spits, each courgette disc drying out and clenching like a tightening fist.

They eat in silence. Tom can taste each individual spice, although he doesn't know their names. The breeze wicks the sweat from his scalp. He's not wearing a bandana today. High above, two large birds circle in the thermals. There's a distant cry from the first nocturnal animal to emerge, attracted perhaps by the unusual odours.

Tom knows Kai is going to speak before she begins. As time has passed, some of her mysterious abilities have become less amazing to him. She hasn't been able to appear out of nowhere the way she used to when he first arrived. Even when he can't see her, Tom often knows where she is.

"Our ancestors divided the natural world into four elements," she begins, throwing a branch into the flames. "Fire was one. Air, or wind, was another." She digs her fingers into the thin soil. "Earth was the third, water the last. Which is the most powerful, Tom?"

There's been another change in Tom. His comprehension levels have increased, the muddy pool of his intellect clearing. He knows he is still a mental pygmy compared to Blue, but he derives joy from this new level of understanding. And so long as he doesn't rush, he can speak clearly. Kai talks so rarely that Tom can relax in her presence, unlikely to succumb to the usual mild panic when attempting conversation.

After half a minute considering Kai's question, he answers.

"The question doesn't make, mm, sense."

Kai washes the dirt from her hands in the stream, wiping them on today's sweatshirt, which reads *farm fresh food,* spelled out in tiny flowers. "Good answer. And yet it is human nature to pit one against another. We make lists, we categorise, we place this above that, label it important; stronger, faster, more worthy of praise. We're impressed by the obvious, the showy, the quick fix. We rarely see what is, instead looking for what we want to see, or what we think we want to see."

She looks up at him. Her grin makes her look twenty years younger. "Yup," she admits. "I practised that speech in my head first. How was it? Good?"

Tom nods. Kai closes her eyes.

"There is another answer to my question about power. It involves the Tao."

Tom looks up at the unfamiliar word. "Dow?"

Kai folds her legs underneath her and lays her hands in her lap.

"The *Tao,* or the *way.* I first heard about it in Malaysia. It changed my life. It saved my life."

She takes a long deep breath in then releases it. "There is no good translation of Tao. Calling it *the way* comes close, but suggests a path, and that's wrong. It's a common mistake. If we are lazy, we think of it as a way, a path, a series of steps we can follow to become fully awake, fully alive."

She puts one small hand palm-down on the dirt beside her.

"Earth. Solid. We stand on it, we build with it, make it into clay. When we die, our bodies become it."

She turns her face towards the fire. The flames dance in her pupils. "Fire is both creative and destructive. It keeps us warm, it allows us to cook food. But it can burn our houses, our bodies, and humans have used it to make weapons of destructive power."

Tom listens. He listens to her words, and the crackle of the fire, the gurgling of the stream. He listens to the call of night birds on the evening air.

"We breathe air. Recycle it through our bodies. Without it, we are nothing. The Hindus call it *prana*. Breath. All life needs it. But the Tao, if it can ever be compared to anything—which it can't—is closest to water. This stream," Kai nods towards the cold rivulets of water running through the rocks at their side, "does not forge its own path; rather it follows the contours dictated by gravity, uncovering the hidden route, going where it should. But it will wear the hardest rock away to nothing, given enough time."

Kai pauses. Tom likes the way she speaks. She deliberates over each word, constructs sentences with care.

"You don't need to study the Tao, or even know it exists, to follow it. Have you ever heard a musician or athlete talk about flow?"

"Mm."

"Good. It's close to a paradox when you try to explain it. Many truths are. Take long-distance runners. They train hard, work on their weaknesses, build stamina. A runner eats the right food at the right times to help her body accomplish tasks regular people find incredible. But listen to the greatest athletes talk about memorable victories, and certain common elements appear. Elements they have in common with musicians, writers, philosophers, and mathematicians.

"During the race, a runner might enter the state of flow. Their preparation complete, they exist in the moment, their breathing fuelling their body, muscles flexing and contracting as their legs push onward. In the flow state, they let go of any conscious effort. The religious among them sometimes describe it as surrender to God, aware that their own will is not enough. Others say it's a perfect storm where each necessary element dovetails. These descriptions sound like the mystical experiences related by holy women and men. But flow is nothing unusual. Or, at least, it shouldn't be. It should be ordinary. The Tao is the most natural state a human being can—"

Kai is interrupted by a sound Tom hasn't heard for over a month. It takes a few moments for his brain to supply the source of the interruption. A high-pitched repetitive trill accompanied by a buzzing vibration. It's coming from Kai's shoulder bag, lying on a rock. It's a mobile phone.

She takes it from the bag, accepts the call and holds it to her ear without checking to see who is calling. Tom is surprised Kai even owns a phone. He's seen no technology smarter than a fridge in the bungalow.

Kai's facial expression remains neutral. She doesn't greet the caller. She listens. After five seconds, the call ends.

Kai stares into the fire. She removes the phone's battery, slides out the SIM and snaps it.

Tom feels the difference in her as clearly as if she'd started screaming and throwing rocks in rage. He experiences a rare moment of certainty. Kai exists in the flow state she described. It's what she's been showing him all these weeks. The menial jobs, the sorting of unwanted possessions at the thrift store, and the long walks with no discernible route. Kai lives her life doing what needs doing next, her attention on what's in front of her, flowing like the stream, wherever the contours of existence take her.

Not now, though. Now, it's as if someone built a dam, preventing Kai from moving forward. Whatever the phone call means to her, it's nothing good.

Kai sits by the fireside and breathes. Minutes pass. When she next speaks, she has returned to her natural state, exactly as she was before the phone call. She stands.

"Time to get back." Kai stretches, kicks dirt over the fire to smother it. "We have about an hour until it's dark. And the moon is nearly full. Tonight will be beautiful."

CHAPTER FOURTEEN

FRIDAY IS A THRIFT STORE DAY. Tom looks forward to taking the bag of clothes to the laundromat. Most Fridays, Angelica is there. They are on first name terms now. Angelica's musical repertoire is narrow, a mixture of gospel and soul classics. Tom has hums along whenever she brings out *I Heard It Through The Grapevine.*

In the kitchen that morning, as he finishes the last of his porridge, Tom realises he has developed a tolerance for the foul stuff. He would never choose to eat it, but he appreciates the way it fills him up for a few hours. It's a cheap source of energy, and easy to prepare. Kai flavours hers with fresh lemon mint from her garden. Tom tried it once. It made him gag.

It's not until he's walking out of the front door that Kai tells him.

"Tom."

She is waiting back at the end of the hallway, outside his room. "You need to pack up your things. I'll wait in the car."

After the phone call, Tom expected something to change, although he didn't know what. But a heavy sadness rolls over him as he trudges into his room and packs his few belongings. As he hoists it onto his shoulder, he hears the Honda start up outside. He takes a last look at the distant hills, the herb garden, the gleaming white barn. Then he walks out of the bungalow towards the waiting car.

As usual, they drive in silence. Kai breaks with the usual routine as they reach the intersection. Instead of turning right towards the thrift store, she goes straight on into the centre of Santa Barbara.

At the bus station, she reads out the destinations and times on the board. Tom recognises a few names. San Francisco. Tijuana. Los Angeles. She buys a ticket, sits on a bench, and pats the seat beside her.

"Let's talk."

A bus pulls in with a hiss of air brakes, disgorging tired-looking passengers. Kai speaks softly. Tom leans in.

"I know you are not the only one who hears my words, Tom. You are fractured, broken. We all are, to some extent. Your condition, however, is extreme.

"The first time we met, darkness obscured you. But when I found you on the boardwalk, I saw *you*. It's why I wanted to teach you.

"A lifetime ago, I left violence behind. I met someone who became my teacher. He taught me about the Tao. How could I deny that to another?"

The huge man and the tiny old woman on the bus station bench attract some odd looks and a few smiles.

"Tom," she says, eventually. "The *other* seeks revenge, but I sense none of that in you. All his intelligence, all his talent—it doesn't belong to him. It's yours, Tom. You can have all of that and more. With no blood on your hands. A violent life comes with conse-quences. It can be hard to leave behind. Impossible, perhaps."

She stands up. "Los Angeles. This is your bus."

Just before he boards, Kai hugs him. "Choose well, Tom."

He finds a spare seat near the back, stows his backpack, and sits down. When the bus pulls out, he looks for Kai, but she's gone.

———

It's twilight when the lone figure approaches the outskirts of the isolated property. The bungalow is in shadow, the bright barn speared by the last of the sun. The figure doesn't hesitate at the turning, taking the dusty track towards Kai's residence.

As he gets closer, he checks the windows. There are no curtains drawn, and no lights on inside. The whole place is in darkness. But he knows she's there. The car is parked between the bungalow and the outbuilding. He walks with near-silent footsteps, and the porch boards make no sound as he transfers his weight to them.

As he steps towards the door, it swings inward. A diminutive figure looks up at him, grey eyes creased with amusement, disappointment, or concern. He doesn't know which.

"How long before you stopped the bus?"

"H-half an hour," says Tom. He walked the eighteen miles back to the bungalow.

Kai gives him a long look. He waits, footsore and dry-mouthed. She doesn't smile but, finally, she nods.

"If you're here, you're here. You'd better come in. Close the door behind you." He follows her down the hallway, and she pours him a tall glass of water, which he drains before refilling it.

"Come with me." Kai walks into her bedroom. He hesitates at the door. He's never been inside.

"Don't be shy."

Kai's room is almost as bare as his own. A single bed, a small desk, and chair. A clothes rail and a dresser. The only marked difference is a large bookcase against the back wall, shelves sagging with novels, poetry, and hardbacks with faded titles on their spines. Tom recognises a few from recent donations at the thrift store.

The bookcase serves another purpose, doubling as a door. Behind it, a space large enough for a chair and three computer monitors. Hanging from a wall bracket are two handguns and a machine gun fitted with a suppressor.

Tom says nothing.

"I wonder what surprises you more," says Kai, taking hold of a small joystick next to a keyboard. "The guns or the technology?"

65

As she moves the joystick, the screens change. Each shows different views of the land around the bungalow. Kai points at the centre screen, which now shows the track he walked down a few minutes earlier.

"Guess your doppelgänger thought I was psychic the first time you turned up. Pot of tea and two cups ready. I was having a little fun. Everyone thinks I'm a klutz around technology, and I don't like to disabuse them of the notion."

Tom examines the screen, which shows the point at which he left the main road. The angle suggests the camera must be at ground level. Kai sees him frowning and smiles.

"That camera's jammed in an old piece of dusty wood. Cameras have gotten smaller. I even hid one in some fake bird shit I bought online. Can you believe that?"

Kai backs out of the cupboard-sized space, leaving the bookcase door open. She leads Tom back into the kitchen and fills the kettle. "An alarm goes off if anybody crosses one of my proximity sensors. No one gets past the boundary without me knowing about it. Plus I have one at the turn off from the highway."

They drink tea in silence. Kai looks at his backpack, then back at Tom. "You can stay tonight. I appreciate your concern, Tom, but I don't want you here. This has nothing to do with you. I'm an old woman, and I can't undo my choices. Just south of here, my Mexican neighbours have a saying that's very Taoist. What will be, will be. It sounds fatalistic to some. But I like it."

She doesn't chastise Tom. He wonders if she can tell he intends to ignore her request, and come back every time she tries to get rid of him.

———

Sleep comes more slowly that night. Tom keeps his curtains open to see the stars and the bright moon. He wonders what kind of people Kai is expecting to visit, remembering the guns in her room. He thinks of his parents, and of those who killed them. He wonders how he would react if he met the murderers when they were old, frail, and long past the violence of their youth. Finally, he drifts into fitful sleep.

He wakes up to a strange sound; a regular low chiming. He is out of bed and dressed in seconds, making his way to Kai's bedroom. Her door is open, and he finds her at her screens. Two of them display nothing but moonlit landscape, but the third shows a pickup truck driving around the fence marking the south-east edge of her property. The night is quiet, and Kai's window is open. Tom listens, but doesn't hear the vehicle he can see on the screen.

"Hybrid," says Kai. "Or electric. About as noisy as a golf cart." She stands and reaches out to take his hands. Tom looks into her upturned face.

"We're out of time, Tom, so I want you to listen and do as I say. Do not argue with me. Do not disobey me. If you do not follow my instructions, you prove you have learned nothing. Don't you dare throw away your life because of some misguided sense of honour. I know you have it in you to make that kind of stupid mistake, and I'm not allowing it. So listen up and listen good. Go get your backpack and meet me in the kitchen."

Tom does as she asks. In the kitchen, the threadbare rug has been pulled to one side to expose a trapdoor in the floorboards.

"Follow the passage, past the first ladder all the way to the second. You'll come out behind the trees to the east. Use them as cover and move south, towards the ocean. When you reach the road, head for town, but take cover if you hear any cars."

Kai hooks a finger through a hole in the wood and lifts. The door pivots upwards to reveal a ladder. The passage beneath is dimly lit.

"Emergency lighting."

There's a handgun on the table, next to the old teapot.

"The guy who built the bungalow was a prepper who died before he could finish a nuclear shelter. I just made some alterations. Go. Now."

Tom has so much to say, but the words can't be forced out by sheer effort of will. He concentrates on communicating as simply as he can. "Mm. You, mm, too."

Kai shakes her head. "No. This is where I stop running. When I found this place, I swore I was done. Every stream ends in the ocean, Tom. Go."

Tom hesitates. Kai sees him eye the gun. She smiles. "Or will I have to shoot you?"

Tom puts his backpack on and climbs down into semi-darkness. Kai says nothing more, closing the door above him. He hears her pull the rug back, then silence.

CHAPTER FIFTEEN

THE PASSAGEWAY IS as simple as the tunnels dug by prisoners of war in black and white movies. It's lit every few yards by low-wattage bulbs behind thick glass. Tom hunches over, the passage not intended for someone his size. When he comes to another ladder, he stops. The passage continues, and he remembers Kai's instructions to continue until he reaches the very end. But it occurs to him where this ladder must lead. The barn. He walks away, then stops. It's as if Blue were whispering in his ear, and that's a voice he's never ignored.

He climbs the ladder.

Tom pushes open the hatch and emerges inside the barn, seeing it for the first time in the glow of similar dim lights to the tunnel beneath.

At first glance, the barn is half-shrine, half-armoury. There are no windows, but the lights increase in brightness. The east wall displays a large map of the world. A small table stands on one side. A black cushion on a small rug faces the wall.

The map is the kind people use when they plan vacations. Pins, each with a tiny red bead at its end, mark specific locations. Tom can't count how many there are. More than twenty. Words sound in his mind as he stares. Blue knows these places. Lebanon, Beirut, Israel. A cluster of pins in the Middle East, two pins next to each other in Dubai. Only three pins in Europe; one in London, the others in Germany and Serbia. Half a dozen in Russia, one in Australia, two in Hong Kong. Kai is too old for this to be a map of places she wants to visit. More likely, places she had been. But there are no photographs, no ticket stubs from trains or planes, none of the day-to-day detritus of travellers. The pins are the only record of her trips.

Tom glances at the table. It holds two piles of paper. He picks up the topmost piece from the pile on the right. It's a pencil sketch of a face, a young woman. Chinese, perhaps. He's not sure. There's a date underneath: February 1988. He flicks through both piles, confirming they follow the same pattern: a drawing of a face with a month and a year.

The cushion on the rug faces the map. Tom looks closer and sees the way years of use have moulded it to fit one particular human shape. Kai must sit there for hours, looking at the map. What significance the drawings might have, he does not know. He's more interested in the wall behind the cushion. It's kitted out like a home improvement display, but the items laid out there are not designed to improve anything. They are weapons. A couple of handguns with boxes of ammunition, and a collection of brutal instruments designed to inflict pain or death. Long knives, machetes, nunchucks. Small carbon throwing-stars. Hiking sticks with sharpened points. A shelf holds small vials of dark liquid, next to a syringe and a perfume atomiser.

On two wooden pallets in the corner, grenades and plastic explosives, with detonators. Some have timers attached, simple clockwork devices common in kitchens. More sophisticated remote detonators sit on an adjacent shelf.

On a low hook, a set of five throwing knives slotted into a leather sheath. Without thinking, hardly aware he's even doing it, Tom picks them up and attaches the sheath to his belt.

Before leaving, he gets an answer to the mystery of the handleless door. The barn's solid metal entrance can only be opened from the inside, judging by the three big iron bolts.

He shrugs off his backpack and lowers it to the floor, drops back through the hatch, leaving it open, and hurries along the passageway, heading for the dim light at its end. Another ladder waits there, and he climbs. This trapdoor is heavier, but there's a pulley mechanism with a hanging rope that allows him to open it easily.

Moonlight pours in as it swings open. Tom looks out. Scattered leaves, the roots of trees. As Kai promised, he emerges among the cluster of dogwoods on the east edge of the property.

Once through, he lowers the hidden door, kicking leaves back over it. He listens. He is breathing fast and his thoughts are unsettled, scattered. Kai is in trouble, but she told him to go. He pictures himself following her instructions, making his way to the road and following it back to Santa Barbara.

Tom looks towards the coast road, a couple of miles to the south. Then he moves to the west edge of the trees. From here, he can see the barn. Beyond, and to the left from this angle, is the decking at the rear of the bungalow, three steps leading down to the herb garden with its raised beds. There are no lights on. He looks for the pickup truck he saw on the computer monitors.

The truck waits on the edge of a copse to the north. It's parked side-on to Tom. The cab is pointing back towards the dirt track leading out. They must have reversed in alongside the trees. Tom doesn't understand why.

Movement. A man emerges from the far side of the truck. He has a rifle on a shoulder strap. In his left hand, he holds a pair of binoculars. He moves slowly, scanning the landscape. The full moon provides excellent visibility. Tom squats as the binoculars swing towards him. For a moment, the man is looking straight at him. Tom peers back through the vegetation at the owl-like glass eyes.

He does not want to disappoint Kai. She's right. Tom is changing. Something he thought he could never happen may now be possible. Kai says he could be whole. He could be normal. She has shown him the flow of things. He is beginning to heal.

But Jimmy Blue, who saved him from a life lived in institutions, makes the decisions. Tom has never questioned this. Not until Kai showed him he has a choice. As he watches the man by the truck, he knows it's time to make that choice.

He embraces the moment.

Does what needs to be done next.

Shuts his eyes and whispers a sentence with no hesitation, no stammer. "She needs you."

It's been weeks since Blue came. Whenever it's been this long in the past, Tom has found somewhere quiet, somewhere he can be alone for however long it takes. And, on those occasions, it's Blue who takes the initiative, who calls Tom. It has never happened this way round. Tom doesn't even know if it's possible.

For an agonising few seconds, there's nothing, just the breeze through the leaves, the skittering of lizards and insects on the hard soil, the faraway yowl of a mountain cat.

Then it begins, slow at first: the thick thump of blood in his veins, a vibration at the base of his neck. Tom looks at the pickup truck in the distance and cannot remember what it's called. Good. His awareness of what's around him evaporates, becomes formless. His knowledge of who, and what, he is follows as rapidly as air escaping from a leaking balloon.

Tom watches his identity scatter like thrown confetti.

CHAPTER SIXTEEN

JIMMY BLUE STANDS, his eyes never leaving the man patrolling by the pickup truck three hundred yards away. He waits until his quarry turns to survey the far edge of his territory, then walks out of the cover of the trees before breaking into a jog, careful not to disturb any birds whose sudden flight would give his position away.

A few seconds later, he increases his pace until he is sprinting. He has around twelve seconds if the man with the binoculars follows the same sequence of checks he made a minute ago.

Kai hasn't marked the limits of her property with a fence, but her neighbour did, and it's this that Blue heads for now, jumping the low wooden slats, flattening himself, and lying still.

No unexpected sounds. He crawls forward, puts his eye between the slats. Binoculars guy is looking at the fence, systematically checking the area. He has made no move towards his rifle.

There's a good chance Blue can get close. He drags himself north-wards behind the fence, staying low. As soon as the binoculars turn away, he stands and sprints again, counting the seconds. When he reaches ten, Blue ducks back behind the fence and continues to advance on his hands and knees. Periodically, he looks back towards the bungalow. No sign of Kai. Why would there be? She is armed; she knows where her enemies are. They might think they have the advantage, but they're wrong. She might not need or want his help. With her ability to move silently, her physical presence undetectable, she could be behind binoculars guy with a knife to his throat before he knew what was happening. But Tom's memory supplies fresh details every second, and Blue remembers the look on Kai's face when she talked about not running, about streams ending up in the ocean.

Jimmy creeps forward. It won't just be one enemy. But there's no way to cross the ground between the pickup and the bungalow undetected. And no one has attempted it since he emerged from the tunnel. So where is binoculars guy's companion?

It takes five minutes of alternate sprinting and crawling to get close to the pickup truck, its grille gleaming in the moonlight.

There's no easy way of getting from the fence to the truck. No cover. If Blue covers the distance undetected, he'll still have a hundred yards to cross when they spot him. If he runs, he risks being heard.

He decides to sprint the first seventy yards, then drop to a walk for the final approach. He visualises each step he needs to take. Slides the first of the knives from its sheath.

Muscles tensing, right foot braced against a root to propel him into a run, he watches binoculars guy, waiting for him to turn.

Something changes. The routine is broken. Binoculars guy turns his head. Jimmy holds his breath. A low sound. A man's voice. Binoculars guy says something back. His unseen colleague must be very close.

Where?

The bed of the pickup truck. As soon as he realises, Blue pictures the second man, face down, a long-range sniper rifle on a tripod, adjusted for wind direction and distance. Watching the windows of the bungalow, waiting for his shot. But surely Kai has seen this in her monitors? She will stay out of sight.

Another sound. Blue recognises it, because Tom heard the same sound every morning and evening for the past five weeks. It's the scraping of wood on wood, as the back door, which always needs a good shove, is pushed open.

No. If Kai comes out, she will be exposed. Blue stands. Moonlight illuminates the bungalow's decking as clearly as a movie set. The door swings all the way open.

When Kai emerges, barefoot, calm, unarmed, Jimmy vaults the low fence and starts running, heedless of the noise he is making.

Binoculars guy has moved to the side of the truck, looking at the bungalow.

Kai walks out to the raised beds of her herb garden. Picks up a leaf from the nearest plant, rubs it between her fingers, and inhales the aroma, her face in shadow. Tom has seen her do this a hundred times. It's Thai holy basil, he knows. He can picture her smile, although she's too far away for him to see it.

She falls half a second before the crack of the rifle sends sleeping birds whirling away from the trees. Even at this distance, Blue knows it's over. Her body snaps back as if hit with a baseball bat and crumples bonelessly to the ground.

Blue throws the first knife, the sharpened steel arcing through the night air towards its target. He's too far away, he knows it, but with every thundering step he narrows the distance. The sniper stands up in the truck.

His first knife falls short, but makes enough noise to alert the enemy. They look up at six-foot-three of muscle, knives, and rage bearing down on them like a crazed rhinoceros.

Binoculars guy moves first, dodging around the back of the truck, scrambling for cover. Smart.

The sniper moves next, but with none of the urgency of his colleague. In contrast, he looks almost relaxed as he topples sideways, Blue's second knife buried to its hilt in his neck. The truck rocks as the body lands.

Jimmy doesn't stop. He pulls a third knife from the sheath as he follows the route binoculars guy took. Even in his rage, he thinks, strategises. Binoculars guy has had enough time to shrug the rifle from his shoulder and hold it ready. If Blue continues to the rear of the truck, he'll run into a bullet. He has a better idea.

At the corner of the truck, Jimmy pitches himself forward. He lands on his front and his momentum carries him past the rear offside wheel. He looks through the underside of the truck to the trees beyond. Once he knows where the target is standing, he'll unleash his blade before his enemy can react.

There's no one there. Blue checks for any cover the man might have found. There's none.

Without warning, the truck lurches backwards. The rear wheel misses Blue's head by a few inches. If electric vehicles had exhaust manifolds, it would have pinned him to the stony ground. The truck passes millimetres over his cheek as Jimmy pushes his head hard to one side.

Binoculars guy is a quick thinker. Plus he knows when to cut his losses. They came for Kai, and they succeeded. No need to hang around. The truck brakes, then lurches forwards.

The electric pickup accelerates faster than its combustion engine driven rivals. As a result, the sniper's corpse and his rifle both slide out of the end of the truck as it bounces over the dirt track.

Blue doesn't hesitate. He rolls over, leans across, and grabs the dead sniper's rifle. He places the tripod on the ground, pushes the stock into his shoulder and puts his eye to the scope. There's no time to adjust anything. He looks at the distance between his position and the bungalow, then swings the weapon to bring it to bear on the rapidly departing pickup. Calculates. The truck bounces across the rough ground, its tailgate banging as it goes.

He controls his breathing, slows it, brings all his attention to this moment. His finger on the trigger, the rifle an extension of himself. The driver's window is rolled up and offers only a reflection of the moonlit landscape. Blue pictures binoculars guy standing next to the truck. Five foot nine or ten. Squat legs and a big, muscled torso. Pictures him driving the truck, swivels the barrel, time slowing.

Now.

Three events. The pickup window explodes. The rifle bucks against his shoulder. The sound of shattering glass reaches him.

At first, he thinks he's missed. Maybe binoculars guy is even smarter than he thought. Maybe he's leaning forward, or across the seats. The truck continues. When it reaches a bend in the track, it doesn't take it, driving straight on. It bounces crazily now on the open ground, hitting rocks and shrubs, slowing all the time. When it comes to rest, the scene falls silent.

Jimmy Blue jogs over, never taking his eyes off the truck.

Binoculars guy has an entry wound above his left ear, and the passenger seat is wet with what remains of the right side of his head. Open tip rounds. Messy, but effective.

Blue tosses the body in the back, locks the tailgate, goes back for the sniper's corpse. There's a shovel in the cab. Thoughtful of them.

He drives back to the bungalow.

———

Jimmy Blue sits in the kitchen for an hour. He doesn't pace the small room; he doesn't talk to himself; he makes no notes. He sits; staring at, but not seeing, the wall.

He might not have much time. Someone will expect a report from the two men he killed. When it doesn't arrive, there will be others. He needs the framework of a plan. Nothing rigid, nothing he can't change in a hurry to adapt to new information. Just a sketch, a series of possibilities and proportionate responses.

The smart thing—what Kai would have called right action—is to walk away. Kai did nothing to prevent her death. She could have met this threat with force. She had the means, and the ability; the weapons and explosives in the barn. But, when the moment came to use them, she chose to die. There is no way to avoid this conclusion. The way she walked out into the moonlight, knowing what awaited her, was a message. Tom's final lesson.

In which case, Jimmy decides, he is about to prove himself a very bad student indeed.

First things first.

Blue walks out onto the rear deck. From here, Kai is visible from the shoulders up. She fell backwards. More accurately, the force of the round punched her backwards. She came to rest six feet from where she started. The pitch of the roof means her face would have been in shadow from the sniper's position, but her body was illuminated perfectly. She knew what she was doing when she walked outside.

Kai knew where the shooter was and stood facing him.

At that distance, a professional would opt for a chest shot. A clear target, virtually no wind, and the mushrooming damage as the bullet passes through soft tissue all but guarantees a quick kill.

What's left of Kai's chest is a grim contrast to the peaceful expression on her face. There's nothing serene about the damage done to the human body by an open tip bullet.

Blue looks at his former teacher for a full thirty seconds. He picks her up and carries her back into the kitchen, laying the body next to the table.

He wonders if he should say something. Tom was her friend, not Jimmy Blue. But he owes her.

"Sorry," he says.

He walks out just beyond the raised beds, takes the shovel from the pickup, and digs two graves.

As he digs, he hums, but the familiar tune brings no joy.

Blue makes sure the graves can be easily seen, beyond the herb garden, mounds of freshly turned earth serving as markers for anyone who comes looking.

When it's done, he moves the pickup truck to the front of the house, the bullet hole in the glass clearly visible.

He pours himself a glass of water, drains it, then goes back to Kai's bedroom, taking the guns from her hidden room. He puts them on the kitchen table next to the sniper's rifle, then drops through the trapdoor leading to the barn.

More of them will come.

He'd better be ready.

CHAPTER SEVENTEEN

IN A MOTEL ROOM fifteen miles out of Santa Barbara, the third member of the Central Intelligence Agency crew looks down onto a dusty parking lot. The space the pickup truck occupied three hours earlier is still vacant. She knows what that means. Should have made the call by now. She's breaking protocol.

Dead flies litter the windowsill. A previous occupant of the room swatted one, leaving a red smear on the glass. The agent looks out towards the coast road, the blacktop smudged crimson by the insect's blood.

Her team calls jobs like this bear hunting, and they take turns playing third wheel, staying behind in case it goes south. Not that it ever does. Easy work and good money, if you have the stomach for it. Although calling this a bear hunt is an insult to bears. At least there's an element of danger when you put a bullet into twelve hundred pounds of gristle and rage. If your aim is off, and it spots you, the game is on. Not so with the ex-agents her team targets. Old, slow, their training forgotten. They're already heading towards the grave; the team just gives them a helpful shove. Their boss calls it sending them to Florida.

The agent works bear hunts three or four times a year. She sometimes wonders if she'll end her days the same way, a bullet in her back. It's the only guaranteed way to buy an agent's silence, particularly one with so much blood on her hands.

On the drive up from Los Angeles, discussing the details, the team stopped calling it a bear hunt. They settled on *chipmunk stomp* instead. The target is a little old woman. Sending three of them is ridiculous.

She picks up her phone, thumbs it on and checks the message thread once last time, despite knowing nothing has changed. The last message read, *we're here*. After that, nothing.

Procedure dictates she reports it ten minutes after they miss the prearranged call. After twenty minutes, she sent a one-word message: *guys?* After forty minutes, she rang both phones and listened to them go through to voicemail.

Sixty minutes after she should have done it, she makes the call. She's not sure what will happen next. These gigs aren't exactly kosher. Sometimes the CIA needs to take action without a paper trail, and, within Langley's bureaucratic structure, there's an invisible hierarchy of agents willing to do the dirty work. They know they'll never climb to the top of the career ladder, but they receive regular performance bonuses of a size that would stun their peers if they ever found out. A flexible approach to morality helps, and a barrage of psychometric tests uncovers the best candidates from every fresh intake.

"It's me. They're not back."

"Last contact?"

"Nine fifty-five."

"You're late. Why?"

She has no answer to that. Because she's covering their backs. Because human beings bond with each other when they find common ground, even when that common ground is killing other human beings. Because she doesn't want them to be dead.

She says nothing. The voice at the other end doesn't ask a second time. "Stay where you are."

While she waits, she puts the television on, stares at a movie about aliens. Flicks through the channels. She catches herself thinking of the three of them laughing in the truck. They're a good team; careful, well-prepared. She doesn't want to accept they're dead, but they're not here. What the hell did they run into?

She goes to the vending machine, gets a bag of gummy bears, takes them back up to the room. Stuffs them mechanically into her mouth, chewing and swallowing, watching a talk show.

Her phone buzzes and she grabs it. A message from one of the team. The relief that floods her makes her hands shake as she thumbs the code to unlock the phone.

Two agents? I'm insulted. I'm not going anywhere. Come and get me. Kai.

She sits on the edge of the bed, gripping the phone in her hand. For a crazy moment, she considers walking away, finding a bus station, sticking a pin in a map and starting again. But she can't move, can't even complete a coherent thought.

The window is open, so she hears the car pull into the space below. She tosses the room key on the bed and walks out, down the stairs, into the warm night air.

It's a standard, characterless agency car. Since everyone assumes the CIA bulk-purchases black SUVs with privacy glass, they've started using pickup trucks and station wagons for bear hunts. No bright colours, but nothing in black either. This three-year-old tan sedan is as anonymous as they come.

She gets into the passenger seat. The driver is someone she's on nodding terms with at the water fountain. Balding, overweight, always yawning. She'd never have guessed he did any off-the-books work.

"You want my report now?" she says, closing the door.

The driver just stares at her.

The guy in the back seat moves fast. As soon as she senses movement the agent brings her hands up, too late to stop the garrotte looping over her head and tightening around her neck.

The sedan rocks gently on its suspension as the agent struggles to breathe, gasping for air that has no way of reaching her lungs. The driver pins her wrists in her lap, his eyes looking into hers with an expression hard to identify as she fights for her life. As she gets weaker, her body twitching in some spasmodic death dance outside her conscious control, she pinpoints the balding man's state of mind.

He's bored.

Four minutes after parking, the sedan drives out of the motel parking lot and heads out of town. It stops an hour later, and its occupants strip the body of phone, ID, and weapon, then bury the surviving member of the bear hunting team an hour before the sun rises.

CHAPTER EIGHTEEN

JIMMY BLUE TIES Kai's body to a chair in the kitchen. Despite the clean dark grey sweater he's pulled over her blood-stained T-shirt, she still looks like a corpse. Her pallor is dull, the head hanging at an unnatural angle.

He hunts around the kitchen for a few minutes, trying drawers and cupboards, then heads out back, past the two graves he dug, to the potting shed. Bamboo canes are stacked in a corner. He takes them, and a roll of twine.

It'll be light in three hours. There will be more of them coming. They've lost the element of surprise, but he doubts they'll risk a daylight attack. Too direct, too visible. Too hard to cover up. Humans have used darkness to cover their worst crimes for thousands of years. This will be no exception.

Before burying the driver of the pickup, Jimmy pressed the corpse's thumb against his phone to send a message to the last number used.

Two agents? I'm insulted. I'm not going anywhere. Come and get me. Kai.

Whoever they send next will expect an experienced, dangerous assassin in her sixties. Blue intends to give them a fight worthy of her memory. But they will be foot soldiers, and he wants whoever gives the orders. Someone from Kai's past life as Elizabeth Murchen. Someone who, years after Kai left the game, decided she should die. Someone with a great deal to lose.

Sooner than they know, that someone will answer for their actions.

To find them, Blue needs leverage. They think Kai is alive. He has to keep them believing it until he can flush out the real enemy.

He lashes the bamboo canes together and ties them to the back of the chair, using them to prop up Kai's lolling head. It still sags to one side, but now she looks unconscious rather than dead.

He drags the chair away from the table, positions it in front of a plain painted wall. Moves some hanging pots to make the background anonymous.

Her mouth is the real problem. It's hanging open, jaw slack. When Jimmy pushes it closed, there's resistance, and as soon as he releases her, the jaw drops open again in a slow-motion yawn.

He considers sewing her lips together, like morticians do. Not something he's ever done before. Likely he'd mess up. No.

He remembers the parcel tape and rips two pieces off, folding them sticky side out. He sticks his fingers into the corpse's mouth and lines the tape across the molars. Puts one hand on the top of Kai's head and the other under her chin. The result isn't perfect—the mouth sags open after a few seconds—but it gives him time to get what he needs.

Blue pulls out his phone and lines up his photograph, framing his subject. When he's satisfied, he returns to Kai's body and pushes the mouth closed, springs back, and takes a burst of shots.

As he reviews the results, Kai's mouth opens again with a sticky tearing sound from the tape.

The photographs aren't bad at all. Three minutes of playing with brightness and saturation settings, and Kai's skin tone looks healthier. Good enough for what he has in mind.

He unties the corpse. It's still dark outside. After slinging Kai over his shoulder, Blue carries her to the old Honda, putting her on the front seat.

In fifteen minutes, he's driving up the twisty road into the hills they walked together. He's unfamiliar with this route. Kai avoided roads or paths on their hikes.

The Honda is the only vehicle on the road. He keeps the headlights off. The moon paints the landscape blue, grey, and black.

A clump of scraggly trees gives him somewhere to leave the car. Jimmy carries Kai and the shovel further up the hill on foot, out of sight of the road. Far enough that he's confident her resting place won't be found.

He digs Kai's grave within sight of the stream where she told Tom about the Tao. Blue works fast, despite the hard, dry earth, digging deep to make sure no wild animals uncover the body. When he's done, he scuffs the surface of the ground with his boots, retreating the way he came, using the shovel to smooth out evidence of his footprints.

Just before the unmarked grave is out of sight, Jimmy Blue looks back. For an instant, Tom is present as clearly as if he were standing alongside him. Blue is aware of a wave of sadness and grief, regret, and loss. He is curious about these emotions and their debilitating effect on the mind. He shuts it all down and turns away.

Any trace of Tom evaporates during the drive back to the bungalow. Once there, Blue parks the Honda where he'd found it.

He intends to use the tunnel as much as possible, but some of his plan means he'll be in the open on Kai's property. Exposed. Ninety minutes until sunrise. Time enough.

In Kai's bedroom, he takes a couple of laundry sacks, emptying the dirty clothes onto the floor. Back in the kitchen, he drops through the hatch into the tunnel and jogs to the first ladder. In the barn, he heads for the cache of weapons and explosives, filling the sacks with the items he needs.

Jimmy checks all the guns before taking them. Each weapon is oiled and immaculately maintained. For someone who lived so simply, Kai's armoury is an expensive anachronism. He frowns at the paradox of a woman who maintained these weapons allowing herself to be killed.

After lowering the bags through the hatch, he pauses. Looks at the meditation cushion, the map, and the drawings on one side; the shelves of weaponry on the other. And he sees it: the choice she was making every time she sat there.

He hadn't understood why Kai—Elizabeth Murchen—agreed to teach Tom when she encountered him on the Santa Barbara beachfront. Why she changed her mind about him, a troubled man who is —in fact—two men.

Now he understands.

CHAPTER NINETEEN

IT TAKES Jimmy Blue most of the night to finish his preparations. He plants explosives at the front and back doors, inside—and under— the barn, and in the footwell of Kai's battered old Honda. The detonators are wireless, each linked to a unique encrypted radio signal triggered by a handset he keeps looped to his belt. He pushes loops of C-4 into the herb garden's raised beds, covering them with loose stones. He raids the recycling box by the back door for bottles, smashing them and scattering the glass over the hidden explosives.

After hiding weapons in nine locations outside, he conceals the sniper's rifle behind the copse where the tunnel emerges, pushing it into a clump of brittlebush.

When he returns to the bungalow, it's nearly dawn.

It takes half an hour on Kai's computer to reset the proximity alarms and check each concealed camera on the boundary. He creates a virtual link so he can access the feeds from his phone. The proximity alarm, when triggered, will send him an alert.

There's a small generator in the hidden room, to power the computer and security system in case of a power cut. Blue fires it up, turns off the monitors, and closes the bookcase to conceal the entrance.

Kai's phone is in her bag. He connects it to his laptop. For a woman with so many secrets, including a false name, Elizabeth Murchen didn't protect her phone with so much as a PIN. Blue finds three recent calls. Two of them are local. The third was received while he and Kai were in the hills. The call that warned her.

A blocked number can always be hacked, but it takes time he can't spare. Instead, Blue logs onto a text-only message board that looks like a throwback to the earliest days on the internet. He leaves a simple coded message, then waits.

Three minutes later, a glowing icon opens a private chat room. The level of security of this chat room might be described as *military-level encryption* if it weren't for the fact that its designer hacked military databases for fun.

To access the chat room, Blue has to answer a question.

36?

He types the answer.

Seedless grapes

The answers are selected at random from a memory training website containing fictional shopping lists. Seedless grapes are the thirty-sixth item on the list Jimmy memorised.

The chat window appears.

bolsteroni
   hey d
   u gud

Blue types his answer.

Darkman
   K, ty. Need help fast. U free?

.   .   .

bolsteroni
  for u
  sure
  If u got something too tough for u to crack ;)

A monthly retainer in cryptocurrency makes the hacker keen to please his favourite customer. Bolsteroni has been teaching him the secrets of data search, paring, and manipulation for five years. Blue is a talented hacker now, but he'll never match his teacher, whom, he suspects, spends most waking hours online.

Darkman
  Nah. I could manage this. But not as fast as you. Time management.

bolsteroni
  what ya need

Darkman
  A blocked number from a SIM

Blue drags and drops the folder into the chat window.

bolsteroni
  that all
  im insulted
  :(

Darkman

Not all, no. Want location of number, also ID of caller if possible. Current whereabouts better still

Bolsteroni
    im on it
    too easy
    will take time is all

Darkman
    How long? I need this ASAP

Bolsteroni
    bad news then
    might take me
    ...
    ...
    one hour
    two at most

Darkman
    Funny. There's more if that's so easy.

Bolsteroni
    shoot d

Jimmy drags in his research on Elizabeth Murchen.

Darkman

When you identify the caller, see if there's a link with this woman.

Bolsteroni
    goddit
    that all

Darkman
    It is. I'll check back in two hours.

Although Blue skips a night's rest occasionally, it reduces his efficiency, blunts his advantage. He'll need to be alert.

With the proximity alarms checked and reset, he rests. On Kai's bed, he tenses and relaxes each muscle, closes his eyes, and falls into the welcoming darkness.

After one hour and thirty-five dreamless minutes, his eyes open at a chime from his laptop. Blue looks at the ceiling, grainy and obscure in morning light through patterned blinds. He sits up, swings his legs off the bed, fully awake. Checks his watch. Eight seventeen.

The online message board has a notification. He logs into a fresh chat with a new memorised item for a password, and waits.

Bolsteroni
    tricky

Jimmy Blue smiles. Leans forward to type.

Darkman
    You can't do it?

. . .

Bolsteroni
> *not what i said*
> *dude*
> *hey*
> *its me*
> *of course i did it*

Darkman
> *Really? Already?*

Bolsteroni
> *yup*
> *cmon*
> *what am i*
> *...*
> *say it*
> *...*

Darkman
> *Fine. You're top banana.*

Bolsteroni
> *the phones are all burners*
> *so no registered owner*
> *no address*

Darkman
> *But you said you'd done it. How can you know who made the calls if they're burners?*

. . .

Bolsteroni
    because im a genius

cellphone triangulation found the grid references
    ran searches on the locations
    didnt take long before something big turned up
    check the news
    i looked into the dead guy
    thats when it got rly interesting
    youll see

Darkman
    What dead guy?

Bolsteroni
    fake id
    pretty good one
    i cracked it
    found the link you wanted
    its all here

A link popped up in the chat window.

there we go
    expires in three minutes
    oh
    hope you werent close or nothing d

Darkman

Thank you.

The hacker logs off before Blue has finished typing. Jimmy opens the link and downloads the folder. The first document contains a name and address. The owner of the burner. According to the medical history Bolsteroni has hacked, Don Parfitt is a fifty-six-year Afro-American weighing two hundred and sixty pounds, not all of which has gone to fat. Mr Parfitt's employment history throws up little of interest. He's a veteran of the Iraq war, has drifted from place to place since leaving the army, and now lives in San Antonio, Texas, having moved there eight years previously.

His photo ID shows a man with a greying beard and a blank stare.

Blue clicks on a map reference. It links to a small trailer park south of the river in San Antonio. On the edge of town, behind a gas station and a Mexican eatery, a small site of about twenty trailers. Jimmy zooms into the satellite image, finds one trailer out on its own, stuck on the far edge of the site like an afterthought, the freeway overpass only yards away.

He types Parfitt's name into the search bar, and clicks on *news.* Finds a flurry of stories from the previous night.

Man feared dead in suspected gas explosion

Questions asked about safety of trailer park after tragedy

Locals identify man who died in explosion as veteran Don Parfitt

The next document is a death certificate for Don Parfitt, stillborn in 1955.

A third document yields a photograph of an army platoon, dated 1986. The location isn't identified, but the vegetation looks tropical. A few adult civilians and a boy in the background. The tall man on the end of a line of grinning soldiers, turning away, could be Parfitt's twin. The caption identifies him as Connor Tyson.

On a hunch, Jimmy zooms in on the group in the background. He squints. Impossible to be one hundred percent sure, but his gut tells him he's right. The boy isn't a child at all. He isn't a boy, either. It's Kai.

Blue scans the rest of the documents. The first few corroborate the evidence of the photograph and death certificate. Connor Tyson has been living under an alias for at least eight years. Until last night's explosion killed him.

The last scan in the folder, a screenshot of an email, contains a list of six names. No dates, no other information. Two of the names are familiar. One is Connor Tyson. The other is Elizabeth Murchen.

Jimmy ensures his location is hidden behind a continually changing wall of VPNs before searching for information on the other four names. It takes twenty minutes to track them down. Three of them served in the US military; the other was a low-level CIA goon with a record so vanilla it had to be fake. All four have one thing in common: they're dead. One hit-and-run, one knifed during a robbery, one shot—collateral damage during a police raid. The last drowned on holiday while deep sea fishing.

And now Tyson and Murchen are dead, too.

Blue checks the time of the phone call made to Kai. If it was Connor Tyson on the other end of the phone, he made that call ten minutes before his trailer lifted ten feet into the air on the crest of a fiery wave, wrenched itself apart in a violent maelstrom of gas, flames, and heat, and left nothing much bigger than a baseball mitt for the fire department to pick over.

Blue scans the news reports of the incident for a few minutes before closing the laptop.

Assumptions are necessary. Not something Blue would normally countenance, but the facts are suggestive. Ignoring this would be negligent. Tyson lived under a false name in San Antonio for eight years. Now he and Kai are dead. Members of a team which has been wiped out. Tyson and Kai were the last of them.

The contents of the barn, and Kai's secret surveillance system, are the clincher. Kai hadn't been affiliated with any government agency. Not officially, anyway. What they did was off the books. Black ops.

Kai's alterations to the bungalow suggest she knew they would come for her one day. That threat hadn't changed, but Kai had changed. Flow, the Tao. Karma. Whatever she called it, it means the same. She talked about always doing the next thing, the necessary thing. Right action. For Kai, that was breaking the cycle of violence, choosing to die instead.

Jimmy Blue makes a different choice.

He closes his eyes, his hand resting a couple of inches from the electronic detonators. Under the house, the car, the barn, and hidden around the land surrounding the bungalow, the explosives wait. Enough explosives to transform Kai's home into a war zone. Enough explosives to send a message.

His fingers twitch on the blanket.

Blue smiles.

CHAPTER TWENTY

THROUGHOUT THE FOLLOWING DAY, Jimmy Blue follows each period of light sleep with a pre-combat regime learned in the Bavarian mountains.

Blue warms up; barefoot, jogging soundlessly on the spot. Places his toes with each step, then rolls back on the ball of his foot, the heel only brushing the floor. His arms follow a pattern that looks like a mixture of interpretative modern dance and semaphore. As he follows the familiar routine, Blue half-sees the other students in Anton's frozen yard, their hardened soles bouncing off the icy ground. Their choreographed figures exercise alongside him now, a memory scratched on his retinae.

Anton liked his Shakespeare, and had adapted a line from *Twelfth Night* to fit his purposes when discussing combat. *"Some fights are already in progress, some you initiate, and some are thrust upon you."* As a variation on a famous line, it was already a stretch, but he'd added an extra element that made it untenable. *"The worst kind of fight is the one you know is coming, but the manner of its initiation is out of your control. You have to be ready at a moment's notice, but have no idea of when that moment might come."*

What Anton's advice boiled down to was this: if someone brings the fight to you, and your only option is to wait for it to start, then you choose your manner of waiting. He recommended a timetabled routine of exercise, food, and sleep.

"Don't bother trying to occupy your mind with anything other than what you are doing that second."

Thinking about it now, after less than two hours' sleep, Jimmy sees the overlap between Anton's advice and the way Kai lived here in Santa Barbara. The difference being that Anton's method is designed to keep the practitioner mentally and physically prepared for combat. Kai had no such objective. She knew how to fight, proving it beyond doubt that first day in the yard. But last night, when the moment came, she chose not to.

Blue recognises the futility of pursuing this train of thought. By doing so, he deviates from Anton's regime, and from Kai's example.

A series of isometric movements keeps his body warm, alert, and ready. Jimmy is careful not to overwork, moving regularly to the next area of the body, allowing the previous muscle group to recover.

He uses his own weight to build strength during the anaerobic section of the routine, performing slow, shallow press-ups, beads of sweat breaking on his skin. Other exercises are variations on those found on the wall of every gym, but slower, more controlled. Harder.

After a cool down and more stretches, he sleeps, but it's a version of sleep lacking a proper description. The way Jimmy Blue rests while waiting has nothing to do with Anton's methods. It's a technique Blue developed when he first emerged as a fully integrated personality. During those initial months of freedom—alive, awake, and in control of Tom's body—he feared unconsciousness. The loss of control, the surrender that comes during deep sleep, the physical paralysis that accompanies the dream-state. Afraid to fall asleep as Jimmy Blue and wake as Tom Lewis. These fears faded, but Blue still finds the sleep patterns he taught himself of use.

Those who study sleep often refer to its different stages as architecture. Blue finds this conceit useful, picturing the stages of sleep as floors in a house. He begins in the attic, level one, the dozing stage. Within ten seconds, he sinks through the floor to the bedroom below: level two, where body temperature drops, heart rate slows, muscles relax, and breathing deepens. This is where he rests for most of his time asleep. The difference is that other people sink into the next level—ground floor—for twenty to thirty minutes at a time, and he can't afford that. Level three is complete surrender. The body relaxes, the brain emitting delta waves. It's the most restorative level, and humans need it. Blue spends time there, but he is its master, not its slave.

The mind and body can be trained to pause the normal progressive stages of sleep on the cusp of deep, non-rapid eye movement. While part of him monitors the outside world, Blue dips into level three for a few seconds at a time, pulling back before the onset of paralysis.

Sleep scientists would, he suspects, find him a fascinating subject. But they would warn him against using his technique. The brain—and the body—needs to spend much longer periods than the short bursts he allows in level three. They would mutter about psychosis and brain damage if they learned he never allows himself to descend to level four; rapid eye movement sleep. Dreams live there. Sometimes, during his brief visits to level three, he cannot prevent himself from being sucked into it, but he always wakes himself up.

Today he can afford no lapses. He stays at level two and keeps each sleep period to twenty-five minutes. He can survive for ten to fourteen days this way without significant effect on cognitive function. A day or two won't diminish his powers.

After sleeping, he eats. Then the cycle repeats, every eighty to ninety minutes.

Exercise, sleep, eat. Exercise, sleep, eat. And so the day passes. No alarm sounds, no police sirens come close. The sun traverses a cloudless sky. Those who intend to kill Elizabeth Murchen, not knowing she already lies in her grave, get closer.

Exercise, sleep, eat.

Outside, darkness approaches, sharp-edged shadows slicing black across the red and orange tones of the sinking sun on the fast-cooling earth.

Night falls.

CHAPTER TWENTY-ONE

NORMALLY, when making a speech, Robert Hanan turns his phone off. Not tonight. Tonight he puts it on vibrate, and spends much of the fundraising dinner absently placing his hand on his breast pocket, hoping the damn thing might respond. He goes to the bathroom more times than a healthy seventy-two-year-old would normally countenance, finding a cubicle and checking the device for messages. He glad-hands, backslaps, laughs, and nods his way through pre-dinner cocktails, and makes interminable small talk with influencers who paid good money to sit at his table. But he can't relax.

When it's time to address the room and he still hasn't heard anything, Hanan brings his famous willpower to bear, and stops thinking about the message he hasn't yet received. The same willpower that saw him through twelve years in the army and, on his return, built a media business that survived the internet age while his rivals fell by the wayside. The same willpower that sent Robert Hanan from small-town politics to the American senate.

Ostensibly, tonight's function is a fundraiser for the cancer charity Hanan founded when his wife died. In reality, it's part of his campaign to secure the vice-presidential nomination. And the ballroom of the biggest, oldest, most expensive hotel in Portland provides the perfect setting.

"Like many young men, I once craved things that weren't good for me."

Robert Hanan isn't a natural orator, but he plays to his strengths. He is still a good-looking man; tall, healthy, with an easy smile. He's old enough now to flirt with the wives without threatening their husbands. Or so they think. He projects a hard-working, straight-talking, easy-going front that voters respond to. And when his party chose a pup in his forties for their presidential candidate, Hanan's stock rose as his party looked to an elder statesman for a running mate.

Hanan leads the pack for the nomination.

"Now, some things that weren't good for me, I grew out of. Most of you know I spent my childhood working in Dad's chestnut farm out at Wilsonville." He gives the audience the lopsided smile that appears on many of his campaign posters. "Not much temptation there. But when I joined up... well. Booze, cigarettes, gambling." He lets his gaze wander, making eye contact with a few of the wealthiest women whose patronage he had nurtured during the past months. "Plus a few other things I'm too discreet to mention." He drops his eyes, gives a little shake of the head, chuckles. It's a gesture Madeline, his public relations manager, suggests he uses once in every speech.

"It wasn't until I lost my wife, over a decade ago..." He swallows before continuing. The silence is gratifying. If his phone vibrated now, he reckons everyone would hear it.

"After Connie died, I gave up the most harmful thing of all."

A decent pause. They're hooked.

"I gave up power, because I knew I was powerless. My entire life, I craved power. In the army, I wanted to give orders, not take them. Back home, I worked for a newspaper here in Portland. But I didn't want to be the guy chasing advertisers, or raising my hand in sales meetings. I wanted to be the name under the masthead. So I knuckled down, learned my trade, climbed to the top. I bought other newspapers, TV channels, and websites. I built an empire. You'd think I'd be happy, right? I should've been happy. I had everything I'd dreamed of. And that's the key, folks. My dream."

A shorter pause here, then a little more energy in his voice.

"My dream was the American dream. The little guy who works hard and rises to the top. But..."

Wistful, now. A touch of regret. Hanan doesn't overplay it. He's no ham.

"Somewhere along the way, I forgot why I chased that dream. And I missed something crucial. A mistake I hope none of you will make. In my early sixties, when I thought I was closing in on the American dream, Connie's illness made me realise my dream had already come true. But I'd missed it. It came true at the age of twenty-seven."

He lifts his hand and wipes a finger along the side of his nose. There's no tear there to wipe away, but it's a suggestive gesture.

"Connie was my American dream. As beautiful on the inside as the outside. We had two wonderful children, and thirty-seven glorious years together.

"I said Connie died over a decade ago."

Hanan looks up beyond the heads of the audience. This is another of Madeline's suggestions and he's practised in front of the mirror enough times to do it justice. It's like he's looking for his dead spouse somewhere above the human realm. It plays well with conservative Christians. "Actually, she died ten years, eight months, and fourteen days ago."

He stares at the floor, then raises his head to make eye contact with as many influential guests as possible.

"Did I live every minute of our marriage to the full? Did I appreciate each moment we were together? No. No, I did not. And I'll regret it for the rest of my life. But I loved that woman as much as my heart could love anyone, and she loved me back. God knows I didn't deserve it, but Connie supported my ambitions, and made sacrifices of her own. Sacrifices greater than mine, but less obvious. And when cancer took her from me, I saw the emptiness of my ambitions, the pointlessness of pursuing power."

Oh, he has them now. Time to wrap up before they lose this

warm, cosy empathy that opens wallets and, if he wants to indulge himself later, legs. He turns his hands palm-up. Psychological research papers identify this as an indicator of sincerity.

"Herein lies the irony, folks. Once I'd worked out—too late—what was truly important in life, when I didn't want power anymore, the American people knocked on my door and asked me to serve my country in a new way."

A smattering of applause for this, a warm affirmation of his humility. They love this horse shit.

"Okay, folks, I won't ignore the elephant in the room."

Madeline shoots him a look, and Hanan moves his left hand, as if simultaneously acknowledging her concern and telling her to stand down. The two of them rehearsed this over and over, filming the movements, analysing the video, practising again and again. It's convincing. The atmosphere heightens as the audience buys into the choreographed moment, believing the senator is departing from his script, to the consternation of his closest advisor.

He milks the moment.

"You've heard the rumours. Me too—I don't live in a cave."

Chuckles. Excellent. He can't mention the vice-presidency tonight, but he can throw them a bone.

"I can't say much, but I will say this. Whatever the American people ask of me next, I promise I will do my best for you, for the state, and for the people of this beautiful country. And I'll do it for Connie. Thank you for your time, your kindness, and your generous donations. Together, we'll beat cancer, and together we'll make the American way of life something worth dreaming about again. God bless Oregon, and God bless America."

Hanan steps back from the mic and nods his thanks while the applause swells and the guests rise to their feet. He counts silently. Madeline says twelve seconds is optimum. Shorter than that, and he looks unstatesmanlike. Any longer, and he risks looking like he's enjoying it too much.

Hanan's hand goes to his pocket again as he leaves the podium. Now the speech is over, he can't stop his thoughts straying to the only two people alive standing between him and the glittering last act of his political career.

Two people who, if they went public, could end all his ambitions. They might not know it, but the clock is ticking. Their time is nearly up. He just wishes it were over already.

He remembers to show his teeth when he smiles. Folk don't trust politicians who smile with their lips together. Besides, dental work this expensive should be on display.

He sticks around for fifteen minutes. Long enough to shake the hands of those with the deepest pockets and the most influence. Then, with a shrug of the shoulders and a comment about an unavoidable conference call, he leaves, pausing for a final wave at the door.

The smile fades as soon as he's certain no one is looking. His features sag, and he looks every one of his seventy-two years. Hanan reminds himself he's on his way to the vice-presidency of the United States, but it doesn't give him the lift it should. Not when he's been so badly compromised. He doesn't feel like a success, he feels like a performing monkey. Still, he reminds himself, an extremely well-paid performing monkey who, after two terms in office, will retire to somewhere with beautiful golf courses and even more beautiful women.

It's not all bad. Not by a long shot.

So long as the two people in question die. Soon.

CHAPTER TWENTY-TWO

MADELINE IS WAITING at the back entrance of the ballroom with Hanan's coat.

"Miss Kalinsky."

"Senator Hanan." She helps him on with the coat, and whispers the amount pledged during the evening. It's a large figure.

Madeline stands a shade under Hanan's six-foot-one. He made her promise not to wear heels around him. Her naked political ambition is intimidating enough. And she's got all the smarts. Once he's on the presidential ticket, he's considering replacing her, not promoting her. A verbal agreement in private isn't a contract, and he won't have any need of her once he's in the White House. Her refusal to sleep with him has no part in that decision.

"I'm beat," he says. "Heading home. You?"

"Oh, I think I'll go talk you up a little more. We want to make the future President's choice of running mate as easy as possible."

"That we do," he agrees. "That we do."

The hotel lift takes him from the ballroom to the parking garage and his Lincoln Continental. It's no substitute for the BMW 7-series he used to drive, but Madeline had been immovable. "American Presidents and Vice Presidents drive American."

"Even if it handles like a turd on a greased skillet?"

"Even then, Robert."

He disables the alarm with the key fob and slides behind the wheel. Finally alone, he raises one leg and lets rip with the fart he's kept in since halfway through his speech.

"Jeez, Bob, do you have to?"

The voice is inches from his right ear. Hanan twists away, cracking his elbow against the window.

"Ow! What the—" his heart is still racing, but he breathes easier when he recognises the broad figure sitting up in the back seat, waving his hand in front of his nose. "Stoppard. Why can't you call me, like a regular person?"

"Because I'm not a regular person. Sneaking around is kinda what the CIA does best, Bob."

Hanan takes longer breaths, regains control over his body before answering. He won't let his voice waver. It would be a show of weakness. He hates being called Bob. Eric Stoppard knows he hates being called Bob, because he told him the first time they met. Stoppard has called him Bob ever since. Hanan needs to remind this blunt instrument who's boss.

"You better have good news."

The agent doesn't answer right away. He exits the car, opens the passenger door, and slides in next to Hanan. Shorter than the Senator, he's built like a Mexican wrestler. He's only missing the brightly coloured mask to cover his glossy black hair, his broken nose, and his permanent half-beard. Stoppard's barrel chest and bulging arms fill the space in a way that seems designed to be intimidating. When Hanan catches the sneer on Stoppard's face, it removes all doubt. It *is* designed to be intimidating. And it works.

Stoppard is half Hanan's age, a rising star poached from the Marines to serve his country in a less accountable way. Hanan knows the type. He once gave orders to men and women like Eric Stoppard. Black ops soldiers. Deniable, lethal, and disposable. Only now, he's not giving the orders.

Stoppard leans in until his face is two inches from Hanan's. The

Senator doesn't flinch, but, to his shame, his right eye twitches. He grits his teeth.

"Senator," says Stoppard. "Just because your empty-headed supporters shake your hand and promise you their votes, don't get any illusions. We own you. You work for us. If you get the nod for Vice President, it won't mean any actual power. It'll mean a bigger house, a better class of dinner party, and the very best hookers in the business. Unless you prefer them skanky?"

Hanan closes his eyes for a second.

"Like I said, Bob, I'm CIA. Of course we know about the hookers. I've seen the footage." He chuckles. "Your life isn't your own anymore. Don't ever forget it."

Hanan hates this icy knot in his stomach. He hates that he's ended up in thrall to the CIA. The CIA, of all people. And he's in this position because of one piece of bad luck. Someone talked, or someone put the pieces together somehow. What did it matter? However it had happened, he's screwed.

Six months ago, Ruben Castle, the deputy director of the CIA, had called to arrange an off-the-record meeting. In a diner favoured by truckers and farmers, Castle tossed a thick file across the table, and ate two helpings of apple pie while Hanan read it. The file contained evidence of Hanan's role in a fatal hunting accident over a decade earlier. The accident that killed Mike Skellern, his only serious political rival in Portland when Hanan was planning his ascent to the Senate. Much of the evidence was circumstantial. When Hanan pointed this out, the deputy director produced a thin folder and placed it on the table. Inside were two photographs: Connor Tyson and Elizabeth Murchen, the two black ops specialists who killed Skellern out in the Siskiyou Mountains. The coroner's report concluded the unfortunate politician had fallen, broken a leg and fractured his skull. The deputy director's photographs of Tyson and Murchen meant he knew different, and had the means to prove it.

Until that moment, Hanan thought no one would ever question the coroner's report. Those two photographs changed everything.

Now, with his videotaped confession as leverage, the CIA are supposed to uphold their end of the deal: tidying up any mess that might spoil Robert Hanan's chances of becoming the next Vice President of the United States.

And tidying up is Eric Stoppard's job.

Hanan swallows his fear, reaches for a little of the entitled arrogance he once took for granted.

"Stop wasting my time, Stoppard. The deputy director and I have a deal. You want me to play ball, you need to keep your promises. Well?"

The CIA man chuckles. Hanan feels the blood rush to his cheeks.

"Sure thing, boss. The good news is, San Antonio has been taken care of."

Connor Tyson is holed up in San Antonio. Hanan thinks back to his only encounter with the two operatives. They looked like a comedy duo: a huge black guy and a tiny white woman. Tyson radiated imminent physical threat. Hanan tilts his head.

"You sure about San Antonio?"

Stoppard laughs; a strange, raspy chuckle that's surprisingly high-pitched. "Tyson really did a number on you, didn't he? He said boo, you shit your pants. Well, don't you worry, Senator. It doesn't matter how mean you are if you're sitting in your trailer when ten pounds of C-4 goes off under your ass. The team brought back bits of his body in a coolbox."

"Jesus. Jesus. Okay."

"He did it himself."

"What?"

"Blew himself up. He knew we had made him. Didn't want to be brought in. He was captured once, in Indonesia. Tortured for weeks. So he opted to go out on his own terms. I can respect that."

"How can you be sure he—"

"It's not your job to worry about details, Senator. The man walked into a shitty trailer with one door. We had eyes on the back in case he escaped through a window. He didn't. Tyson was in that trailer when it lit up. And we have lumps of barbecued meat to prove it."

A trickle of sweat slides from the end of Hanan's eyebrow. He tilts his head to stop it running into his eye. He will not allow himself to look weak in front of Eric Stoppard. "And Santa Barbara?"

The CIA man doesn't answer.

Hanan presses his hands onto his knees, afraid they might tremble. His voice sounds tight and strange to his ears.

"I told you Tyson and Murchen are the best. I said you should take a big team."

"We know what we're doing, Bob. We did our homework. Murchen got out of the game years ago, changed her name, left it all behind. Growing herbs and volunteering at a thrift store. There's no way she could have known we were coming."

"But?"

In answer, Stoppard takes out his phone, scrolls through some photographs. "The agency rerouted a satellite this morning. These pictures were taken nine hours ago."

Hanan squints, tries to understand what he's looking at. The roof of a bungalow, a car to one side, a pickup truck out front. Out back, rows of greenery and two brown trenches, the earth freshly turned over. No, not trenches.

"Are they...?"

"Uh-huh. And the pickup truck matches the model our team used. We're assuming the worst. But she's still there. Crazy bitch."

"Christ." Hanan pictures Elizabeth Murchen the way she'd looked at their only meeting. She hadn't spoken. It had been Tyson who'd asked for the information he needed, then given Hanan instructions for payment. Tyson and Murchen were part of a team working off the books for various government agencies. The buddy who recommended them died in a car crash three weeks after Hanan's meeting with the CIA. That leaves Tyson and Murchen as the only people alive who can link him to the hunting accident.

Now there's only Murchen. And Hanan's starting to think he should have paid more attention to the quiet, watchful woman who'd let her colleague do all the talking.

"Wait," he says. "What do you mean, she's still there? She knows you've found her. She'll run."

"Nope." Stoppard scrolls through the messages on his phone. "She used one of the team's phones to send this."

Hanan squints, then reaches into his breast pocket for his reading glasses. He doesn't like wearing them in front of voters.

Two shooters? I'm insulted. I'm not going anywhere. Come and get me. Kai.

"Kai?"

"She changed her name."

"She's baiting you. Guess you underestimated her, son. What now?"

Stoppard's smile falters at *son*. Hanan savours the minor victory.

"It's a secluded location. No near neighbours. She should have run. Once our team go in, this is over."

"You sound confident."

"I am."

"You sounded confident when you sent the first team."

A big hand slaps his shoulder and squeezes. It's like being trapped in a vice. Hanan bites back a whimper.

"She got the jump on us, Senator. And I lost some good people. Now, you and I don't get along. We both know that. But we're adults. We have to work together, so we put aside our personal differences, right?"

Hanan nods. Stoppard's grip on his shoulder is excruciating, and he doesn't trust himself to speak without betraying the pain he's in. Doesn't want to give the younger man the pleasure.

"That said," continues Stoppard, "let me make something clear. When I joined the agency, I understood that meant I'd have to do things that don't fit into a narrow view of morality. Bend a few rules here, break a few limbs there. All in the interests of keeping my fellow citizens safe. But this job gives me a bad taste in my mouth. You're as self-serving a piece of shit it's ever been my misfortune to encounter. I'm cleaning up after you because my boss told me to do it. He thinks you'll be an asset for us in the years to come. Me? I'm not so sure."

Stoppard squeezes harder. Hanan's shoulder bones scrape together and he gasps.

"One thing I've learned in this game," continues Stoppard, "is that things change. Always have. Always will. And I want you to know, Bob,"—he leans in close enough for Hanan to identify the brand of hot sauce he'd squirted on his tacos that evening—"that when things change next, I'll volunteer to scrape you off the CIA's shoes. And I'll relish every second."

He releases Hanan. The Senator groans with relief.

The passenger door opens and Stoppard gets out. Before shutting it, he bends down and looks in at the ashen-faced driver.

"Once our business in Santa Barbara is done, you'll have a clear run at the White House, and a few fun years in office. After that, who knows? Good night, Senator."

Hanan waits a couple of minutes before driving away. Stoppard is more than a thug. He's one of the most dangerous individuals Hanan's ever met. He massages his shoulder, knowing he'll have bruises in the morning. Then he starts the engine and guides the Continental out of the parking garage and towards home.

As he negotiates the familiar streets, he thinks of Elizabeth Murchen. She may have taken out the agents sent to kill her, but her message is the work of a suicidal lunatic. She can't hope to prevail against the amount of firepower coming her way.

Hanan sweeps into the long drive leading to his house, clicks the remote to lift the garage door, turns the engine off and sits in the dark. When his hands stop shaking, he gets out of the car and unlocks his kitchen door. Pours himself a large whiskey on ice. Sleep will be hard to find tonight. He'll sleep better when Elizabeth Murchen is dead.

CHAPTER TWENTY-THREE

JIMMY BLUE TUCKS a pistol into a shoulder holster, loops the strap of a machine gun around his shoulder. Picks up his backpack and stuffs the laptop inside.

In the kitchen, he fills a bottle with water. Hesitates at the entrance to the tunnel. Turns back to the shelves, selects a chipped bowl, puts a pan on the range.

In Kai's kitchen, sitting where Tom always sat, opposite the empty chair, he eats porridge. Slow-release carbohydrates. He might need them. He ignores the taste.

Afterwards, he leaves the empty bowl on the table, drops through the hatch, and lowers it behind him. Picks up the lump of plastic explosive he left in the tunnel. Shapes it so the charge will be directed upwards, moulding it around the trapdoor's bolt, the detonator pushed into the putty.

Blue jogs along the tunnel past the ladder to the barn, exiting in the copse. The final plastic explosive charge goes across the hatch. He covers the trapdoor with leaves and dirt.

He checks his phone. None of the alarms or cams have picked up any movement. He climbs the nearest tree and surveys the land. Sees nothing troubling. From this vantage point, he can pick out the places where he concealed weapons. If not for Kai's interest in gardening, there would be few options. As it is, the land is studded with small bushes, saplings, and raised beds.

He runs over to the brittlebush and the sniper rifle, attaches and adjusts the sight, selecting night vision. The scope's green-and-white rendering turns the scene into a vintage video game. From here, Jimmy has an unobstructed view of the barn, Kai's car parked alongside. The north and east sides of the bungalow. To the west, the pickup truck. He checks the point at which the track meets the highway. There's no wind.

He adjusts the backpack on his back and settles down to wait. Used to extended periods of inactivity, Jimmy expects a long night broken up by regular stretching to prevent cramp. He'll use the time to practise some of Kai's lessons; lose himself in the landscape by becoming part of it, instead of putting his ego at the centre.

To his bemusement and annoyance, he finds Tom is better at this than him. Blue wants to keep his senses alert while his mind rests in the comfort of the deep shadows. But his internal darkness stops him letting go. Or is he stopping it himself? Whichever, he finds he can't yet replicate Kai's trick, which Tom was getting close to mastering, of disappearing into his surroundings.

Less than an hour after reaching the brittlebush, he snarls in irritation and shakes his head like a wet dog coming in from the rain. His sense of self is too solid, too engaged. So be it. If it means letting go of the darkness, he'll never completely master the technique. He and the darkness merge like strands of DNA, or the moss that hugs the trees in South London's parks.

The hours pass. His daytime cycle of short bursts of sleep means he can get through the night without dozing. Every forty minutes, Blue stretches out each limb, tightens and releases muscles aching with the effects of inactivity. Reptiles scuttle and slide from rock to rock, the insect chorus ebbs and flows like arrhythmic electronic music. When the wind is right, he can just hear waves breaking on rocks along the coast.

The alarm chimes once while Blue waits. He scrolls through the cam feeds on his phone, starting with the one that triggered the alarm. Sees nothing more suspicious than a racoon. Uses the scope from the sniper's rifle to check the area. There's no movement.

Four a.m. passes without incident. Five a.m. too. Jimmy Blue is on high alert during that period. Police and military alike are fond of pre-dawn raids, when human evolution instructs brain activity to slow down, and bodies to rest. He fights the dimming of his intellect, and his will prevails.

He looks east, towards the hills and Kai's resting place. The light is changing. Dawn approaches, a grainy reality increasing in definition every second. When it's light, he'll go back through the tunnel to the bungalow. Repeat the routine. Be ready for tomorrow night.

And if they don't come then? He can't wait forever.

One more night. If they don't show, he'll take a bus to Los Angeles, fly back to London. Become Tom, find some hod-carrying work on building sites again. Most of the pieces are in place for the revenge he's planned. The twentieth anniversary of the night he lost everything is no longer a speck on the horizon, it's four years away. The Forger, the Traitor, the Executioner, and Robert Winter himself. They are out there. He has to be ready. He will be ready.

As Jimmy sits, a bubble of contentment, a sense of belonging, seeps through from Tom's memory. Tom found acceptance in this corner of California, a chance of a life that didn't involve avenging his parents. With a cold shock, Blue sees how close he came to being diminished, his power ebbing away, during Tom's stay. Darkness shifts and coils around Blue as realisation turns to anger. He has always been able to draw on Tom's memories, see what he has seen, remember that which Tom has forgotten. It sometimes works the other way, if Jimmy Blue pushes a memory to the front of his mind, leaving it there for Tom to find. He can remind Tom why he is here, why Blue exists, why he has put mind and body through rigours, tests, and torturous physical abuse for years. He can deliver these reminders to Tom in dreams, in ghostly images he sees out of the corner of his eye, or even as brutal, unannounced flashbacks.

Blue channels his energy into picturing the faces of those who murdered his parents. Watches again as a criminal boss delivers a death sentence to his mother and father. Breathes in his own terror as a man pours petrol onto his mother while she struggles against her bonds, eyes fixed on her twelve-year-old boy. He reads the message there—*run*—and, seconds later, with his father dead and his mother burning, he does it, doesn't look back, pelts up the stairs, hears his pursuer, reaches the bedroom, slams the door shut behind him. Safe in his bedroom, where his mother or father tucked him in, read him stories.

In the seconds before the door behind crashes open, as he shakes with fear and horror, he doesn't see his familiar room. He sees his parents die, over and over. Rhoda Ilích, Marty Nicholson, John Strickland, and Robert Winter would pay for their murders. He relives the details associated with sudden death; the way an arm falls unnaturally, the slack emptiness of a mouth that will never speak again.

When Marty Nicholson, the Forger, points the weapon at his head, the child in cotton pyjamas stares into the darkness of the barrel, and stops shaking.

Maybe that's where Jimmy Blue was born. Not in the hospital where Tom lay in a coma, but there, in the pregnant void before death, the split second before the gun bucks, flashes, and Tom is punched backwards into the wall.

Blue thinks of that, and he hears one of the folk songs his father loved.

This spirit white as lightning
    Would on me travels guide me
    The moon would shake and the stars would quake
    Whenever they espied me
    Still I sing bonnie boys, bonnie mad boys
    Bedlam boys are bonnie
    For they all go bare and they live by the air
    And they want no drink nor money

                    .   .   .

A muted bell chimes.

His father slumps on the chair; a hole in his head and his brains on the wall.

A bell chimes.

His mother's head twists away when her attempt to hide her agony fails. She twitches and shrieks through her gag while her legs, then her torso, burn. The heat reaches Tom on the far side of the room.

A bell chimes.

Jimmy Blue opens his eyes. Grey half-light bathes the Santa Barbara countryside. He remembers who he is, why he is here. Takes out his phone, which chimes every four seconds.

It's the proximity alarm at the highway turn-off.

They're not coming tonight. They're smarter than that. They figured their quarry would expect an assault in the early hours, so they waited until Kai would be at her least alert after a night waiting for their attack.

They're coming now.

He stretches his limbs, tenses, and relaxes his muscles again. Takes his time, does it properly. Stares towards the distant highway. And, while the darkness inside him rises to counter the hopeful rays of dawn, he answers his own unspoken question. Why is he doing this? It's not loyalty, outrage at the loss of an innocent life. Whatever else she was, Kai was no innocent. Tom is the loyal one, like a dog too dumb to leave its dead owner's side, eventually starving to death.

No. Blue has no interest in loyalty. But he understands the pure justice of revenge. And he burns to deliver that justice.

Whoever's come here to kill Kai isn't human. Not to Jimmy Blue.

They're practise.

CHAPTER TWENTY-FOUR

THE LIVE FOOTAGE from the highway camera is distorted, but clear enough to give Blue what he needs. The camera, mounted on a road sign advertising a weekly market, offers a wide field of view from a fisheye lens. The vehicle that triggered the alarm is parked to one side, a dark Jeep. Two SUVs roll off the highway, tiny, long and wide, then tiny again as they pass under the camera. The dawn sun flashes off their windshields. A line of trees and a dip in the landscape means the vehicles won't be visible from the road. They're cautious, staying out of sight of Kai's property.

Every door opens simultaneously, and he squints at the people sent to finish Kai. The message he sent from her phone has done its job. Whoever wants her dead is sending a hammer to crack a nut. Good.

There are ten of them. Four in each SUV, two in the Jeep. The SUV teams congregate at the back of their vehicles, unzipping heavy canvas bags. The two from the Jeep talk while the team members tuck handguns into holsters and sling automatic weapons over their shoulders. Jeans, big light jackets, sunglasses, baseball caps.

They gather round the Jeep. Blue frowns at the phone's screen, wishing the resolution was better. The smallest figure is giving the orders. Female, he thinks. She spreads out a piece of paper on the ground. A map. Her pep talk takes forty-five seconds. They return to their vehicles and start their engines.

Jimmy is wearing khaki trousers, and a faded white T-shirt. He scrapes his fingers into the dirt and rubs it into his scalp, his face, his arms, and clothes. On-screen, the vehicles kick up dust; the convoy approaching at speed. He hears them now, engines revving hard. This attack isn't about stealth. It's shock and awe all the way. They've already lost the element of surprise, so they're coming in hard and fast, ten against one in a coordinated attack.

There's no external darkness to help Jimmy Blue, but he calls on the pitch-black maelstrom at his core, his senses heightening, muscles tightening. The tickle of air on his face, the sour dirt on his lips. Everything extraneous, everything unrelated to the task ahead of him sloughs off, dead skin falling away. Power hums in his veins as he channels his fury. If there was ever any fear in him, it's gone now. He won't stop until he finishes this. Or until someone stops him.

Let them try.

His energy swells with the roar of the approaching vehicles.

The convoy comes into view, the vehicles building speed as they round the sweeping bend. Once they're through the un-gated entrance—the proximity alarms chime redundantly to confirm it— the vehicles split up. The Jeep pulls over to allow the others through, stopping a hundred and fifty yards from the building. One SUV skids to a halt, the other heads to the rear of the bungalow. No one exits, but a stubby, wide barrel emerges from the open passenger window of the SUV. Blue recognises the class of weapon. It's a riot gun, used to launch stun grenades or tear gas canisters. Blue hears Uxbridge's voice in his head. The ex-SAS officer who played such a large part in Blue's firearms training would have pushed him for details.

"Identify the bastard thing as specifically as possible," he'd insist, punctuating his sentences by whacking his walking stick against his prosthetic leg. Blue had once watched Uxbridge—in a crowded underground carriage—slice up an apple, then stab himself in the leg, leaving the knife there while he ate. He had a dark sense of humour.

"Thing is, sonny, details can save your life. Say you're pursued by someone with a rifle, and they stop to take a potshot at you. If you know the range, calibre, and accuracy of the weapon, it will inform your next move. If it's a jungle carbine, keep running, because that thing couldn't hit an elephant in a playpen. However,"—another whack on the leg—"if it's a L115A3, you might as well shoot yourself and save them the cost of a bullet."

Blue, eye to the telescopic sight, checks the size of the muzzle, the length of the barrel. It's a general penetration device, a phrase Uxbridge never uttered without a smirk. Not just designed to launch canisters into a crowd, but to punch through windows, fences, or home-made shields.

A puff of smoke, and Kai's bedroom window explodes, followed by a muffled *woomph* inside. Smoke fills the space and pours out into the yard. The hostiles move the moment the riot gun fires, four of them diving out of their vehicle, gas masks in place. They carry sub-machine guns. Good at close quarters. The leader and her tall companion remain by the Jeep, handguns drawn, while their four colleagues spray automatic fire at the front door, kick it open, and disappear inside.

Jimmy swings the scope. The second SUV has stopped nose-on towards the porch, at the end of the herb garden, and two men walk towards the back porch, handguns held ready. The other two hang back, sub-machine guns ready. If Kai were inside, instead of buried on a nearby hillside, she would be trapped. Unless, of course, she had an underground tunnel leading to an armoury, and a hidden escape hatch.

It's a solid attack strategy. No finesse, but that's unnecessary. They're taking on a lone opponent in her sixties. Trained, capable, and dangerous. That's why they deviated from a night-time assault, instead striking at a time any covert operative would consider too blatant, too visible. That's what makes the strategy solid. Blue is glad.

Killing people is more satisfying when they prove themselves intelligent adversaries.

And these are intelligent adversaries. Just not *that* intelligent.

Blue unclips the remote detonator pack from his belt. The C-4 buried in the herb beds is too far away from the crew to be lethal, but the loose stones and broken glass will cause confusion and, he hopes, injuries.

He triggers the bomb. The beds rip apart in the blast, and a shock wave full of soil, stones, glass, and Thai basil lacerates the closest hostiles. All four, plus the SUV, disappear in a cloud of dirt.

Behind the open door of her Jeep, the leader screams into a radio and waves her hands. Too far to hear, but Blue is confident it's something like, "run away." She and her colleague take their own advice, and fling themselves away from the building, keeping their vehicle between them and the bungalow. Heads down, arms pumping.

"Run away" is an excellent tactical decision.

But too late.

He triggers the detonators on the remaining explosives in the bungalow. The windows go first, as the first explosion shatters the glass and sends it flying outwards; subsequent blasts driving the tiny shards far enough that they catch the light, twinkling as they drop near Blue's hidden position.

There's not much left of Kai's home once the smoke clears. A pile of grey rubble. No matter what colour they were, every bombed building ends up the same grim shade. A couple of internal walls still stand. The saucepan hanging on one, now as grey as everything else, looks almost comically incongruous.

Four hostiles were inside when the C-4 exploded. There's no movement in the pile of rubble. That leaves six. Jimmy angles the scope towards the back of the bungalow. One of the two men near the herb beds lies flat on his back. His right leg sticks out at an unnatural angle and is bleeding. His colleague wasn't so lucky. He's lying face-down in a pool of blood. The two operatives at the car are unhurt.

In the past half minute, ten enemies have become five. Four, effectively, as the guy with the shattered leg has just passed out.

Blue prepares to improve the odds further. He swings the rifle's scope back to focus on the leader and her wingman.

The adrenaline courses through his veins, but he remains in control. His hands don't shake, and his breathing remains even. His heart elevates past its usual languid resting pace to settle at seventy beats per minute. This is Jimmy Blue's domain now. When he set out on his path, he knew he would have to become a weapon. He has pushed his mind and body past the point where others would have given up, crumbled, failed, died. He's killed, when necessary. Blue doesn't believe in rehabilitation. Some people only make the world a better place when they leave it, and he's prepared to help them on their way.

The Jeep conceals the leader and her colleague. Blue waits for one of them to move, his finger resting on the trigger.

It doesn't occur to him that his absolute confidence concerning how the next few minutes will play out is contrary to Kai's lessons with Tom. He is not taking the next action as it arises, he is imposing his will on the situation, certain he will prevail.

He has never been wrong before.

Movement behind the car. He closes his left eye.

He has no doubts.

Someone stands up. He holds his breath, pulls the rifle's stock against his body.

Blue is right about it being over in a few minutes. He's wrong about everything else.

CHAPTER TWENTY-FIVE

THE TALL MAN'S head appears above the roof of the Jeep. The smoke from the explosion is clearing, helped by a south-easterly breeze.

Cross hairs centre on the man's head. He is in his thirties, clean-shaven. He's chewing gum.

Blue squeezes the trigger, the rifle twitches, and bucks, held tight against his shoulder.

As the bullet leaves the chamber, the target falls.

Too soon. He falls too soon.

There's no jerk backward as metal meets bone; no tell-tale pink cloud.

He didn't miss. But the way the man fell was wrong. His head didn't drop straight down. Its trajectory was diagonal. Blue considers likely explanations. Only one makes sense. Someone swept his legs from under him. The leader. She's good. Really good. Thinking on the fly, and smart with it. The bungalow was a trap, so she's wondering what her adversary might do next. She's concluded—correctly—that whoever planted the explosives in the bungalow is waiting to pick off the survivors.

Jimmy keeps his eye pressed to the scope. The Jeep's passenger door opens, suspension rocking, the hostiles staying low. He could try a shot, but it might not penetrate the metal doors. Since every shot risks giving away his location, he needs to make them count.

Instead, he swings the barrel of the rifle back towards the SUV at the rear of the bombed bungalow. Curses under his breath. The men are following new orders from their leader and are running. By the time Blue tracks them, both men have rolled behind their vehicle.

The Jeep's engine roars into life.

Jimmy considers his options. Do they know where he is? There are six or seven bushes, copses, and natural dips in the land to provide cover for a sniper. Pretty good odds. He should stay put.

The Jeep swings north, its wheels spraying dust and stones as the tyres skitter across the dry surface.

Blue's eyes widen. It's heading directly towards him.

The tall guy's meerkat impression got a fix on his location. They know his position.

A second engine joins the first, and he takes his eye away from the scope. The SUV bounces over the uneven ground but doesn't turn towards the copse. It's cutting off the rear, making sure he has nowhere to run if he breaks cover.

They think his options are binary: stay put, or run.

The Jeep will be on top of him in ten seconds.

He takes the third option.

He has time for one shot. As expected, both driver and passenger are hunched low. He fires low, and the Jeep slews sideways as the tyre explodes.

Dropping the rifle, Jimmy Blue pulls out a handgun, breaks cover, sprints towards the copse.

The Jeep's shredded tyre pitches the vehicle onto the bare rim. As a result, something in the suspension snaps, throwing the occupants into the windscreen as the wheel rim bites the earth and drags them to an abrupt halt.

It buys Blue the seconds he needs to cross the ground. He throws himself into the trees feet first, sliding like a baseball player trying to complete a home run. Once inside, he risks a look back.

Both hostiles are out of the Jeep. The woman sits down hard, blood on her face. She brings her hand up to it, stunned.

The tall guy, while not the brains in the outfit, compensates for intellectual weakness with dumb bravery. He runs towards the copse.

Towards Blue.

They've seen me now. They know they're not fighting Kai. I can't let that information get back to whoever sent them.

He lifts the trapdoor, drops inside, and makes sure he has the right detonator button on the remote primed and ready.

He sprints for the barn, listening for the sound of the hatch behind him opening. It won't take the man long to search half a dozen trees. Once he's done that and found nothing, there's only one other explanation.

Blue pictures it as he runs. He wants to time this right. As he climbs the ladder and emerges inside the barn, in his mind's eye, the tall man has finished his search of the small area and is looking up into the branches, assuming his enemy has climbed a tree.

Blue throws back the three bolts on the barn door and steps outside. From here, he's hidden from the others. He clicks off the safety mechanism on the detonator. The tall man must have found the trapdoor by now.

Jimmy pushes the button and the explosive charge detonates. While his remaining adversaries are distracted by the fiery remains of the copse, he glances around the corner of the barn.

The leader, blood wiped from her face, stands by the stricken Jeep, staring at the debris from the blast. Tries to put together an explanation for what just occurred. The explosion has felled every tree, leaving devastation behind. No one could survive it. The facts suggest this new enemy, whoever he is, has spectacularly killed himself after wiping out half her team. She shakes her head and gets moving. Wipes the blood from her face and runs toward the trees, gun held low in a two-handed grip, looking for anything she's missed.

The SUV from the rear of the bungalow brakes to a stop fifty yards away from the smoking bombsite. The two men emerge and jog towards their leader. She holds up a warning hand and they slow to a walk. Blue hears her voice for the first time, notes a Hispanic lilt. The wind carries her words as she gives orders.

"Unknown male, Caucasian, six-foot two or three, black bandana."

One of her subordinates answers, but Blue can't make out the words. Whatever he's saying, his boss cuts it short with a wave of the hand.

"Assume nothing. He knew we were coming. Murchen could still be here. There may be more booby traps. Proceed with extreme caution."

They search the area. Blue thinks fast. If he's lucky, debris from the explosion has covered the entrance to the tunnel. If so, the theory that he died in the blast will gain traction. That gives him more options. If he's not lucky, the explosion will expose a hole in the earth leading to the tunnel beneath.

He's not lucky.

One man shouts, pointing at his feet. The leader jogs closer, gives an order Jimmy can't make out. In response, the hostile fires a burst of fire into the tunnel from his sub-machine gun. He waits a couple of seconds, then takes a step forward and disappears into the tunnel. Jimmy hears another burst of automatic fire, muffled this time. Time is running out.

The leader stays on the edge of the trees now, giving orders. She asks a question, and when she hears the reply, her head snaps up and she looks at the barn. Blue pulls back behind the wall.

He has two detonators left. The one in the barn and the one in Kai's car. Within a quarter mile of where he stands, there are hidden guns, grenades, and a crossbow. But he can't reach them without being seen.

Three enemy operatives remain. Four if he counts the hostile with the shattered leg. The man can't move, but if he's conscious, he can fire a gun.

They know about the tunnel.

They're coming.

He readies himself for the next few moments, descends into his obsidian heart, draws his strength from the certainty he finds there.

Looks back at the smouldering rubble, and at the other SUV near the bombed bungalow. Sees another option.

Takes that option.

He runs from the shelter of the barn, out into the open.

CHAPTER TWENTY-SIX

BLUE RUNS with the barn at his back, keeping it between him and the burning copse. The injured man behind the bungalow has the clearest view, so Jimmy stays low. He sacrifices speed to use the technique Anton taught him in Bavaria, placing each heel and rolling the foot forward so that it can respond to any unevenness in the terrain. An expert can run at a reasonable pace—about nine minutes per mile—in near silence, with reduced risk of injury.

If he sprints, Blue estimates the time to the SUV at four to five seconds. Stay low, and broken leg guy won't get a clear shot—but running hunched over will add a second or two to his time. Seven seconds of exposure. One man is in the tunnel. They know it leads towards the barn, so there's every chance they'll be watching the bright white building.

He is ten steps from the point at which he needs to break right, losing his cover. He needs a misdirection, but blowing up the barn and the car will draw everyone's eye towards him, and he already knows the leader has excellent reactions.

Five steps. Time slows as he decides, visualising what he needs to do. Sees every step before it happens. Concludes it is likely to work. If it doesn't, he'll be dead.

Two steps. He looks for a piece of debris the right size. Sees a half-brick alongside a splintered table leg.

One step. He bends, scoops up the brick, draws back his right arm. Sends the brick sailing over the rubble, behind the stricken hostile. It drops behind him, and he reacts as Blue had hoped.

When the brick lands, the man swivels his shoulders, brings his weapon to bear. His reactions are slow. He's bleeding out. He squeezes off a burst of automatic fire towards the sound.

Blue breaks from cover the moment he hears the brick hit the ground. Pictures the scene from the leader's point of view. At the burst of gunfire, her attention will switch towards the sound. As she looks, she will catch a sudden movement in her peripheral vision. Her head will turn towards the sprinting figure.

Jimmy Blue squeezes the remote detonators' triggers at the moment just before he anticipates the leader spotting him. Two seconds until he's close enough to dive behind the SUV.

The Honda goes up with a roar, its tired suspension screaming when it smacks back to earth.

Kai's barn is a much smaller structure than the bungalow, but the C-4 he placed on the trapdoor sends the main shock wave towards the south wall, where she kept the weapons of destruction she had forsworn. The wall containing grenades, mines, and explosives.

The weakest point of the barn is the wooden roof, and it erupts, ripping itself from the building, driven by a fireball so hot Blue feels it on his back as he dives for cover behind the SUV.

The explosion not only sends debris into the sky, it flings jagged broken bricks and red-hot metal shards outwards in deadly ripples from the epicentre. There's no way Blue can dodge the debris; where it falls is down to chance. Chunks of masonry hit the vehicle, smaller pieces drum on the roof like lethal rain.

Before he can drag himself further into cover, his left foot jerks to the side. There's no pain, but he knows the body can respond to severe injury by blocking signals to the brain. He flexes his foot, wiggles his toes inside the boot. Everything seems normal, but he needs visual confirmation. He rolls onto his side, hunches. Lifts himself up on one elbow, half-expecting to see his limb end in a bloody stump. It doesn't. He raises his leg, twists his foot. Can't see anything wrong at first. Then he spots it. On the heel, a straight line cut through, a half-inch chunk of rubber missing, torn off by something hitting it at speed. It could have been his foot.

There's no time for *could have beens*.

He sits up, presses his back against the side of the SUV. The world falls quiet in a way familiar to anyone who's seen active combat. Few people experience that uncanny peace that isn't peace at all, the deep, immediate silence brimful with the potential for sudden change. Every soldier, every fighter knows the cliché that you never hear the shot that kills you. They also know it's not always true. They've seen comrades fall after a bullet puts them down, heard the shot that did it, watched them gasp for breath, twitch and cry as their life runs out of them.

The smoke from the explosion is already clearing. Sound returns to the scene; the strange creaks and cracks of stone, brick, wood, and metal cooling after the burst of white heat. There are no shots fired, no shouts. If the leader is giving orders, she's doing it quietly. She's lost another team member in the collapsed tunnel under the barn. Discounting the dying man by the herb beds, she now has one colleague left. The odds still favour her. She'll keep coming.

Jimmy reaches up. Opens the door. Pulls himself into the driving seat, staying low. Finds the ignition key. Doesn't stop to acknowledge his relief. The hostiles' mission was a full frontal assault. They planned to be in and out quickly, leaving a corpse, probably setting a fire to cover their tracks. They were always going to leave their keys in the ignition, ready to go.

He turns the key, pulls the gear shift into drive. Doesn't look ahead, just plants his right foot on the accelerator. There's nothing more solid than a bush to hit for half a mile. He bounces on the seat, still lying on his side, as the SUV picks up speed. Shrugs off his backpack, undoes the strap, reaches inside, finds the grenade he tucked in alongside his laptop.

They're not firing at him. She's too smart for that. Knows better than to waste time taking potshots at this distance. He raises his head high enough to see out of the passenger window, looks through the drifting smoke. The tunnel has gone, along with the hostile inside.

The second SUV is on the move.

He confirms with another look. Two of them in pursuit, both in the second SUV. Not fast enough to cut him off before the highway, but they might get close enough for sub-machine gun fire to rip through his tyres and—possibly—him.

He sits up when his SUV bounces off the rough ground onto the flatter track between the bungalow and the highway. He's heading west now, towards the unseen ocean. Before reaching the highway, the track curves south around a rise in the ground substantial enough to conceal the road beyond.

As he rounds the corner, Blue braces the steering wheel between his knees, wraps his fingers around the grenade's pin. He's never thrown a grenade in combat before, but the design is straightforward. The pin is thick metal, substantial. In the movies, he's seen people pull it with their teeth, but he suspects his teeth would come off worst in that encounter.

In the rear-view mirror, the pursuing vehicle lurches onto the track behind. He adjusts the steering wheel as the curve tightens. Leans his elbow on the button to open the window. He'll be out of sight for half a second. The timing needs to be perfect.

His fingers tighten on the pin. One more check in the rear-view mirror.

An unexpected movement, out of focus. He looks back at the road ahead.

Sees a mirror image of the SUV he's driving. A third black, bland, accelerating mass of metal. Coming straight at him. Driver's face hard set, ready, not surprised. Passenger window open, barrel of a machine gun.

She had backup waiting on the highway.

Shit.

CHAPTER TWENTY-SEVEN

ANTON'S TRAINING SAVES BLUE. Instinctive reactions he's systematically unlearned and recalibrated. Bavaria taught Jimmy to remove his ego in life-or-death situations, bypassing the biological imperative for self-preservation.

He jerks the wheel right as the SUV passenger opens fire. Makes the angle awkward for the shooter. Bullets ricochet off the front and side, a headlight shatters.

He pulls the grenade's pin as the pursuing Jeep and the approaching SUV skid sideways to follow. The world lurches and settles as something gives way in the SUV's suspension. The front left tyre deflates, fragments of torn rubber littering the dusty soil.

He drops the grenade.

It rolls into the footwell, knocks against his right foot. No time to think. Only a body and mind trained past most human limits, and the dark core that drives him.

Not today, not like this.

The SUV's broken suspension screams. He kicks the grenade. A flick of his foot propels it up the side of the footwell and into the air. He bats it out of the window, aware of the three to five second count that began the moment he pulled the pin. If it's closer to three seconds, his upper body and head will absorb the worst of the explosion through an open window.

He drives on. Another second passes.

The backup team is closest; the driver of the SUV near enough to see the object that emerges from the car in front, bounces once, then disappears beneath their front wheels.

Fragment grenades, when they detonate, push most of the explosive force upwards. Here, the detonation punches a hole through the underside of the car, and sends the engine block through the front cabin and the fragile human bodies within. The SUV rolls three times and comes to rest on its side, rear wheels spinning. The front wheels, still attached to the axle, bump away from the devastation.

Breathing hard, caught in the buzz of moment-by-moment survival, Blue is looking at the wrecked SUV when the leader's vehicle hits the rear right-hand corner of his vehicle, spinning him round and throwing him forward. His skull whips toward the steering wheel, which blooms white when the airbag deploys, expanding to fill his vision. His face hits it hard, the material folding around his head. There's an odd squishy sensation when his frontal lobe, slowed further by the thick fluid protecting the brain, smacks the thick bone of his skull and ricochets away. He bites his cheek, tastes blood.

The airbag saved him, but a concussion could still prove fatal. He has the classic signs—ringing in the ears, disorientation, and an urge to vomit—but can't afford to give in to them. He has to... has to...

Jimmy Blue shakes his head. Can't remember why he's there, behind the wheel of this wrecked car. Heartbeat raised, senses on fire. He's in danger. Has to get out.

He grabs his backpack from the floor, opens the door, and half-falls onto the sandy soil. Looks left and recognises a pattern in a group of rocks by a bush. There's a crossbow in the bush, he knows, picturing himself concealing it there, although he can't remember why. Does he need it?

Blue puts his hand to his head. The bandana is missing, but the only injury his fingers find is the ridged scarring of the old bullet wound. His sense of imminent danger comes from the far side of the SUV, so he scoots backwards and sideways towards the bush, handgun held shakily in front of him.

His breathing comes in ragged gasps. He wants to hear what's going on around him, so he takes a breath and holds it. The ringing is in his right ear. He tries to tune it out, pay attention. Hears footsteps; cautious. Lowers his head to the dirt, looks through the gap under the SUV. Two pairs of boots. Classic pincer manoeuvre. The car's wrecked suspension sags. One pair of boots disappears behind the collapsed front wheel.

Lying on his side, he steadies the gun, aims at the other hostile, squeezes off a shot. Hits one boot square on. Its owner hits the ground hard, ends up facing Jimmy who fires two quick shots into the man's chest. He rolls, ready to—

"Toss the gun." She's early forties, Hispanic, dark hair cropped close, her mouth a thin line. She's holding a sub-machine gun, ready to fire.

Two consecutive actions are necessary for Blue to prevail: sweeping the gun across to her, then pulling the trigger. She only has to tighten the grip of her right index finger to send twelve to fifteen rounds per second into him.

He thinks about it. He's fast, but no one's that fast. Shrugs. Throws the gun to one side.

If she wanted to kill him, it would already be over. His short-term memory flags up some useful information. He has a seven-inch blade in one sheath on his belt, five throwing knives in the other. If she gets close enough, he is certain he can kill her hand-to-hand.

She doesn't come closer. Doesn't look back at her dead colleague. Betrays no emotion, just an icy determination.

Jimmy Blue respects her focus. She gets straight to the point.

"Where is she?"

It's the obvious question. The leader came to kill a retired black ops assassin. There's no sign of Murchen. An unidentified man no one mentioned in her briefing wiped out her team. Ten arrived, now two remain, and the injured man has gone very quiet. She'll have to report to someone, admit they failed. To survive, Blue must convince this woman Kai is still alive.

He needs the leader to come closer.

There's blood in his mouth. He pushes himself up on one elbow, feigning severe discomfort, keeping his movements slow and awkward. Coughs a little, then more loudly, wincing. Spits blood onto the ground. Whispers, as if struggling to breathe.

"She's in the hills," he says, far too quietly to be understood, his breathing a series of shallow gulps. Let her believe he's punctured a lung. Force her to get close enough to hear. Close enough to grab.

The thin line of a mouth tightens further. "You're gonna die out here today. But I can make your death slow and agonising. So don't fuck around with me. Where is Elizabeth Murchen? Where is Kai?"

He hesitates, spits a little more blood. Whispers something incoherent.

She lowers the weapon to point at his groin. "Speak the fuck up," she says, "or lose your cojones. Your choice."

Blue visualises sequences of actions and reactions, considers the consequence of each. The only one with any chance of success is to succumb to a desperate coughing fit, using it as cover to grab a throwing knife from the sheath at his back, releasing it with a sideways flick. A throat shot is too risky. Too likely she'd take him with her. No. Aim for her hand, push the muzzle of the gun aside so she can't fire, then follow up with a second knife to the throat.

He's not operating at his physical best. The concussion has impaired his reflexes. He estimates his chances of success at around twenty-to-one. She's too good.

Twenty-to-one is better than nothing.

He draws breath to cough. Looks up at her. She takes two quick steps towards him and delivers a kick to the side of his head that sends him crashing back into the dirt.

He blinks, tries to think. She'd been close enough to grab. He'd done nothing.

Maybe the odds are fifty-to-one.

"Last chance," she says. She raises the gun to her shoulder, aims at his chest.

She's changed her mind. He sees it in her eyes. She's going to kill him.

CHAPTER TWENTY-EIGHT

Sixty hours earlier
San Antonio, Texas

Connor Tyson picks up his target coming out of a liquor store with a fresh pack of smokes, watches him light one before starting the five-minute walk home. Tyson falls in step fifteen yards behind.

Jobs like this for Big Tony help Tyson stay as far off-grid as it's possible to do in an American city. He doesn't need to visit a bank when sufficient cash comes in from the local drug dealers. Big Tony stands five foot six in platform shoes. Small-time San Antonio crime bosses and their crews display little wit when coming up with nicknames.

Tyson keeps his quarry in sight, follows the river south, then turns onto an anonymous street a bit more run down than its neighbours. The gang signs are there if you know how to read the graffiti. It's still light, so people with regular jobs are coming home from work. In ninety minutes, when darkness falls, it'll be a different story. Walking these streets at night appeals only to those with a death wish.

Tyson doesn't have a death wish. But he knows how it feels. There was a time, after he left the wet-work business, when the idea of nothingness held an appeal. But sticking a gun in his mouth means letting them win. And his old paymasters are too used to winning. Well, not this time. Every morning Connor Tyson wakes up alive is a minor victory.

He stops outside the address. Looks up and down the street. Sees nothing to give him pause. Tyson wears his usual uniform; black hoodie with a baseball cap, raincoat over that. Belted with string. His boots are mismatched, the ends of his pants frayed. His body odour is none too fresh. Tyson's general appearance and size —tall, broad and solid—means most people give him a wide berth. The occasional drunk teenager, egged on by friends, gets too close sometimes. Most of them laugh at the way he talks to himself, or imitate his shuffling gait and facial twitches. On the rare occasion it goes further than a bit of cruel teasing, Tyson lets them push him around a bit, even absorbs the odd punch or two. If they persist, a quick elbow to the throat or heel to the kneecap stops it from escalating.

Poor, ragged, desperate individuals are invisible. It's why he became one.

He approaches the door and listens. He knows Crust—what it is with these ridiculous nicknames?—lives alone. Tyson took the usual precautions when following Crust, but he wonders why he bothered. The tall Mexican wears oversized headphones while walking, head bobbing to music only he can hear. Oblivious. Tyson could have followed him at the head of a marching band waving pom-poms, and Crust wouldn't have noticed.

Tyson raises one massive boot and delivers a kick hard enough to shatter the lock and splinter the wood. Stands in the hallway. Lets the door swing closed behind him. It's dark in here. Dingy. Damp.

Silence. No. Not quite. The tiny hiss and tick of loud music leaking through headphones. Jesus. The kid can't even hear someone kicking his door in.

Tyson puts his hand in his coat pocket, through the lining and onto the butt of a gun strapped to his thigh. He doubts he'll need it, but it helps make an impression.

With the gun in his right hand, he walks down the hall and through the first door he sees.

Crust looks like he's auditioning for the part of small-time drug dealer in a low-budget movie. He's on a low sofa, jacket unzipped to reveal a hairless bare chest adorned with three gold chains. Hunched over a glass coffee table, snorting a line of cocaine through a twenty dollar bill. Alongside the coke, a pile of cash and an open beer bottle complete the cliché.

Crust doesn't realise he has company until Tyson pushes the muzzle of a SIG Sauer into his forehead. His head jerks up, his eyes go wide, and he darts at a glance at the cushion next to him.

Tyson motions at him to remove the headphones. The Mexican complies, looking again towards the cushion. He might as well wear a badge saying *I have a gun under that cushion.*

"Lift that cushion," says Tyson. "The cushion, Crust. That's right. Lift it up, nice and slow, slow as you can, gentle and slow."

Crust does as he's told, shivering now.

There's a Glock under the cushion. It's in pitiful condition. Likely to blow up in his hand rather than hurt anyone else. Tyson picks it up, drops it in his left pocket.

"You've been skimming. Lining your pockets. Not good, bad idea, don't do it. You're going to stop. Cease and desist. That's the message from Big Tony. Tony, Big Tony."

Crust looks sick. Tyson concentrates on using fewer words. He can feel his mouth running away with him. Bites down, crimps the ends of unnecessary sentences. "I'm here to pick up the eight grand you owe him, and break one of your fingers."

Crust chooses denial. A poor decision.

"I'm not. I swear. I—"

Tyson holds up his hand. "Shh. Quiet. Be quiet, don't speak. If you lie, that's another finger. Now I have to break two. Don't lie again, okay? Because you might run out of fingers. Don't."

The Mexican thinks about this. Makes a better decision.

"All right. Okay. I'm sorry. It was just to tide me over. I was gonna pay it back."

"Don't care. Pay attention, listen up. You did wrong. You take the consequences and Big Tony lets you carry on dealing. Harsh but fair, cruel to be kind."

Crust looks up hopefully. His eyes are wet. Jesus. Is he crying?

"Thank you. I won't let him down, you tell him that."

"He knows. Do it again, and I kill you. Murder you. Shoot you in the head. Maybe beat you to death. Strangulation? Not sure."

"Right, right, it'll never happen again. Never. I swear it. But I don't have the money. I have four thousand. I can get the rest tomorrow, okay? Okay? You tell him I swear I'll have it tomorrow."

"Yes. Big Tony thought you might say that. Tomorrow is fine, the day after today, two days from yesterday. Tomorrow."

Crust looks amazed he's getting off so lightly. He scoops up the money on the table, reaches under the couch. Tyson cocks the gun and he squeals.

"Woah, chill. Please! It's just the money, man, I'm getting the cash."

Tyson nods and Crust pulls a shoebox from under the couch. He keeps his money in a shoebox under his couch. The man is an idiot.

Crust counts out four thousand. It disappears into the same pocket as the confiscated gun.

"About the fingers," says Tyson.

Crust looks unhappy at the prospect of two broken fingers. Time for the bad news.

"Big Tony said if you came up short, not enough, some of the money gone, it was one finger per missing grand."

Crust goes very pale and looks at his hands. Tyson guesses he's trying to calculate how many that comes to altogether.

He hopes the Mexican doesn't rely on his fingers for counting.

———

Tyson walks back down the drug dealer's street and retraces his route along the San Antonio river. It's dusk. In the nature magazines and

140

books he reads at the library, he's learned about diurnal and nocturnal animals. Day creatures and night creatures. They stick to their patch. You don't see a bat in daylight unless it's sick. And the squirrels that scurry around the trailer park disappear at night.

At dusk, one shift ends, and another begins. He likes this time of day. Tyson stops to watch the green and brown riverbanks, and the water between them, turning black and grey as the light fades. Is there a name for animals who are both diurnal and nocturnal? *Omni-urnal?* Tyson doesn't think it's an actual word, but he likes it. Tries it out loud as he rounds the long curve of the river, the sound of the water swallowed by the freeway.

He likes words these days. Never used to. But the act of turning words over in his head, or—even better—forming them with his lips, helps keep the bad juju at bay. Holds back the tide of memories. Prevents a flood of reminiscences, a deluge of remembrance. And the pills, of course. The medicine. The drugs. They help too.

"*Omni-urnal. Omni-urnal.*" It has a rhythm that pleases him.

He is close enough to the freeway to see the nocturnal humans of his neighbourhood occupying the dank, shadowed spaces beneath its concrete ceiling. They sell meth, crack, coke, or horse. Newer drugs Tyson hasn't heard of. Those who don't sell drugs or stolen goods— mostly phones and jewellery—sell themselves.

The underpass where he placed his battered, run-down trailer is the kind of location folk avoid; grimy, its inhabitants fizzing with dangerous resentment. Local papers run biannual news columns describing such areas as shameful; a blight on the city. The nocturnal creatures who ply their trade in the shadow of the concrete are collectively referred to as scum. Tyson knows the truth, same as he knows the truth about the evil enemies he once killed in the name of the USA. They're people. That's all. Just people. As confused and messed up as the journalist who writes those columns, and the readers who shake their heads while reading them.

When Tyson spots Pharrell leaning up against a graffiti-tagged wall, smoking, he slows his pace, waits for the signal.

He has an arrangement with the dealers, the pimps, the fences, and the hookers. When he first towed his trailer close to their territory, Big Tony, who runs the district, sent a couple of his crew over. They asked him to move. He refused. They insisted. Tyson sent them back with empty wallets, a few bruises, and a broken bone apiece. He went easy on them. Next day, he introduced himself to Big Tony, who hid his surprise well when a stranger walked into his bedroom, having incapacitated five armed men en route. When Tyson explained his offer, and how little he wanted in return, Big Tony was quick to agree. It was good for business to have Tyson on his crew.

Pharrell looks over, registers Tyson's familiar silhouette shuffling along the river path. Instead of the all clear—both hands shoved into his pockets—he combs his short bleached hair with his left hand, then scratches his nose.

It's the signal Tyson hoped he would never see. Strangers. Looking for him. Instead of continuing towards his trailer, he skirts the far side of the underpass, slips into a malodorous alleyway behind a shuttered pawnbroker, and waits.

Pharrell sends a kid over. They start young. The kid who appears is ten or eleven, trying to hide it with a slo-mo swagger and permanent frown. The facial expression, Tyson guesses, is meant to project an aura of menace. Looks more like he's constipated.

"Yo, Parfitt, my man." Since moving to San Antonio, Tyson has been known only as Don Parfitt, an identity he paid good money for when he first dropped off-grid. He holds up his fist and follows the series of gestures the underpass crew use. Humans need tribal rituals of belonging, he knows that. No point telling them it's a lie, that everyone dies alone.

"Dwayne, right?" Tyson is good with names. When he hears one, he rolls it around his mouth for a few minutes, tries it out.

The boy shakes his head. "Ice-bone."

Tyson's mouth stops moving. "Ice-bone?"

"For real."

A gang nickname means Dwayne is a full member now. Tyson has a flash of sadness at the thought. He's old enough to be this kid's grandfather. Half the gang members he'd watched come and go in the underpass end up in prison or dead. Is that the best this poor kid can hope for?

He pushes the thought away. It's unhelpful, and it's distracting. No room for that. Not now, not ever. Some people get softer as they get older. Not Tyson. If that happens, he's finished. Was a time he might have cared about someone else, but it's long gone, and he can't afford the luxury.

"So. Ice-bone. What's the score?"

"There's two of them. One's white, one's a brother. Old dudes. In their forties." Dwayne catches the older man's eye. "Sorry. Er, you know, middle-aged. Acting casual, like they's looking to rent a trailer. Gram gave 'em a tour of the park. They asked questions and shit, but you could see what was going down. One of them faked a phone call, but he was using the camera, getting shots of your trailer. They were in Gram's office twenty minutes. Gram just scored enough horse to keep him high a month. Looks like he came into some money, know what I'm saying?"

"Sure. I know, I got it, *capiche*, understood." It's over. He has to leave San Antonio. How did they find him? And why now? What's changed?

He peels off a couple of twenties from a roll in his pocket. Doesn't look like Big Tony will get Crust's money. "Where are they now?"

"They split up, came back in two cars. Watching the entrances. Waiting for you. You wanna know the models and registrations?"

"No. Thanks, Dwayne. Ice-bone." He hands over the bills. "Get me a phone, will you?"

The kid grins, looking his age. "Just so happens I have a spare. It's yours, man." Hands over a black plastic rectangle. Tyson looks at it.

"How do you make it work? I need to block the number too. Can it do that?"

Ice-bone smothers a giggle, takes the phone. His fingers dance across the screen.

"What century you living in, Parfitt? They say you don't even own a TV. That right?"

Tyson frowns at the kid's naivety.

"All electronic equipment is connected. Signals, out there, traceable. They send a picture to you, damn sure it's sending a picture back. Use a phone, they can find you, track you, any time they like. They got a file on every one of us. Even you. You think I'm crazy, out of my mind, losing it? I know what I'm talking about. You're the crazy one. Buying phones, watching TV, using computers, giving them everything they need, giving it all away, letting them use radio microwaves to send you orders, keep you down. I..."

Tyson catches the look on Dwayne's face. Stops himself. Remembers the two men looking for him. Focuses. Leans on his training. The kid hands him the phone.

"Number's blocked. What ya gonna do about these guys, Parfitt? Break their heads? You want any help?"

Tyson puts his hands on the kid's shoulders.

"Hey!" Dwayne squirms, tries to break away. Tyson holds him fast and the kid registers the iron strength in those big hands. He knows Parfitt's reputation. He stops struggling, all swagger gone.

"What ya doing, man? Let go of me."

"I need you to listen up. Listen real close. It's important, life or death, got it?"

Dwayne nods fast. "Yeah. Yeah, I got it. What you need?"

"Carlos in his spot yet?"

The kid shakes his head.

"Good. Go find him. Tell him I said he needs to find somewhere else to be tonight. If I see him, I'm gonna be very, very disappointed. Upset. Angry. Violent. You got that?"

There's genuine fear in Dwayne's eyes now. No one wants to get on Parfitt's bad side. They've seen the injuries sustained by those who did. And they've heard rumours of worse. Tyson needs Dwayne scared. He needs Carlos—who sells meth from the pitch at the rear of Tyson's trailer—to sense that fear when Dwayne passes on the message and stay away.

"Tell him it's just for tonight, this evening, the night-time. Then he can come back."

Carlos might wonder what he's done to upset Parfitt. By tomorrow, it won't matter.

Tyson relaxes his grip. "Tell everyone else to stand down. You see these two guys, ignore them. I'll deal with it my way. You got that?"

"Got it, man. Shit, you lift weights with yo fingers or what?" He rubs his shoulders, turns tail, and jogs away.

The day has come.

He has to warn Kai. Has to follow protocol.

He dials a memorised number. Waits for it to be answered. Doesn't speak; stays on the line for a count of five, then ends the call. Closes his eyes for a few moments. They're the last, Kai and him. And whoever wants to tie up this loose end has made a mistake. They should have left them alone, let them live the rest of their lives with some dignity. Some privacy.

Now he's gonna have to make someone pay.

CHAPTER TWENTY-NINE

A FADED BLUE Dodge Charger waits at the trailer park entrance; dented, suspension old and sagging. Window rolled down. The guy inside is smoking.

A hot rush of anger passes through Tyson, watching from the shadows of the playground opposite, where no kid ever plays. They only sent two agents to finish him. Two. And they're journeymen, not bothering with basic precautions. These guys don't expect Tyson to present much of a challenge. A quick, easy hit, and home for a late supper. The anger threatens to morph into fury. He squats behind a slide, spits out the thoughts that might slow him down; clears them out of his system. Purifies himself.

"I've been out a long time, but they have my files, know about the hospital, there but not there, breakdown, breakdown, breakout, broken. Not sure, for sure. That's not me. They think this is the real me; wasted, scared. Mad Parfitt, collecting soda bottles for pennies, days in the library talking to himself, the man who isn't there, living like a bum, in a shitty old trailer, no soap and the booze stink. A pair of desk jockeys sent to finish me. No point wasting a good team, follow a sick old crazy into his hovel and beat him to death, kick him when he's down, make him bleed, every rib broken, dance on his body, pour liquor over it, toss a match, watch him burn. Another no-hoper who upset the wrong gang, got what was coming for him, waste no tears, criminal scumbag. Okay, fine, that's good, works for me, works for me, it's good, it's all good. Play along, planned for this, play my part, the crazy guy who used to be dangerous. Mustn't kill them. Need witnesses. C'mon, man, c'mon, be full dark soon. Move. Move out. Move along."

Equilibrium restored, Tyson leaves the playground and walks through the trailer park, passing under the street lamp. He pauses his shuffle long enough to look over his shoulder, check the goon is paying attention. Their eyes meet. The goon looks away as if disinterested, but a second later, Tyson hears the door of the Dodge clunk open.

Five seconds later, and the man is out of the car, and moving. Good. Tyson injects a note of panic into his performance, stumbling in his haste to reach sanctuary.

At the trailer door, he stops, key in hand. Looks back. No one. The agent hangs back in the shadows. His partner will watch the back. Not in the underpass—too visible. Parked up top, eye pressed to a night vision scope, best guess.

Once Tyson is inside, they've got him. They think.

The trailer sits on a low brick wall, purpose built. It means no one can get underneath, no one can *see* underneath.

A thick chain and a heavy padlock secure the door. It's under Big Tony's protections. All part of their deal.

Inside, he flicks on the light and draws two thick bolts in place. Moves fast now.

If anyone other than Tyson ever stepped inside this trailer, his reputation for eccentricity would skyrocket.

There's no bed other than a thin mattress and a sleeping bag. No kitchen, and the only furniture is a sun lounger. Two tiny windows, both of them boarded up. In the single room is a metal implement the size of a small spade, a flashlight, a scuba diving jacket, oxygen tank and regulator, and a large chest freezer, secured with a second padlock. Bags of empty beer, wine, and hard liquor bottles line the far wall.

Tyson walks around the freezer, using the side of one boot to kick down the catches on the wheels underneath. Pushes the freezer against one wall, revealing a bolted trapdoor beneath.

The padlock on the freezer has a combination lock. Tyson spins the dials, thinking of the last European job he did for the agency. Fifteen, sixteen years ago? It was just him and Kai, which was often the case. She was still Elizabeth Murchen then. They had almost given up finding their target when Kai uncovered the concealed entrance to a tunnel beneath the five hundred-year-old house. Its only weakness was the fact it was a dead end. Strategically, that was suicide.

He lifts the lid of the freezer. Inside, curled up like a pregnancy photograph, is a man's body. Tyson doesn't know his real name. Everyone knew him as Irish Harry. He was one of the lost; a homeless drinker waiting to die. Hypothermia took him two winters back. Tyson found his corpse under a bench. A big man, his grey beard matted and nicotine-stained, Irish Harry is unaware of how useful his afterlife is about to become.

Tyson tips the freezer on its side and drags the corpse out, sliding it along the floor. The body wears a raincoat tied with string, a fashion statement Tyson copied to prepare for this day. He hoists Irish Harry onto the lounger, and returns the freezer to its upright position, pushing it against the wall.

The Glock he took from Crust makes a nice extra touch, although Harry's thumb snaps when Tyson forces it around the grip. He peels the front of the raincoat from Harry's chest; tucks Ice-bone's phone into his pocket. If a piece of it survives, it has Connor Tyson's finger-prints all over the screen.

He estimates he has five minutes, not that he needs them. They'll expect him to be armed, so they'll be cautious. Plastic explosive on the door to blow it off its hinges. Follow up with a grenade. No need for subtlety. A couple of bribes dropped into the right pockets, and it's a gas leak.

Tyson lifts the trapdoor, revealing the real reason he moved the trailer. A metal cover leading to the oldest part of San Antonio's sewer systems. He drops the three feet to the ground, inserts the metal implement, leans back. The cover lifts, and he nudges it to one side with his boot.

He shrugs on the scuba jacket and the tank, twists the canister on. Grabs the flashlight, puts the regulator in his mouth, climbs three steps down the iron ladder. Breathes through his mouth, sucks in the air from the pressurised tank. Pushes the trapdoor back into place. A long press on the button of the kitchen timer screwed into the trailer's underside. It flashes up *2:00, 1:59, 1:58, 1:57*.

Tyson pulls the cover back. As it drops into place, he is plunged into absolute darkness for a split second. The usual terror squeezes its claws around his heart. He's ready for it, but it's never easy.

Complete darkness pulled him apart, piece by piece, when he was captured on a solo mission in Indonesia. He never found every piece needed to put himself back together. Seven weeks in a pitch-black hole before Kai found him, led him out of a basement, past a dozen dead men, onto the street, into a car, and through the pre-dawn streets to a safe house. Ten days before he could talk, another two weeks before he could board a plane home without screaming.

The flashlight kills the shadows. He thinks of Kai. Thanks her. Adds a prayer that she'll take his call seriously. She needs to run. If someone is retiring what's left of their team, they won't stop. Too dangerous to leave any of them alive.

At the bottom of the ladder, Tyson reaches into a hole in the wet brickwork, pulls out two plastic bags. After tying them over his boots, he drops into the sludgy liquid that runs along the underground system of old sewage pipes, walks north, his pace brisk. He breathes from the tank. The rats won't kill him, but poisonous fumes might.

This stretch of the sewers, slated for modernisation, dates back to the city's founding. Back then, they used canals to dispose of waste. A handful still survive.

At the first junction with another tunnel, he turns west. Tyson's body clock tells him two minutes are up. He stops. Waits. Hears only the scratch and scurry of rodents, the drip of foul water. Tastes the rubber of the regulator. Blinks away the sting in his eyes from the sulphuric reek of the sewers.

Listens.

When it comes, the explosion registers as a low, booming thump, once it's penetrated the dampening effects of asphalt, concrete, and soil.

Irish Harry—or his scattered remains—is poised for a short period of notoriety. After an anonymous couple of years in Tyson's freezer, the city will identify him as Don Parfitt. Others will identify him as Connor Tyson.

Tyson plods down the tunnel, his pace slower now. His face twitches into an unfamiliar smile. He's out. For good this time. Somewhere in Langley, there's a database with his name on it. Tonight, or tomorrow morning, he can picture some clip-on tie office drone, crisp white shirt and a buzz cut, ticking a box that moves his name from one column to another. From inbox to outbox; from jobs outstanding to jobs completed; from active to deceased.

It feels good to be dead.

CHAPTER THIRTY

RV Heaven Motorhome Sales occupies a large plot half a mile south from Connor Tyson's trailer park. Huge billboards advertise its location, and no San Antonio cable channel runs more than twenty minutes without showing an *RV Heaven* commercial.

The pearly gates aren't a prop made for the commercial; a huge entrance, spray-painted gold, welcomes all visitors. Brand new RVs arrive every month, lined up where they can be seen from the freeway. Trade-ins and second-hand vehicles join the ranks through a less ostentatious rear entrance. They come and go regularly. All but one, which the owner—Big Al Crawston—tells his employees he's looking after for a friend. It's close to the truth. The motorhome tycoon's daughter would be dead if it weren't for Tyson, and Big Al takes that debt seriously. He wouldn't take a cent for the motorhome Tyson chose, and he didn't ask questions when his daughter's rescuer told him he wanted it parked, long-term, in a specific place on the lot. Every Saturday morning, when Al comes in early to catch up with paperwork, he checks the exterior of Tyson's motorhome personally, making sure it's still roadworthy, then starts it up and drives around the lot for a few minutes.

It's a ten-year-old Phoenix B-class rig favoured by Mom and Pop vacationers who rack up the miles and run down their kids' inheritance. Tyson appreciates its bland anonymity. It's not a rich person's plaything, and it's not a wreck. Traffic cops pass dozens of identical vehicles every day all over America.

He emerges from the sewer between the Phoenix and a neighbouring RV. Waits. The chances of anyone hearing the ironmongery slide aside is slim, but Tyson hasn't lived this long by taking unnecessary risks. Once sure he's alone, he finds the magnetic box under the wheel arch, takes out the key, and unlocks the rear side door.

Every window has blackout cloth taped across it. He turns on the interior light, performs his customary checks. Dials in the combination on one of the padlocked cupboards, looks over the weapons he keeps there. Chooses a shotgun for the rack over the driver's seat.

It takes two minutes to remove all the blackout material. He leaves the windshield until last. Sits in the driver's seat and looks across the lot towards the freeway. Half a mile away, a cloud of smoke punctured by headlights and the flashing blues and reds of the emergency services.

Don Parfitt and Connor Tyson's funeral pyre.

He starts up the van, headlights off. *RV Heaven* has security lights bright enough for him to navigate through the ranks of vehicles to the back entrance. Once there, he leans out of the window, punches in a six digit code and waits for the dark iron gate—quite the contrast to the gaudy customer entrance—to slide open.

He puts his lights on when he reaches the road, joins the traffic heading for the interstate. The first news station he finds mentions the explosion just south of the San Antonio river, but offers no details. It won't be long before they release Don Parfitt's name. For a couple of days, his face will make the local news. Even phones can show the news these days. Kids watch movies on them, on screens the size of their palm. And they call Tyson crazy.

Best to lie low for the first twenty-four hours, let the media move on to something else. He can't move on until tomorrow night, after his follow up call to Kai.

Tyson figures they sent the B-team to kill him. Maybe even

further down the pay grades. They believe his documented break-down means he's compromised, that he can't out-think them. So they assigned a couple of losers with lazy habits and paunches to kill him.

They won't do the same for Kai. A legend when operational, if some pen-pusher has decided it's time to retire her, they won't take risks. He thinks through how he and Kai would have approached the gig: concealment, surveillance, then a clean hit. Fast, uncomplicated, efficient. A high-velocity round from a Steyr SSG 69 at about eight hundred yards out. The Austrian rifle had probably been replaced as long-distance weapon of choice by now, but Tyson liked it. Reliable, well made, accurate. That's how he would do it.

But Kai knows that too. She'll be ready for them. He's sure of it.

———

A motorhome driving the perimeter roads of Canyon Lake, forty-three miles out of San Antonio, is not an unusual sight, even late at night. Tyson passes seven vehicles similar to his own as he circum-navigates the body of water heading around to the north-west shore. He's glad of the dark; it means he doesn't have to raise a hand in cheery salute at every vacationing couple he sees.

The RV provides perfect camouflage, but Tyson doesn't look right. A solo male dressed—and smelling—like a bum will attract attention in areas popular with retirees and families. And he's aware of how badly he handles even basic conversation. Better to avoid people. Tomorrow he can change his appearance.

His last scout of Canyon Lake was six weeks ago, as one of the four bolt-holes he'd picked out for an emergency. A mile and a half after crossing the Guadalupe River, he passes a sign for a boatyard. He slows the Phoenix to twenty miles per hour, counts the trees on the passenger side of the road. When he reaches fourteen, Tyson checks his mirror. Nothing coming. He pulls off the road, bumps the van between the trees, counts another three, four, five, takes a sharp left and enters a small clearing where he kills the engine, flicks the lights off, gets out.

Collecting a broom from a storage bay at the rear, he jogs back to the road. Checks both ways again, then shines a flashlight into the trees. No sign of the parked Phoenix, and no giveaway reflections from its windows and mirrors.

The soil here bakes hard and dusty in summer. It's a two-minute job to rearrange the loose top layer to cover the evidence of his egress. Tyson retraces his route to the van in reverse, bending branches back into shape, kicking over his footsteps as he retreats. The result wouldn't fool a professional, but a casual glance from the road won't give him away.

Back at the van, Tyson grabs a sleeping bag, hunkers down, finds a suitable spot a few feet from the rear bumper. Spreads out the bag, takes a quick walk around the clearing. Listens for the nocturnal animals, hears nothing yet. The twenty-two thousand pound metal box on wheels has spooked them. Give them twenty minutes and they'll be back, providing a first-rate alarm system. An alarm system Tyson is tuned into. He'll wake at the slightest disturbance in the lake's wildlife.

Feels good to sleep under the stars. There's a moment, eyes heavy, before the usual fitful rest, when a rare childhood memory jolts him. His lips are moving as usual—slower now, the stream of consciousness fading into sleep—and, of a sudden, he's seven years old, Mama's hand resting on his back while he kneels at his bedside. Some prayers come back to him as he blinks up at the glory of an unpolluted night sky, but he pushes his lips together. He's seen too much pain, known too much loss to believe in a merciful god. The best he can hope for when he dies is true, dreamless oblivion. If Tyson thought prayer worked, that's what he'd pray for.

CHAPTER THIRTY-ONE

DAWN COMES peaceful and slow to Canyon Lake. The water is a soft, deep blue blanket; placid, patient. Only at one spot, on its north-west shore, is the surface ruffled, the stillness disrupted.

A naked man stands waist-deep in the shallows, the water foaming white around him as he washes. The grime is deeply ingrained, and Tyson uses a stiff-haired brush to scrub his body—which is heavy and broad, and not as lean as it was when he killed people for a living.

His skin shines with scars from cuts and burns, the legacy of weeks of torture. His right nipple is missing, and the angriest scar—running from his missing nipple to his hip—is obvious even now, because his torturers, after sewing it up, reopened it the next day. They repeated this over and over. When he didn't break, they left him in the dark for so long he forgot what the sky looked like; or a tree. The sea at sunset, the curve of a breast. He believed he would never go outside again. Then Kai came for him.

His entire body prickles with goosebumps as he wades back to shore, picks up the towel he left hanging on a branch. Still naked, rubbing the towel across his chest, he goes back to the Phoenix. He could have showered there, but no point using the water tank when there's twenty square miles of it on his doorstep.

Back in the lake, as far out as he could throw them, his old clothes —tied inside his jacket, weighed down with rocks and his old boots— rest on the bottom.

After hacking off as much beard as he can with a clasp knife, Tyson boils water on the stove, makes instant coffee with a finger of tequila, and, dipping a razor in the saucepan, scrapes away at his chin until the wing mirror of the van reveals a stranger.

Coffee finished, he steps into the van, opens drawers, dresses like Cory Davenport, a man who—until the moment he slides a new ID from the compartment behind the shower—doesn't exist. Canvas pants, blue cotton shirt, olive baseball cap.

Cory Davenport, according to online records available to all but those with clearance to dig deeper, is a fifty-five-year-old heating engineer from Fort Worth. As with Don Parfitt, Tyson wrote Cory's backstory in a small black notebook; a fictional life touched by the average amount of joy and tragedy. He learned the details by heart so he won't get caught in a lie.

He pulls on a pair of new hiking boots. The final touch is a pair of thick-rimmed black glasses. Along with the clean-shaven chin, they lift attention to the top half of his face. The glasses are oversized, the kind he's seen older musicians wear.

Tyson stares at his new face. It took months to become Don Parfitt. Months of studying, making sure he had relevant dates and details at the front of his mind. Answering to his new name, burying Connor Tyson deep, not sure if he'd need him again. His mind was foggy then. It's worse now; more confused. His intellect, once sharp, lithe, and strong, has been away by his demons. Time is supposed to heal. In his case, time has dismantled him. His thoughts have a momentum, an agenda, of their own; they pull Tyson from place to place, never letting him settle. It's why he talks to himself. To regain control. When he can't mumble the thoughts away, pictures run free in his head, his body remembers the pain, the frightened child screams in the dark.

"Cory," he whispers to the mirror. "Cory Davenport. Out of Savannah, Georgia. My wife and I planned to travel the entire country when we retired, but cancer took her last fall. So I took the trip on my own. Forgive me if I talk too much. Martha was blind. I always described new places, new people to her. Still do. Not sure I'll ever be able to break the habit."

That works. It even explains him talking to himself. Wouldn't do for folk to think him crazy. Wouldn't do at all. Grief is an excellent cover story. Grief makes even regular people crazy for a time.

He fishes for his breakfast in a cove masked by trees, pulls out three largemouth bass. Blackens them over a flame. Tears white flesh from the bones of the first; washes it down with another coffee and a second finger of tequila. Without the alcohol, he'll sweat and shake. Not good for his new image.

The day passes slowly. Waiting is a condition familiar to every soldier. Waiting is, by far, the biggest part of the job. Everything else is a distraction: training exercises, briefings, nights drinking and fighting, tempers running hot, the illusion of eternal brotherhood mending temporary rifts between comrades. Behind it all the waiting, always the waiting. Waiting to kill or be killed.

He tries to read. All he has is a couple fishing magazines, a Sports Illustrated. He flicks through the pages, tosses the magazines into the footwell. Thumbs through the black notebook, scans his own handwriting. He can't remember writing the notes on Cory Davenport. Can't remember the last time he scribbled anything longer than a faked signature.

In the afternoon, the notebook joins Parfitt's clothes in the lake. He paces his domain like a tiger in an invisible cage.

Afternoon gives way to the evening, a purple bruise of sunset. Tyson eats the other two fish, supplemented with ramen from the van's store cupboard. Drinks more coffee, more tequila. The light fades. He talks, mostly to himself, but once to a cottonmouth snake looping lazily through the shallows.

Midnight arrives, and Tyson switches on the burner he keeps in the glovebox. This phone is an older model with physical buttons. It doesn't stop him finding the device inherently untrustworthy, but at least it's not a smartphone. He skips setting the time and date, dials the second memorised number, then stops.

Midnight in Texas. Ten p.m. in California.

He turns the phone off, stuffs it in his pocket. His grunt of frustration sends a creature in the bushes scurrying away. Paces out another two hours.

Two a.m. Tyson dials the number, checks it on the screen before pressing the call button. With the phone at his ear, he looks out across the silver water and listens to a phone fourteen hundred miles away ring and ring. Protocol means he should hang up after the fourth ring, but he doesn't. There's no answer.

Which means...

Which means nothing. Not necessarily. He stares into the night, seeing a locked basement where he once thought he would die. He sees Kai, her silhouette at the top of the concrete steps like an avenging angel. Her face, when his eyes adjust to the return of light, striped with the blood of their enemies.

The phone stops ringing; becomes one long tone. He presses the button to hang up, then dials again. Listens to it ring and ring.

Enough. Tyson takes the phone apart, snaps the sim card, tosses it and the battery into the lake, throws the rest into the bushes. Goes back to the van for the broom, uses it to brush away his footprints.

There are maps in the van. He figured out the best route to Santa Barbara the same day Kai told him where she lived. Didn't think he'd ever have cause to use it. Some friends, when you say goodbye, your gut says you won't see them again. That's how it was with Kai. They'd shared enough horror, enough death. Time to leave it behind.

Problem is, some things can't be left behind.

It's a long drive, and he'll have to eat, shit, and sleep. The calculation Tyson makes is rough, but it helps him form a plan. If he drives for eight hours, sleeps for three, then repeats, his third driving session will get him to Santa Barbara around dawn.

When he and Kai set up their protocol, they agreed an unanswered second call meant it's over; they were dead or captured. No heroics. They're professionals. The best in the game.

Revenge is for amateurs. He knows this.

As hard as he tries, he can't imagine a world without Kai. She's too dangerous, too deadly... too *alive*. It's New York Harbour without the Statue of Liberty. Frisco without the bridge. But imagining her captured is even harder than imagining her dead. She'd slit her own throat first.

What does it matter? Kai didn't answer. And he has to know why. Maybe it's stupid. Maybe it's amateur. But he's retired now, so he guesses that means he is an amateur. Not sure Kai would agree with the distinction, but to hell with it.

Tyson starts up the Phoenix, puts the lake at his back, and drives up the gravel track, keeping his speed low until the tyres grip the blacktop beyond.

There's little chance of trouble, but he's close to San Antonio, where his face—still bearded, of course—will have been on the news, so he takes the smaller roads west to begin with, adding fifteen miles to the fourteen hundred ahead.

There's no sound other than the rumble of tyres on asphalt, but Tyson keeps hearing the ringing phone that Kai didn't answer. His lips move while the ghost echo of the sound afflicts him like tinnitus. He speaks aloud, lets the words come.

"Kai could slaughter a platoon on her own, one hand tied, no one gets the jump on Kai. She gutted them and hung the bodies from a tree. No way she's dead. She ain't dead, that's the end of it. No way. No how. Not Kai."

The Phoenix joins the I-10 at a town named Comfort. Tyson doesn't miss the irony.

CHAPTER THIRTY-TWO

SENATOR ROBERT HANAN checks his watch. He's three minutes early for his reservation in one of Portland's many lunch spots. Since he's meeting Madeline, a subordinate, political etiquette dictates he arrives five minutes late. However, since his relationship with Madeline doesn't fit with the norm, there's no point playing games. The maître d' shows him to a private room, and Hanan orders a drink, wondering if it's at all possible to get Madeline Kalinsky into bed. He knows he shouldn't indulge himself in this kind of speculation, but he can't help it.

He thinks back to their first meeting in Washington DC. Madeline, to his shock and dismay, already knew of his legendary libido when she pitched her proposal to run his campaign. She closed with a statement he will never forget.

"Now, Senator, if you're the man I think you are, you have two questions. I'll answer both. I'm one of the sharpest political advisors in Washington. So, question one is, why did I pick you?"

There was no point in challenging her. Her statement wasn't arrogant. He'd heard her name more and more over recent years. She'd achieved the rare distinction of gaining the respect of senior politicians without making enemies. Well, that wasn't quite true. But

Madeline Kalinsky's enemies had one thing in common: they all ended up in the political wilderness.

Madeline nodded at his lack of denial. "Well, there you go. That lack of reaction is one reason I'm here. You're a pragmatist. You know I could work for whomever I choose. There's enough bullshit in politics. I promise you I'll keep it out of our working relationship. That's a quality you'll appreciate over the next few years."

She held his gaze. Steady, assured, not challenging.

"Senator, I'm a thirty-six-year-old woman. Politically, that means I work twice as hard as you. You're a rung on the political ladder I'm climbing. An important rung, Robert, but a rung nonetheless."

He raised an eyebrow, but said nothing.

"Circumstances handed both of us an opportunity we shouldn't pass up. You'll never be president. We both understand that. But I can get you the vice-presidency. Which will draw the attention of those who can facilitate my next move. Are you okay with that kind of ambition?"

Hanan treated her to one of his avuncular chuckles.

"Well, Miss Kalinsky," he smiled. "You've done your homework. I prefer plain talking and a direct approach. Yes. I can see how a partnership would be mutually beneficial. As long as we both agree who's in charge."

Madeline nodded at that. In retrospect, Hanan realised it wasn't necessarily in accordance with his own thoughts on the subject. "You said I'd have two questions," he reminded her. "I have many more. But what did you think I'd ask?"

Madeline smiled, her full lips parting.

"It's not a question you're ready to ask today. Even you wouldn't be so bold. Still, I can read your signals. They're obvious. We'll need to work on that if you ever want to see the Oval Office outside of a tour."

Robert stopped chuckling.

"Let me answer before you ask." Madeline leaned forward. Hanan fought the urge to look down her shirt. "The closest you get to my panties is when our luggage is in the hold of the same airplane. Are we clear?"

Hanan is still smiling at the memory when Madeline enters the private lunch room. He looks at his watch. She's six minutes late.

Madeline slings her bag over the back of the chair and sends the server away for a large Bloody Mary. Doesn't apologise for her tardiness.

"We'll keep this brief, Senator. I'm leaving for Washington this afternoon."

"Where's the fire, Madeline?" She's not his type, he reminds himself. She's too tall, athletic rather than curvy. Brunette, not blonde. And she's made it plain she's not interested. Also, he's going to fire her once he's in office. Unless she loosens up.

"It's our golden boy. He's about to make a mistake. Well, his team is. We need to stop it. When did you last speak to Grant?"

Hanan sits up straighter. "Wednesday, no, Thursday night. Ted's talking about tax in his CBS interview next week. He wanted to go over the details, make sure we're on the same page."

Ted Grant is the closest to a dead cert for president in a generation. On-screen, he comes across as energetic, handsome, warm, and empathetic. A straight talker, a natural leader. Since on-screen is the closest ninety-nine percent of voters will get to Grant, they don't know that away from the limelight he's lost without his team of handlers. For the man who runs that team—Ross Dacre—Grant is the culmination of a political project developed over two decades. Dacre has groomed three presidential candidates, but Grant is his best shot at the most powerful job in the world.

An African-American grandmother completes Ted Grant's election-friendly picture. No one can accuse the party that approved his nomination of racism. He's the perfect frontman for the ageing white cabal that intends to continue running the country.

Madeline isn't saying anything. Waiting for Hanan to join the dots. Tax is the hot topic right now, after a New York Times piece on the current administration's proposed cuts for billionaires went viral. Grant has to walk a dangerous line if he wants the White House. He can't condemn the policy—it's his own party's, after all—but unquestioning support risks losing the trust of middle class Americans. Not a demographic any presumptive president wants to mess with.

As a multimillionaire himself, tax cuts for the rich would make Robert Hanan richer still, but his wealth is an Achilles heel in the race to be Grant's running mate. But none of this is news. What's making Madeline scurry back to DC in such a hurry?

"Shit," he says. When the server sets down Madeline's Bloody Mary, he sends him back for another whiskey and soda. "Jackie."

"Jackie," Madeline confirms. Jackie Cartland, senator for Maryland, and Hanan's only rival for the vice-presidency. An outside bet, her appeal is narrower than Hanan's. Her name is still in the hat because her supporters are organised, enthusiastic, and predominantly middle class. She's strong on the economy. You won't find Jackie being caught out by a trick question from a clued-up financial reporter. She runs rings around them. Her grasp on other issues is shakier. She's a one-trick pony. The problem—for Hanan's campaign, at least—is that her trick is tax. Whereas Hanan is strong on security, law and order, prisons, and foreign policy, he is happy to leave the economy to Grant and Ross Dacre.

"What's she saying?"

"Nothing. She's being smart. The noise about tax cuts gets louder and louder, and she's nowhere to be found."

The server hands him the whiskey, and he takes a long sip. "What's her play?"

"She wants Dacre to see her as the safer choice for VP. The longer she leaves it—assuming the story doesn't go away—the better she looks as a running mate. Putting her on the ticket sends a strong signal to the middle class that someone is listening. Someone has their back."

"But—" All thoughts of bedding his advisor gone, Hanan takes a gulp and puts the glass aside. "She's a fucking liability, Madeline."

"Sure. I know that. You know that. Dacre knows it, too. Doesn't mean shit if their boy's shiny image looks tarnished."

Hanan nods, smooths back his white hair, a gesture Madeline

advises he only uses in private as it makes him look vain. "You're right," he says. "What do we do about it?"

The server returns for their order. Madeline raises a hand to stop him. "The special looks fine. Two of those. No bread. A pot of coffee to follow."

"Of course, ma'am." The man leaves.

Madeline takes a thick manilla envelope out of her bag. Hanan is uncomfortably reminded of his meeting with the deputy director of the CIA. But Madeline is smiling, and she's on his side. Isn't she?

"Senator Cartland," she says, drumming shiny red fingernails on the envelope. She makes no move to open it.

Hanan bites.

"You got something on Jackie?"

"Maybe."

His dormant libido twitches. There really is something indefinably arousing about Madeline Kalinsky.

"I thought you didn't play games," he reminds her.

"I don't. Robert, if we go down this road, things will get dirty. So, once we've discussed the contents of this envelope, I'm going to ask you a question you already answered. I won't apologise for that. You may have lied to protect your ambitions. Not this time. I want the truth."

"I never lie to you, Madeline," lies Hanan.

"Really?"

Hanan shrugs. "What do you want me to say? You know me better than Connie did. The bad and the good. Where are you going with this? What do you have there?"

Madeline taps one finger on the envelope.

"This contains proof that Jackie Cartland took a bribe back in Los Angeles, in her City Hall days."

"That's great!" Hanan coughs, adjusts his tie. "I mean, that's appalling. I'm shocked to my core. It's our public duty to bring this to light. Excellent work."

"Not so fast. It's more complicated than that. This is your decision, Robert, but you need all the facts."

"Enlighten me."

Madeline looks at the view that adds twenty percent to their bill. Downtown Portland's high-rises are sparkling in the sun, watched over by a snow-capped Mount Hood.

"It happened a year after her husband died. Her son needed experimental treatment. He had a terminal illness. Insurance wouldn't pay for anything not FDA approved. Unlike you, Senator, Ms Cartland doesn't come from money."

Hanan doesn't flinch. Okay, he was lucky; Granddaddy Hanan made his fortune in oil, but—as the Senator reminds reporters and voters alike—he can't be blamed for that. He worked damned hard to get where he is. Still does.

"So she took a bribe to save her son." Hanan thinks over what he knows about Jackie Cartland. "Oh. Shit. The treatment failed, right?"

"Right. He died."

"Jesus." Hanan leaves an appropriate pause to register the human tragedy. Four seconds feels about right. "So how do we use this to screw her over? Go to the press?"

"Terrible idea."

"Why? It'll finish her."

"Yes it will. But the timing is terrible. After the feeding frenzy, the press will wonder how this information came to light just before Ted Grant announces his running mate. They'll ask who benefits most from the timing. Then they'll dig around some. It could blow up in our faces. No. There's a better play."

Hanan doesn't rise to the bait. He waits her out. Enjoys the tiny win when she speaks first.

"Jackie is an honourable woman. If I go to her with this, she'll resign. It's a crime, after all. If it's made public, she'll go to prison. Even if folk sympathise with her reasons, she still took a bribe as a government official. Her political career will end. Worse—she won't get any job better than stacking shelves once she's out of whichever white-collar penitentiary they send her to. No. I confront her, she resigns, and, in her statement to the press, she mentions you by name as her preferred candidate for the vice-presidency."

"Wow." Hanan toys with his cutlery. "You figured it all out. Question."

"Shoot."

"How can you be so sure how she'll react?"

"That's a great question. Before I answer it, I want to ask my own. As promised."

Hanan loses patience. Shakes his head. Madeline speaks again.

"No games, Robert. I need to know."

"Fine, Madeline." He doesn't hide his irritation. "Whatever you want."

"Good. Senator, you've been candid with me about your sexual habits, and some financial dealings close to the edge of what many consider ethical. I need to know that's everything. If you're hiding any skeletons, bring them out, because if you keep anything from me, I will bury you so deep, you'll never feel sunlight on your face again. So. Last chance. Is there anything that, if it comes to light, could compromise your candidacy?"

Hanan doesn't give it much thought. Connor Tyson, incinerated in a San Antonio trailer, is no longer a problem. Elizabeth Murchen, on the other hand... But Eric Stoppard says he'll take care of it. What can one woman do against a CIA black ops team? It's only a matter of time. Elizabeth Murchen and Connor Tyson are dead.

He twists a napkin around his fingers. Who the hell does Madeline Kalinsky think she's talking to? It's bad enough being beholden to the spooks, without his own advisor treating him like a clueless ingenue.

"Watch your tone, Madeline. You're good, but I could take a piss out of this window and soak a dozen political advisors who'd love your job."

Madeline ignores him.

"I'm waiting for an answer, Robert."

"Fine." He swigs the last of the whiskey. "There's nothing. I'm disappointed you asked me again."

"Noted, Senator. I can live with your disappointment. Here's the answer to your question. For the past couple weeks, I've been talking to the Cartland camp. Jackie wants me to work for her. I told her I'd think about it. That's what I've been doing, Robert. And I didn't decide until a few seconds ago."

Hanan's fingers are throbbing along with his pulse. He looks down to see he's twisted the napkin so tight, the tip of his left index finger is white as the snow on Mount Hood. He relaxes his grip.

"Ms Kalinsky, you are the most scheming, ruthless, cold-hearted bitch I've ever met."

"Thank you, Senator. Now, where's that food? I'm starving."

CHAPTER THIRTY-THREE

TYSON'S EYELIDS droop heavy before dawn. He blinks at the blacktop spooling under the headlights, rubs his face with the back of his hand.

The roads are quiet, the cabin warm. The cruise control is on, and he's covering the ground at a steady fifty-five miles per hour, keen not to attract the attention of any patrol cars.

Twenty minutes after passing Fort Stockton, he pulls off the I-10 into a rest area with a truck lot behind. Fills up the tank at the quiet gas station, watched by a straggly bird of prey which perches on a telegraph pole when he walks across the forecourt to pay.

He uses the restroom, splashes water on his face. Dries himself with paper towels, which he drops into an overflowing trash can. In the store a bored middle-aged woman with purple lipstick ignores him while he fills a basket with protein bars, chocolate, nuts, and energy drinks.

He saw security cameras outside. Inside, two more cameras: one over the door and another behind Purple Lips. She rings up his purchases, calling out the total in a monotone. Tyson frowns at her earbuds. Wireless. Fat white grubs burrowing into her brain. Whispering to her. Telling her what to do.

As he counts out the cash, he realises he's thinking out loud, sharing his stream of consciousness in a mumble.

"And who's in control now, anyway? The government? Maybe not, maybe not, maybe it's the corporations that got so big, so powerful, they can buy and sell entire countries if they want to, and who can stop them when the world bends over for whoever has the most money? Even if they still call the shots, the government ain't gonna stand in the way of big tech, big pharma, they get to do whatever they want, sending subliminal messages, binaural signals telling you what to buy, what to eat, who to vote for; that's how the revolution happens, not a riot, not a war, but some corporate asshole whispering in your ear until you're a soulless drone like the rest of them..."

He bites down, tooth on tooth, stops the flow. Most gas stations cameras don't have audio, and a quick glance identifies it as a cheap black and white model. Still, if someone watches this looking for Don Parfitt or Connor Tyson, they'll be interested in any big black guy, especially one who talks to himself.

Purple Lips puts the cash in the register, ignoring him, lost in her private soundtrack. For the benefit of any future audience, Tyson smiles at the top of her dyed-blonde hair, nods as if acknowledging something she said, replies silently, acts like he's listening, then fakes a soundless laugh. Just two tired strangers sharing a joke, is all.

The cashier looks up as he ends this performance. Hands him his change, expression implacable.

"What ya listening to?" says Tyson, tapping his ear. Purple Lips stares back for a second, then turns away as if she didn't hear, or doesn't care.

Tyson, put off his game by the woman's blankness, shuffles towards the door, reminds himself he's Cory Davenport now, straightens his shoulders, and crosses back to the van with an easy lope. When he opens the door, the watching bird drops from the telegraph pole, snaps open its wings, and powers away.

He parks up outside at the end of a row of silent trucks, the motorhome hidden behind them. He's about halfway through his first driving shift.

There's a clockwork egg timer in the glovebox. Tyson sets it for twenty minutes, puts it on the dashboard, leans back and closes his eyes. He's asleep almost immediately, but the ticking timer keeps him from going too deep.

It doesn't stop the nightmares. Normally, he'd take Valium and prazosin. Valium opens the door to sleep, prazosin prevents the trip to hell that follows. A doctor at a veterans' medical centre prescribed prazosin to ease the nightmares caused by post-traumatic stress disorder. Tyson liked the guy, who gave him none of the usual warnings or scoldings about his misuse of drugs. He just wrote a scrip and wished him luck. The doctor's legible handwriting meant Tyson knew what to steal when assembling his stash for the Phoenix.

But there's no point using either of his sleep aids for a twenty minute nap when he's on the road. So he spends his dreams in the familiar concrete basement, his mind hoisting him out of the driving seat of the van, locking him up where the sun can't find him. Where a tiny hatch opens once a day to deliver tasteless gruel. Where, if a key turns in the lock, they've come to kill him. Which he welcomes.

When the buzzer sounds, he snaps awake, heart racing. Before he can acclimatise, the truck parked next to him starts its engine, air brakes hissing. Tyson jumps at the noise, goes for a holster that isn't there, then unsheathes the knife at his ankle, holding it in front of his body as he scrambles across to the passenger seat.

Heart punching his ribs, panting hard, eyes darting around the truck park, he spins the knife blade down; a grip better for side-on slashes that sever tendons and ligaments.

The thick-framed glasses are on the dash. He picks them up, hands shaking, puts them on his face. It helps. Cory Davenport. Out of Savannah. Vacation. Wife dead. No children. Retired. Harmless.

Tyson puts the knife away, starts the van, follows the diesel-coughing truck west onto the highway.

The next four hours pass without incident. The sun rises at his back as he drives towards New Mexico. He ignores the protest from his internal compass when turning north to Las Cruces, before the I-10 once again heads west. Stops at the first truck stop he finds, climbs in the back for a hundred and eighty minutes of chemically assisted sleep.

After that, it's rinse and repeat. At least, that's the idea. Drive for four hours—or however long it takes for the road signs to dance and blur—pull over for protein, an energy drink, and twenty minutes on the kitchen timer. Another four hour-drive, then three to four hours' sleep.

It doesn't work out quite that simple.

In Arizona, hippies in RVs, pickups, or hanging out of wood-panelled nineteen-seventies station wagons, slow traffic to a crawl for three hours as they head for some desert festival. Not wanting to break speed limits to make up lost time, Tyson adds a couple hours to the next stage, pulling over half-blind with exhaustion, not much before midnight, sixty miles west of the Colorado River marking the California border.

Like so many bad ideas, he doesn't recognise it until it's too late.

The truck stop looks like all the others. The diner doubles as a bar. It has a neon sign advertising Bud, and the thump of live music spills out into the desert-hot air. It's not RV territory, more a sawdust-floor throwback for long-haulers, judging by the couple of boarded-up window panes and discarded bottles out front.

Tyson is starving, and bored with protein bars. He eyes the neon sign. Where there's beer, there's chicken wings and hot sauce. His stomach grumbles. He needs the energy, then he needs to sleep. Figures he can afford twenty minutes. He'll be no good to Kai if he turns up weak and dead on his feet.

Mind made up, he crosses the lot to the concrete apron outside the bar. The noise gets louder when a laughing couple spills out of the door. Country music. Of course.

It's busy inside. What day is this? If he called Kai on Thursday... Saturday. Saturday night. That explains the packed room, the height-ened fug of pheromones, sweat, and alcohol. Hard wooden floor, scratched and old, sporting a patina of stains, worn shiny along the route miniskirted waitresses follow to the tables and booths. The band at the back is butchering a Tammy Wynette standard.

Tyson finds a seat at the end of the bar nearest the door. Checks the exits, scans the faces, looks for anyone out of place, anyone on edge. Force of habit. After half a minute, he stops himself. He doesn't need decades of experience to see who's out of place here. It's him. All the men look like they shop in the same store, which only sells check shirts, blue jeans, boots, and belt buckles thick enough to stop a bullet. The women dress the same, mostly. There's a wagon wheel on the wall and photographs of cowboys. The whole place looks like it opened in the seventies, and neither it nor its clientele have any desire to change.

In his hipster glasses and button-down shirt, he looks like a movie extra who wandered onto the wrong set.

The prediction regarding chicken wings turns out to be accurate. There's corn, too, plus rice and beans. He washes it all down with a coke. No alcohol now. Not until this is over. The pills are a different story, but years of self-medication means he knows his limits. He's an addict, but addiction is better than the alternative. Better for everyone.

His limbs are heavy when he slides off the bar stool. Four hours of restorative sleep. Then back on the road.

He's opening the door when his instinct and experience send him a message about a potential problem his conscious mind was too tired to recognise.

At a table alongside the far wall, a stocky red-faced man in his thirties is on his phone. Nothing strange about that. But Tyson's subconscious supplies more information. Four minutes ago, when he finished his food and asked for the check, there were three men at that table. Big guys, too, one in particular. Cowboy hats, all with the same raw-beef complexion A thousand micro-signals, from the way they eyed the customers, an expectation of preferential service, and the dismissive way they treated the staff paints an ugly picture. Local crime, probably. Either they own the joint, or—more likely—they run the protection racket.

Tyson hesitates at the door, lets it swing closed. Turns back towards the bar, patting his pockets as if worried he's forgotten something. Checks the mirror behind the bar. The guy on the phone is putting it away, standing up. He eyes the door, then Tyson, who makes a show of finding his wallet in his back pocket, smiling with relief.

A quick review of available information. The two missing men left their drinks on the table. Their friend, falling in behind Tyson as he opens the door a second time, leaves his drink too. Not worried that someone might sit there while they're gone. Confident no one would dare. Also confident they won't be away long.

Tyson needs to sleep, then drive. But he reads the signs. He's been sized up, evaluated. A tourist who picked the wrong place to eat. An easy mark, a wallet full of cash and a motorhome bound to contain some valuables.

Things are about to get messy.

CHAPTER THIRTY-FOUR

TYSON HITS THE PARKING LOT. The Phoenix waits thirty yards away, tucked behind a couple of rigs. Force of habit, parking out of sight. Also means he can anticipate the likely scenario about to play out.

He's past the second row of cars, halfway to his van, when the bar door bangs shut a second time. That'll be Red Face following him. Three on one. Perhaps Tyson's size made them nervous. Maybe they're small-town bullies who like the numbers to be in their favour because, beneath the arrogant, cruel, tough guy facade are three scared boys who never got their asses handed to them.

The exhaustion lifts as the adrenaline pumps fresh energy into Tyson's limbs. He doesn't hurry, keeps his pace at a cautious amble. Stays in character. Cory would be out of his comfort zone. Nervous. Alone in a place he and his wife would have avoided. Glad to be on his way.

The training kicks in. Tyson stops paying attention to his inner voice. The other Tyson, the soldier, the specialist, takes charge now.

The biggest of the three men leans against a truck, back in the shadows. Good place to hide, unless you wear a polished belt buckle the size of a side plate that reflects even the tiniest amount of light.

The second man will cover the rear of the Phoenix to block any escape. When Tyson goes to unlock the driver's door, he'll find himself boxed in by the beefsteak cowboys. If they're smart, they'll state their business, ask for his wallet, point a gun at him while their friend searches the van, then send him on his way. No doubt the local police department will be unhelpful, should he be tempted to bother them. They'd advise him not to press charges and be thankful he can still walk.

But they're not smart. The arrogant display inside made that pretty clear. Which means they're probably planning a beating.

Another five seconds and he'll reach the Phoenix. Tyson's lips are still moving. If any of the cowboys got close enough to listen, they might have experienced some doubts.

"Mustn't kill them, too messy, don't need the attention, the trouble, just hurt them. Put them down, nice and quiet, quick, no killing."

And he's there. At the door of the Phoenix. Hears the second man move, coming around the Phoenix, the third guy walking faster behind him. They're trying to be quiet. He nearly laughs at their incompetence, but he does what Cory Davenport would do. Puts his hand in his pocket, takes out the key. Instead of holding the key like Cory would, he grips it in his fist, the metal protruding between his knuckles.

Lifts his hand towards the door.

The first guy moves. Tyson's guess is good. There are smart thugs and stupid thugs. The beefsteak cowboys have sworn allegiance to the second group.

Three steps towards him, picking up speed. The first guy is using his bulk—he weighs over two hundred pounds—to gain a quick advantage. He's expecting to piledrive the tourist with the big glasses into the side of his motorhome, deliver a punch or kick to the gut, then join his friends in a workout that's part-business, part-pleasure, as the three of them kick their victim into unconsciousness.

Tyson moves the minimum amount necessary to avoid the oncoming challenger. Pivots on his toes, sweeps his right arm up and across. Judges it perfectly. Beefsteak cowboy number one, a charging mass of beer and testosterone, gasps in surprise as Tyson's key rips across his face, opening up a deep gash between his upper lip and right eye. His momentum, unchecked by the expected impact with Tyson, carries him into a side panel, and his neck takes much of the impact. It doesn't break, but the pop and crack of tendons giving way can be heard over the bang of his skull denting the Phoenix.

The sensible play for the remaining two would be to retreat, pull their guns, regain the advantage. But amateurs don't always make smart choices under duress. And these boneheads are amateurs. They remain committed to administering a good kicking.

They keep coming because it's two on one. Most demonstrations of flat-out unthinking male aggression occur in company. Solo thugs are a rare find indeed. It's all about hormones and peer pressure. The idiots in the parking lot perfectly illustrate the theory. They roar as they close in.

Space is tight between the van and the neighbouring truck, so the third cowboy has to wait before getting his shot. Tyson doesn't keep him long. He delivers a *sokuto geri* to the second cowboy, speaking the name of the technique aloud as he unleashes a downward kick. It strikes the second idiot in the knee, giving that leg the unusual ability to fold both ways. The man drops, whimpering like an overtired toddler.

The third cowboy wises up to the changed situation, which is, he now realises, precarious. He skids to a stop, eyes flicking from his supine colleagues to the man who caused their condition. Tyson can almost see the testosterone evaporate, leaving a very frightened bully, aware of the fragility of the human body and keen to keep his own undamaged.

Nine seconds have passed since beefsteak number one rushed him. Tyson doesn't expect much resistance from the last man, but he doesn't want him to run. He grabs a handful of checked shirt, pulls him close.

The man bursts into tears.

"Please don't hurt me. I'm sorry. I'm real sorry. I didn't want to do it. Chad makes me join in. Please. I have money."

Tyson slaps him, open-handed, leaves a pale imprint of fingers on one gammon cheek.

"Give me your gun. Nice and easy."

The cowboy sobs harder, lifts his shirt away from his pants. Tyson takes the gun. "Which one's your car?"

"We came in Chad's pickup, sir. It's just over there." He nods towards the end of the next row of vehicles.

Tyson points the gun at him. "Get Chad's keys and bring the pickup. You even think about running, I will shoot you, and I will shoot to kill. You got that?"

The third cowboy looks like he might be about to shit himself with terror. "Yes, sir. I'm sorry. Please—"

"Go." Tyson raises the gun. "Quickly now."

Cowboy number one groans when his friend reaches into his pocket, pulls out a key. Tyson watches the weeping man walk stiffly across the lot—maybe he *did* shit himself—climb into a Ford and drive it back. He orders him out, and supervises while, with a good deal more crying, the sweating cowboy drags his leader away and boosts him into the back of the pickup. His broken-legged friend pales and sways when, with some help, he stands up, but joins his colleague in the back with only a couple of stifled screams.

"Wallets."

The third man collects them, tosses them over. Tyson lifts out an ID, scans it.

"Yeah, yeah, okay. Now I know your names and where you live. Drive straight to hospital, tell them five guys jumped you. It was dark, so you can't describe them, but you think they left in a Toyota. Or a Honda. Nothing specific, but make it one of those. I'll be listening to the police band, and if I don't hear about it in the next hour, I'm gonna delay my vacation long enough to pay you all a visit and slit your throats."

Tyson watches the pickup drive away, then runs his fingers over the fresh dent in the side of the Phoenix.

"No blood to clean off. That's good, I guess. But gonna have to find somewhere else to park up, get my sleep, get my rest. Running on empty, man. Running on empty."

He smiles as he pulls out of the parking spot. It's been a long time. He's delighted he stopped before killing anybody.

———

Although he promised the cowboy he'd monitor the police band, Tyson doesn't do so. The terrified man's hands shook so badly he struggled to get the key in the ignition. Tyson has no doubt he's doing exactly as he was told. He might even be considering a change of friends. As for the others, their brawling days are over. Their leader will need a neck brace, and may never look over his shoulder again. The second guy might lose his limp one day, but Tyson's seen breaks like that before. They heal slow. Cowboy number two will have plenty of time to consider his life choices.

He pulls over in a lay-by, hiding the Phoenix behind a big sign advertising the Joshua Tree National Park. He's strung out, jittery, and the hit of adrenaline from the parking lot isn't helping any. Six or seven hours of rest would help, but he can't afford it. Kai could be under attack right now. Or she's already dead, and his trip is dangerous and pointless. Either way, Tyson plans to sacrifice half of his allotted sleep to get to Santa Barbara before dawn. The roads are quiet. He can crank down the window. And when you spend your life talking to yourself, you're never short of conversation to keep you awake.

Two hours' sleep goes by in a surreal, stretched-out moment Tyson hasn't experienced since he was on active duty. On one level, he's convinced only a few minutes have passed since he set the timer, pulled the curtain between the rear compartment and the cab, and leaned back on the soft leather armchair. On another, his memory tells him he's spent days, maybe weeks, curled up in the dark on a concrete Indonesian floor. He wakes staring at the metal ceiling of the Phoenix. It takes a minute to make sense of where he is. What he's doing. Where he needs to be.

Two minutes after opening his eyes, the motorhome rolls onto the blacktop, its lights sweeping the empty landscape. The dull yellows, greens, and greys of the California desert are monotonous by day. By night, the landscape takes on an other-worldly character, ominous and alien. Tyson catches himself humming the five note phrase from *Close Encounters of the Third Kind*. The tyres rumble. Cold night air wicks the sweat from his forehead.

He drives on, racing the sun.

Three and a half hours later, the headlights pick out a sign for Santa Barbara Zoo, and Tyson slows. The leaden sky brightens. He looks left. Sees the ocean. The past few hours passed without him noticing.

In a well-kept rest area he steps behind the van, stretches, pisses over a guard rail towards the distant water. Helps shake off his exhaustion with a couple of uppers and an energy drink. Brings up the map in his head. The one he memorised. Thinks like the enemy. If he were to attack Kai's bungalow, how would he go about it?

He turns from the ocean. On this stretch of the Californian coast, the Pacific lies to his south. He looks north-east, where Kai's property lies less than three miles from where he's standing. Beyond her land is a big swathe of nothing, then the hills. Easy to defend, because anyone approaching would be spotted miles away. The enemy would assume she had cams, alarms, tripwires, and they would be right.

Tyson looks back at the ocean; a natural defence. In darkness, hostiles might leave a vehicle on the coast road and close in on foot. Or drive in and circle round, find some cover, set up a sniper position. A car engine might be heard though.

There's always the direct approach, a frontal assault. Fast, unexpected, but only useful if you have overwhelming firepower and numbers. Would they send overwhelming firepower and numbers to deal with a senior with a herb garden?

If they knew Elizabeth Murchen, they might.

Back in the van, Tyson dresses in camouflage gear, dials in the combination on the storage unit under the bed. Takes out a rifle and scope, plus spare ammunition. Climbs in front and drives.

He has no plan, not really. He's one man, damaged, dangerous, talking to himself, and wearing a stupid pair of hipster glasses.

So he'll improvise.

CHAPTER THIRTY-FIVE

THREE MILES from Kai's bungalow, he sees the smoke.

A black SUV squats on the shoulder two hundred yards from Kai's turn-off. Two men inside. Engine running. Judging from the dark smoke inland, the assault is already in progress, which means they're backup.

Tyson drives past, doesn't slow, doesn't respond when he sees the driver turn his head to check him out. Keeps his monologue going as if he were singing along to the radio.

"Just another senior in an RV, pal. Spent all my life getting up when it was dark to go fix boilers, promising myself one day I'd be free to do as I please. Retired now, so I get up early, drive someplace pretty, and stare through the windshield while eating beets from a can. Oh, and don't you worry about that dent in the side. That's where I half-killed some idiot redneck last night. Made a mess of my paintwork, didn't it?"

He checks his mirror as he rounds the next corner. The driver is talking to his colleague.

As soon as he's round the corner, Tyson pulls over. No time to conceal the Phoenix. He's out of the door and running before the engine fan kicks in.

There's a slight rise leading from the road, and when he reaches the top, he throws himself flat, brings the rifle to his shoulder, and scans the area with the telescopic sight.

It ain't pretty.

Kai's bungalow is a smouldering ruin. A twin of the SUV he's just passed on the highway sits in front of a smoking heap of bricks, glass, and wood. Tyson never saw Kai's home, but she described it to him after moving in.

Behind the wreckage, an injured man holds a sub-machine gun. He's bleeding from various injuries and his leg is a mess. Won't last long.

Tyson sweeps the scope east to west, talking to himself, describing what he sees. The next figure he spots makes him pause. Outside a freshly painted white outbuilding, a big white guy wearing a bandana is pressed hard against the wall. Knees bent, staying low, out of sight of the wounded man.

Tyson looks further north, finds a female and a male near the perimeter, behind an SUV. A second plume of smoke rises from a patch of bushes and trees. What little remains of the vegetation is burning.

Tyson guesses the woman is CIA. Black ops. Deniable, but on the payroll. He'd bet his house on it. If he owned one. Three vehicles, including concealed backup, teams briefed to split up, all classic manoeuvres straight out of the Company playbook.

Which leaves the solo guy. And he's a mystery.

The wetwork Tyson did for governments, corporations, and private individuals was almost always subcontracted through US agencies who couldn't get their hands dirty. CIA mostly. He knows the type. This guy isn't one of them. A freelancer like him and Kai? It's the only explanation that makes any sense, and it'll do until Tyson has more intel.

Something in the guy's hand. Not a gun. Tyson squints until he's sure, then his throat dries, his whispered monologue falling silent. It's a detonator. Did this guy blow up the bungalow? Whose side is he on?

Whoever he is, he knows what he's doing.

Tyson follows the big man's progress as he breaks from cover. He runs in that weird crablike way soldiers do when they have to stay low, but he's quick. And sure-footed, despite the rubble-strewn terrain. There's something about the way this man places each foot without hesitation, making rapid progress. Something Tyson has seen before. Something he tried to learn himself. Only a handful of people in the world move that way.

Bavaria. This man has trained with Anton. Which makes him one of the elite. Ninety-nine percent of whom are attached to governments, unofficially. They are the deadliest of secret weapons. Kai trained with Anton. She'd shown Tyson the techniques. Whatever else, this guy probably knows what's happened to Kai.

Tyson loses sight of his quarry through the scope, lowering it as this new information spools across his conscious mind. There's a burst of automatic gunfire and he brings the sight back up. The white outbuilding is the easiest landmark to find, and he focuses on it.

An old car parked in front explodes.

The first white-hot flash of the blast makes Tyson drop the scope, cursing. Then the building behind goes up too, roof lifting off like a rocket, consumed by fire as it ascends. The walls blow outwards.

Tyson moves the scope and finds the big man, safe, behind the SUV. He's reaching up to the door, pulling himself in, starting the engine. He's outgunned, outnumbered, and there's nothing left to blow up. The explosions, gunfire, and smoke will bring fire crews and police soon enough. They'll all want to be gone when that happens.

And he's watching near the only exit. The action is about to come to him.

The rise where Tyson is lying is too exposed. If they look his way, he's in trouble. He needs cover, and the sparse vegetation of the Californian scrub doesn't offer much.

There's a bush big enough to conceal him about forty yards away. At a sprint, he'll be in the open for six seconds. Tyson gets into position to launch himself. His knees crack and his ankle has a touch of cramp. Ah. Maybe fifteen years ago he'd make it in six seconds, but not now. No choice, though. He might make it in ten.

Tyson runs. Rifle held at the bottom of the barrel. Arms pumping, legs powering across the stony ground. Ten seconds, he concedes, as everything starts to hurt and his lungs insist they are not fit for purpose, was wildly optimistic. After fifteen yards of torment, he'll be happy to reach his goal without triggering a cardiac arrest, whether it takes ten seconds or ten minutes.

For half a minute after he flops onto his belly and crawls into position, anyone watching might have thought they were witnessing a mirage, as Tyson's heaving attempts to get his breath back make the whole bush rock back and forth.

When he's wiped the sweat away, found a sitting position that won't bring on cramp, and readied the rifle, the sound of his own blood pumping in his ears recedes enough for Tyson to hear the roar of two engines getting closer.

Two SUVs. Mystery man driving the first one, the Company goons in pursuit. Accelerating towards the highway. Bad idea. Tyson can hear the backup SUV joining the fray. The odds of the stranger getting away narrow by the second.

The stranger hasn't seen the other vehicle yet. He's rounding a bend in the tracks and he's pushing the SUV hard. Tyson waits for the inevitable collision as the backup vehicle rounds the same corner from the opposite direction.

Tyson grunts in surprised respect at the near-instantaneous twitch of the steering wheel that sends the pinned SUV off the track and bumping across the ground. The backup team responds and gives chase, but they've lost ground.

Mystery man's advantage is only temporary. There are now two SUVs in his tyre tracks, and the closest passenger is shooting at him.

Tyson considers moving. They're not heading towards him, but a slight change of direction could change that. In another five or six seconds, it'll be too late to change his mind. But if he breaks cover, he'll be seen. Both sides will assume he's an enemy. Which means everyone will try to kill him.

He stays put. He's been in tighter spots.

Even as Tyson wonders what other surprises the stranger might have, the pursuing vehicle rears up like a horse meeting a rattlesnake, its front axle riding a wave of fire. The boom of the grenade follows. What's left of the vehicle hits the ground hard. No one walks away.

The team leader has reflexes as sharp as her enemy. She altered her course while the vehicle in front kept their quarry busy, cutting across, anticipating the turn the stranger would have to make to avoid a ditch. She may have lost two men in the explosion, but it bought her a distraction that means her enemy has no idea where she is until the front of her vehicle ploughs sideways into the rear of his.

Mystery man's vehicle rocks and spins away, out of control. The impact is severe. The Company goons would have been braced for it, seat belts on. Not so their enemy.

Tyson brings the rifle's scope to his eye. A hundred yards. An easy shot. The stranger scrabbles backwards on his butt. His bandana has gone. He's bald. On one side, his smooth skull is marred with a mass of old scars.

The stranger has a backpack in one hand, a gun in the other. Staggers across the sandy ground, using the car as a shield, keeping it between him and his pursuers, who exit their vehicle, guns held ready.

He might be disorientated, but the stranger is dangerous. Tyson sees him grip his gun with both hands and squeeze off a shot. Tyson swings the scope across in time to see the male goon take two more to the chest.

Then the stranger's luck runs out. The leader didn't take cover when he opened fire. She ran towards the danger. While the stranger was shooting her colleague, she rounded the vehicle and now points a gun at him. It's over. The big guy knows it too and makes no suicidal effort to shoot her. He tosses the gun away, and she steps closer.

Close enough for Tyson to read her lips.

He was never the best lip reader, but he kept up his practice of the technique, despite not needing it for many years. He'd stare in at the televisions in the electrical store window, check he could still do it.

His accuracy is about sixty percent. No conversational nuances, but good enough.

The stranger has his back to him, so he keeps his attention on her.

She wants to know where Kai is. Tyson smiles, lets out a long breath. Still alive. The Company woman doesn't like the answer she gets. Threatens to kill him. Asks about Elizabeth Murchen. Steps forward and delivers a brisk kick to the head. Mystery man raises a hand to protect himself, but he's too slow. It's all a bit one-sided.

She brings up her weapon. Says something else. Sights down the barrel.

If Tyson is going to get involved, he needs to act now.

Her shoulder tightens. She's going to shoot him.

It has to be now. Now. What would Kai do?

Tyson doesn't have the first idea what Kai would do.

He tightens his finger on the trigger.

CHAPTER THIRTY-SIX

JIMMY BLUE REACHES behind his back for a knife. Every move he makes is too slow, too late.

He can't die out here. Not now. Not while his parents' killers still walk, eat, and breathe. He's believed so long that death will not come until he has taken revenge, that even now—when this woman is about to shoot him—he does not believe he will die.

What happens next does nothing to dissuade him of this belief.

The leader makes an odd noise, a kind of animal grunt of surprise. Her head jerks left and drops forward onto her chest, a spray of blood emerging from an exit wound above her right ear.

He witnesses the moment when her eyes change, all intelligence gone, leaving a meaningless husk of meat that drops to the ground.

Jimmy sits up opposite the corpse. His head is still full of cotton wool. The darkness calls him back to heal, to regroup. But he can't. Not yet.

He looks south. The bullet came from that direction. There's no one there.

Less than a hundred yards away, one of the scattered brittle-bushes moves. A shape within it stands up. A big man in glasses holding a rifle with a scope. He keeps it in front of him as he approaches. Cautious. He glances at the corpse of the leader. Moves closer to Blue. Peers down at him. Jimmy has seen his face before. The name that goes with it eludes him.

The man's mouth works, even when he isn't saying anything. His face twitches and he cocks his head, as if listening. His stubble is coming through grey and black, and, above the neck of his T-shirt, Blue sees scars; old and deep. The glasses are black, the frames thick and heavy. They look incongruous, a fashion statement. When he speaks, the words are not what Blue expected.

"She alive or dead? Tell me the truth now."

No need to ask who he means. The rest of his face is in motion, but the stranger's eyes are hard and still. No way of knowing whether he's friend or foe. Jimmy probes at his usually helpful and accurate memory, but it won't cooperate. He has seen this face before. Recently.

The rifle's barrel rises until it's pointing at him. "Answer me or die. Your choice." The mouth chews silently, then he whispers, "his choice, his choice."

Blue tells the truth.

"Kai's dead."

The rifle doesn't waver. The man talks to himself. "Yeah, makes sense, cos she never picked up on the other number, burner two. Didn't answer. Shoulda known when she said she wouldn't run no more. We ran together that day, though, didn't we? She came back for me and we ran and ran. They never caught us. Now I'm too late. I warned her. She picked up the first call. She knew they were coming for us."

He keeps looking at Blue, staring through him. He blinks.

"You know that expression, 'the enemies of my enemies are my friends'?"

Blue nods in answer.

The big man's lips move for a couple of seconds, then his expression clears, and he looks younger.

"Yeah. Well, in my experience, it's bullshit."

He flips the rifle, holds the stock towards Jimmy.

A name skims closer to the surface. Almost close enough to reach for. Jimmy Blue looks the man in the eye.

"I know you. You're her friend, right? Heard you were dead."

The man presses his lips together. His forehead wrinkles in confusion. Or anger.

"You heard wrong."

He lifts the rifle. Brings it down, fast.

Blue registers the sound of wood hitting flesh, the back of his head hitting the stony earth. A brief flash of pain, then he's back in the darkness.

CHAPTER THIRTY-SEVEN

IT TAKES Connor Tyson six minutes to run to the Phoenix and drive back to the stranger on Kai's land.

The RV draws up alongside the unconscious man. The dead black ops agents, an abandoned SUV, and the smoking remains of another are nearby. Beyond, what's left of Kai's bungalow still smoulders, and flames lick the wreckage of the barn. It looks like a war zone. The agent on the far side isn't moving anymore. Probably bled out while the rest of his comrades were picked off.

The black ops team sent to kill Tyson in San Antonio were CIA, same as these goons. He would bet his last dollar on it. Which means this big scarred white guy is likely on Kai's side. Maybe even tried to save her. But he can't be sure.

Hard to believe Kai's dead. Always thought she'd outlive him. He pushes a wave of grief away.

The stranger groans, rolls onto his side. That was some smack Tyson gave him, and the guy was already in a car wreck. Tough son of a bitch. He kicks the man onto his front, sticks a boot on his back. The big guy grunts while Tyson secures him with heavy-duty hand and leg cuffs. Tyson drags him into the RV, which takes every bit of strength he can muster. The stranger is big, but none of it is fat. It's like lifting a bagful of rocks.

The big guy dozes in the back while the Phoenix rumbles towards Los Angeles. Tyson scans the police bands as he drives. There's no chatter about any incident in Santa Barbara. He checks every twenty minutes until he's past LA, then turns the radio off. He's read it's impossible for anyone to track him through an RV antenna, but why take chances?

In the rear-view mirror, Tyson watches the guy move; quiet, cautious, testing the strength of the cuffs. After a few minutes of silent exertion, the man quits, slides his legs up, rolls onto his knees.

"You stay right there, right there, buddy. Right there." Tyson shakes his head to reaffirm the point. "Right there." He mouths a few soundless words, then pushes his lips together to stop the flow.

"I need a piss."

"Hey! British, right, you're British, from England, Britain, the UK, right? The Queen, cricket, Shakespeare, Winston Churchill. The guy who played House in that TV show, he was a Brit, can you believe it? What was the name of that show? The one about House? The one with House in it?"

"House," says the stranger.

"House! That was it. OK. Bathroom. Sure. Yeah. You need to go, need to go. Fine. You go. It's behind you, on your left."

The guy stands up slowly, lurching sideways. Steadies himself against the bathroom door. Waits for the dizziness to pass. Or he's faking it. Impossible to say.

"I'll give you something for your head. But don't try anything, bud." Tyson puts his hand on the passenger seat, waves the taser in the air. "You can sit in that chair when you get back. Sit your ass down there, down there. But you get any closer, I zap you good, make you dance the funny dance. Electric boogaloo, man, electric boogaloo, you get it? You understand? You focused? You with me?"

"I get it," says the stranger, and shuffles into the bathroom.

Tyson hears the snick of the lock and returns his attention to the road. He needs to sleep. Even his experience with uppers and downers won't prevent a crisis if he doesn't rest soon. It's not just the slowing of cognitive processes that worries him, it's the fragmentation of personality that goes with it. Tyson has trouble interacting with the outside world as it is. At first, his separation from others, his life on the street, was a choice. He was playing a part. It was a way to disappear. But at some point, the crazy vet who talked to himself stopped being an act.

The stranger emerges from the tiny bathroom, shuffles forward and sits on the rear chair.

Tyson takes a blister pack of pills out of a pocket, rips two off the strip. Tosses them into the big guy's lap.

"These will help."

Watches him dry swallow them without checking what they are. Smart. If Tyson wanted him dead, he'd be lying in a storm drain with a bullet in his skull.

"Where's my stuff?"

Tyson leaves the question unanswered. He turned off the stranger's phone and laptop and locked them in a storage bay. All the bays and cupboards are lined with foil. It stops transmissions getting in and out, even the advanced technology the government copied from the Russians. Or aliens. Tyson read about that in the library.

He's got the stranger's ID in his pocket. British passport and driving licence. Tom Kincaid. Probably fake. Good fakes, top of the line. Roach will find out who this guy really is.

Two minutes pass where Tyson looks out at the road, watching the hills rise on either side of the interstate north-east of San Bernardino. With a twitch of shock at his lack of attention, he checks the mirror, his hand closing around the taser.

There's a trained killer sitting behind him and he forgot he was there. That's only ever happened once before. It's a trick Kai pulled the last time he saw her. She sat so still he plumb forgot she existed. Which is hellish weird, considering Kai is the most *present* person he's ever met.

Was, he reminds himself. Kai is dead. And this Brit does the same trick, kinda. Not as good as Kai, but spooky all the same.

He drives with one hand on the taser after that.

He needs to find a payphone. Roach owes him. Time to call in the favour.

Tyson pulls off the highway, climbs in the back, and opens the smaller of his two medicine cabinets.

The hospital pharmacist he stole the meds from said their shelf life was four years. That was six years ago. Will an out of date general anaesthetic work?

He fills the needle and taps it. Not sure why, but they always did it on *medical shows.*

"I got business to take care of, a call to make, spin the wheels, get intel. This will make you sleep."

The big guy leans forward, shoulders hunched. He's trying to break out of the cuffs again. Ain't gonna happen. He relaxes, sits back.

"We're on the same side, Mr Tyson."

"How do you—? That's not—" Tyson clamps his errant mouth shut, points the taser.

"Gonna inject you now. Not gonna kill you. You'll wake up in a couple hours. Feel much better. Don't make me zap you."

It's a lie. This much anaesthetic should put him out for twenty-four hours. Easy. Long enough for Tyson to get some rest.

The stranger sighs. When Tyson is close, he speaks without looking up.

"Kai was my friend. I killed her murderers. At least tell me where we're going."

Tyson thinks of the miles ahead. It's a forty-hour trip, and he can't do without sleep the way he used to. Can't concentrate for long enough either. Gonna need to sleep soon.

"Pittsburgh first. Then Langley, Virginia."

"You planning on paying the CIA a visit?"

"Something like that," replies Tyson, blinking away a tic in his eye. "Something like that."

Tyson injects him in the neck and the big man goes limp as grilled cheese.

CHAPTER THIRTY-EIGHT

THE JOURNEY IS A NIGHTMARE, and when Tom sleeps, more nightmares come. Hours pass like an infinite flipbook of anxiety, grief, and fear.

Grief is the hardest to deal with.

Anxiety is part of Tom's normal existence, always there, a psychological tinnitus. He takes longer than others to understand something, and the world moves faster than he can cope with. People talk too quickly, use words he struggles to understand, and rarely have the patience to explain when his expression clouds in response to their questions. Being anxious is as natural as breathing.

Tyson's muttered monologue from the driving seat seeps into Tom's dreams. The droning voice continues as day becomes night becomes day.

When he wakes, his captor lets him use the tiny bathroom. Gives him water and a protein bar. He is dull-headed, drowsy. When he sits down, the needle pricks his neck again, and he sleeps.

In the periods of wakefulness, some of what Tyson says is clear enough to understand. He mumbles, 'let's see what's really going down', and 'we'll find out the truth about this summer bitch. Find out who killed Kai.' Tom doesn't know who the summer bitch is, but

Tyson isn't happy with her at all. But two men in a pickup truck killed Kai. Men with guns. Not a woman. It's the last thing Tom remembers from Santa Barbara. Then Jimmy Blue came. After that, there's nothing. Well, not quite nothing.

His nightmares provide out of context flashbacks that terrify him. Scenes of destruction, explosions, gunfire, and death. He's not sure which are real. Something bad happened.

Other dreams are kinder. Mornings sorting clothes in the back room of the thrift store. Long, silent walks with Kai in the hills. The terrible porridge. Then—and as hard as he tries to turn his mind away, he can't—the way she fell, crumpling like laundry. All the life gone in one instant. All the knowledge, the kindness, the wisdom.

That's why the grief is so hard. Tom knows what he has lost, and it makes the grief a twisting, grinding blade mangling his insides. Kai *saw* Tom. She saw him. And Tom changed. Because he saw himself through her eyes. A lost, lonely, desperate child-man with no friends, no family, who had shut himself away from any attempt to reach him. After his parents were murdered, he had visited the border between life and death, set up camp there, unsure of whether to go on, or come back. And when he returned, it wasn't to embrace life. It was to bring death. To seek revenge. Because Tom wasn't alone when he came back from that border. He brought Jimmy Blue with him. His time with Kai made Tom see Blue differently. For the first time since his childhood coma, he has doubts. Maybe Blue isn't the protector, the loyal companion, the only one who understands. Maybe the darkness he brings means Tom, like Peter Pan, can never grow up.

With Kai, the world looked different. Not the bleak, brutal, unforgiving place Blue lives in. Somewhere better. But she had left him, too. Life may be full of good things, good people, but they will be taken away.

For a while, in Santa Barbara, Tom experienced doubts about Blue's version of justice. There are other ways to live. Then someone killed Kai, and Tom realised the truth lay in the darkness after all.

Jimmy Blue is resting, getting stronger. And when he returns, Tom will welcome him.

There's just one hitch. Every time Tyson stops to rest, after hours of driving, he injects Tom to make him sleep. And the drug that makes Tom sleep pushes Blue down, stops him coming close. Locks him away where Tom can't see or hear him. While Tom is awake, Jimmy Blue starts the journey back, but he never reaches his destination before Tyson puts another needle in his neck.

Tom's existence shrinks to the tiny space in the back of the motorhome. Two chairs, a couch. Locked cupboards. A bathroom he can barely squeeze into, where his handcuffs and chained ankles make it difficult to do what he needs to do. Tyson threatens him if he takes too long, and Tom can't stammer out the words to explain he's trying as hard as he can.

Although Tyson frightens him, Tom recognises the damage in his new companion. He knows how that feels. The older man twitches and flinches, spills out his words, fighting to keep his monologue at a level Tom can't hear. Despite this, and maybe because of the pills he tosses into his mouth as he drives, Tyson sometimes becomes coherent for long enough for Tom to pick up disturbing details from his thoughts.

He often mentions Kai. Sometimes, he calls her Murchen. Tyson wants the same thing Blue wants: revenge. Tom tries to tell him they both want the same thing, but the words swell and thicken, drying when they reach his lips. During his stay with Kai, he spoke in sentences, without the customary tightening of his throat when language deserts him. Now, his speech reverts to the level when he first emerged from his coma. The right words aren't always there, and —when they are—he can't push them past his lips.

Tyson drives on, too suspicious of his passenger to release him, and Tom can do nothing to convince him otherwise.

The injections mean Tom loses track of time. His watch isn't working, its screen cracked and blank. His phone is missing, as is his laptop. When he asks Tyson where his backpack is, the man doesn't answer. This provokes a flutter of panic. Blue needs the phone, he knows. There's something important about it.

One morning, as Tyson pulls down the visor against the rising orange sun, Tom looks out at a transformed landscape. Hard to believe he's in the same country. The desert ochres, oranges, and reds are gone. Instead of yellowing shrubs eking out their existence in an arid landscape, trees line the road; tall, lush, green. For a second, Tom thinks he's back in Britain among the oaks and poplars, but the cars are wrong, the road is wrong, the air coming through Tyson's open window is wrong.

Tom looks at the signs, wishes he could interpret the black letters, force them to make sense. He stares anyway, scanning his surroundings. Jimmy Blue will understand it all later, will read the writing that Tom sees as meaningless patterns.

He sleeps, he wakes. Even without the aid of an injection, Tom finds his eyes getting heavy through the sheer nightmarish monotony of the journey. His life has shrunk inside the van, in this space too low to stand up in. He paces the few feet Tyson says he's allowed to. Tyson doesn't speak to him much, so Tom plays games. He looks for red cars, giving himself a point for each, but keeps losing count. Whenever he sees a yellow car, he's supposed to punch the driver on the arm—at least, that was what Dad used to do on long car journeys —but since Tyson would probably shoot him, Tom punches himself in the arm instead. Mostly, he dozes, head snapping up every few minutes in mindless panic, then sinking back onto his chest.

Tom is asleep when Tyson leaves the interstate, but his body registers the change in the road surface beneath the tyres. Deep in the darkness, Jimmy Blue is awake. Alert. Paying attention. Listening.

The motorhome follows a smaller road for a few miles, then turns onto an uneven surface barely more than a dirt track. Tom sleeps on, but his eyes open half an inch.

It's early evening. The sun reflects silver-white from the sides of vast metal silos and chimneys belching white smoke. The track they're on brings them behind the industrial site—it might be a mega-farm, a gasworks, or a factory of some sort—to an incongruous wooden gate. Beyond it, a cabin like something out of *Little House On The Prairie*. Smoke curls up from its roof from a miniature version of the massive chimneys they've just passed.

When Tyson opens the door, Tom hears the metallic rhythm of the industrial site, the grind and groan, the scrape and roar carried on the breeze. He sits up, awake now.

A traditional American mailbox perched on a wooden pole makes Tom, in his exhausted, drug-addled state, suspects the whole place is a television set. He looks for cameras and finds one on the side of the mailbox. It's no tv camera, though; too small. Tyson looks into the lens. Says nothing. The wooden gate swings open.

Tyson doesn't get back into the driving seat. He opens the rear door, gun in hand. Tom has his eyes closed. Tyson kicks the sole of Tom's boot. When he does it a second time, Tom opens his eyes, blinking.

It's only a few hours since Tom was last anaesthetised, but he knows the drill. At a gesture from Tyson, he moves from the chair to the couch. Waits there while his travelling companion spins the dials on a padlock, opens a cupboard, takes out the needle. You're supposed to use a fresh needle every time, Tom knows, but Tyson doesn't. He fills it from a vial, sliding the needle under Tom's skin and pressing the plunger.

There's a moment, barely there before it's gone, when Tom and Jimmy Blue meet. He never remembers this when he wakes. It's only now, when it happens, that Tom knows this isn't the first time. Blue waits in the depths that rush up and swallow Tom. The needle comes out of his neck and he slumps back. His eyes flicker, and every muscle in his body relaxes. His awareness of his surroundings drops away, and he does not stir when Tyson opens a cupboard, taking out his backpack.

Tom encounters Jimmy Blue in that horrible instant. Blue is desperate to wake, fighting to make it happen. Tom stands at the top of a cliff, stretches out his hand. Even as Jimmy Blue grasps it, the anaesthetic rushes through them like a torrent of water, washes him away into the deep, deep, deep.

At the fringes of consciousness, he is aware of the Phoenix rocking as it drives through the open gate, which clicks closed behind it.

Hours later, he stirs as someone puts a hand on his arm. Then the sharp scratch of another needle, and he falls away again, dissolving.

Tom sleeps. Far below, Blue climbs, undeterred, never giving up. Even in the murky blackness of drugged sleep, Tom senses a new desperation in Jimmy Blue. Something has changed. Blue is raging, summoning all his power to fight the effects of the drug, but the cliff he scales is glass and his fingers are coated with oil.

Jimmy Blue is afraid.

CHAPTER THIRTY-NINE

WHEN TOM WAKES, he is alone. He's lying on his side. He rolls into a sitting position, his right arm hanging limply. It's as if it belongs to someone else; a heavy lump of dead meat hanging from his shoulder. Then the fingers of his right hand tingle, and he clenches his fist a few times, the feeling returning to his limb in a prickly, uncomfortable rush of blood.

"Ow." Tom rubs his face, scrapes crusted sleep from his eyelids, groans as his body aches in protest. How long was he asleep for?

Light streams through the motorhome's windscreen. From this angle, all Tom can see is trees and, through their branches, blue patches of sky.

He badly needs the bathroom. When he stands up, he groans again, legs cramping after a long period of inactivity. He shuffles the few feet across the width of the van, the chain between his ankles dragging. Too shaky to stand for long, he sits on the cold seat and regards his haggard reflection in the mirror. He looks terrible; dark, heavy circles under his eyes, facial hair somewhere between stubble and a beard.

It's quiet. Quieter than it's been for days. Tom listens. He hears a breeze moving through leaves. Birdsong. Further away, traffic on a distant highway. Two sounds stand out. The crackle, spit, and pop of a fire. And, in counterpoint, running water, a river. Accompanying the sounds is a smell—fried fish—that dominates everything. His mouth produces saliva and his stomach flexes with hunger.

Tom washes his hands, shuffles to the rear of the van. Puts his hand on the metal handle. Twists as gently as he can, then pushes outwards. It's unlocked. The door swings open.

Because of the chain on his ankles, Tom has to jump from the small step, landing on thin grass and dirt. He nearly falls, then steadies himself.

The motorhome is parked just inside a tree line. There is no sign of a road, just a badly maintained track with one set of tyre marks. Tom sees the source of the sounds he heard from the bathroom. A wide river, blue-brown water flowing fast. On the bank, flanked by trees, Tyson sits cross-legged in front of a small fire. Two smoke-blackened fish hang from an improvised spit above the flames.

"Breakfast," says Tyson, without turning. "Lunch and dinner, too."

He picks up a tin plate, lifts and shakes the spit until the cooked fish slide onto it. Puts the plate down. Digs into his pocket and brings out a key ring, which he tosses towards Tom. It lands at his feet.

"Figure you'll be more comfortable out of those cuffs. Freedom, take them off, a key for the lock."

It's awkward getting the key into the lock while handcuffed, but Tom manages it at last and the metal bracelet springs open. The other key fits the padlock on his legs and he steps out of the chains. He rubs his wrists, rotates his ankles, doesn't know what to say. In the end, he says nothing, just sits down beside his captor, picks up the nearest fish, and immediately drops it again.

"Let it cool a bit first. Fish, freshly cooked. Nothing better, best way to start the day, even in the afternoon. Good to be out in the open. Forgot how much I enjoy being out of the city. Forgot how quiet it was. Thought I didn't want quiet, that I needed other people close by. Maybe I was wrong, maybe I was wrong, don't know."

During their interminable journey, Tom had grown accustomed to Tyson's stream of consciousness, although the older man had fought to keep his monologue to a mutter. Not any more. Along with releasing him and cooking breakfast, this new, more relaxed, Tyson is a little unnerving. Tom doesn't get too close. Is this some kind of trap?

When the fish cools, Tom strips away the flesh and stuffs it into his mouth. It's the best thing he's ever tasted. When did he last eat?

"Time for us to have a talk, I reckon," says Tyson. He's clean-shaven again, and looks rested. The sun isn't high. Tom would have guessed at midmorning, but according to Tyson, it's afternoon already.

Tyson pours two cups of black coffee from a thermos, handing one over. Tom finishes the fish, stripping the last piece of flesh from the bones with his teeth. The coffee is strong and bitter.

"Sorry I had to chain you up like that. Thing is, I learned not to trust anyone until I'm sure they're not a threat. And it's kept me alive, so I keep doing it. Still here, still alive, not dead yet. Things to do, things to do. Had to know more about you. Who you're working for. What you want. Back in California, I called Roach. Told him I needed to see him. Not his real name. Roach knows things. Knows people. Knows secrets about people. And he loves technology, won't listen to me when I warn him they're listening, they're watching. Maybe he's right, maybe he's smart enough to keep himself safe, hide in plain sight, keep them looking somewhere else, never on their doorstep. Visited Roach yesterday. Had to knock you out, couldn't let you come with me, hope you understand. Roach found out who came for me. Who came for Murchen. Kai. Who came for Kai. It was the Company."

Tom tries to keep up with the words, but it's too hard. Tyson is connected to Kai. He remembers that much. A photograph. Tyson with a group of men; Kai in the background.

Tyson is still talking. "But you're not CIA. I phoned through your ID to Roach. He says it's fake, not real, forged, get out of jail free. Pretty good, but wouldn't stand up to his analysis. I told him you were one of Anton's, a graduate of the German mountains...."

Tyson pauses here, with some effort, head tilted, expecting a response. Tom stares back, wanting to help, to gain this man's trust, but he can't find the right thoughts to put into words.

Something about the name Anton chimes with Tom, as does the thought of mountains in Germany, but, while everything he sees and does helps Jimmy Blue, it doesn't work the other way around. Tom slept through much of the last five or six years. Blue was in charge, occasionally stepping back for Tom when safe to do so. Tom has opened his eyes in Paris, Stockholm, Florence, Kyoto, Toronto, Mumbai, New York.

Now he's here. Wherever here is. Tom screws his eyes shut, making it dark for a moment. That's where Blue lives. In the dark. But there's no one there. Tom fights the tears that threaten to come.

Tyson throws dirt onto the fire to smother it. "I'm not good with trust, like I said. Seems you're the same way. Self-preservation, I get it. Course I do. Learned the hard way, the hardest way, learned my lesson for sure. Don't trust people, they let you down, they turn their backs. Leave you to rot. Not Murchen, not Kai. She was the best of us."

A big bird skims the surface of the fast-flowing river. A heron? Tom used to see herons on the Thames. This bird is too far away to identify, but Tom labels it as a heron, and the link with home reduces his anxiety to a simmer.

Tyson keeps his eyes on the ground. "I know you're not with the CIA. You killed the agents who killed Kai."

Talk of killing makes Tom's discomfort and anxiety more pronounced. He watches the dying fire. Tyson leans forward.

"The name on your ID card is Tom. That what you want me to call you?"

Tom nods. Waits for his throat to relax, pushes the words up and out. "Mm. Y-yes. Mm. Tom."

"Good. It's a start. So, like I said, we know who you ain't. Not CIA, and Roach says he can't find a link to any nation state. You're a puzzle. A conundrum, riddle me this. So what is it, Tom? Corporate work? Freelance? What brought you to Kai?"

Tom shakes his head in frustration, the tears spilling from his eyes. Wipes his face with the back of his hand.

Tyson watches him, mumbling to himself.

"Okay, Tom, okay. I'm sorry. You're not what I expected, man. Most folk in our line of work... well. We can't do what we do and stay normal, right? See the things we see, then go back to our family, throw ball in the yard with the kids. If we go to the movies, we check the exits first. In diners, we sit where we can see the whole room. Expecting trouble. We're not normal, we don't belong."

Tyson stands, picks up a broom that was lying by his right side. As he talks, he backs away from the fire, motioning Tom to do the same. With a practised sweep, he removes evidence of their stay.

"I haven't seen Kai in a long time. Long, long time. She's the only one I stayed in touch with. She... she saved me once. How did she die, Tom?"

Tom jumps when he hears his name. The older man sometimes forgets he's talking to someone else and his voice drops to a whisper. But that last question was clear enough.

The pickup, the man in the back with a long-barrelled rifle. These images Tom recalls, but there are more in his dreams. Kai rubbing Thai holy basil between her fingers. Kai falling, lifeless. Then hot, crazed, unstoppable rage.

"Th-th-they, mm, they shot her. From, mm, f-far away."

Tears slide down Tom's cheeks. Tyson leans the broom on the side of the Phoenix. Reaches down and pulls a knife from his boot. Five-inch blade, sharp, not serrated. He adjusts his grip, the tip pointing at Tom, who goes still.

When Tyson moves, it's with a speed and fluidity Tom would never have expected from someone his age and size. He steps forward, the knife coming up from waist-level, heading for Tom's exposed throat.

Tom flinches backwards, stumbles, cries out. Tyson's other hand grabs the neck of his T-shirt, stops him falling. The blade is a cold, hard point scratching his Adam's apple.

"N-n-n-no. Mm, p-please. Kai, mm, w-was m-my, mm, my friend."

Tyson looks him in the eye, the constant movement of his lips stilled for the moment. He moves the knife away, releases his grip on Tom, puts a hand on his shoulder.

"I believe you, son. I do. Who are you, exactly? You ain't the same guy I found in Santa Barbara, are you? I mean, you are, of course you are, but you ain't neither, right? I heard about this multiple personality shit, not like the movies, real deal, right? That you? That what's going on here, Tom?"

All Tom can manage as he struggles to understand Tyson is a shake of his head. The older man sighs.

"Well, whatever you are, you ain't gonna be much use to me or Kai like this. No use at all. Not a fighter, just a kid, a scared kid, and kids get hurt, get killed. C'mon. I'm sorry about the knife. It was a kinda test, you know? I had to see. Now I've seen. Complicates things."

He opens the passenger door. "You can ride up front. Would you like that?"

Tom hesitates. Will Tyson attack him again? Should he run? He looks towards the river, as if Jimmy Blue might wade out of it and make the choice for him. In the shadows under the trees, he senses, rather than sees, something move, a deeper darkness. The anaesthetic is wearing off. Blue has begun his climb back towards wakefulness.

Tom hoists himself into the passenger seat. Puts on his seatbelt. Tyson scrapes the broom across the ground as he walks around the front and climbs in alongside him, tossing the broom into the back. He starts the engine.

"Roach told me who sent the teams. I'm gonna find that guy and I'm gonna kill him. When Roach tells me who gave that guy his orders, I'm gonna find them and kill them too."

The engine ticks over. Tyson places both hands on the steering wheel.

"Kai changed. She did what we all want to do, but none of us can. We thought it was impossible. She got out, and she changed. Became someone different. Someone useful, someone kind, someone wise. She changed, Tom, she changed. I talked to her about revenge once, you know what she said? She said revenge is wasteful, revenge hurts everyone, and no one wins. She said revenge is stupid."

Tyson turns to Tom, and there is such intensity in his expression that it's like a physical force, a wall of pain and anger pushing against him. It's all Tom can do not to slide away across the seat. But, even as his mouth dries with fear, he is aware of a different response from deep inside; a recognition, a kinship with this damaged, dangerous man.

"She's right, of course," says Tyson. "Always was smarter than me, but here's the thing. Revenge may be stupid, but it's straightforward. And I like straightforward. You find out who needs to die, then you go kill them. Right?"

Tom thinks of his parents, and of the men who killed them. Of the young, scared-looking guy who chased a terrified child upstairs, raised a gun, and put a bullet in his head. Tom's parents are long dead, but their killers still walk the streets of London. Tom fears Tyson's intensity, the violence so close to the surface. But Jimmy Blue is close.

Before he knows he's going to speak, Tom finds he's already answered.

"Right."

CHAPTER FORTY

THE PHOENIX EMERGES from a bumpy track between the trees onto a narrow, poorly maintained road. Ten minutes later, they pull onto a highway.

Tyson mutters the whole time, his monologue peppered with threats against Kai's killers. He's quieter now, his voice a whisper.

Tom risks a question. "Mm, wh-where's, mm, m-my backpack? I n-need it."

"Sorry, kid." Tyson rips a packet of jerky open with his teeth, clasps a couple of inches between his molars, twists and pulls until it breaks, then starts chewing. He offers the packet to Tom, who shakes his head. "Roach has your stuff. I left it with him, it's there, he's looking after it. Checking it. Wasn't sure about you. Computers are his thing, he's good with them, crazy, but he won't listen. We can go back when we're done, pick your stuff up."

Sometimes, Tom can tell when someone's lying. Tyson's doing it now. For whatever reason, Tyson doesn't believe they'll ever go back to that picture postcard cabin Tom glimpsed behind the huge industrial site.

Losing his phone, his only link to home, adds to Tom's discomfort. He has Debbie's number on that phone, the police lady who checked in on him every few months since he was a kid. He hasn't called her for years. It makes him sad, but Tom knows it won't be forever. When he returns to London, it'll be to stay.

Tom looks across at the man gripping the steering wheel, his jaw working while he stares out at the road ahead. And he knows what Tyson lied about, and why. He doesn't believe he'll ever see his friend Roach again. He thinks he'll die avenging Kai. And he's accepted that.

"Stoppard," says Tyson. "Eric Stoppard. That's his name. Summabitch."

So the summer bitch is a man.

"Roach told me he was the one who sent in the teams to kill Kai. I know Stoppard. Or I knew him. He was on the way up when I last saw him. Climbing the greasy pole, the company ladder, doing the dirty work, not asking questions, carved himself a niche, got comfortable there. Smart guy, but not smart enough to play politics. Enjoys getting his hands dirty too much. Some people, they enjoy killing, get a rush. Gives them a thrill. That's how it is with Stoppard. Saw for myself. He's ruthless, but he does as he's told. He attached himself to a real slimeball back in the day—Ruben Castle. Was his right-hand man. Loyal lieutenant, old faithful. Stoppard chose him because Castle knew how to play the game. He took Stoppard with him when he got promoted. You heard of Ruben Castle?"

"N-no."

"He's Deputy Director of the Central Intelligence Agency, the slimy piece of shit. Always figured he would get to the top. One more rung to go, I guess. If Stoppard sent those teams, Castle gave the order. But Roach says it's off the books. The director of the CIA knows nothing about it. Figure Castle has some side-game of his own going. Whatever. I don't care why, not important, doesn't matter. World gonna keep turning either way. Just want Stoppard and Castle. And if it goes higher, I'm coming for them too."

The more Tyson says, the less Tom understands. But he thinks Tyson needs to speak, so he listens until he stops talking. He wants to help this man, but the promise of violence scares him.

"Wh-, mm, wh-what do y-y-you want, mm, me to d-do?"

Tyson smiles, and Tom sees another man for a moment, capable of kindness. "You? You don't need to do nothing, kid. Nada. No. You've done enough. I owe you. You're done now. Go home, forget all this. That multiple personality thing you've got going? It could get you killed. All finished, thank you, gracias."

Tyson flips open the glove box, revealing a heavy handgun. Next to it, Tom's wallet. Tyson nods, and Tom takes it.

You got money? That credit card good?"

Tom nods.

"We'll be in Washington soon. I'll drop you at a motel near the airport. The Company doesn't know who you are. Let's keep it that way, keep you safe, get you home, Tom. You've done enough. This is my fight."

Before Tom can respond, Tyson flicks the indicator, pulls off the road, drives half a mile, then slows when they pass a tired-looking row of stores. It's getting dark, and the doors of a pawnshop, clothes store, and accountancy office display shut signs. Tyson parks out front. Points at a phone booth.

"I need to check in with Roach. Here." He takes a roll of cash, peels off two twenties, and hands them to Tom. "There's an all-night store across the street. Go get us some food, some chow, will you? Whatever you like. I'll only be a few minutes."

Tom jogs across the street and looks over his shoulder before going into the store. Tyson waves before turning to the phone booth.

There are the usual sandwiches and wraps inside, but Tom heads straight for the counter at the back, which offers freshly made hot dogs. The smell alone makes his mouth water. He orders two large hot dogs from a small man in a hairnet. The store has the brand of jerky Tyson likes, so he picks up two packs.

"Onions?"

Tom doesn't realise the hairnet man is speaking to him. "Hey! Bandana guy. You want onions on these?"

"Mm. Er, mm..." Tom loves onions on a hot dog, but isn't sure about his travelling companion. He heads to the front of the store, holding his forefinger up to the hairnet man, who has a hot dog in one hand, and tongs full of soft browned onions in the other.

At the door, about to push it open, Tom stops. Takes his hand away. Stares across the road. Tyson has finished his call and is smashing the phone receiver into the wall. Bits of plastic fly off until what he's holding is unrecognisable. He kicks the machine until it sags. Then he stares at the shattered receiver. When he turns towards the store, Tom backs away guiltily, despite having no reason to feel that way. He goes back to the hot dog counter.

"Onions on both, please."

By the time Tom has paid, Tyson is back in the Phoenix.

Before Tom can walk round to the passenger side, the driver's window lowers.

"In the back, kid. We'll pass some security cameras. Stay out of sight, keep down."

Tom hands Tyson a hot dog. Gets in the back. Tyson doesn't turn to look. He seems calm now. Hard to believe he's the same man Tom witnessed destroying the phone booth in a rage.

They eat in near-silence, Tyson's monologue more sparse than usual, and spoken in a whisper too quiet to understand. Tom gives him the jerky and his change. Tyson doesn't thank him, placing the items on the passenger seat without comment.

Tom wonders if he might have offended the older man. He tries to remember what they've spoken about, but—as usual—the effort yields no usable results. His memory isn't good with specifics.

While he tries to clear the fog, Tyson starts the Phoenix, then swings around in his seat, smiling. Tom returns the smile hesitantly. Perhaps he's wrong about Tyson's change of mood. Maybe trashing the phone booth was an outburst of grief for Kai.

"Change of plan," says Tyson. "Roach found a flight to London. Booked you a seat. I'll take you to the airport now. You leave in a couple hours."

Tom doesn't know what to say. This is wrong, somehow. He should be pleased, but he's not. And something about Tyson is different.

"Here." The older man tosses a blister pack into Tom's lap. Two pills.

"Mm, mm, w-what are th-these?"

"There's random drug screening at the airport. If they pull you in, they'll find traces of the drugs I used to keep you asleep. Not exactly prescription drugs, not over-the-counter, illegal, you know what I'm saying? These pills will flush out the anaesthetic. You'll be clean. Good to go. No trouble."

Tom stares at the packet, then back at Tyson, who nods. "Take 'em."

There's no reason not to trust this man, Tom reminds himself. He's Kai's friend, and—once he discovered Jimmy Blue was fighting the people who came to kill her—he let Tom out of his chains and stopped drugging him.

He unscrews a bottle of soda, pops the pills out of the pack and swallows them, chased down with lemonade.

Tyson turns away without another word, flicks on the headlights, and backs out of the parking space.

Tom looks at the lights of the city as they rejoin the highway, surprised they're driving away from them. He looks up front. Tyson is watching him in the mirror. "Airport is out of town a ways." Tyson's voice sounds strange, like he's at the end of a tunnel.

Tom shakes his head, yawns to pop his ears. The rumble of the van fades. He claps his hands to make sure he can hear the sound. At least, he tries to. His arms are leaden, his muscles weak. He looks back at Tyson, but can't raise his head. His neck can't handle the weight of what feels like a bowling bowl balanced on top of it. When his head falls forward onto his chest, Tom can do nothing to stop it.

He looks down at his feet as his eyes close. He has no choice. His eyelids come down like the shutter in the storage unit he keeps in Soho. All he has left of his family is in that unit, and—as everything slows and blurs—he fights off unconsciousness by picturing his mother's old writing desk, seeing her sitting at it in her home office, fountain pen in hand. She turns towards him, but her face won't come into focus, and her hair is dissolving, and he can't remember who this woman with his eyes is, as heavy, dreamless sleep rushes up to envelop him.

CHAPTER FORTY-ONE

IT'S LATE, and Robert Hanan is drinking alone. The flat-screen television above the fireplace provides the only light in his den, daubing the walls a kaleidoscopic monochrome.

He stands behind the leather recliner, looking at the screen. It shows a rolling news channel, but he's muted the sound. His cell phone is on the desk. Hanan walks over, picks it up, as he's done at least once a minute since he came down here three hours earlier.

No messages. No missed calls.

It's not his usual phone. It's the burner Eric Stoppard gave him when they first met. If either needs to contact the other, they send a blank message. Hanan sent his third blank message since dinner thirty minutes ago.

No messages. No missed calls.

Stoppard told him he would be in touch when everything was taken care of. *Everything*, in this context, means Elizabeth Murchen, and *taken care of* means killed. Stoppard's silence means she's not dead. She's still out there. She could resurface. What has she got to lose? If she were to hand herself in to the FBI, they'd relish the opportunity to embarrass their rival agency, and destroy Hanan's shot at Vice President. Unless Stoppard and his people end her, now.

No missed calls.

Hanan checks the clock. It's nearly one. Since Connie died, if he's alone, he's always in bed before midnight. If he's drinking, he stops at eleven. There are good, practical reasons for this regime. Drinking into the early hours can be habit forming. He's seen friends go down that road and lose their way. Also, one trip to the bathroom per night is plenty. Lastly, he needs six hours of decent sleep to maintain the level of mental stamina necessary for his job.

Tonight is an exception he already regrets. His thinking has become fuzzy and paranoid, his tongue thick and clumsy, numbed by whiskey. Is this who he is? A nervous old man, hiding with a bottle, scared his past is catching up with him?

He puts the whiskey away, closes the cabinet. Where's the compartmentalisation Connie used to admire? She'd tease him about it, the way Hanan could fall asleep like a baby nights while she stared at the ceiling worrying about the kids, the country, or the planet. But, really, she loved his ability to fence off areas in his mind, not allowing them to contaminate other areas. She envied it. So why isn't it working tonight?

When his phone vibrates, he turns so fast he almost falls. It takes a couple of seconds to realise the sound is coming from his jacket, draped over the chair, rather than the burner on the desk.

He slides it out of the pocket, looks at the screen. Castle. Why is the deputy director of the CIA calling him at this hour? His heart flutters as he thumbs the button to answer.

"Hanan."

"Senator, we have a situation. Nothing we can't handle, but I've sent a couple of agents over to your place. We're moving you to Washington for your own protection. Pack a bag for a couple of nights. They'll be with you soon."

"A situation? Do you mean—"

Castle's baritone stays infuriatingly calm. "Senator, it's best we don't discuss this on the telephone. Certain information has come to light, suggesting a credible threat. Until we eliminate that threat, or prove it false, it's in your best interests to put yourself under our protection. I hope you understand?"

"I do." Hanan ends the call, grabs his jacket, and heads upstairs to pack.

He understands all right. Castle won't discuss anything incriminating over the phone. The precautions the man takes before sharing information would be paranoid in anyone else. The fact that he's deputy director of the Central Intelligence Agency makes that paranoia frightening. As Hanan folds shirts, placing them in a small suitcase, he glances around the bedroom he shared with Connie for nearly thirty years. Wonders where the bugs are. Where the cameras are hidden. Are they in every politician's house and office? In their cars? When the intelligence services spy on their masters and each other, who's running things? Is anybody?

When the doorbell rings, he looks out of the window, remembering to turn off the lights first. That's a lesson learned at his first security briefing as a US senator. If your drapes are open, the lights are on inside and it's dark outside, you may as well stick a note on your head saying PLEASE SHOOT ME.

Two agents. A big man and a small woman. For an appalling second, he sees Connor Tyson and Elizabeth Murchen. Then he remembers Tyson is dead, and—even if Murchen came for him—she would hardly put on a suit and ring his doorbell.

Downstairs, he puts his eye to the peephole, and the agents hold up their identification before he unlocks the door. The small woman is Asian, half Murchen's age. She takes his bag and directs him to the dark sedan at the kerb.

"You guys get a discount on black cars or what?"

Neither of them smiles at his feeble attempt to make light of the situation. The male agent walks ahead, opens the door for him. The Asian woman drives. No one speaks.

After ten minutes of silent travel, the woman takes the filter lane for the freeway and the airport.

Hanan pulls the burner out of his pocket.

No missed calls. No messages.

———

Another taciturn pair of agents meets Hanan at Dulles and chauffeur him downtown. Their destination is an anonymous building used only by the politically powerful. Certain hotels in Washington don't advertise. They owe their continued existence to a stipend, paid out of the budget of a government subcommittee with a long name. A handful of lavish suites kept in readiness for a very short list of possible guests. Other suites, less lavish, are available to the heads of America's security agencies. It is to one of these that the silent agents deliver Senator Robert Hanan, leaving him in the care of a courteous night manager who shows him around the rooms. Hanan doesn't offer a tip. It's not that kind of place.

Ten minutes after arriving, as Hanan stares out of a floor-to-ceiling window made of glass tough enough to withstand a mortar strike according to the night manager, the deputy director of the CIA arrives.

"Hanan."

"Castle."

It's not unusual for powerful people to despise each other, and neither man pretends to enjoy the other's company. The deputy director makes this clear by not removing his coat. Hanan doesn't offer him a drink.

"What's this about, Castle? I assume we're safe to talk here?"

"We are."

"Stoppard told me he was sending a team to take care of the Santa Barbara situation. Now he's not returning my calls. What the hell's going on?"

Castle crosses the room, puts his briefcase on the desk, takes out a laptop. Opens it, and waits. Hanan grits his teeth and joins him.

Castle is a small man, balding, with old-fashioned wire glasses. Hanan looks down at the younger man's head and scowls. He reminds himself not to underestimate Castle, who points at a grainy black and white image of a dark RV waiting at a traffic signal.

"Is this supposed to answer my question?"

Castle sighs. "I'm going to ask you to shut the fuck up and listen, Senator."

Hanan takes a breath and holds it. He fights an urge to slap the expanse of accessible scalp within reach. As unpalatable as it is, Castle as good as owns him. The evidence the deputy director amassed concerning his use of Tyson and Murchen's peculiar talents gives Castle enough leverage to run Hanan any damn way he pleases. No point being naïve. Better to accept the unchangeable, and wait for an opportunity to redress the balance. There's always an opportunity, eventually, and Hanan is good at waiting. He'll see Castle suffer one day. Assuming he lives long enough. He folds his arms, pins his hands to his sides. Castle puts one podgy finger over the right arrow key, but doesn't press it.

"Stoppard told you about the first team he sent to take out Murchen. The second team went in at dawn on Sunday. More of them, better armed, well-prepared, led by one of our best. All twelve are dead."

Hanan takes a second to process what he's just heard. "Sunday morning? That's nearly three days ago. Where the hell do you—"

Castle bangs the flat of his hand hard on the table and Hanan stops talking. The deputy director doesn't raise his voice, but hisses through clenched teeth. "I told you to shut. The. Fuck. Up."

He waits. Hanan, to his horror, realises that this man is all that stands between him and Elizabeth Murchen. He hasn't yet considered her as a physical threat, only a potential disaster for his run at the vice-presidency. Twelve agents. She killed twelve agents. How is that even possible?

"It's a mess," says Castle.

Hanan, obeying the order to stay quiet, doesn't point out the understatement. He lets Castle talk.

"But I've taken charge of the operation personally. This is why."

Castle presses the arrow key, then the space bar. The image changes. The same RV, parked by a row of stores. It could be anywhere in America. It's not a photograph, as he first thought, it's a video, which becomes clear when the figure to the left of the screen becomes animated. He repeatedly smashes a phone and wrenches the metal body half away from the wall. He's big. Tall. Black, bald, wearing heavy-framed glasses. The freeze-frame catches three-quarters of his face.

"He's been very, very careful around cameras. He thinks the CIA has facial recognition devices linked to security cams. Naturally, if that were true, it would break dozens of laws, and breach the trust of the American people. Which is why we don't talk about it."

Hanan wonders if Castle is attempting humour, but decides he's not capable.

"On this occasion, he was agitated, and made a rare mistake. The database picked up a match, but the operative thought it was a computer error. It wasn't. Here's the same image, enhanced."

There's a chair by the table. Hanan sits in it, gaping like a fish.

It's Connor Tyson.

"But. But he's—"

"Dead? Yes. So we believed. Apparently not. Connor Tyson is very much alive. And he's heading this way."

"To Washington?"

"It would appear so. We—Stoppard and I—think he must have obtained Stoppard's name. They know each other. I think Tyson's coming here to kill him."

Hanan isn't sure how to respond. The inside of his mouth is furry, but he wants another drink.

"That's not everything, Senator."

Jesus. What else is there?

Castle taps another key, bringing up a map with a highlighted route crossing the country.

"Tyson didn't come straight from San Antonio. We ran a search on the vehicle, picked it up in several locations. Enough to make it clear he stopped off en route."

"Where?" croaks Hanan.

"The California coast. Santa Barbara. They're working together. Tyson and Murchen."

Robert Hanan, who has enjoyed an easy command of the

language ever since he uttered his first word—*wallet*—at nineteen months, opens and closes his mouth.

Castle closes the laptop. "Fortunately, we now have an advantage over our psychotic friends. We know they're coming. And this time, we have bait."

Hanan can't formulate any actual words, but something in his blank stare, from a face shining with cold sweat, must adequately convey his question, because Castle answers it for him.

"We have Eric Stoppard."

Hours after Castle has left, lying in a bed large enough to accommodate five adults, Hanan's brain catches up with the implications of that word: *bait*. What if dangling Stoppard in front of Tyson and Murchen doesn't work? What then? Might the deputy director decide he needs a backup plan?

The room is eerily silent. The mortar-proof glass stops all sound as efficiently as bullets and bombs.

If Stoppard fails, only Castle and Hanan have skin in the game. And Castle just moved Hanan to Washington. In the middle of the night.

Moved for his own protection. To Washington, where two highly trained lethal killers are headed. They know Stoppard sent the teams, but surely they don't know who sent Stoppard. If they find out...

Bait.

CHAPTER FORTY-TWO

TOM LIES ON A CLIFFTOP, head hanging over the side. The cliff is made of glass. Despite the lack of light, Tom knows the drop is long. No mountaineer, however experienced, would try to climb this face as there is no flaw in the glass surface: no ledges, no cracks, no purchase at all.

Despite this, far below, Jimmy Blue climbs towards him. Tom can't see him, but his own fingertips throb with the pain of each handhold as Blue pushes through the glass; flesh pierced as he pulls himself up. Every inch of his progress is agony. His ascent is too slow, and Tom hears the echoing roars of desperation as Blue turns his implacable will to the task.

Jimmy Blue is coming. But he won't get here in time. A scream of primal rage sounds inside Tom's head, terrifying him. He peers down into the abyss, seeing nothing at all.

It gets a little lighter. Shapes form. A soda bottle, cap off, its contents spilled. The familiar thin brown carpet of the motorhome, stained darker by the liquid.

He thinks he's still asleep at first. The Phoenix is on the road, the engine note lulling Tom as he emerges from the fog of the drugs. It takes a few minutes for any kind of understanding to return. Then he remembers. The pills weren't what Tyson said they were. They sent him to sleep. Tyson lied. Why?

Tom is on the floor. He does not know how long he's slept. It could be minutes, or hours.

It's night. They're not on the interstate. This road is narrower, quieter, lined by trees.

For the first time on this trip, his fellow traveller isn't talking.

Tom's hands are pinned under his body, so he moves a few inches to release them. He has pins and needles. Wiggles his fingers, clenches and unclenches his fists. Moves his hands apart, then stops. Can't go any further. The familiar, but unwelcome, sensation of metal against his wrists.

Tyson has handcuffed him again.

Tom sits upright, tilts his neck one way, then the other. Rolls his shoulders. The chains on his ankles stop him from stretching, but he brings his knees to his chest, then extends his legs, feeling the burn in his stomach muscles. Repeats the exercise. Looks forward at the driver, wondering at this change in behaviour.

Tyson hasn't stopped talking at all. If anything, he's talking more than ever, his jaw tense as it works, his lips spitting sentences into the night. But he's turned the volume down. The effort this takes makes sweat bead on Tyson's brow like condensation on a window; fat drops running into his eyes or down the side of his face into stubbled cheeks.

For a few minutes, Tom watches Tyson, wondering why the man is fighting so hard to stop his internal monologue being spoken aloud. Whatever he's saying, he doesn't want Tom to hear. And the effort is costing him.

Tyson shifts his head, glares at Tom in the rear-view mirror. Looks away again. Doesn't offer a bottle of water or anything to eat. Twitches and whispers, drives on.

The minor road joins a bigger road. Houses appear on either side. There are retail parks, fast-food outlets, billboards. Thousands of lights from tiny windows in distant buildings. It's a city, but Tom doesn't know which. Not Washington, surely. There are very few vehicles on the road, the stores they pass shuttered and quiet.

He knows they've been driving east pretty much the entire trip. New York is east, but he doesn't think that's where they are. New York has the Statue of Liberty and the Empire State Building. The Chrysler Building, too. One institution Tom remembers from his teens chose posters of New York landmarks to decorate the dining room. None of those landmarks are here.

The Phoenix pulls onto a bridge across a wide, fast-flowing river far below, lit by a crescent moon. Halfway across, Tyson brings the motorhome to a stop. Before opening the door, he pulls a backpack from the seat beside him, slings it on his shoulder.

Tom frowns in confusion. It's his backpack.

The back door opens. Tyson doesn't come in.

"Out," he says, then whispers something, his voice harsh and strained.

Tom stands and shuffles to the door, hops out, almost falling. Tyson doesn't help. He moves forward, stands at the waist-high guard rail.

Tom stays where he is. When Tyson turns, Tom holds up his handcuffed hands.

"Yeah," said Tyson. "I can explain. Come here."

Tom doesn't understand. He shuffles forward to join Tyson at the guard rail.

The water is a long way down. Even this high, he can hear the rush of the current.

Tom's backpack is at Tyson's feet.

"That's mm, th-that's m-m-my, mm—"

Tyson interrupts. "Yeah. It is. After talking to Roach, I didn't know what to think, who to believe. Told him I needed to see for myself, check it out, find the truth. My own eyes, my decision. So I drove back out here to Pittsburgh and he showed me."

Tyson bends down, takes out Tom's phone. "Funny. Roach said he spent more time on your laptop. Looking for clues about who you are, who you're working for. But he says you're smart, that nothing is stored on it. He did whatever the hell hackers do, data strings, hard drives, thread analysis, he told me, but he may as well speak Klingon. Says you use remote servers, and memorised passwords, which means they can't be cracked by an algorithm. Like he said, smart. But maybe not that smart."

He presses the phone, swipes, and taps. "No password on your phone. Nothing. Opens for anyone. Roach, me. Anyone. Guess you don't keep secrets, nothing to hide?"

This is all wrong. The way Tyson talks, the way he's standing, the tension in his body. Everything is wrong. There is danger here. An echo of his dream reminds him of how frantically Jimmy Blue wants to get back. He remembers the fear, the desperation.

"But you take photos sometimes, don't you?"

Tyson has become still. Tom needs to respond, but doesn't know how. He's scared, and he needs to pee.

Tyson holds up the phone, its screen towards Tom. It's a photograph of Kai, in the bungalow kitchen. She's tied to a chair. Her eyes are closed.

Tom does not know when this terrible photograph was taken, and how it got onto his phone. It's vital he communicates this to Tyson, but he can't do it. Not here, handcuffed, scared, upset, the tears already pooling. Not with his throat constricting around his vocal cords, and his mind unable to form a sentence. His eyes widen and his mouth opens in mute appeal to Tyson to accept that this is a misunderstanding.

The older man drops the phone back into the backpack. Looks out across the river to the darker bank, lined with evergreens.

"I like you, Tom. I do. And I know what you're trying to say. That this wasn't you, right? That you didn't take this photograph, this picture, of Murchen, of Kai, yes? It must have been someone else."

Tom nods frantically.

"I believe you, Tom. I believe you."

Tom's body sags with relief. Tyson understands. The relief is so profound, he doesn't understand what Tyson says next until it's too late.

"Thing is, Roach can find out if a photograph was sent in a message, or uploaded from a memory card, a stick, whatever. Not this photograph, Tom. Someone used your phone to take this photograph the night after I called Kai. Not you, Tom, not you."

Tom can't unpick the conflicting messages. Tyson's words sound like he accepts Tom's innocence, but the tension in his voice and body send a different message. Tyson places a hand on Tom's back. The guard rail pushes into Tom's midriff.

"I believe you, Tom. But who else is in there with you? Do you know anything about them? Do you remember things they did? The other personalities? I guess you need help. Treatment. Doctors. Shrinks. Medicine. Electric shocks. I don't know. But someone in there killed Kai."

Tom shakes his head, can't speak.

Tyson steps behind Tom. "Can you swim, Tom?"

Thursday mornings in the municipal pool with his class, float held out in front of him. Someone pushing him under. A mouthful of chlorine. Coughing a thin stream of vomit onto the tiles.

Finally, he speaks. "N-n-n-no."

"Good," says Tyson. A pair of powerful hands on his shins, thumbs behind gripping his calves, then Tom is tilting, pivoting on the guard rail, handcuffed arms windmilling. He senses the moment his weight transfers, then Tyson shoves, chest pushed against the soles of his feet, and Tom is launched away from the bridge, and over the river.

It's oddly familiar, almost comforting, the sensation of being caught between two states, held in the moment before one reality is replaced by another. Then gravity, and panic, claim him and, end over end, Tom falls towards the ever-louder water.

The drop is long enough for one near-perfect somersault, meaning he enters the river feet-first, a fact that might have saved his life had Tom been a strong swimmer, and if he wasn't in shackles.

The water slaps him with a cold, powerful, giant hand. There's a silty, gritty breath—half air, half river—then he's under, and it's dark, and Tom, after a couple of kicks which send him deeper, gives up.

He tries to picture his mother again, but it's Kai sitting at the old writing desk, tied to the chair, her head sagging. Her eyelids snap open, but she has no eyes, just pools of liquid darkness that suck him out of the world and away from everything he has ever known until there is nothing left to see, hear, feel, or taste.

There is no Tom, no Jimmy Blue. There is only the river, and, high above, a motorhome driving across the bridge, heading towards Washington.

CHAPTER FORTY-THREE

AT FOUR A.M., an hour after a raucous party ran out of steam after all the girls either went home or paired up with other guys, two brothers sit on the hood of a Chrysler a few years older than either of them. They stare out at the water and pass a joint back and forth.

"Levi? What day is it?"

There's no answer from his brother, so Dale digs him with his elbow. "I'm serious, man. I can't remember. Mom and Dad fly in Friday. Is it Wednesday morning or Thursday morning now? We've gotta clean up before they get back. Levi?"

Levi grunts. Dale knows he's still pissed that Vanessa Cross disappeared upstairs with the film studies guy. Levi has lusted after her for months, timing his daily workouts to make sure they crossed paths on campus, his muscles bulging under a lifter's vest. Turns out she's not into jocks. Levi will sulk for days, Dale knows.

"Who cares, man?" is Levi's eventual rejoinder. He takes another long drag at the blunt before handing it over. He takes three tokes to Dale's one and keeps the beer on his side of the hood. The perks of being the older, taller, bulkier sibling. Levi may be only fourteen months older, but he's twenty pounds heavier than his younger brother, and makes the most of that discrepancy.

"And what about the booze? We gotta replace it before Dad sees. He'll go batshit crazy, man." Dale googled the bourbon Levi had liberated from the drinks cabinet. It cost a couple of hundred bucks.

"You worry too much, little brother. It'll be okay. Have a beer." This is Levi's way. He hasn't changed since they were toddlers. Nine times out of ten it was Levi who broke something, took food from the refrigerator, or 'borrowed' money from Mom's purse, but when it came to the reckoning, he invoked the solemn fraternal code. This meant both brothers sharing the blame. And he's still doing it.

Dale takes the can from his brother and sips tepid light beer, looking out across the Allegheny river. It's flowing fast and dark. Occasionally, something disturbs the surface. A fish, or an otter? Do they have otters in Pittsburgh? If he'd paid more attention in school science lessons, Dale muses, he'd be studying to be a veterinarian now. He'd always liked animals. Instead, he'd barely got his diploma, and the only reason he's at college at all is because of Levi's wrestling scholarship.

They parked facing the water. A long, tidy garden slopes down to the river. There are still some lights on in the house, but Levi's bulky outline blocks Dale's view.

Hey, he thinks. *I'm literally in my brother's shadow.*

He shifts along the hood to find his own space, and that's when he sees it. Out in the shallows. A dark shape moving with the current. Was he right about the otters? No, it's bigger than that. Can bears swim? Of course they can. They eat fish, don't they? But you don't get bears in Pittsburgh, and this one isn't swimming, it's floating on its back.

And it's wearing handcuffs.

"Levi!"

Dale slides off the Chrysler's hood, stumbles down the bank and is knee-deep in the cold water before he even realises he's moving. "Levi! Help me."

Dale hooks his hand around a clammy forearm, tries to stop the body floating past. The current is strong, and it's slippery underfoot. He scrabbles around for purchase, digging his heels into the silt, but the pressure is relentless, his grip is loosening, and the river wants to keep its prize. He's about to give up, let go, when Levi splashes past and slides his hands under the body's armpits, pulling it towards the shore.

The corpse is big and heavy, the sodden clothes, handcuffs, and chains around his ankles adding to his natural weight.

The brothers flop onto the ground, panting, staring at the body.

"Reckon he's dead?" Dale looks for movement, finds none.

"Course he is." Levi scoots closer, shakes the man's shoulders.

"I don't know," says Dale. "He might just be unconscious. He needs to be on his side. Recovery position. Help me, will you?"

College ran mandatory first aid classes once a year. Dale took his this semester. When Levi rolls the body onto its side, Dale pushes the legs up the way they'd demonstrated in the PowerPoint. He looks into the drowned face. The man is wearing a bandana, a dark line visible where it's ridden up his shaved head. Dale pushes it back further to reveal old scars, like someone had taken a hammer to his skull.

"Shit. Check that out."

Levi doesn't respond. When Dale turns, his brother holds up a sodden wallet.

"Who is he?" says Dale.

Levi shrugs, pulls out a handful of bills. "I don't care. Whoever he is, he's paying to replace Dad's bourbon."

"Jeez, Levi, what the hell's wrong with you? We need to call 911."

Dale checks his phone and groans. It had been in his pocket when they pulled the body out and is now ominously dark. The power button changes nothing.

"Give me your phone, man."

"You crazy?" Levi waved the cash in front of him. "It's too late for this loser, but he can still help us. We call this in, we're spending tomorrow answering questions. We're both drunk, we're both stoned. No. I don't think so. Let someone else find him. Come on, let's go."

He walks back towards the car. Dale protests, but, for once, Levi is kinda making sense. Not that he'll split the money fairly. Dale follows his brother, then stops.

"Shit. The cops will know we were here."

"What are you talking about?"

"Think about it. They'll interview everyone at the party. People saw us park up. Tyre marks, footprints, DNA, all that shit, it's everywhere, man. We're screwed."

Levi blinks stupidly. Nods. "You're right." Jogs back down the bank. "Come on, give me a hand."

He squats next to the body, shoves the wallet back into the man's jeans pocket. Puts his hands on the upper back, and pushes. "Come on, Dale. Some help here."

"What are you doing?"

"What the hell does it look like? We push him back in, he floats another mile or two, we're free and clear."

"Jesus, Levi, we don't even know he's dead. I'm calling 911."

Levi glares over his shoulder. "You gonna be a pussy your whole life, Dale? Get your ass over here and do as I say."

Dale hesitates. Levi's right. He is a pussy. He never stands up to him. He should do it. Tell his brother no. Be a man.

"Fuck's sake, Dale. Now!"

Dale hurries forward, kneels in the mud, pushes. He'll make a stand next time, he promises. This is the last time he'll let Levi push him around. But his brother is right. Someone else can find the body.

And that's the moment that the corpse coughs, throws up a couple pints of water, then collapses.

The brothers back away in a rush, trip, and sit in the squelch. They stare at the body, then at each other.

"Did he just—?"

"Did you hear?"

"Is he—"

"Do you think he's not d—?"

"What the hell?"

Levi recovers first. The bald guy isn't moving. "I heard about this. Bodies fart in funeral homes, or burp. Cough. Happens all the time, Dale. It's natural. Don't let it spook you. It's nothing. Come on."

Levi moves towards the body, slower this time. Dale hangs back a little. His brother's voice had shaken, and his lips are trembling.

When he's close enough to touch the man's shoulders, Levi stops.

"You know what? You're right. We should call it in. Let the cops deal with it." He lowers his voice to a whisper. "No one has to know about the cash."

Relief floods Dale's body. Yes. This is the right thing to do. He's about to agree when the body moves again, fast. It rolls over, and the cuffed hands shoot out, yanking Levi's ankle, sending him sprawling. Dale is so stunned, he can't move for a couple of seconds, and—by the time his body responds to the imminent danger—it's too late. The big guy rolls onto his knees, then stands up.

Levi gets up, too. Squares up to the waterlogged figure towering above him. This guy is tall. Built like a tank, too. Dale feels a flush of pride at the way his brother sizes up the threat, and doesn't retreat. Levi might be a bully, but he's no coward. He's tipped to be on the State wrestling team this fall. He can handle himself. This dude should have stayed drowned.

Dale holds his breath as Levi edges a little closer, staying low. Recognises his intent. He's going to lift the guy, use his own weight to knock the breath out of him when he hits the ground. He's seen Levi do this a hundred times, and it never fails. He'll follow up with—

Levi's eyes roll back, and he drops backwards into the mud.

Dale's brain reconstructs what he missed the first time. The cuffed hands shooting out, hands pressed flat together like he's praying, fingertips jabbing hard into a spot under Levi's ear.

He looks across at his brother. Is he dead?

"He'll live," says the big, bald guy, taking a shuffling step closer. He has an accent. Not American. South African?

Dale looks into those eyes and wishes he hadn't. There's a look actors use when they're playing the bad guy. A dead stare, like they're looking through you. Like you're a worm, you're nothing, your life is meaningless. Dale thought it was a Hollywood thing. Now he knows different. Those actors must draw on something genuine, because this is the real deal, and it's not on the other side of a screen. Dale's limbs go loose, his teeth literally chatter with fear, and he thinks he might be about to shit himself.

The bald guy holds up his handcuffed wrists, nods towards the car. "You got any tools in there?"

————

It probably only takes five or six minutes to get the toolbox from the trunk, place the flat blade of a chisel on the chain, a rock beneath, and smack it as hard as his shaking hands allow. With every smack of the hammer on the chisel, Dale wonders what the stranger will do once he's free.

The Chrysler's headlamps give enough light to work with, but he keeps missing, his hands shake so much. But Dale perseveres, and sparks fly as metal meets metal. He doesn't look up. He can't look up. Can't lock eyes with that... thing again. Levi always said the boogeyman was real, kept Dale believing it long after exposing Santa Claus as a fraud.

On this one subject, it appears Levi wasn't lying.

The hammer comes down again, the chisel bites into the metal, and the chain parts. Dale looks up, then quickly away again.

The bald man grunts. Sits down. Lifts the padlock securing his ankle chains.

"You got some wire?"

Dale goes back to the car, comes back with a paper clip from the glovebox.

The stranger prods around inside the handcuffs' locks until they pop open, then turns his attention to his feet. While he bends over his task, Levi sits up ten feet away, looks towards the car. Gets to his feet. Walks over, placing every step with exaggerated caution, taking it real slow.

The big dude doesn't notice. Dale plays his part, starts apologising to the bald guy, insisting—whatever he might have heard while he was lying there in the mud—that they would have helped him. They pulled him out of the river, didn't they? Saved his life.

231

Levi picks up a rock the size of a bag of sugar. He's four, maybe five, steps away now. He moves even more slowly, and Dale, keeping his eyes on the stranger's feet as he works at the padlock, hears his own voice tighten, raising in pitch, as his body tenses.

Levi's arm goes up.

Make it a good one. Hit him hard. Fuck this up and he'll kill us both.

The rock comes down, fast. Dale stops breathing. Closes his eyes. Anticipates the sickening slap of stone on flesh. When it comes, he waits for the sound of the body slumping to one side.

Nothing.

Dale opens one eye. The bald man looks right at him. It's too dark to make out the colour of those eyes, but Dale imagines the near-black of dried blood. He'll see those eyes in his nightmares. Pitiless. Blank.

He drags his gaze away, looks along the man's left arm, which now holds a rock the size of a bag of sugar. Levi still grips the other side of it, and his body is shaking, whether with an attempt to regain control of his improvised weapon, or with terror, Dale can't be sure. Levi's face is a contorted mask; mouth open, eyes staring, neck muscles bulging with effort.

The bald man continues to manipulate the paper clip with his other hand. The padlock pops open with a click as ominous as a tolling bell.

Without releasing his grip on the rock, the stranger gets to his feet. When he breaks eye contact, Dale sags, fighting an urge to sob with relief.

The sweat on Levi's face makes it shine in the moonlight. When the stranger draws himself up to his full height and looks down at him, the most feared student wrestler in Pittsburgh lets out a noise like a lost kitten.

The stranger's voice stays level and calm. Dale keeps swallowing, but his spit has dried up.

"It's been a trying few days," the bald man says, releasing the rock. Levi holds it in the air as if glued to it. "Don't make me lose my patience. I have a question. Answer that and I'll be on my way."

Levi is still shaking. His expression doesn't change.

"Yes, sir," squeaks Dale.

"Good. There's an industrial area near here. I need to get there."

Ten words into the bald man's description, and Dale knows where he means.

"It's a steelworks. Outta town a few miles west. Just off the highway. Easy to find, sir."

He gives directions, eyes down, aware that Levi is still frozen, the rock held out like it's a crucifix and the stranger is a vampire.

"Car keys?"

Dale pats his pockets, although Levi has never once let him drive the Chrysler. Then he looks at his brother.

The stranger walks around the outstretched arm, reaches into Levi's pocket, and pulls out the keys. Levi, his breath coming in quick gasps, doesn't move. He's like one of the human statues outside the malls in summer, except he's shaking so much he's almost dancing.

"Thank you. Oh. One more thing."

The bald man turns to Dale, but he can't meet those eyes. Not again.

"Best you forget this ever happened, wouldn't you say?"

"Yes, sir. Thank you, sir."

The Chrysler's lights sweep across the two brothers as it reverses up the bank before swinging away and up the drive. The strange tableau it captures—two young men, one kneeling, eyes down, the other standing, holding a rock at arm's length, and shaking—remains the same until the engine note has long faded.

CHAPTER FORTY-FOUR

THE OLD MAN in the wheelchair sits at a large drawing board, the sketch pad resting on it illuminated by two floor-standing lamps behind him. He is using charcoal for this portrait, and each deliberate stroke reveals more of his subject; a bearded face, hollow-cheeked with a widow's peak, staring out of the page with a subtle expression that's hard to place. It might be boredom, amusement, or—perhaps —a challenge, issued by someone who has no fear of his opponent.

The artist reaches for the glass by his side, raises it to his lips. It's empty.

"Do me a favour? The vodka bottle is on the shelf to your left. There's another glass there, too. Please join me."

Jimmy Blue's astonishment only lasts a moment. He crosses the room from the doorway, lifts the vodka bottle and glass, and moves into the pool of light supplied by the lamps. He pours a good measure into both glasses before setting the bottle on the desk. Only then does the man in the wheelchair face him.

"Na zdorovie." Blue holds his glass still. The old man has a neat, squared-off white beard, hooded eyes, and white hair thin enough to reveal the liver-spotted scalp beneath. His watery blue eyes are huge behind oval tortoiseshell glasses.

"It's good stuff. From St Petersburg. An old friend sends me a crate each Christmas. As I get older, I appreciate every small pleasure." He tilts his glass, looks at the transparent liquid inside. "You're supposed to drink it ice-cold, of course, but Dmitri never did, and he's been a bad influence, I fear. Please sit down."

"I don't have the time," says Blue, not moving, "and I haven't decided whether to kill you."

The old man smiles. "Well, sitting down won't make much difference, will it? Humour me."

When Blue pulls up the only chair and sits, his host examines him quickly with a practised eye.

"Rough night?"

"You could say that. Your friend tried to drown me."

"Ah. I thought he might react like that. Still, you murdered his friend. Which is a mystery. You're obviously talented with technology. The way you covered your tracks on the laptop was elegant. Leaving those photographs of Murchen on your cell phone doesn't fit. It's fascinating."

"How did you know I was here?"

The old man turns his head, taps his right ear. There's a flesh-coloured button inside. "I've always had a first-rate security system, but when my eyesight worsened, I realised there was a better way to protect myself. Everyone looks for cameras and alarms. A common thief might cut the power or disable the cameras. If that happens, I can seal my private quarters and alert my security people. They are fifteen minutes away, should I need them. I'm not concerned about burglars, Mr Kincaid."

Jimmy doesn't respond. The old man takes another sip.

"Since I know your most recent alias, you must call me Roach. Everybody does. Now, then. A highly trained individual might not cut the power or sabotage the alarms. Instead, they might study the pattern followed by the security cameras as they sweep back and forth. If they identify the four-second gap, and are physically exceptional, they can get inside without triggering the alarm. One specific route across the roof to the back allows a gifted intruder to enter through an upper window. Only a handful of men and women could make it this far. My secondary alert system kept me appraised of your progress. My eyesight may be awful, but my hearing is adequate, and every floor in every room contains a hidden microphone. You're only the second person to try getting in by this route. And the first to succeed. Well done. Why did you kill her?"

"Why sit and wait if you knew I was coming?"

Roach seems irked to find his own question answered with another. "Isn't it obvious? Did Tyson tell you nothing about me?"

"Only that you're good with computers. And that you had the information he needed. Now I need the same thing. Tell me where I can find the man who sent the black ops teams."

Roach ignores Blue's command, still following his own line of thought.

"Information is my trade. That's why I waited. Anyone with your level of skill always works for a nation, a corporation, or a powerful lobby group. I know them all. My death will trigger the release of revelations that would end careers, and lives. But you? None of that applies, does it? You don't work for anyone but yourself. You're unique. Unknown. And knowledge is somewhat of a compulsion for me. I have to know who you are."

"Even if it means risking your life?"

"Certainly."

Roach points at his drawing. "Sir Francis Walsingham. Elizabeth the First's spymaster. There were spymasters before him—humanity is inherently distrustful—but he founded modern spycraft. Double agents, misinformation, propaganda, code breaking."

He stares at his work for a few seconds. Jimmy Blue, off-balance after Roach's casual dismissal of his break-in, reaches inside to reconnect with the darkness there. He cannot afford to waste time.

"I'm not interested in hearing about your role model. Tell me what you told Tyson. Where is he?"

Roach raises bushy eyebrows in surprise. "Role model? No, no, it's quite the opposite. I worked with people like Walsingham my whole life. With very few exceptions, they start out as idealists. But they are beholden to the worst ideals, and they lie to themselves, misidentifying their idealism as realism. They believe their work, however distasteful it becomes, has to be done. A minority of people—some, unfortunately, innocent—must suffer to protect the majority. It's an insidious, deadly falsehood."

Roach doesn't turn away from his sketch. Shows no fear of Jimmy Blue. It's never happened before.

"Possibly," continues Roach, "Walsingham might even have done some good. Left his country a better place than he found it. Who knows? But these days? No. The modern world's spy network is a ludicrous, dangerous affair, and those who run it play a game they can't master. So much time wasted by agencies chasing their own tails. The NSA suspects the CIA, who have moles in the FBI, who believe a double agent in the Secret Service might pass information via the NSA to Iran, and so it goes on. It might be funny if it weren't for the lives lost during their blinkered skirmishes."

"So what does that make you? The agencies you're talking about are still here. Still doing their thing. If they are so dangerous, why are you sitting in the dark drawing pictures?"

"Portraits," corrects Roach. "And they help me relax. I see my role as damage limitation. If any agency gets too powerful, those in charge lose sight of the moral imperatives they should uphold. I keep information on all of them. I threaten to leak morsels when necessary to stop their excesses. In Kai's case, I'm afraid I was too late. I am only one man. Until Tyson turned up, I had no idea the Company was trying to erase that team. Now Tyson is the only survivor."

Blue remembers the files Bolsteroni uncovered.

"They were black ops. Tyson and Kai. Murchen."

Roach drains his glass. "The blackest of black, yes. But, as always, the foot soldiers suffer while the generals remain untouched."

Jimmy Blue stands, takes a step closer. Bends over the wheelchair and grips the sides, his face six inches from Roach. The old man doesn't flinch.

"Where is Tyson?"

"There's no point trying to intimidate me, Mr Kincaid. I'm an old man. If it's my time, it's my time. I want to know why you killed Elizabeth Murchen. Given the information I found—that you killed the two-man sniper crew, then wiped out the team sent to clean up—I admit I'm confused. The pieces are all there, but they don't fit together. Complete the puzzle, and I might tell you."

Darkness swirls around Blue. He draws it in through his nostrils and it fills his bulky frame, swelling muscles, instilling its dread purpose. He is on the edge of surrender, standing on the precipice. To fall means becoming his true self, a beautiful creature with the instincts of a predator and the calculation of a chess grandmaster, intent on destruction and death.

But it's not time. Not now. The darkness is always there, but Jimmy provides the mould for its molten power. Many apex predators, rejoicing in their dominion over all others, end up staring glassy-eyed from some oak-panelled wall in a London club. What elevates Blue is his mind and his will. His mind, diamond-hard, multifaceted, as focused as the white-hot tip of a welder's flame, is driven by a will before which all obstacles fold, snap, or crumble to dust.

He lets go of the wheelchair's metal arms, bent out of shape where he gripped them. Picks up the vodka bottle, pours two generous glasses. Sits down. Drinks, while Roach does the same. The old man's hand shakes.

"I'll tell you who I am," says Blue. "Then you'll tell me who sent those teams. If you don't, I'll snap your neck like a twig."

———

Roach listens without comment while Blue speaks about the night Tom Lewis saw his father shot, and his mother sent alight. The night Tom crawled, half-blind with the blood from the bullet hole in his skull, through his bedroom window and away from the burning house. The night Tom journeyed to the place everyone visits, but few return from. The gates of hell. The Abyss. The pit of despair. The river Styx. Humans have given the source of their darkness many names.

Jimmy Blue remembers Tom's school assemblies. The local vicar took them once a week. "The light shines in the darkness. And the darkness can never extinguish it." Back when Tom travelled to the border of that undiscovered country, the Bible verse came to mind, an echo from his old life, and he knew it for a lie. Everything he loved had been taken from him.

When Tom had reached the banks of that great, eternal river, he spoke no words, swore no oath. But the man that made the long journey back to a broken body in a hospital bed was not the child who'd explored the badlands between life and death.

When Tom returned, Jimmy Blue came with him. And his darkness would shine in the light, and the light would never extinguish it.

Blue lays out the facts for Roach. He betrays no emotion as he describes the way his parents died. He uncovers his scar and Roach's rheumy eyes don't linger on the angry wound.

Confronted with a man devoted to learning the art and practice of violence for the purpose of revenge, Roach becomes solemn, his fingers tracing the bent metal of his wheelchair where Jimmy gripped it.

When Blue stops speaking, he nods once. "The puzzle is complete. I know it means little, but I'm sorry, Tom."

"Sorry won't bring them back. And I'm not Tom."

"Yes." Roach drains the last mouthful of vodka. "That's what I'm sorry about."

Jimmy Blue sees pity and despises the old man for it.

"Kai helped me," said Blue. "She was my teacher. She was already dead when I took those photographs."

Roach drops his gaze, looks at the floorboards. Grunts in surprised respect. "Of course. Smart. Very smart."

He pivots away from the drawing board, wheels over to a keyboard and monitor. There's no computer tower visible, but a cable disappears into the wall.

"This is Eric Stoppard. He sent the teams to kill Tyson and Murchen."

Blue stands behind the wheelchair, looks at the image on the screen. Stoppard is Hispanic, thuggishly good-looking, his nose broken more than once. The text underneath his name identifies him as a senior agent in the CIA, but annotations to one side detail a series of operations that don't appear in official records. Assassinations, armed incursions into hostile countries, kidnappings, extortion. His government wage is supplemented by lump sums paid into an account in Panama.

At the bottom of the page, an address. Blue memorises it.

"I wasn't always in this wheelchair," says Roach. "The knife an assassin stuck in my back was supposed to kill me. When they came to the hospital to finish the job, Connor Tyson killed them and gave me a safe place to stay. I owe him. He thought you murdered his friend."

"I'm not going to kill him." Jimmy looks out past the portrait of Walsingham to the window. Soon it'll be dawn. "I'm going to help him."

He pictures the battered Chrysler he'd arrived in. Looks at Roach doubtfully. "Don't suppose you have a gun you can lend me, do you? And a car."

Roach smiles at that. "I might have a couple of toys lying around that will help."

———

Ten minutes later, Roach is back in his hub—a hidden room between rooms, humming with computers, a vast desk dominated by three screens. He watches the middle screen now, tapping to expand the feed from one of his cameras. The image shows his guest leaving on a Japanese motorcycle, his jacket bulging with two German handguns. Roach doesn't believe in buying American, he believes in buying the best, whichever country it came from. He's lived long enough to witness the ugly side of national pride, and he wants no part of it.

Long after the man who called himself Tom Kincaid has gone, Roach, unable to sleep, sits in front of the electronic equivalent of Walsingham's spy network, and tries to regain his mental equilibrium. In the end he gives up, opens another bottle of vodka, starts typing. He puts a hold command on every piece of clandestine work he has running worldwide. Roach coded algorithms for the Company before anyone called them algorithms, and his skills have improved since his disappearance. He knows better than anyone that, whereas it's possible to conceal information, hiding it at the end of labyrinths few have the skill to explore, it's impossible to expunge it completely. There's always a trail.

His computer system is more powerful than that of some large corporations, and Roach hides his online presence by attributing a little more bandwidth use to every one of the hundred and five terminals in the steelworks next door. He uses all of that power for one task now, booting up a ghost algorithm to parse tiny shreds of information in the CIA database. There's always a pattern. Hard to find when it's based on absence of information, but it'll be there. And Roach enjoys a challenge.

Within thirty minutes of Kincaid—or, he reminds himself, Lewis —leaving, he has a list of twenty-seven names. Each name may have ordered CIA off-the-books operations. Certainty is a rare luxury in Roach's world. He has confidence in the results. Nations have gone to war on poorer intel.

The next search is simpler, but time-consuming. Cross-referencing Stoppard and Castle's movements with the names on the list. If they were in the same state on the same day, they filter into a new list, which tightens the search criteria further, narrowing the geographical radius of potential meetings, extracting dates and names from public and private diaries. Everything is cross-referenced again, filtered again, the information distilled over and over. Finally, like the vodka he sips while he works, what remains, while not absolutely pure, is as good as it gets.

When the process is complete, five names remain. Now Roach uses a technique Walsingham would have been familiar with. He checks each name, looks for what's changed, what might provoke the violent closing down of a black ops team years after they ceased active service. Find out who has the most to lose if their connection to that team becomes public.

Roach pours himself a fresh glass and gets to work.

As he stares at the screen, he keeps seeing those dark green eyes, and the creature that stared out from them. As if something had painstakingly hollowed out all his humanity, leaving nothing but a brutal purpose and an absolute commitment to achieving it.

God help anyone who stands in his way.

CHAPTER FORTY-FIVE

TYSON PARKS the Phoenix in the lot underneath a large, midrange hotel. In the lobby, he replaces the number plate with that of a memorised Plymouth, filling in its make and model on the check-in form. It's an old trick, designed to buy time. The CIA doesn't have the resources to check parking lots on foot, and a call to this hotel will draw a blank.

He takes a cab to the edge of the suburbs, half a mile from the target. When the car is out of sight, he strikes out on foot across a golf course.

Tyson shins up a tree by the bunker on the fifteenth hole. Takes a rifle scope from his inside pocket, checks the adjacent streets first. No movement. Cars parked in driveways, a few on the street. Four vans. Can't be Company vehicles because no one thinks he's coming. He's a dead man, blown to bits in a San Antonio trailer park.

According to the records Roach shared, Eric Stoppard is divorced. No kids.

No collateral damage.

He turns the scope to Stoppard's house. The lights are off. He searches for the alarm system, finds it under the eaves. Cheap. Typical goon. Doesn't buy the best security system, because he thinks he can handle anyone foolish enough to break in. Alpha male. Stupid.

Tyson is muttering, muttering, the words spilling out as quietly as he can make them, but he can't stop them coming. He relaxes his throat, reduces the sound to the faintest whisper. Checks his handgun. Replaces it in the shoulder holster. Pats the knife on his ankle, reassured by the blade. Truth be told, he prefers knives to guns, and he prefers bare hands to knives. Combat has changed in the era of modern warfare. A sniper's bullet inserts distance between killer and victim, deed and consequences. Shoot someone point blank, and you'll be walking around with pieces of them spattered over your shirt and pants. Drones are the latest toys. The kids who fly them have never fired a gun in combat, taken a punch, or watched a friend bleed out.

What will happen to these fresh-faced killers when the consequences of their actions settle on their untested shoulders? Because it will happen. The dead, even when cut down by someone pushing buttons on a joystick thousands of miles away, will make themselves known to their killers. In dreams at first, then scratching at their minds whenever they relax their guard. Demanding to be seen. Consequences. Tyson survived the way he was trained: he closed himself off. Built a wall. But the dead are patient, and, when in that dark Indonesian cellar, as he waited to die, they crawled through cracks in the walls and sat with him. Told him who they were, what he took from them and their families. Since then, Tyson talks all the time, fearing if he stops they might speak again.

Kai found another way to survive. Showed redemption might be possible. Dismantled her wall, laid herself open, and didn't succumb to the razor blades, the bullet, or the bottle. Tyson never told her he loved her, but it's the truth. The best kind of love. Like a child for its mother, but like a father for his child, too. For a man with so many words, Tyson never found the right ones for Kai. Now he never will. He hopes she knew. She knew most everything, it seems.

Tyson sets his teeth together. The world doesn't work the way it should. In a just world, Eric Stoppard would be dead, not Kai. Nothing he can do about Kai, but it's time to fix Stoppard.

There's a fence between the golf course and the street. He walks a hundred yards and climbs it, approaching the house from behind. Shins the neighbour's fence, gets close enough to smell the air, listen, look for signs of trouble. Finds nothing to concern him.

The easiest door to force leads onto a paved area with a barbecue. Tyson has seen movies where thieves pick locks using hairpins, or slide a credit card into the crack. Truth is, front doors are the ones built to deter burglars. Take the time to investigate, and you'll usually find a flimsier target.

Cupping his hands over his face, he checks the interior. A dining room. Dirty plate on the table, a half-full coffee pot next to a cup. Kitchen through an arch to the right. Closed door ahead leading to the front room.

He puts a shoulder against the wood. One good push should do it, but he knows it will be noisy. The closed door ahead will absorb some sound, but not all. If Stoppard investigates, Tyson will wait behind the closed door. Close enough to use the knife as he steps inside. Tyson half-hopes Stoppard will wake up. But the risks are fewer if he doesn't, and Tyson mustn't lose sight of his goal: Stoppard has to die. Then Castle. Killing the deputy director of the CIA is a suicide mission, but Tyson never expected to get old anyhow. This way, he might not die happy, but he'll die satisfied.

He retreats from the door, then shoulder-barges it, directing all his weight at the lock. The cheap wood splinters and gives; the door swings open. Tyson steps inside, holds his breath, and listens. A second later, he hears something move upstairs. A man turning over in his sleep, perhaps. He waits longer, but the sound doesn't repeat. After thirty seconds, he lets out his breath with relief, not because he can't hold it, but because, faintly, so faintly, the dead are congregating, turning their dry, drained eyes towards him.

The interior door doesn't squeak, opening over a carpeted floor. Tyson moves across it using the technique Kai taught him. He never quite mastered it. Kai could cover ground like a ghost. Tyson is more cat-like, impressive for a man his size. Tom could probably move through this house as undetectably as Kai. He had run across the wasteland of her property sure-footed and fast, reading the terrain.

He hopes the Brit drowned quickly. The thought of Tom suffering troubles him, but the monster inside him had to die. How had he won Kai's confidence only to betray her?

There are cushions on the couch. He picks one up as he passes.

The stairs are wood, but each step has a layer of thin matting made of rough hemp wrapped around it. He places his foot precisely, transferring his weight little by little. The groans and shudders of the wood as he climbs are no louder than the distant sound of traffic, or the wind through the leaves. Throughout, Tyson speaks his monologue in silence to an unseen audience, his eyes fixed on the landing above as, second by second, more of it comes into view. He's glad of the cloudless night, the grey wash of light that precedes the dawn.

His gun slips into his hand, easy, familiar, and his brain turns all attention to what is about to happen. He heard no other sounds from above as he approached. If Stoppard moves now, Tyson is close enough for a rush to be effective. Three or four yards separate him and any of the four half-open doors he sees from the top of the staircase.

Nothing. No sound. From here, Tyson can see two rooms, both to his right. One looks to be a study. Computer, desk, big leather chair. The desk is a mess; magazines, a glass, discarded candy bar wrappers, and a couple of mugs competing for space with the keyboard and mouse.

The next door leads to what might be a guest room. The bed has no sheets on its mattress, which is covered in cardboard boxes. He guesses Stoppard doesn't have many guests.

To his left, two more doors. The room ahead looks out onto the back yard. Tyson takes two slow steps, looks inside. Bathroom. A sink and faucet, a couple of empty shelves above. Folded towels on top of a hamper. A mirror reflecting a bathtub. All neat and tidy.

One room remains over the garage. Tyson pauses by the half-open door. Sees clothes slung over a chair, a T-shirt on the floor.

Tyson turns sideways, steps smartly through the door and points his gun at where he expects the bed to be. It's a good guess.

There are heavy curtains in the bedroom, but they're not fully closed. The light isn't good enough to pick out details. Tyson sees the shape under the duvet. Stoppard isn't moving. Another step sideways, the gun always fixed on its target. No movement from the bed. A third step, and something changes. Tyson doesn't look down, but what he thought was a rug is, in fact, plastic sheeting. It wrinkles and stretches under his boots, making a sound like the peel of a fresh bag in a grocery store.

Stoppard sleeps on. Outside, a few streets away, someone's pushing a bike engine hard, its note rising as it screams up through the gears. Tyson takes one more step, stands at the foot of the bed, careful to roll the heel of his foot onto the toe. He wants to wake Stoppard up, see his face, but he was a professional killer far too long to succumb to temptation.

He raises the gun, holds the cushion over the barrel. The screaming engine is closer. He can't stop himself from saying something.

"This is for Kai."

This killing is not a message. No need for two taps to the chest, one to the head. No need for anything other than certainty. Tyson empties four rounds into the biggest area of the body—the upper torso. He repeats the same words, one to accompany each bullet.

"This. Is. For. Kai."

As he fires, the air between Tyson and the bed fills with white absorbent cotton, wispy miniature clouds of the stuff. Between the third and fourth shots, two events occur, one interior, one exterior, both bad news.

The interior event is Tyson's assassin's brain, rusty with under-use, supplying vital information that would have been more useful half a minute earlier. It's a deduction based on the way Stoppard lives. The man is a slob. Dirty plates downstairs, cardboard boxes on the guest bed, candy wrappers, and glasses on the desk. Clothes on the floor of the bedroom. Which means... which means the immaculate bathroom is all wrong. It doesn't fit. Stoppard doesn't use it. Tidy bathroom out there, plastic on the floor in here. Shit.

The exterior event is Stoppard emerging from the bathroom he uses; the en suite. Gun in his hand. Firing.

Plastic on the floor for Tyson's blood. No need to ruin the carpet.

Tyson swings left towards the danger but there's no chance to fire again. The first bullet hits him in his left shoulder and spins him further anticlockwise. He's been shot before, but it still feels like a giant smacking him with an iron baseball bat.

Stoppard is a courteous neighbour. He's using a suppressor. There's enough light for Tyson to notice he's smiling.

Three more bullets, all centre mass. Stoppard, like Tyson, is a professional. This isn't personal. He intends to take Tyson down. No mistakes. A tick in a box on a CIA database against the final living member of a black ops team that can no longer haunt its commanding officers.

Tyson drops face forward onto the plastic.

———

Blue knows he's probably too late. He pushes the Honda as hard as he dares from the cabin on the outskirts of Pittsburgh to Eric Stoppard's address, weapons stuffed into his jacket pockets.

A subtle approach isn't an option. When he enters Stoppard's neighbourhood, he notes the anonymous black vans parked near intersections. Their occupants glance up as he passes, but a big white guy on a motorbike isn't what they're waiting for.

Tyson has walked into a trap.

On Stoppard's street, there's only one van. Jimmy slows as he passes it. The faces within watch him for a second before returning their attention to the house. He rounds the next corner, lays the bike on its side in a hedge, and sprints back to Stoppard's street.

Approaching the rear of the van, his gaze flicks between the two wing mirrors. He's exposed for around five seconds. If either agent checks a mirror, they'll see him. Once he's in their blind spot, he

pauses, visualises the next ten seconds. He has to be quick and efficient. It'll only work if their door is unlocked. He figures that's likely,
since they are on active duty, ready to cross the street at speed when
needed. They're expecting a trained assassin to show up. Possibly two
—the second being Elizabeth Murchen.

What they're not expecting is Jimmy Blue.

Blue walks alongside the van, pulls open the passenger door, and
punches the guy in the sternum. He jumps onto his lap, leaning over
and wrapping his fingers around his partner's throat. She goes for her
gun, but he increases the pressure, shaking his head. She drops her
arm back to her side.

Meanwhile, the first agent is gasping for air that won't come.

"Try to relax," says Jimmy. "Your diaphragm is in spasm. It will
ease off soon." He reaches under the man's jacket, removes his gun,
takes out the clip one-handed and drops both out of the window.
Releases the woman and does the same.

"In the back."

They comply, climbing over the seats. Blue pulls out his own
weapon, a well-maintained Glock from Roach's collection. He waves
it at them. A phone rings from the female agent's pocket.

"Don't answer. Toss your phones into the front, both of you. Try
anything and I'll shoot you. Go."

They do it.

"When I say so, leave the van by the rear, close the doors behind
you and start running. Use the sidewalk."

He shifts into the driver's seat, starts the engine. "I'll be watching
in this mirror. If you're not running, I'll mow you down. I'm going to
drive this van across the street. When I get out, if you're still in sight, I
will shoot you. Clear?"

The winded agent repeats, "Clear," his breathing now close to
normal.

"See?" says Blue. "Temporary discomfort. Now piss off."

They run as instructed.

Blue turns the steering wheel, points the van at the house across
the street. Behind that anonymous suburban exterior is Stoppard, the

man who ordered two teams to murder Kai, and Tyson, the man who tried to drown him.

The phones ring, first one, then the other. He looks in the wing mirror. The two agents have reached the corner. He pulls the shift into drive, waits until they're out of sight, then stamps his right foot on the accelerator.

CHAPTER FORTY-SIX

ERIC STOPPARD FIRES as he walks, pumping shot after shot into Connor Tyson. The first is the only one that goes wide, as some kind of sixth sense makes Tyson turn, too late. It still hits the target, but it's not enough to stop him, although blood sprays from the old assassin's shoulder as he twists and stumbles, ending up facing away from Stoppard. Every other shot hits pay dirt, driving Tyson forwards one step, then another, then he's falling.

"One down," he says. "Now where's your friend, Murchen?"

He whistles as he heads downstairs. Castle was right about Tyson. He said he would come for Stoppard. Castle may be an arrogant prick, but he's smart, good at his job, and he's kept Eric Stoppard close as he's climbed the CIA ranks.

He grins at the rush of adrenaline flooding his system. Some agents have a coke habit, but, in Stoppard's opinion, nothing comes close to the killing buzz. Castle may have supplied the intel, but it was Stoppard who baited his own trap, who ordered the two agents to park out front in plain view, forcing Tyson to the back of the house. From there, it was just a question of sitting on the john, his laptop propped on the laundry basket, watching the crazy bastard take fifteen minutes to climb a staircase. Stoppard has read Tyson's record, and knows better than to underestimate the man, but watching him hold a silent conversation as he climbed the stairs was eerie.

"Nut job," he says, stepping over the body, picking up the gun. He thumbs the last-dialled number on his cell phone as he jogs downstairs. He puts Tyson's gun on the bookshelf. When no one picks up after the third ring, he cancels the call, presses the second number, gets the same result.

He goes to the front room window, peels back enough curtain to glimpse the street. The van is still outside. Engine running, the morning sun a white-gold glare on the windshield. Stoppard reloads his gun while squinting through the gap in the curtain. Can't see either of the agents in there, and they're not answering their phones. Not a good sign. Not good at all.

Everything is quiet, but he's familiar with Murchen's redacted file. She was the best the Company ever employed. Some kills credited to her look impossible on paper. That she achieved them at all is impressive. The fact she got home afterwards without being caught is close to miraculous. Stoppard is outclassed and he knows it. But this is his home turf, and he has eight bullets in the clip. Let her try.

He drops the curtain back into place, then freezes. The dining room door hangs open. The skin on the back of Stoppard's thick neck prickles. She's behind him. He's a dead man. He doesn't know whether to swing round firing, or turn and face her. Stoppard opts for the latter, but his breath comes in rapid gasps while he does it.

The room is empty. He waits for his breathing to deepen, then heads into the dining room, weapon held ready. Also empty. The splintered lock means he can't secure the room. Stoppard pushes the table over, pinning the door closed. It won't hold anyone for long, but he'll hear her coming.

He calls Castle's private number. If the deputy director ever sleeps, no one has produced any evidence to prove it.

"Is it done?"

"Not quite. Tyson's down. Murchen's here. Burcher and Stagg aren't responding. I need backup. Now."

"Already in place. I'll tell them to move in. Good job."

They're already here? A cold wave washes across Stoppard's body. He's been played. Castle has placed other pieces on the board beside the two agents outside. The game is over for Elizabeth Murchen, and the deaths of agents Stagg, Burcher, and Stoppard are a sacrifice worth making for her elimination.

Stoppard figures if he can stay alive for the next ten minutes, he might make it.

An engine starts up, a vehicle moves outside. Scrape of tyres in a tight turning circle. Crossing the street. A bump as wheels hit the bottom of Stoppard's drive. Brakes squeal, the engine dies.

He's heading for the front door when he hears a noise upstairs. Stoppard crosses the front room. Someone bangs on the front door. "Stoppard! She's out here. Murchen. Open the door. Agent down, agent down."

The voice is male. Stoppard throws the bolt with his left hand, his gun still pointing at the staircase. He put four bullets into Tyson, three of them into his back. If he survived, he won't be much of a threat.

The key sticks as usual, but as soon as it gives, he grabs the handle and pulls. It's only as the door opens to reveal a stranger that Stoppard questions the unfamiliar voice. And who says, "Agent down" outside of a movie? He tries to push the door closed again, but the intruder—big, solid, capable—anticipates this and delivers a kick to the wood that almost rips it from its hinges.

"No!" Stoppard's gun drops from numbed fingers as the heavy door smacks his arm into the wall. It's a clean break, the ulna and radius snapping within milliseconds of each other, the enclosed space making the sound echo like castanets. Stoppard sinks to his knees.

The big man shuts the door. Picks up the gun, drops it in his pocket.

"Where is Connor Tyson?"

This guy is what Castle would describe as a variable. Stoppard hates variables. On a flip chart before an assignment, a variable is a number, a guess; a percentage chance assigned to the likelihood of something unexpected occurring. The goatherd in Slovenia had been a variable. The family at the picnic spot in Mexico had been a variable. And now this guy. The goatherd and family had moved from the variable column to the collateral damage column, but that's not happening here. This giant wearing a bandana isn't acting like a variable. He looks like a professional. Maybe Stoppard is the variable.

Still. Stoppard is at the top of his game. He won't be intimidated, broken arm or not. "Who the fuck are yo-aaaggghhhh!"

The man's expression is impassive as he leans closer, extends a massive hand as if about to introduce himself, and squeezes Stoppard's arm, rubbing pieces of bone together among the muscles, ligaments, and tendons.

"He's upstairs," hisses Stoppard.

The big man looks down. Stoppard can't meet his eyes. Something primal stops him, something he couldn't name if he tried. His head drops, but a fresh burst of agony accompanies another squeeze.

"Don't pass out." The big stranger looks out towards the street. "I saw two more vehicles. How many agents are here? Lie, and I'll shoot your left kneecap."

Stoppard knows he means it.

"I didn't organise the backup, just the two out front."

A pause for a calculation.

"Castle?"

"Yes."

"Call him. Say whatever you have to say to stop them coming in here."

Stoppard takes out his phone. "I can only delay them."

The barrel of the gun moves towards Stoppard's knee.

"Okay." He dials. Castle answers. He speaks over him. "The backup, sir. Call them off, get them to withdraw. Tyson's still alive, but wounded. He'll take me to Murchen, but only me. Yes. Yes, sir."

He ends the call before Castle can ask any more questions.

"They'll stand down. But only for ten minutes."

"Phone." Stoppard hands it over.

Thirty seconds pass. A van approaches, slows. The bald guy raises the gun to point at Stoppard's head. The van accelerates away, the engine fading as it turns the corner. Castle's calling them off, but they won't go far. He might still get out of this alive.

The variable scoops up the suppressed handgun. At the foot of the stairs, he shoots a glance back at Stoppard, who is eyeing the front door. Even with the broken arm, he figures he can get it open, make a run for it.

The variable comes back.

The man examines the door, closes it, and throws the bolt. Looks at Stoppard. Bends down.

"Please," says Stoppard. "Don't."

What happens next is the result, Stoppard acknowledges, of another calculation. For whatever reason, this man doesn't want to kill him yet. But he doesn't want him walking out the door while he's upstairs.

Stoppard's right arm is useless. The variable takes his left thumb, bends it back like he's throwing a switch. It snaps. Tears spring into Stoppard's eyes.

"I liked Kai," says the variable, pointing the gun. He puts a bullet through Stoppard's right foot. Stoppard slumps against the wall.

The variable climbs the stairs without looking back.

Stoppard hovers on the brink of passing out. If he remains still, the pain stays just short of agonising, but even breathing hurts. His thumb, after the initial white-hot flare of distress, is a throb of minor discomfort compared to the signals coming from his mangled bones. He reduces his inhalations to sips of air. His running shoe—chosen to reduce the sound he made when coming out of the bathroom behind Tyson—fills with blood.

Time morphs to a shifting, odd, dancing illusion. Stoppard is a soldier. He's used to this happening under extreme stress. Never been this bad, though. Something deep inside believes these are his last minutes on Earth, and faces, voices, and smells from his childhood, adolescence, and early army days crowd his senses. He fights the confusion, comfort, and distraction that accompany the memories.

He is better than this. He will not succumb. Eric Stoppard is a survivor. He has to think, fast.

He's not dead because the variable wants something from him. Should be able to work out what. He said he liked Kai—Elizabeth Murchen. Which means what? That she's dead? In which case, who the hell killed her? And who is the variable working for? How does he know Tyson? What's their relationship? No. Don't waste energy on that. What does this guy need that's worth keeping Stoppard alive for? Yes. Focus on that. If bandana guy is working with Tyson, he's helping him wipe out the people who sent the black ops teams. Stoppard has the name he wants. Two names, in fact. Castle. And Senator Robert Hanan. Tyson already knows who Stoppard works for. He would have been content putting a bullet in Stoppard's brain, then going after Castle. Perhaps the variable suspects this goes higher than the deputy director.

So. The longer Stoppard can dangle the information he has without giving it away, the longer he'll stay alive. Long enough for the back up to arrive, without getting himself killed? Doubtful. But it's all he's got.

When the sounds from upstairs filter through his thoughts, he looks towards the staircase, trying to come up with any explanation that fits what he's hearing.

Because it's the sound of two men fighting.

CHAPTER FORTY-SEVEN

JIMMY BLUE STANDS in the bedroom doorway. There's blood on the wall. From the arc of the spatter, it looks like whoever supplied it was moving fast when it happened.

He takes a step inside. More blood on the floor. Plastic sheeting on top of carpet. Only one explanation. Stoppard knew Tyson was coming.

How? Tyson is supposed to be dead. Did Roach give him up? No. Blue doesn't trust anyone, and the old man is no exception, but it's a question of logic. If Roach betrayed Tyson, he would have betrayed Jimmy too, but the agents in the Company vehicles staking out Stoppard's place weren't looking for him. Roach provided his transport, meaning he arrived at dawn on a bright yellow Honda Fireblade. Hard to blend into the background. But he'd passed the dark-windowed vehicles without incident. The look in the female agent's eyes when he grabbed her throat wasn't just fear, it was surprise, and confusion. They were expecting Kai, not him.

No. Roach hadn't betrayed them. So how did Stoppard know Tyson was coming? Did someone see Tyson on their journey between California and Washington, and call it in? Maybe the CIA had sent his photograph to every gas station. Not if they wanted to deny any connection between Tyson and the Company.

The most likely explanation is that Tyson got caught on a security camera. Blue spent most of the trip shackled in the back of the Phoenix. If his theory is correct, he's still unknown to the CIA. Or, rather, he was. By now, the two agents he'd met would have reported back.

Should have killed them.

He'll need to remove that last vestige of conscience before taking on the scum who killed his parents. If he shows any weakness in his pursuit of Robert Winter and his allies, it'll be the last mistake he ever makes.

From his position in the doorway, he can't see Tyson's body.

He steps inside.

The curtains hang slightly open, meaning he sees sunlight flash off the blade as it jabs at his neck. At close quarters, with milliseconds to react, he registers the threat, and takes the only course of action open to him with a chance of success. Evasive action won't work: jerking his head back would take too long. It's not a decision Blue makes with his forebrain, it's a decision hard-wired into his brain stem, reinforced by thousands of hours of sparring with the most vicious fighters in the world.

He's already moving forwards, so he accelerates, dipping his head as he does so, dropping to a crouch, twisting to his right.

The edge of the knife opens the flesh at the base of his skull, but he barely registers the shallow cut. He's already punching, aiming for his assailant's armpit. From that angle, punching upwards, he can't get much force behind his fist, but the blow is accurate, landing in the mass of nerve endings. The result of the punch is predictable. The burst of pain produces the anticipated agonised gasp, and—as the arm goes numb—fingers lose their grip on the knife and it drops onto the plastic.

"You."

Tyson, his left shoulder a mess of blood, and his right arm

temporarily out of commission, tries to kick Jimmy in the face. Blue sways out of range, grabs the boot and yanks it hard. Tyson falls, but is rolling immediately, trying to get up. Blue stands, puts a foot on Tyson's back, pushes him to the floor. The older man won't stay down, jackknifing his knees underneath his body, so Blue grabs a fistful of jacket and propels him into the wall head-first. It's plaster-board and Tyson's skull is hard, so two inches of his head disappears into the hole it makes.

Tyson lies still for a moment. Long enough for Blue to speak.

"Kevlar?" He'd felt the bulletproof material when he'd grabbed Tyson.

Tyson pulls his head out of the wall, pushes himself up into a sitting position. The bullet wound in his shoulder isn't as bad as Jimmy first thought. Looks like it passed right through. It needs patching up, though, and the more Tyson fights, the more blood he'll lose. The man won't give up. He's flexing the fingers of his right hand, preparing for another attack.

"Stop it. I didn't kill Kai."

Tyson's lips move fast as he mumbles. He's looking at Blue, but not seeing him. Not listening, either.

"I don't have time to explain. Roach knows the truth. He said to show you this, to prove you can trust me."

Jimmy pulls a dagger from a sheath at his back. Three-inch blade, non-serrated, pointed tip. A weapon made for stabbing, not slashing. A black pommel bearing a Chinese character printed in red. At first, Tyson won't look. Blue holds it out, waiting. The mumbling slows a little, the eyes lose that tormented glaze. Tyson looks at the knife. Takes one deep breath, then another.

Roach told Blue it was the blade that severed his spinal cord and almost killed him. Tyson recognises it because he'd found Roach face down, the distinctive hilt buried in Roach's back.

Tyson nods. For the first time, he looks properly at Blue.

"The pictures on your phone?"

"Later. We need to patch that up."

Jimmy ducks into the bathroom, returns with a thin hand towel. After folding it, he binds it around Tyson's injured shoulder. It's enough to stop the bleeding. Tyson watches while he applies a decent field dressing.

"You're not him, not the kid I spoke to. You're not Tom."

Blue shakes his head.

"You're... one of the other personalities. Someone else, we are legion, right?"

"There's only one of me."

"Okay. So what's your name, your handle, what do I call you?"

Blue had no name. When he had first tasted self-awareness, first known he was alive, awake, distinct, there had been no one to name him. The fragments of memory, dark sparks that first ignited his nascent personality, then fanned the first flames into a black blaze, were violent, traumatic, bloody. Other memories—less defined, less important—informed and refreshed the visceral images he fed on as he grew, drawing strength from the promise of revenge. One memory was a song his father loved. An old nickname when Tom was ten or eleven.

"Jimmy Blue."

"Sure. Whatever. Can't say it suits you. Not really. Did you kill Stoppard, Bluey?"

Bluey? Jimmy let it go.

"Not until we get some information. Why is the CIA wiping out every member of a black ops team that disbanded years ago? Someone needs you to disappear. Stoppard knows who that someone is."

Tyson tries to reach into an inside pocket, but his right arm won't cooperate. "Would you mind? A little help? A favour?"

Jimmy Blue reaches in, brings out a phone. Shoots a questioning glance at Tyson. "You're carrying a phone? What about being traced by the government? What about mind control?"

Tyson flexes his fingers, clenches them into a fist. "Yeah, it's real funny until they come for you. Think about it for more than a couple seconds and you'll see it makes sense. We're all being watched, Bluey, and the sheep help them out by using phones, connecting to the internet. No thanks, no can do, ain't gonna happen. Roach vouched for this phone. Only reason I have it. Nothing but essential functions. They can't track me through it."

Blue drops it into Tyson's hand and he punches in a four-digit code. Turns the screen to show the only message.

I have the name you want. Call me.

"Roach came through. We don't need Stoppard," says Tyson.

"So call him," says Blue.

Tyson shakes his head. "Payphone. Safer. No cell phone is completely safe."

"Naturally."

Blue extends a hand, pulls Tyson to his feet. Sees the wince as the older man takes a deeper breath. A Kevlar vest can stop a bullet piercing flesh, shredding internal organs, but it's not magic. The kinetic energy has to go somewhere. Each shot at close range is a punch from a heavyweight boxer.

"Stoppard?" says Tyson.

Jimmy points downstairs. Tyson frowns. Blue reaches into his pocket, pulls out Stoppard's gun, hands it over. "You're a tough old bastard."

"Funny. That's what Kai used to say."

They go downstairs, Blue first. Stoppard watches them come. When he sees Tyson, his eyes drop to the bulletproof vest. He swallows twice. He's ashen-faced, trying not to move. Looks like he spent the last few minutes thinking, getting his speech ready.

They stand in front of him. Stoppard looks at his own gun in Tyson's hand. Swallows again.

"I can get you to Castle. But he's wiping out the team to protect someone else. Someone high up. You'll never get to him. But I can. He knows me. He trusts me. Let me live and I'll give him to you."

It's a desperate pitch. All three men know the best Stoppard can do is buy time. Most people will do anything to extend their lifespan by a few hours. A few minutes, too. Seconds, even.

Blue looks at Tyson, Kai's friend for decades. This is his decision.

Tyson raises the gun. The barrel doesn't waver. Neither does his voice. "Kai was better than us, Stoppard. She changed. She really changed. All of us could do it, if we chose to. That's what she taught us. But we chose not to."

Stoppard focuses on the barrel, then Tyson. "You really think I choose..." he nods at the gun, holds up his broken finger to point at his bleeding foot and Tyson's wounded shoulder "... all of this? We're the same, you and me. We're in too deep. We're not allowed to change. It's too late for us."

Tyson leans down closer. Grunts. "Yup. That's the truth."

The muffled sound of the suppressed gunshot belies the mess made when the bullet penetrates Stoppard's skull and blows blood and gore out of the back of his head.

Tyson stands up, inspects his handiwork. For once, his lips don't move. He makes a gesture as if crossing himself, but on his face, ending by tapping his nose.

"T-box," he says, his gaze flicking to Blue's bandana, where it conceals his old scars. "Shoot there. Never fails."

"I'll remember that."

The van is parked up close to Stoppard's house. It's getting light fast now.

"The Phoenix is downtown," says Tyson. "Hotel parking lot, underground, safe enough. Weapons, ammo. Your phone."

He gives Blue a pointed look.

"Bluey, there are at least six agents within a few blocks ready to kill us."

"I bought a little time." Blue checks his watch. "We have about eight minutes."

Tyson's jaw works as if chewing an invisible stick of gum. "I had a plan, a scheme, knew what to do, kill Stoppard, then kill Castle, after making him tell me who else was involved. But it kinda relied on the element of surprise. They knew I was coming, Bluey. We're screwed."

He unscrews the suppressor from Stoppard's gun. "Never liked these things. You hardly know you're killing someone. You should know. Right? You should feel it. Okay. Guess we go out in a blaze of glory, gunfight at the O.K. Corral, High Noon, Gary Cooper. Unless you have a better plan, Bluey?"

"As a matter of fact," says Jimmy, "I do."

CHAPTER FORTY-EIGHT

IT'S the second time in twelve hours Robert Hanan has met the deputy director of the CIA, and the mix of disgust, anger, fear, shame, and guilt the sight of the man provokes makes him want to take a second shower, reclean his teeth, and get the hotel rooms fumigated. The view of Washington is stunning from up here, but Castle's presence makes it impossible for Hanan to enjoy it.

Castle walks to the table, puts his briefcase on the surface. Places both hands on the oak surface, leans over, and glares at the polished wood.

Hanan had breakfast an hour ago, but there's coffee brewing. Hanan pours himself a cup without offering any to his guest. He senses the impending crisis, and, for no good reason he can name, feels oddly distanced from it.

Finally, Castle breaks his silence.

"Fuuuuuucccckkkkk. Fuck. Fuck."

He's still staring at the table. Hanan's sense of separation from reality continues. It's plain Castle is about to deliver bad news. Bad news that will have a negative impact on Hanan's life. Yet he's enjoying witnessing Castle beleaguered, lost, dishevelled. Out of control. Above all else, this man is a control freak, seeing the world as a series of problems to be solved by his superior intellect. Well, maybe not this time, buddy.

This brief period of *schadenfreude*, as enjoyable as it is, dissipates in a hurry when Castle moves on from expletives.

"Stoppard's dead."

This is it. The worst news possible. Eric Stoppard had been a smart, brutal killer. Which means whoever killed him was smarter and more brutal. And coming for the two men in this room.

"Tyson? Murchen?"

"Tyson for sure. And he had help."

Castle moves now, pushing himself away from the table, swinging around to face Hanan. He doesn't look scared or angry. He looks bewildered. He's gone to war with these people and he's losing. Losing is not in Castle's vocabulary. Hanan can only pray he's a quick study. The last vestiges of disassociation fall away to be replaced by a cold lump of fear in his belly. He needs Castle. He needs him thinking straight, making decisions, taking action.

"Help? What kind of help?"

"Some asshole who came out of nowhere. Six-foot-three or four, built like a quarterback, possibly bald, dark green eyes. Mid to late twenties. Neutral accent, hard to place. Trained, dangerous, special forces, Mossad, I don't fucking know. Do you? Any of this sound familiar, Senator?"

"Doesn't sound like anyone I know."

"Great. That's great. Jesus. Give me a coffee, will you?"

Castle is breathing a little easier, and his voice is closer to normal. He's not shouting, at least. Hanan, keen to keep him that way, pours a coffee and brings it over to the table. The shorter man takes a sip, followed by a series of long, deliberate breaths.

There's an obvious question, although Hanan worries it might set Castle off again. But he has to know.

"What happened? Stoppard was the bait for a trap. How did Tyson and this bald guy escape?"

The yoga-style breathing stops. Castle's face reddens. Hanan prepares for another episode of shouting. It doesn't come. Castle masters his temper, resumes the deep breaths, and takes his time before answering.

"The fuck do you care? This is my turf, Hanan."

"Sure. Don't tell me. But I'm ex-army. And politics is a dirty game. I might be able to help."

He sees the logic of his statement register on the deputy director's face.

"My agents established a perimeter around Stoppard's property. Stoppard told me Tyson was taking him to Murchen. One of our vehicles left Stoppard's house. Our agents picked it up at the next corner and followed. After twenty minutes, it pulled into a parking lot. Our agents found a sixty-seven-year-old army veteran by the name of Harold Quentin behind the wheel. No one else. Mr Quentin lives opposite Eric Stoppard. He was wearing a bandana given to him by a bald man who paid him five hundred bucks to do it."

"Five hundred dollars to drive a few miles and park up? Didn't he ask questions?"

Castle took a gulp of coffee. "Tyson identified himself as a fellow vet. Mr Quentin, judging from the signs on his lawn, is not a fan of the current administration. I suspect he believes he was helping stick it to the man."

Castle is drawing this out. Not getting to the point. Probably because the point is that two—no, three, now—trained killers are still at large. Hanan's guts churn, and he tastes acid bile.

"And Tyson?"

"Four agents went to Stoppard's house, found his body. As they approached, Mr Quentin's Corvette reversed onto the street. The driver, a big man wearing a Stetson, asked what was going on. They waved him back for his own safety. He drove away. I expect Tyson was lying on the back seat."

Castle drained the last of the coffee. Crossed the room and refilled his cup before returning to his station at the table.

"We found the Corvette downtown. The keys were on the rear wheel. Wiped down, no prints. No sign of the two men."

Hanan moves to the toughened glass window, leans his forehead against it. Castle had made wiping out the old black ops team sound easy, everyday, trivial. Now the last of them are in Washington, anonymous among five million people, very much alive. And they want Castle and Hanan dead.

His phone rings. Madeline Kalinsky.

"Robert? Where are you?" Something strange about her voice. Tight. Higher than usual.

"Washington," he says. "What's wrong?"

"Wrong? Are you taking a break from the news? Gone cold turkey on twitter?" She's talking faster, too.

"What are you talking about, Madeline? You're not making sense."

"You near a television?"

Hanan finds the remote, presses it, has to wait while automatic panels slide aside to reveal a huge flat-screen on the north wall. "Which channel?"

"Any news channel. I'll wait."

Ted Grant's handsome features fill the screen. He's smiling, as usual, showing that straight line of white teeth. A press conference. Called in a hurry, as it's outside Grant's campaign office. A text box announces that it's live.

"Madeline? What's this about?"

"Shh. Turn up the sound."

Hanan does it. Grant's relaxed baritone fills the room. Castle looks up from the table.

"Well, I don't know where you got that email, and—"

A *Post* reporter interrupts. Hanan recognises her. Steph Tulles. Politicians on both sides of the floor know her as the Ferret. She is immune to Grant's famous charm.

"So you don't deny the email is genuine?"

Grant holds out his hands. *Hey, I'm just some guy. No different to the rest of you.* "I get hundreds of emails a day, Steph. I honestly don't remember this one."

"You don't remember an email from a senior advisor referencing a conversation about your possible running mate for the White House? An email that concluded Jackie Cartland was the smart choice?"

Grant looks like he's forgotten the script. He has a tell. When flustered, he looks over the heads in the room, as if spotting an old friend at the back. He's doing it now.

"Shit," breathes Hanan.

"Wait." Madeline's voice still has that odd tightness.

Ross Dacre steps up. Whispers in Ted Grant's left ear. Hanan's eyebrows shoot up. Never seen that before. Dacre keeps his briefings private. He hates being seen prompting Grant, and avoids being in shot at press conferences if possible. Not this time. He's standing at Grant's shoulder. Grant says something back and Dacre nods.

Meanwhile, Hanan reads the text scrolling across the bottom of the screen, which changes everything. As he does so, in an unlikely feat of synchronicity he reflects on later, he is distracted by a helicopter approaching the hotel.

He looks back at the scrolling news feed.

... follows leak of internal email suggesting Cartland about to be named as Grant running mate for election. Senator Grant yet to comment. Breaking: Jackie Cartland resigns Senate seat, drops out of Vice-Presidential race, claims personal reasons. The announcement follows leak of internal email...

"What the hell?" says Hanan, but the Ferret has another question.

"Mr Grant. *The Post* obtained a copy of the leaked email at around four a.m. Jackie Cartland resigned three hours later. What's going on in the Grant presidential campaign? It sounds like chaos."

"Not at all, Steph. Far from it, in fact." He's looking at her now. Dacre has steered him back on course. "The email you have, if it's genuine, was never part of any discussion. We're running the most important campaign of our lives out of this office. In November, the American people will decide who leads this wonderful country for the next four years. They want someone they can trust. Someone dependable. Someone who appreciates the privilege of living in the greatest country in the world."

Steph is about to interrupt. Other hands go up like a double speed whack-a-mole game. They've heard the sales pitch before. They don't want this, they want something with meat on it. Then Grant surprises them by giving them just that.

"But it won't just be me in the White House, if I'm elected. No man is an island, and I will rely on a talented, experienced, and patriotic team. The most senior member of that team is, of course, the vice president."

The press corps, restless and desperate to ask their questions, grow still, sensing an announcement.

Grant delivers.

"I'll be calling Senator Cartland later today to offer my support and wish her well, but—as much as I respect and admire Jackie—I believe the media has done her a disservice by constantly suggesting she will be my running mate. Our announcement was due tomorrow night, but let's put an end to the speculation. My running mate is one of the most hard-working, talented, and decent men I've ever had the honour to call a colleague and a friend."

Hanan's phone beeps. He glances at the screen. Ross Dacre is calling.

"My running mate for November and, I hope, the next Vice President of the United States, is the Senator for the great state of Oregon, Robert Hanan."

"Jesus H. Christ." It's one thing to work towards a goal this lofty, but—as Hanan discovers—it can be quite another to achieve it. He sits down on the nearest couch. For a moment, he forgets the three people set on killing him.

"You said it." Ah. So that's how Madeline sounds when she's excited. Shame he never found out the way he'd hoped. Still, he would be Vice President before Christmas. Even Madeline Kalinsky's sexual principles might become more flexible once he's in office.

"The leaked email? It kinda forced their hand, coming so soon after Jackie's sudden resignation. You know anything about that?"

She laughs. Ignores the question. "A nice coincidence, wasn't it? You were the obvious choice once Jackie dropped out, but I think Dacre was still lobbying for someone he can control. Like Ted. This way, Grant had to announce or appear weak. Did you see Dacre's face? Bet he's mad as hell."

"Reckon so." Hanan's phone buzzes with the voicemail notification. He'll be working with Dacre soon. Best not to piss him off by not taking his calls.

"I gotta go, Madeline. Outstanding work. I'll see you at the dinner tomorrow?"

"You know it, Mr Vice President." Is he imagining it, or has a note of flirtation just entered the conversation?

He hangs up, smiling, looks at Castle, and stops. The hotel phone rings.

"Wait," says Castle as he goes to pick up. "This will change things. You're public property now. That'll be your Secret Service detail."

He steps back from the phone. Hanan answers it. Castle's right.

———

Twenty minutes later, Hanan's in the air above Washington, a helicopter transferring him to the Olympus Hotel. The Olympus is new, opulent, centrally located, and patronised by those in the most rarefied political circles. Some of them invested in the hotel, and their choice of name is revealing. Men like Ted Grant might claim to be an ordinary Joe, a people's champion, but he was throwing a party at a joint named after the mountain home of Greek gods.

Hanan feels safer already. Hard not to when he's flanked by three serious-looking men and one serious-looking woman. They wear the uniform of the Secret Service: white shirt, black suit and tie, lapel mic, coiled earpiece. Polite but distant, all four of them. They introduced themselves, answered Hanan's questions, but used as few words as possible, and rarely looked directly at him. In fact, they looked everywhere else instead, which was disconcerting at first, then reassuring. They treated him like the most important person in the world and were ready to protect him. Willing to die for him. No, for the Office of the Vice President. Willing to die for an ideal. Hanan experiences a brief flush of shame, holding up his own self-interested pursuit of power alongside their dedication. It doesn't last long. They don't have the imagination or the drive to be like him.

It's a brief ride, the helicopter lowering itself onto the landing pad atop the Olympus six minutes after they took off.

Ross Dacre's voice message had been pithy. *There was a leak. Ted had to announce early. Don't talk to the press. We're sending a chopper. I'll call you later. Oh. Congratulations.*

Delivered through gritted teeth, no doubt.

When he releases his seat belt, the female agent holds up her palm. "One moment, sir." She's short and wide, older than Hanan had first thought, her brown hair flecked with grey. Two agents take up positions outside. Their jackets are cut loose, the buttons down the front lower than normal. It creates an unnatural bulge in the material at chest level where the garment hangs away from the body. Easy to access a shoulder holster in a hurry.

The lead agent listens through her earpiece, responds too quietly for Hanan to hear, steps out of the chopper, and waves him forward. The last agent falls in place behind, and they exit the chopper. Every agent constantly scans the roof and the sky for potential threats.

Hanan's head is a little higher, his step lighter. He read the report on Tyson and Murchen. Both dropped out of their violent professions years ago. Murchen became some kind of hippy, and Tyson—when they tracked him down—was living like a bum.

What chance did they really have against the Secret Service?

He glances at his watch. Just shy of nine-thirty. Too early for a drink? Maybe he'd call Madeline. They had much to discuss.

CHAPTER FORTY-NINE

TYSON STARES at Jimmy Blue's phone screen, shaking his head, fists clenching and unclenching.

Blue cleaned and dressed Tyson's wound back at the Phoenix. A sling would help speed his recovery, but neither of them suggest it as they don't know what the next twenty-four hours will bring. Going to war with one arm bound up is not an option.

"Explain this to me," says Tyson, nodding at the images of Kai, slumped on the chair, tied up. "And make it good, convince me, tell it like it is. Roach says I can trust you. I need to know what happened. Hear it from you. Talk."

Blue points at the image, tapping the sweater he pulled over Kai's body to conceal the bullet wound and blood beneath.

"Look at her trousers."

Tyson frowns.

Jimmy clarifies. "Her pants. See the dirt on them? Her hands and the side of her face, too."

"I see it."

"They shot her, Tyson. Open-tip bullet, three hundred yards out. No wind. A three-oh-eight Winchester. After I killed the sniper and his buddy, I brought her back into the kitchen. Put a sweater on her to cover the wound. Wanted her to seem alive. See where the blood is coming through?"

Tyson's mouth moves as he examines the photo. The dirt on Kai's clothes and face where she fell. The darker patch on the grey sweater.

"I see it. And I watched you slaughter those assholes in Santa Barbara. It makes no sense that you killed her. But when Roach told me what he found on your phone, these photographs, what you did to Kai... what it looked like you did, I snapped. Wanted you to suffer. Wanted you dead."

Tyson hands the device back to Jimmy. Nods. That's all the apology Blue is getting for Tyson trying to drown him.

"Why tie her up, Bluey? Don't understand, don't get it."

Blue puts the phone in his pocket. "I did my homework on Kai. When she was an active agent, she was the best. But someone still found her, killed her. Found you, too. Whoever is behind this, makes sense they're powerful. Well protected. Hard to get to. I thought I'd need leverage."

"Leverage?" Tyson repeats the word as if he'd just bitten into an apple and found it full of maggots.

Jimmy turns his dark green eyes on Tyson.

"Leverage. While they still believe Kai is alive, the photographs give me a way in. Even if it's the deputy director of the CIA. I don't have to track him down. I send him the pictures, he'll come to us."

There's silence in the Phoenix for a full minute.

"Wanna ask you something," says Tyson.

"Sure."

"Tom can't think too well, gets confused real easy, got less street sense than most five-year-olds. But when Tom was here, you were somewhere inside, buried, waiting. Watching. And now you're back, and you've got all the smarts. And I don't see Tom anywhere. Is he in there? Or is it just you, only you, Bluey, the one-man killing machine? The guy, when he sees Kai get killed, who thinks about leverage?"

"She was my friend, Tyson."

The older man looks up at him, jaw working, eyes wet but fierce. "*Your* friend?"

Blue accepts the correction without rancour. "She was Tom's friend. She refused to help me. But when she met Tom, she took him in."

"And what does that tell you?"

The phone in Jimmy's pocket rings. He takes it out, holds it to his ear. Listens.

"Yes. He's here. Wait. I'll put you on speaker."

He places the phone on his knee. Roach's voice comes out of the device.

"There's a lot of chatter on the CIA servers. You boys have been busy. You holed up somewhere safe?"

"Safe enough for now," says Tyson. "Won't be here long. Got to finish the job. You got a name for us?"

"Yes, I have a name. But it's not good news. You need to drop this. Stoppard was expendable. Castle will be harder to get to. But the guy whose mess they're cleaning up? Forget it."

Jimmy Blue's face leans closer. "The name."

Even with two hundred miles between them and no connection other than a cell phone signal, the words carry a menacing weight. Roach stops prevaricating.

"Hanan. Robert Hanan. Senator for Oregon."

"So?"

"*So?* Either of you ever watch the news?"

Tyson and Blue shrug.

Roach's voice crackles out of the phone. "Ever heard of the internet?"

Tyson frowns, shakes his head.

As if he can see him, Roach responds. "Yes, I know, Tyson, they're watching you, they'll trace you. OK. Fine. Robert Hanan is going to be the next goddam vice president."

He let the information sink in. "You're not just up against a deniable branch of the CIA anymore. You go after Hanan and you take on a secret service detail whose only job is to keep their boss healthy, even if it means dying."

Jimmy, clicking on his phone, turns the screen towards Tyson, who flinches at the idea of interacting with an electronic device. Then he sees the photograph Blue has found online.

"Oh shit. Can you make that any bigger?"

Blue zooms in.

Tyson nods.

"I remember him, this guy, the politician. One of the last jobs we did before Indonesia." He clams up, points at the phone, shakes his head.

"Makes sense," says Roach. "I guess whatever you did for him, if it became public, wouldn't be good for Hanan."

For once, Tyson keeps his answer short. "Good guess."

Jimmy Blue thinks of home, of what waits for him there, the culmination of nearly seven years' preparation. His parents' killers are criminals. Successful, violent, well-connected criminals, but not impossible to get to. No one is impossible to get to. No one is impossible to kill. The difficult bit is escaping afterwards. If he goes after the next Vice President to avenge someone he barely knew, he might as well paint "Death to America!" on his bald head and run across the White House lawn with a machine gun in each hand.

Tyson looks like he's reached the same conclusion.

"It'd be crazy to go after Hanan."

"Yes," agrees Roach.

"Well," says Tyson, "I never figured I'd die in my sleep, surrounded by grandchildren anyhow."

He looks up at Blue. "Not your fight, Bluey. Thanks for coming this far."

Blue says nothing.

Roach is the sole dissenter. "Tyson, don't do anything crazy. Please. I know what she meant to you, but—"

"It's my call, Roach." Tyson speaks over his old friend. "I can't let him walk away from what he's done. I won't."

"Even if it means..."

"Even then."

Blue understands Tyson's decision. Approves. That some bastard on the other side of the country could end Kai's life because an old connection might derail his political career, disgusts him. Worth killing for? Absolutely. Worth dying for? For Tyson, yes. Of course Blue understands. How could it be any other way?

"Roach?" Jimmy surprises himself by speaking. "Send me everything you have on Hanan. Background, associates. Any exploitable weaknesses. And his movements for the next few days. Can you do that?"

"I can."

"How long will it take?"

"I already have a file on every Senator. Three or four hours to make sure it's all current."

"Stand down," says Tyson. "Both of you. I appreciate your help. Don't get me wrong, I owe you, in your debt, you went above and beyond. Enough now. Stop. You're done. Kai is dead. My friend. My fight. It's up to me now."

Tyson ends the call. Puts a hand above Jimmy's shoulder, changes his mind; lets it drop to his side.

"It's over, Bluey. You've helped me more than I can say. You've honoured Kai's memory, shown respect. Like I said, I owe you, man, but Santa Barbara was different. We're on their turf now. It's Washington DC, Bluey, and they know we're coming. They saw your face, too. Go home. Kai wouldn't want you to die, not here, not like this. Not for her. It's different for me. Go home, okay?"

Jimmy doesn't answer. He should walk away, but he won't. The same boundless rage that screamed him into existence, that pulled Tom Lewis back from the brink of death, has turned its pitiless gaze on those who killed Kai, and he finds he can't leave. Not yet.

"How long are we safe here?"

Tyson shakes his head. "Thirty-six hours, forty-eight if we're lucky."

"I'll risk it if you will. Give me until this evening."

"For what, man? What are you thinking?"

"I'm thinking logically. You should, too. Our chances of getting to Hanan are slim. But I can deliver Castle to you, with little risk to either of us. If you choose to chase Hanan afterwards and get yourself shot, that's your lookout."

Tyson is still shaking his head and muttering. "No, no. My fight now, my fight."

"Tyson." Blue stands. "I'm staying."

"No. You're leaving. It's over."

Jimmy Blue drops the veneer of humanity, allowing the darkness to expand. It starts in the pit of his stomach, ash-black, formless, a roiling, shapeless fog that swells within him. He doesn't speak. He doesn't have to. The temperature inside the cramped conditions of the Phoenix seems to lower, the atmosphere thickening; congealing.

Tyson stands, confusion written on his face, jaw hanging open, eyes staring.

He looks at Jimmy Blue. Meets his eyes for less than half a second. Stumbles backwards until pressed against the side of the van. Turns his face away.

Blue lets the darkness fall back, regains control. He never lets it engulf him. He's not sure what would happen if he did. Nothing good, probably.

"I'm staying," he says.

The phone rings, and the two men resume their seats as if nothing happened.

It's Roach again. Blue puts him on speaker.

"I found something," says Roach. "Or, rather, someone. There might be a way."

"Castle? Or Hanan?" Tyson's voice is dry and husky. He coughs, licks his lips.

"That's why I'm calling." There's a new authority in Roach's voice.

"What if you don't have to choose? What if you could get both?"

CHAPTER FIFTY

ROACH WHEELS himself up the shallow incline into the minivan, then presses the button to retract the ramp. He adjusts his tie in the rearview mirror and starts the car. It's been a while, but the minivan starts on the second attempt, and he reverses out of the garage, using the remote to close the door.

A while? he thinks, and tries to remember the last time he left his sanctuary. Six years. *Goddam.*

The plan isn't over-complicated, but each of its constituent parts has to work for the whole thing to succeed. Roach, Tyson, and Blue each have their tasks to complete in the next thirty-six hours.

The clock is ticking. Four hours after outlining the bare bones of his idea to the others, then listening in awe as Kincaid—or Bluey, as Tyson refers to him—turned that initial idea into a coherent plan, Roach is keenly aware that everything depends on him. If his instincts are off, if he baits this hook poorly, they'll lose the only chance they have of pulling this off. Worse: they'll show their hand to their enemies.

He's already typed the message into his phone, but doesn't press *send* yet.

Downtown Washington's streets are as busy as he remembers.

One of the few advantages to being a wheelchair user is the availability of decent parking spots. He pulls into a space close to the restaurant he booked. Looks out through the windshield at the lunch crowd hurrying from one place to the next. He wonders how many of the frowning suits feature in his databases. A small number, probably, as the top Washington power brokers don't lunch in this neighbourhood. It's the reason he chose it for the meeting. Close to the Hill, but further than overfed senators want to walk.

Roach checks his watch. Twelve-fifty. He doesn't want to give the recipient of the message much time to consider her response.

This is the moment it could fail. If his judgement is ill-placed, if she isn't as ambitious as he thinks she is, it'll all fall apart. He will have risked being exposed for nothing.

He takes a deep breath. The adrenaline pumps. When he was last in the field, it was a different century.

He presses *send.*

———

Madeline Kalinsky can't stop smiling. The child of Polish immigrants with high hopes—and higher expectations—for their daughter, she has plotted, manoeuvred, and grafted to get here. It took a level of determination few possess. People think they can make tough decisions, put their personal life aside in order to advance their career, but when it comes down to it, they baulk. Madeline started her first internship with a cohort of bright-eyed, idealistic political ingenues who wanted to change the world. At first, they embraced seventy-hour weeks, all-nighters, and cancelled vacations. Later, they endured them. After a decade, idealism morphed into disillusionment, complaints and whining.

Not Madeline, though. She said nothing when her contemporaries spoke of five- or ten-year goals. They thought her silence revealed a lack of ambition, and their smiles were one-quarter pity, three-quarters self-satisfaction. But Madeline had goals, and her silence hid her contempt for her peers' lack of perspective. Sixteen years later, her career plan just passed its halfway point.

Madeline has heard the expression *work/life balance*, even nods politely when others mention it, but she doesn't understand the concept at all. By choosing not to have children, which evidently saps the sense and life-force out of capable women faster than a tequila binge, she can focus on pursuing power. Madeline doesn't have her parents' faith in an afterlife, and romantic love strikes her as an unnecessary addendum to the uncomplicated sexual encounters that fulfil her needs.

Her short-term goals, updated on the first of every month, continue to be crossed off as planned. Hanan is an important landmark in her life plan, but he is far from its zenith. Accompanying a Vice President into power begins the real work. Once in the White House, she will forge new alliances, put down foundations for the political empire she intends to build.

She looks around her downtown office. Too small for her needs now. Not in practical terms, of course. She has all the space she requires, and the White House is only four blocks away. But status is a matter of perception, and no top-level mandarin or power broker can be taken seriously in a building like this, shared with bankers and lawyers.

She moves out in two days. The morning after the big fundraising party at the Olympus.

Everything is in place, and Madeline Kalinsky is content. Not happy. Happy suggests a spring in the step, a simpering feeble-mindedness. Far better to be content; pages of tasks ticked and completed longhand in a small journal bought for the purpose. She does it now, flicking through the previous pages before putting the book away, enjoying the sight of hundreds of ticks.

Her phone pings. No phone number accompanies the message, and when Madeline reads the four brief sentences, her smile disappears.

Hanan is hiding a scandal from you. I have all the details, but I will only wait until one-thirty. After that I go to the press. Half Moon Diner, ask for Walsingham.

————

Madeline isn't sure what she was expecting, but it wasn't this. The busboy points her towards a distant table set aside from the booths. At the back wall, watching her, is an old man in a wheelchair. His white hair is thin. He is the whitest man she has ever seen, and Madeline works with some very white men. His eyes, blue and bloodshot, lock onto hers when she reaches the table, alerting her to a keen mind behind the benign exterior.

"Please, Miss Kalinsky, sit down." He holds a pair of thick glasses to his face and inspects the menu. "According to reviews, this place has the best omelettes in the city. A well-cooked omelette is one of life's great pleasures, don't you think? I'm going to indulge. You?"

"I'm not here to eat, Mr Walsingham."

"No, no. I understand. Straight to business. You'll join me in a coffee, though? Humour an old man."

He keeps talking while they wait for the coffee to arrive. Walsingham, whoever he is, has an excellent grasp of Washington politics. Not the gossip anyone with enough time and a decent internet connection can pick up, but a nuanced understanding rare in even the sharpest advisors. A couple of details about the current administration are news even to her, and Walsingham's casual display of knowledge impresses in the way he'd doubtless planned it to. She's intrigued. Hooked. A little scared.

The waitress sets down two coffees and a jug of milk. Time to take control.

"Mr Walsingham. You're obviously well-informed, so you'll be aware I'm a very busy woman."

The old man chuckles at that. Behind her faint smile, Madeline grits her teeth.

"Yes, I am aware, Miss Kalinsky. I'm also aware of the chess game you've played for the last eighteen months to get yourself close to

Robert Hanan, then nudge him towards the Vice-Presidential nomination. Grant will win this election. You play the game brilliantly, Miss Kalinsky. My findings suggest you've only used bribery twice, and blackmail three times."

Her body stiffens, but Madeline fights the instinctive reaction, picking up her coffee, coolly sipping it while raising an eyebrow at the old man. She thinks about leaving, but the thought comes and goes before she seriously considers acting on it. Walsingham gives her a tiny nod, as if aware of the direction of her thoughts. She's angry and scared, but the fear is greater.

He chuckles. "Your blackmail of Jackie Cartland was a masterstroke."

Madeline forces a smile, as if this man's conjecture is of no interest to her. Sweat prickles the base of her spine. "You said you had information."

Walsingham returns her smile. He seems genuinely relaxed. "I do."

He pulls a slim folder from a pocket on the side of the wheelchair.

"Read it here," he says. "It'll only take a few minutes. I'll wait. I won't leave it with you."

Madeline opens the folder. Within twenty seconds, she knows enough, but she keeps reading. Robert Hanan's career is over. It was over before she met him, because he's not his own man. The CIA owns him. But that's not important. It's what this means for her that's important. And what it means is the end. Of everything. She might as well go home, pack a bag, and move back to Brooklyn. Mom and Dad might let her work in the store, help with deliveries. She can marry a local boy, give him a litter of brats. Forget about this crazy dream.

The rage surges hot and fast, then subsides, leaving a kind of weightless emptiness.

She doesn't know she's crying until Walsingham hands her a napkin.

Madeline closes the folder. They sit in silence for a while. She regains her composure. It takes longer than she'd like, but she waits until she is certain her voice won't waver, or her throat clamp tight. She is still in control of herself, if nothing else.

"What do you want, Mr Walsingham?"

"I want to prevent you making a mistake that will torpedo your promising political career."

She gulps a laugh at that, swallows it quickly, scared she won't be able to stop. "A little too late, don't you think?"

"As it happens," says Walsingham, folding his hands in front of him on the table, "no. Not at all. You can still make this go away and increase your political capital at the same time. I'm going to tell you how. But—"

"*But?*"

Madeline looks into those pale eyes. Is that amusement she sees there?

Walsingham waves at the waitress. "But I haven't eaten since supper yesterday. I'm going to order one of those omelettes."

CHAPTER FIFTY-ONE

FRIDAY MORNING DAWNS sunny and bright. As the sun creeps up the side of the skyscrapers, downtown Washington is awash with commuters slurping cappuccinos from cardboard cups, yapping into phones, spilling out of trains, buses, and cars.

Tyson leaves thirty minutes before Jimmy Blue, merging with the flow of foot traffic outside the hotel, boarding a bus to take him into a neighbourhood most folks on the Hill pretend doesn't exist, only crossing the river when their official duties take them to the National Cemetery.

Once the bus clears the Anacostia River into southeast Washington, Tyson relaxes. They drive through the projects, past graffiti-speckled walls, stores with bars on their windows. Even the ice-cream truck looks like an armoured vehicle, painted military grey, although it still plays the usual tinny song as it plies its trade.

Tyson disembarks on Good Hope Road, heads south. He is aware of a few pairs of eyes turning his way as he enters their territory, but he looks big, mean, and—crucially—poor, so their interest wanes.

He reaches the body shop without incident, making it as far as the office door before a mechanic in oily overalls, that might have once been red, calls after him.

"Help you?"

Tyson can't stop an unfamiliar smile from appearing on his face. The mechanic is in his teens, the resemblance unmistakable.

"Your dad here?" The kid narrows his eyes, grip tightening on the heavy spanner at his side. Tyson nearly laughs, the similarity is so startling. "I served with him."

"Tyson? That you?"

"Pez?"

The kid returns to his work, not curious to witness a reunion between his father and an old army buddy.

The two men regard each other. Henry Penn, variously known as State, Dispenser, Pez Dispenser, then—finally—Pez, has changed in the nineteen years since Tyson last saw him. He's kept his hair, but it's grey. His eyes are red-rimmed and watery. One of the smaller men in their unit, Pez stands hunched now, looking even shorter. His right leg—shattered by a landmine—is supported by a metal stick that ends with three rubber-tipped feet.

"You look exactly the same."

"You haven't changed a bit, you old bastard."

Both men speak over the other, laugh at how ridiculous their statements sound, then clasp hands.

"You said you'd be shit at staying in touch, Ty."

"I'm a man of my word."

"Come on in. Have a drink with me."

The two men talk about the old days for twenty minutes, passing a hip flask of bourbon back and forth across a metal desk cluttered with invoices, bolts, screws, tins of oil, and unidentifiable pieces of engines. Tyson compliments Pez on his boy. Pez doesn't ask if Tyson has a family. When the safe subjects run dry, Pez nods at his old buddy.

"You do that a lot? Mumbling to yourself? That a thing?"

Tyson brings his fingers up to his mouth, as if only now aware he's still talking.

"You drink every morning? That a thing?"

The silence isn't companionable, but it's not awkward, either.

"Why you here, Ty?"

Tyson takes another pull at the hip flask. It's warming, but it's rough, cheap gut-rot.

"You still in business, still keeping a sideline going? Still boosting?"

"Sometimes."

"I need this to be one of those times. And it's easy money."

"That's my favourite kind."

"Here, listen up, call this number." Tyson reels off Roach's burner number while Pez dials. It's a brief conversation, and two minutes after it ends, the phone on the metal desk, its digits smudged with grime, rings with an automatic message from the bank.

"Sonofabitch." Pez replaces the handset in its cradle. "What are you into, Ty?"

It's the sort of question he doesn't expect an answer to, and Tyson doesn't disappoint.

The kid is draining oil from an old Chevy truck when Tyson leaves. Pez limps alongside his old comrade.

"The vehicle will be there by seven. The plates come from long-term airport lots, so no red flags with local law enforcement. Second set of plates in the trunk."

"Good. You did good. I appreciate it, Pez. Be seeing you."

"Hey."

Tyson pauses underneath the sign. Some letters are missing, so it reads *Pe Bod Sh.*

"Whatever you've got yourself into, be careful, Ty."

Halfway down the street, Tyson looks back over his shoulder. Pez has limped back inside out of sight, but his kid is sitting on a box, and he watches his father's old friend until he turns the corner.

———

Blue heads for a neighbourhood full of men's outfitters. He can't go too downmarket, but what he needs has a specific look. He finds it in the fourth place he tries, trying on a black suit with enough room for a holster. A black tie and a white shirt at the next store, then a hunt around the thrift stores to find a used pair of black shoes in his size. He also picks up a pair of sweatpants and a hoodie.

A brief visit to an electronics retailer, then the wig store is his last stop. He looked it up online. He wants a business that appeals to clients in denial about their hair loss, and phrases like hair 'enhancement', or 'replacement' means discreet staff and a convincing product.

Jimmy is familiar with hairpieces and knows he'll have to spend money to get believable results. A good wig can cost a thousand dollars, a great one as much as a compact car.

He emerges from the store eight hundred dollars poorer, but with a hairpiece that would stand up to scrutiny without him looking like a bit-part actor in a daytime soap.

Before heading back to the Phoenix, Blue finds a cheap motel, pays cash, and takes a long shower, shaving his face and head with a disposable razor. He prepares his scalp for the hairpiece, then glues it in place. It's a little long, but the shorter the hair, the harder to make it convincing. The colour and style work well; dark brown with a neat side parting.

He dresses in the sweatpants and hoodie, and leaves through a fire exit.

Tyson, back at the RV forty minutes after Blue, gawps.

His reaction satisfies Jimmy. He turns back to the mirror, darkening his eyebrows to match the hairpiece.

Tom's hair never grew back properly over his scars. Left for a few weeks, dark blonde hair grows in again, but it's coarse and irregular around the ridged scar tissue, drawing attention to the old wound. Staying bald, and favouring bandanas, caps, and hats, means fewer glances, fewer questions. And a good wig means he can become someone else for a few hours or more. A head of hair, a pair of contact lenses, careful choice of clothes—they all combine to create characters Blue fleshes out with acting techniques learned from one of the best teachers in Britain. The way he stands, the way he moves, the way he talks, even how often he pauses mid-sentence, all add up to a coherent picture. No one he meets will think they are talking to a work of fiction.

"You've done that before, not your first rodeo." Tyson checks Blue's reflection. "All of this to get the guys who shot you and killed your parents? The weapons training? The fighting techniques? Disguises? All for them?"

Blue shades his eyebrow with a make-up pencil, checks it against the hairpiece. It matches.

"You don't know who I'm dealing with, Tyson. What they're capable of."

Blue stands, takes the new suit from the wardrobe, places the electronics purchases in his outer pocket.

Tyson nods his approval. "Looks convincing, you'd fool me. The car will be delivered in a couple hours."

"Good. Let's check the weapons; go over the schedule."

"Yeah, sure, let's do it." Tyson pulls one of his locked boxes from under the bed, spins the combination. Takes a long rifle with a night scope. Loads and unloads it, checks every moving part until satisfied. Dismantles it, and places the pieces into a sports bag, zipping it up.

Jimmy checks his handgun, accepts a spare box of ammo from Tyson.

They talk through the details. When they're done, an hour remains before Tyson is due to leave.

"Right," says Blue, opening the make-up kit again. "Time for your photo shoot."

CHAPTER FIFTY-TWO

RUBEN CASTLE SITS in the dark in an unfamiliar apartment.

Tonight, across town, the party celebrating Robert Hanan's confirmation as Ted Grant's running mate is underway. The real celebration should be Castle's. Hanan is his ticket to power. With the current CIA director retiring in six months, the top job is within reach. The Company's influence, under Castle's leadership, will grow as never before.

Before he can celebrate, he has to tidy up Hanan's mess. Stoppard failed, but Stoppard didn't have Castle's intellectual agility. The endgame will trigger when Murchen and Tyson make their move. Soon, Castle knows, because the longer they wait, the more chance they'll be found.

Two agents watch the front, another two cover the rear of the Company-rented apartment building. A sniper watches from the roof opposite, which is why the drapes remain open. The front door is steel, four inches thick. There's a safe room behind the closet. Castle doesn't think Tyson and Murchen will risk a frontal assault. They will want to draw him out. Good. He's ready.

Something chimes. Castle looks through the window towards the spot on the roof opposite where his sniper waits. A second chime, and he turns. His phone glows on the arm of a chair. He picks it up, opens the message.

There are two photographs. One of Murchen, the other of Tyson. The accompanying message has a concise clarity he admires.

Your agents saw me at Stoppard's place. I now control both of the assets you need. I want $10m. Wire 500k deposit to the account below now and I will give you Murchen tonight. The balance by midday tomorrow and I will give you Tyson. Go to the Potomac Overlook park at 9:45pm. Coordinates to follow. Wait by the fire hydrant. Alone. Transfer the money and I will bring Murchen to you.

The photographs are doozies. Murchen tied to a chair, head slumped to one side. Tyson hog-tied, his face a mass of purple bruises, lying on a concrete floor.

At least this answers some questions about the variable. He wasn't at Stoppard's place to help Tyson; he was there to kidnap him, having already grabbed Murchen. A rogue agent, maybe even one of their own, taking a chance for one big score. A vicious opportunist. Castle can respect that.

His phone buzzes with the coordinates for the meet. He checks the time. Eight-fifty. Whoever he is, the variable knows what he's doing. Not enough time to secure the meeting place. And five hundred grand is the perfect amount to ask for as an advance. Castle can authorise it without going any higher up the chain of command. As for the other nine and a half million, it doesn't matter. No one will be getting that.

Leaving the variable alive would be a mistake. He knows too much and is obviously capable. He's succeeded where the black ops teams failed. If he brings in Murchen, that's two-thirds of Castle's problem solved. He likes those numbers.

He looks up the coordinates online, checks the street view. It's a popular spot. This time of night there might be tourists, some joggers. If he clears the area, the variable won't show. The variable chose a public place to protect himself. His first error. Any witnesses will be told they were present at a terrorist incident, and their signature on a gagging order will ensure their silence.

Castle makes a call, wires the money. Books a cab. Lastly, he picks up the phone to the rooftop sniper.

"I'm sending you an address. It's surrounded by trees. Find a suitable spot, check you're not being observed. Look for a white male, six-foot two or three. Probably bald. If he makes contact with me, take the shot."

"Yes, sir."

———

Andy 'Headshot' Hodge isn't an agent of the Central Intelligence Agency. He doesn't appear in any database linking him to Ruben Castle. Hodge gained his nickname on tour in Afghanistan and, on returning home, was recruited by Pathforger, a private security company. While no one else seemed interested in his skill set, Pathforger offered a generous salary, healthcare, and the chance to keep doing what he loves.

Hodge is one of the few snipers who can guarantee a kill at distances greater than two thousand yards. His other talents include the ability to take orders and fulfil missions without asking questions. He enjoys doing something he's exceptional at. Hodge isn't stupid. He knows Pathforger works for the CIA, and he knows, since the George W. Bush administration, that certain private contractors aren't subject to Congressional oversight. As far as he's concerned, he lucked out when he left the army. He gets to live back home most of the time and occasionally demonstrates his skills in return for a very comfortable lifestyle.

Tonight, his rifle dismantled and inside his backpack, following a hiking trail into Potomac Overlook Park, Andy Hodge isn't happy. For several reasons. One is the lack of preparation time. It's nine-twenty. The target is due to arrive at nine forty-five. Twenty-five minutes is not long enough to check the location fully, find the best spot. He doesn't like to be rushed. And more time means he can check out potential problems. Is there anything blocking his view? Will the wind increase, drop, or change direction? Are there any other hostiles nearby? Locals?

Worse still, and the real reason Hodge scowls as he reaches the coordinates and scouts for the best position, is how easy this is going to be. Anyone capable of holding a gun the right way round could make this shot.

The fire hydrant marking the meeting place is in a clearing twenty yards from a cabin. The road forks here. The sun set about forty-five minutes ago.

Hodge takes five minutes to pick his spot, circling the area once. Lots of trees offer a clear shot. A mature white oak by the cabin is straightforward to climb, with plenty of foliage.

There's no natural high ground, and no skyscraper offers a better vantage point, but, on the far side of the river, a tall crane sits astride the foundations of a new housing development. Hodge makes some educated guesses, based on extensive experience, and estimates the crane's cab sits a hundred and fifty feet above the street. Given a couple of hours to prepare, he would have chosen that crane. Great visibility. Plus, when the shit hits the fan, he could pack up his rifle three-quarters of a mile away, with the Potomac between him and the target.

He spits on the ground, leans against the trunk, waits for a couple of joggers to pass, then swings himself up onto the lowest limb. Shimmies to a point halfway up where a thick branch gives him a decent perch. He takes twenty-six seconds to reassemble the rifle. Hodge checks the scope, attaches it, and takes position. Even after adjusting the sight to account for the short range, the fire hydrant fills his vision when he stares down the barrel. It's so close, Hodge is ninety-nine percent sure he could make the shot with a handgun.

For a man of his talent, this job is a professional insult. Still, Castle has promised a handsome bonus, so maybe he'll treat himself to that Harley-Davidson Dyna Wide Glide he's been eying. Yeah, why not? A few hours putting that baby through its paces, and he'll forget about the time he was asked to snipe someone so close he could hit them with a well-aimed rock.

Hodge remains still for twenty minutes. Five joggers, three dog walkers, a cab—which comes back three minutes later—and a convertible carrying four pot-smoking teenagers provide scant entertainment.

Castle arrives on foot at nine forty-two. Not from the obvious direction—the city below—but from the road above. He must have been in the cab. Hodge sees the sense in this. Castle, approaching from higher ground, has a good view of what he's walking into, and he's staying off the road, keeping to the trees.

Nine forty-two. No sign of the target. Castle hangs back in the darkness, invisible to anyone without a nightscope like Hodge's. The sniper is relaxed but ready, his rifle held loosely. It'll be the work of a second or less to bring the butt into his shoulder, put his eye to the scope, and squeeze off the shot that'll buy him a premium motorcycle.

Nine forty-five. All quiet. No dog walkers or joggers. Hodge checks the wider area, finds nothing. He listens. No approaching engines, no footsteps.

Nine forty-six. He catches a movement from Castle. Raises the scope to see the deputy director take out his phone. Hodge is still watching when Castle's left eye becomes a crater, his head lolling crazily on a neck no longer trying to support it. Castle's body falls into a bush already wet with the blood blown out of the back of his skull.

Hodge freezes, but only for a moment. His soldier's brain calculates the angle of the shot, considers the fact he didn't hear it, and knows where the shooter is. Too late, he accepts that one of his perceived strengths—taking orders—might also be a weakness. Castle told him what to do, and he'd accepted it. Followed orders like a good soldier. But this isn't a war zone. No one has his back.

He swings around in one fluid movement, lowering the rifle as he turns, then bringing the scope back up to his eye as he completes the manoeuvre. His left fingers are on the scope, twisting, adjusting for the extra distance. He's already thinking about wind direction and speed—north-easterly, and how it picked up a bit in the last couple minutes—when the operator's cabin on the crane comes into focus.

The figure kneeling inside is a blur, but clear enough to see a mirror image; another rifle, another scope, another sniper. The mirror sniper has already made all the calculations for an accurate shot; and he's good, Hodge knows he's good, because hitting a target in the eye at a thousand yards isn't easy, so turning round in his perch on the tree might not be the smartest idea, since it brings him out from behind the trunk, unless the other guy hasn't seen him and—

Hodge's rifle flies out of his numb hand as the wooden stock shatters, smacking every branch on the way down before thumping onto the grass. A huddle of middle-aged joggers comes to an untidy stop at the sight of the weapon. One goes for his phone. Another, a woman sporting a luminous orange headband Hodge associated with the nineteen-eighties, screams, pointing at Castle's splayed feet on the path. She takes a step closer and her scream goes up three octaves and eighty decibels when she sees what's left of his face.

Time to go. This operation is off the books, and Pathforger will deny all knowledge. Hodge is on his own.

In the last few minutes, Hodge has learned that blind obedience to your superiors isn't always wise, that if a mission is so easy he thinks there might be a catch, there *definitely* is a catch, and—in a situation where there's a five-foot thick tree trunk between him and a distant sniper—it's probably best to keep it that way.

Now he adds another life lesson to the list: when grabbing a branch with which to swing to the ground, ensure you still have all your fingers. The numbness in Hodge's hand gives way to pain, as bloody stumps try, and fail, to make a fist. Three of his digits, including his trigger finger, are lying on the grass below. Hodge joins them face-first. He flings his left arm across his body as he falls, meaning his shoulder dislocates on impact.

He tastes grass, soil, and defeat, rolling over with a moan to look up into the barrel of his own rifle.

"Been a while since I shot anyone," says the unsmiling, silver-haired jogger, "but I reckon I can still remember how. You lie still, friend."

He hears sirens. Passing out presents itself as an available option, and Hodge gratefully accepts.

———

The wind is stronger at a hundred and sixty feet up, and Tyson doesn't rush his descent of the crane's metal ladder, placing his hands on each rung. Halfway down, he smiles at the flashing blue-and-red snake on the far side of the river.

Back at street level, he walks to the pickup spot, takes his time, sticks to the main streets, mingling with the tourists. He wears his hipster glasses and a black baseball cap. He's shoved a pair of white earbuds into place. There's no music playing, but no one else knows that, and it gives him a reason for his constant mumbles. He nods along to his imaginary soundtrack, and no one gives him a second glance.

If he takes a direct route, he'll be at the pickup spot early, so he turns a two-mile walk into four, and arrives a few minutes before eleven.

Tyson can't help scanning the street as he walks, checking the passing traffic. He's thinking about Senator Robert Hanan. With Castle's help, Hanan tried to bury his past. Literally. But some bodies won't stay buried.

Tyson has done his part. Now it's up to Bluey.

He scans the traffic again. Doesn't see what he needs. Thinks back to when he pushed the kid off the bridge. Wonders if he's been a fool to think Bluey would help him.

The cars keep passing. None of them stop, or even slow down. Tyson puts his hand on the gun in his jacket pocket, flexes his ankle to feel the reassuring solidity of the five-inch blade strapped there.

One car slows as it approaches. If he's been sold out, he'll know in the next few seconds.

Either way, Tyson thinks, it will be over soon.

He stops walking, turns to face the car as its headlamps wash over him.

CHAPTER FIFTY-THREE

WHATEVER CRITICISMS MIGHT BE LAID at the door of Washington's political class, no one can deny they know how to throw a party.

Hanan arrives fashionably late, descending from the aptly named Presidential Suite with Ted Grant, Ross Dacre, Madeline Kalinsky, and four Secret Service agents. As they walk into the ballroom, the hum of the partygoers swells into applause and cheers. The big band's sax player, mid-solo, works a few notes of *Hail To The Chief* into his improvisation when the guests of honour approach the stage.

Hanan follows Grant up the steps as a melange of tuxedos and ballgowns waft from their tables and hurry towards the band, cramming shoulder to shoulder, turning the area in front of the stage into the world's richest mosh pit.

All thoughts of Castle, Tyson, and Murchen float away like bubbles as Hanan bounces onstage alongside Grant, buoyed by the palpable goodwill and excitement in the room. This is it. This is what he's craved ever since he made his first campaign speech as a newspaperman taking his first step into politics. The inner circle. The real deal. Power.

Grant's press secretary is already at the mic. As she speaks, Grant and Hanan shake hands. Cameras flash and the cheers get louder, so she leans into the mic.

"Ladies and gentlemen, the next President and Vice President of the United States of America, Ted Grant, and Robert Hanan."

The cheering and applause last for three minutes. Hanan inhales the rush, the instant high; zings with it. Even though he knows ninety percent of the adulation is meant for Ted Grant, he doesn't care. Did Buzz Aldrin resent Neil Armstrong for being the first human on the moon? Later on, surely, but at the time? When he looked back at Earth from its satellite, standing on the surface of that alien landscape? Hanan doubts it.

The ballroom, which holds two thousand, is decorated like a millionaire's New Year's Eve party in blinding white, silver and gold, from the draped chairs and tablecloths to the balloons, hundreds of which fall from a net on the distant ceiling. They drift down onto the delighted guests, and pyrotechnics provide a shower of sparks from a dozen canisters dotted around the room.

Hanan slaps his future boss on the back and beams out at the guests. Among the females in the closest group to the stage, he spots a few potential conquests; women he would have considered untouchable before his confirmation as Ted's running mate. He has often enjoyed liaisons with the bored partners of his fellow politicians. Many of his peers, male and female, do the same. It's an unofficial club, its members confirmed by a knowing smile. But Hanan has reached the top tier, and is emboldened by the certainty that his sex life, in his seventies, is about to enter an exciting new phase.

The only unsmiling faces belong to the dark-suited men and women of the Secret Service, who treat every rich party donor as a possible assassin, and give the trays of canapes a once over as if they contained tiny grenades. Hanan finds their professional mistrust reassuring.

Grant makes a speech. Hanan makes a speech. Half a dozen notables make speeches while their future leaders work the room. Hanan shakes hundreds of hands, kisses hundreds of cheeks. On half a dozen occasions, his hand slides from the small of someone's back to cup a willing buttock, the last of which belongs to the much younger wife of the Senate majority leader.

He can't remember the last time he was so happy. He thinks about making a move on the owner of one of the buttocks, but decides anticipation will further sweeten the experience. A few months of campaigning remain before the election. In January, he'll move into Number One, Observatory Circle, where he plans on indulging his urges as often as he sees fit. He will need to relieve the stresses of office, after all.

And, he reflects while a nobody from Maryland presses a card into his hand and talks about his daughter's desire to be an intern—*daughters, there'll be daughters, too*—he'll have eight years to enjoy the perks, since only an idiot would bet against Ted Grant being a two-term president. By the time he leaves office, Hanan will be eighty-two. Maybe his libido might do the decent thing and subside at that point. Probably not.

One missed conquest is a little distant this evening. Madeline, always clear about the professional nature of their relationship, doesn't look like thawing any time soon. Quite the opposite. After the phone call yesterday, and Hanan's subsequent move to the Olympus, Ms Kalinsky has been unusually quiet. Half a dozen one-line messages or emails, but she didn't show up in person until an hour before the party.

Madeline is also working the room, coming within nodding distance as she strengthens old alliances and puts in the ground work for new ones. She hides it well, but Hanan can see she's preoccupied. Whatever it is, she's keeping it to herself. He'll call her out on it tomorrow. Tonight is about enjoying the moment, and what a moment it is.

Just when he thinks he couldn't be happier, Madeline Kalinsky catches up with him as he's telling an anecdote from his newspaper days to a small crowd. They're laughing as if they've never met anyone blessed with this much natural wit, and he smiles at their naked attempts to get noticed by the future Vice President. Madeline slips an arm into his.

"I've heard this one before," she says to the fawning guests. "They found the cow in the public library, eating a first edition Robert Frost. My apologies, folks, but I need to borrow the VP."

The ingratiating crowd applauds as she steers him away. They actually *applaud*.

A tiny bit of Hanan's good mood dissipates like a slow leak in a balloon. He anticipates bad news, some criticism of the way he handled someone, or a heads-up about an upcoming problem. He doesn't want to know. Not tonight. She needs to let him savour the moment. Just because she doesn't know how to enjoy herself doesn't mean she should spoil his fun.

Madeline steers Hanan to the quietest part of the room, near one set of swinging double doors through which servers pour with trays full of food and drink, or debris, depending on the direction of travel. Despite their speed, they never collide, hitting the door with their shoulders and spinning into the room beyond.

"Madeline," Hanan begins, before she speaks. Then, when he looks at her, he stops. He's already noticed how great she looks tonight. He'd have to be unconscious not to. Rather than a ballgown, Madeline has opted for the classic black cocktail dress, an item of clothing which hides little of her lithe figure. But, since she's made her unavailability clear, and he needs her political machinations, he keeps his eyes above shoulder level. *Needed,* he reminds himself. He *needed* her machinations. She's done what she set out to do. The White House is in sight. Only if she continues to be useful will he keep her on his staff.

"What is it?" he asks. Her lips are parted, and her eyes are shining. She looks scared or excited. It's hard to tell which, as he's never seen Madeline this way. A strand of dark hair has detached itself from the silver grip at the back of her head, and that single hint of disorder is enough to revive his dormant sexual interest.

Surely not, he thinks.

She leans close. She's wearing perfume. Heady stuff. Another first.

"Robert." Her voice shakes a little. The buzz of the ballroom

300

diminishes to a murmur. He focuses all his attention on her words. "I made the nature of our relationship very clear to you, correct?"

Hanan's mind races. Has he done, or said, something inappropriate? Nothing that he can bring to mind.

"You did, Madeline. You did. I hope I've given you no reason to doubt my intentions. The matter is closed. No need for further discussion."

Madeline leans closer. "I'm afraid that's where you're wrong, Senator."

Hanan is not an unintelligent man, and the breadth of sexual experiences that accompanied his rise to power led to a reputation euphemistically describing him as *worldly*. But with Madeline's lips almost touching his left ear, he's floundering amongst a barrage of mixed signals.

"Wrong how?" he manages, barely breathing.

"A one-time offer," she whispers. "Never to be repeated. But we both deserve to let off some steam tonight, don't you think?"

Hardly daring to believe he's heard correctly, Hanan stands up straight, taking half a step backwards. She holds his gaze, and he sees the anticipation there, the hunger, a sexual urge so naked it could be misinterpreted as anger.

"Are you suggesting..."

"I am," she confirms. "But I'm not risking my reputation."

"And what about mine?"

His attempt at a joke falls flat.

"You're a white man who can trace his ancestors back to the early settlers. I'm a second-generation immigrant from Poland. And I'm a woman. If anyone ever finds out we fucked, my career is over. You'd get a few knowing winks and slaps on the back."

The erotic effect of hearing that Anglo-Saxon word on her lips is negated by the sense of an ephemeral opportunity slipping away, Hanan holds his hands up. "I'm sorry. Bad joke. You're right. We must be discreet." He can actually feel his heart thumping.

Madeline scans the room as if looking for someone.

"I'll leave first," she says without turning. "Give me ten minutes.

Then come find me. Not the suite. Go through the kitchen. There's a service elevator. Take it to the ground floor. Turn right, follow the corridor. I'll be in the laundry room."

Hanan is glad he already has a reason to smile, as he can't prevent the grin that follows her words.

"You've planned this, haven't you? Naughty girl."

She half-turns at that. "One more thing. The two agents assigned to you?"

They're easy to spot. A big blonde guy, back to the wall, watching the room. His boss, the short female agent who had accompanied Hanan in the helicopter, stays in motion, moving through the guests, never more than five or six yards away. The Olympus ballroom is a secure location, swept for bombs and weapons that afternoon. Every guest has been identified and vouched for, but the secret service agents remain alert, suspecting everyone.

"What about them?"

"They'll follow you unless you give them a direct order not to."

"Understood." This close to the White House, he can give orders to the secret service. A taste of power. And Madeline Kalinsky on a plate. Tonight can't get any better.

"Good. Laundry room, alone, ten minutes."

Before leaving, Madeline steps forward, and—for one glorious second—her body presses against his. Then she's gone, weaving through the crowd towards the exit by the stage.

Hanan doesn't waste time. He waves over the female agent, fishes for her name.

"Crawford?"

"Stafford, sir."

"Stafford. I have a private meeting in ten minutes. It's a very sensitive matter. I'll be gone for—" He pictures Madeline Kalinsky, her dress tossed across a laundry sack, waiting. "Shouldn't be more than an hour." The image sharpens in his mind, prompting a re-evaluation. "Probably less."

"Sir." The agent is hard-faced with disapproval. "Our job is to protect you. We can't do that if you—"

"Understood, Crawford. Stafford. But it's not a request, it's an order. I'll be back before you know it. Try one of the shrimps on a stick. They're delicious."

"Not while on duty, sir."

She speaks into her collar as he walks away, and her blonde colleague listens via his earpiece. Neither of them looks happy.

Hanan ducks into the kitchen seven minutes later. No one challenges him as he walks through, and the elevator is waiting, smelling faintly of cabbage. He presses G, and it shudders into life.

He whistles as the numbers blink down to the ground floor. Just for a second, Tyson and Murchen, absent from his thoughts, rise up like vengeful spirits. Tomorrow, he'll call Castle for a progress report. The thought of the black ops killers and the slimy CIA man threatens to spoil his good mood, so he pushes it away. Tonight is about celebration.

Madeline Kalinsky, he thinks as the elevator bumps and settles, the doors shuddering open. *Well, well.*

CHAPTER FIFTY-FOUR

THE LAUNDRY ROOM is easy to find. Hanan checks his watch outside the anonymous white-painted door. Wouldn't do to be early. He waits while the final twenty seconds tick away, then steps inside.

To his disappointment, nothing matches his mental image. The laundry sacks are piled into huge plastic containers on wheels. The room is laid out like a small-town library, with laundry instead of books. Shelves on the left side hold clean bedding, tablecloths, uniforms. To the right, wheeled boxes line up in pairs, like the grid in a motor race.

There's no sign of Madeline, and her dress is conspicuously absent from the nearest pile of dirty laundry.

"Madeline?"

The mystery of the dress is solved when Madeline emerges from behind one row of shelves, still wearing it. She has a phone pressed against her ear, and—when she sees Hanan—her expression proves deflating in every sense.

"What's the matter?" he says.

"I understand." Madeline, speaking into the phone, holds a finger up to stop him. Her hand is shaking. "Of course. Yes, I'll tell him. How long? Of course. Send it to the staff entrance. He'll be there."

She hangs up. Her hand still trembles. She holds the phone between her palms to stop it shaking.

As part of his media-friendly campaign, Hanan visited an elementary school. The TV crew spotted a game of Jenga. They filmed Hanan playing against a cute little girl with a wide gap between her front teeth, and an even wider competitive streak. The clip went viral, particularly Hanan's dramatic wide-eyed gasp at the moment the entire wooden structure wobbled and fell, his fingers still clutching the offending block.

The tipping point, the moment unstoppable events are put into motion. He pictures that pivotal wooden block when Madeline speaks again.

"How well did you know Ruben Castle?"

Did?

"I, er, that is..." Is there any good way to answer? How much does Madeline know? Hanan comes back to that word: *did.* "What happened?"

"Shot dead. Earlier this evening. Potomac Overlook."

"What?" Hanan can't prevent the shock showing on his face. He stumbles, puts his hand flat on the wall for support. Is aware of Madeline watching his reaction. Fights for control. Fumbles for the right way to react. "That's terrible. Give me a second here."

His mind races between possibilities. With Stoppard and Castle dead, where does that leave him? Castle was—discounting himself— the most nakedly ambitious man he'd ever met. Maintaining such a rapid climb to the top of the CIA meant running a tight ship and controlling the flow of information. Castle's rise relied to a large extent on secrets uncovered, leverage exerted. Hanan doubts the deputy director shared the file on Tyson and Murchens' team with many others. It's possible he told no one. If trying to install a compromised Vice President was Castle's solo project, then his death might not be such a disaster. If not, then the tower will fall, and there's not a damned thing Hanan can do about it.

A sense of devil-may-care returns. Hanan recognises this might be down to shock. His libido remembers why he came down here, and he wants nothing more than to pin Madeline against one of those shelves.

He needs to get her mind off what's happened.

"It's a tragedy, Madeline. I'm shocked. Listen." He takes a step closer. "I know it's a cliché, but life is short. We're alive, here, now. And we want each other." Another step closer. She's flushed, breathing fast. "We're alive, Madeline."

Then she pulls out the next wooden block and everything tumbles. She speaks quickly, her eyes on his face.

"It's not just Castle. I've just spoken to the head of the secret service detail. He says there's a credible threat to your life, Robert. Linked to Castle. They've been sent descriptions of two suspects, and they've confirmed that individuals matching those descriptions were seen inside the hotel tonight."

"What?" Hanan can't process the information fast enough. "My life? Two suspects?"

"Yes." Madeline looks into his eyes. She's not shaking anymore, but he barely notices. "A tall African American male, and an older Caucasian female."

"Here?" Hanan's voice is a croak. "In this hotel?"

"Yes."

"Oh, Christ, oh Christ, what the hell am I going to do? They're killers, Madeline. We have to get out. The secret service will take care of it, right? They're the best. Get hold of Crawford. Tell her she needs to shoot on sight, shoot to kill. They won't get a second chance. We have to leave, Madeline."

"Senator."

Hanan is babbling, he knows, but the fear that squeezes his chest tight also loosens his tongue. He can't stop himself from filling the silence with words, as if saying them aloud will bring about the result he desires. He needs Tyson and Murchen finished. They left a pile of corpses as they got closer and closer. Now they're in the building. They've come for him. He needs to leave. Now.

"Madeline, where's your car? Do you have your keys with you? Go get it. You'll be safe, they don't know who you are. I'll hide here until you get back. Don't tell anyone where I am."

Her voice is calm now, in stark contrast to his own wheezing hysteria. All the excitement, the breathless anticipation he'd put down to arousal, is gone.

"Senator."

He's on the brink of hyperventilating. Hanan takes some deeper breaths, keeps his eyes on Madeline's face.

"Madeline, we need to go."

"We will. Or, rather, you will. It's all being taken care of. They're getting you out."

"Oh, thank God."

"They're sending a car. I directed them to the staff entrance. You'll be taken to a safe place until the situation is resolved."

"Right. Thank you. Right. Good."

She heads out of the door and Hanan follows, flinching as he exits as if Tyson or Murchen are lying in wait. There's no one there. The corridor is empty. As he hurries to catch up with Madeline, the raw fear subsides enough for him to review how much he might have revealed by his reaction. It's only days since he swore to Madeline Kalinsky there were no skeletons in his closet, nothing in his past or present that might damage his run. Now, he assumes, she knows he lied.

"Madeline. Madeline, wait up."

She slows her pace a little. He's out of breath, sweating. Thinking fast, reaching for the usual easy half-truths, but they're not there, not when he's jogging down a hotel staff corridor, evading two trained killers. He has a supple, limber intellect, but right when he needs a cogent sentence or two, his synapses fire off into a vacuum. Nothing helpful comes. He improvises.

"Castle warned me about a pair of home-grown terrorists. Antifa. Zealots. Part of a group that, er, that the CIA has monitored for years. They've become more dangerous in the last twelve months, but Castle had to keep it secret because he suspected there was a

Company mole. An inside man. Or woman. I couldn't tell you about it. Need to know basis. I'm sorry, Madeline."

Hanan isn't sure if what he's saying makes much sense. And Madeline's neutral expression gives him no clue as to whether she's buying it. He reaches for something else, some convincer, but there's nothing. He puts a hand on her arm, and that expression is back on her face. Not desire. Anger. Definitely anger. Something else, too. If he was thinking clearly, he'd be able to interpret those signals, but he's floundering.

He's saved by someone banging on the door. He responds with a strangled shriek, side-stepping to put Madeline between him and the threat. She flashes him a look before approaching the door, and its meaning penetrates the fog. It's contempt.

"Senator Hanan? Madeline Kalinsky? Secret service agent Bruce Grayson. We need to get you out."

Madeline opens the heavy door. There's no handle on the outside. A dark-haired agent fills the frame, the familiar curled wire leading from his ear to his jacket. He speaks into his lapel.

"Echo four-oh-five confirming pickup."

An engine idles outside. The big agent steps to one side, motions towards Hanan.

"Senator?"

Hanan hesitates. Now he's with the secret service, some of the fear subsides. Has he convinced Madeline to stay onboard, at least until he comes up with a better story? Her face remains blank.

The agent speaks again.

"Roger that. Picking up the Goose now. Confirmed. Goose safe."

Hanan is still looking at Madeline. "Goose?"

"Code names," she says. "Didn't you know? Everyone under secret service protection gets one. Grant's is Eagle. Yours is Goose."

"Oh."

And that's how they part. From the promise of a sweaty tumble in a pile of laundry to a stony-faced farewell.

It's warm outside, but the air conditioning in the secret service vehicle belts out a cold breeze. The agent closes the door, and the privacy glass presents him with a darkened image of Madeline Kalinsky superimposed on his own sweating face. Her arms are folded. He doesn't look away until the hotel door swings shut.

The car sags as the agent gets in, then they accelerate along the service road and into the late-night Washington traffic.

———

Madeline Kalinsky stares at the door long after Robert Hanan walked out of it. She retraces her steps back to the service elevator, riding it past the ballroom level, back to the floor where she's been given a suite for the night.

The Olympus, along with almost every hotel ever built, conflates status with altitude, meaning the largest, most opulent suites take up the topmost five floors of the building. Advisors, however powerful, are never allocated a room up there. The hierarchical flooring arrangement means Madeline is eight floors below the helipad. Her accommodation—a *junior* suite, as if she might not already have got the message—is bigger than her apartment. The view across to the river, where flashing police and ambulance lights still strobe across Ruben Castle's final resting place, is breathtaking.

It's been a harrowing couple of days. All her ambition, the years of sacrifice, deal-making, sixteen-hour days, weekends spent tweaking her plans to fit changing circumstances, seemed for nothing.

Unless, as Walsingham pointed out at lunch, she took action to prevent the imminent disaster.

Downstairs, the party continues. It'll be hours before the evening winds down, the final drunken stragglers spilling out of the elevator and into their rooms. Dacre has the suite next to hers. A deliberate gesture of respect. He might not like her, but he respects someone who plays the game as well as himself. Better actually, although he doesn't know it yet. The revelations due in the next twenty-four hours, and where all the pieces end up afterwards, may change that.

She pours herself a large vodka, neat, sipping while she looks down at the tiny cars, one of which contains Hanan.

Finally, after eighteen minutes of silence, she speaks.

"Goose cooked."

CHAPTER FIFTY-FIVE

WITH EVERY YARD that opens up between him and the Olympus, Hanan relaxes a little more. The power of coherent thought returns, and he sees that, far from the disaster he feared, the situation remains salvageable.

Castle is dead. That's good news rather than bad. The more he thinks about it, the more Hanan convinces himself Castle had likely kept his blackmail to himself. Yes, he had dirt on Hanan. Proof that a prospective US Senator had paid for a rival to be killed. If that evidence turns up in Castle's effects, it will doubtless damage Hanan's career. However, it might not ruin it. Not now. Not after his confirmation as Ted Grant's running mate. Ross Dacre is far too experienced a strategist to allow his choice for vice president to be exposed as a liar, a cheat, and a murderer. He'll lean on the CIA, they'll make a deal, and it'll go away. Instead of answering to Castle in his tenure at the White House, Hanan will answer to Dacre.

"The more things change, the more they stay the same."

"Did you say something, Senator?"

The dark-haired agent has an accent he can't place.

"Just thinking aloud. It's a French expression." He repeats it. He doubts the young man understands or cares, but the agent nods politely.

"You're probably right, sir."

Hanan looks out of the window. He expects them to head out of town, but they've circled around the centre of Washington, crossing the Potomac once, and now recrossing it across the Fourteenth Street bridge.

"Where we heading, son?"

"A safe house, sir."

"Where?"

"I'm not allowed to say, Senator. It's for your own protection."

The agent looks at his watch, hangs a left. The traffic, even this late, is heavier around the tourist spots.

Hanan looks around the interior of the car. Bland, big, and anonymous. Leather seats, plenty of space. Black, privacy glass, anonymous. Exactly what he'd expect from a secret service car. Multiple antennae on the roof. But when he leans to one side, he can only see a CD player.

He frowns. Something else odd.

"Aren't you guys always in pairs? Like penguins?"

"Yes, sir."

A moment of doubt. Nothing serious. They needed him out in a hurry. Maybe this guy's partner was taking a leak.

"We're picking up my colleague before going to the safe house, sir."

"Ah. Good." Hanan sits back, satisfied. After the events of the past hour, he allows himself the latitude to be paranoid. The fear won't dissipate until he sees photographs of Tyson and Murchens' corpses.

"Any news from the hotel? About the terrorists, or whatever they are?"

"Officially, Senator, no. Nothing yet."

Hanan leans out again. "Unofficially, then."

"Well, sir..." The dark-haired man taps his earpiece. "I've been listening to the chatter."

"And?"

In the rear-view mirror, a pair of dark green eyes lock onto Hanan's. For no good reason, his stomach clenches and the terror-fuelled adrenaline, receding since he left the Olympus, returns in a horrible rush, made worse by the fact he can find no reason for it. Looking into the driver's eyes bypasses millennia of conditioning and triggers a survival instinct buried so deeply Hanan didn't know it existed. This instinct sends a barrage of messages to his brain demanding he run away, escape by whatever means, throw himself out of this moving car if necessary; anything rather than spend another millisecond in the company of the creature whose predatory gaze pins him to his seat.

Then the moment passes, and Hanan's higher brain functions come back online, damming the torrent of emotions, reintroducing a rational narrative to his crazed consciousness.

It's a secret service agent. One of the good guys.

He forces himself to break contact. When, heart hammering, he looks back again, the young man winks. He's singing to himself. Not a song Hanan's familiar with. The odd phrase is clear enough to make out over the noise of the engine. Something about Satan's kitchen, and murdering giants.

When the car slows, pulling over to the kerb, the sweat droplets are glistening on Hanan's forehead, pushed along his skin by the freezing air still blowing from the vent. He puts his shivering down to the ambient temperature.

A dark shape outside. The door opens. Not the front passenger door. A big man slides onto the seat next to Hanan. The car pulls away, the central locking snicking back into place.

"Hello, Senator. I've been looking for you, trying to find you, hunting you down. And here you are, in person, so it's me and you, mano-a-mano, just the two of us, at last."

Hanan doesn't want to turn, doesn't want to look, but he does it anyway. Strangely, when he does, the terror gives way to something else. A kind of placid calm. An acceptance of the inevitable.

"Hello, Mr Tyson," he says.

CHAPTER FIFTY-SIX

Mrs Henrietta Burton is weary, footsore, and content. She figures she's walked three miles today, and her joints ache. Her knees hurt the most, although her lower back has joined the chorus of complaints, offering little jolts of pain unless she sits up as straight as a child at first communion.

The bench faces Lafayette Park and, beyond it, the White House. Henrietta's eyes are damp as she faces the most famous building in America. Always promised herself she would come see it one day. Took eighty-seven years to make good on that promise.

She drinks water from the metal flask she bought for the trip. It keeps the water cold all day somehow. Henrietta wishes she'd bought the flask back home, instead of in the city. Six dollars is daylight robbery, but the doctor warned her to keep up her fluid intake, and she won't throw away money on plastic bottles full of water she can get for free in her hotel room, no sir.

Her right knee is the worst offender. She stretches it out, holds it for a count of ten. Right up until she retired from teaching, she walked the three miles to school and back again before making Matthew's supper. Now she can't even take a gentle stroll without her legs threatening to seize up.

The thought of Matthew makes her smile. He'd promised to take her to Washington, never laughing at her dream, never suggesting they save up for something more exotic, or use the money for a new pickup truck. They used to lie in bed and talk about the day they'd sit on the steps of Congress, eating ice cream. She'd done just that yesterday afternoon.

She remembers the other promise he'd made, which had reduced her to fits of giggles in the old iron double bed that had belonged to his parents.

"I'll call ahead," Matthew had said, his hand stroking her hair, fingers lost in her tight curls. "Speak to the White House staff. Explain who's coming to town. They'll roll out the red carpet for you, Henny. I expect the President will insist on meeting you."

"He'll insist, will he?"

"I reckon so."

"And I reckon you're a fool, husband."

"You knew that before you married me, woman."

"Well, I didn't marry you for your intellect, Matthew Burton. I was only after your money."

They both laughed at that. Henrietta had almost drifted off to sleep when Matthew spoke again, his voice soft at her ear.

"You're right, though. The President is a busy man. He won't meet you personally."

"No?"

"No. I reckon he'll send the Vice President."

Henrietta smiles, then blushes a little when she remembers what followed that conversation. She looks out across the beautifully maintained park towards the White House. The building is brightly lit, and Henrietta wonders how the President can get to sleep when his home is constantly illuminated. If his bedroom is this side, his drapes must be a sight heavier than the muslin hanging at her own windows. She lives in a one-room apartment across from the school where she taught history for fifty years. It was all she could afford after selling the smallholding she and Matthew had worked all their married life.

315

She dabs her eyes again. Matthew would have loved this. Not because he'd yearned to visit the way she had, but because her dreams meant more to him than his own. The man was no saint, but he did love to see her happy. She'd been unsurprised, but still profoundly moved, when the letter arrived from the insurance company a month after Matthew's death with a cheque for six hundred dollars from a policy called *Washington Trip*.

That was twelve years ago. It wasn't until Henrietta woke one morning a week back, with her heart fluttering in her chest like a trapped bird, that she picked up the telephone to book the vacation. It felt like a betrayal, taking the trip without him. Now she's here, Henrietta admits she was a fool to wait.

When she checks her watch, eleven o'clock has come and gone. If she doesn't get her old bones moving soon, she might not get up at all.

Henrietta stands, hissing out a long breath as every muscle, tendon, joint, and bone from her hips south conspires to pitch her onto her butt. Steadying herself, she shuffles along the length of the bench hand over hand like an infant gaining confidence before its first steps.

Just as she prepares to tackle the three-block walk to the hotel, a black car pulls up, disgorging two men from the back seats. The first of them, big, dressed in dark clothes, a baseball cap pulled low, is talking to the second man, who's wearing a tuxedo. He's old, white, frail. The first man guides the second over to a tree on the sidewalk. They hug. The younger man lowers his companion to the concrete.

When the car leaves, Henrietta starts the fifteen-yard trip to the older man, sitting with his back against the tree, looking right at her. Her legs and her hips may be past their best, and her hearing has deteriorated to the extent that she had to stand under the loudspeaker at the train station, but her eyesight is still twenty-twenty. And she recognises the man in the tuxedo. She saw his picture on the television that morning. At eighty-seven years old, getting dressed and dabbing on a bit of foundation takes so long, Henrietta caught two news cycles, the weather reports, and half an episode of Cheers before getting out of her room.

Somehow, Matthew had kept his promise. Or as good as makes no difference. The man she's looking at—sitting legs splayed, a wine spill on his white shirt—will be, unless something catastrophic occurs to prevent it, the next Vice President.

She's covered half the distance when she asks herself why one of the country's most prominent politicians is sitting on the sidewalk late Friday night. Then she realises the stain spreading across Senator Robert Hanan's chest is too dark for wine. Her smile falters. Closer still, and it's clear he's not looking at her at all. He's looking past her, past the benches, past the lawns and the statues. He's looking at the White House.

A yard away and she can hear him; the laboured, gasping, wet breaths. A young couple stop and stare. The woman looks once, then away, then back again. She screams. Her companion takes out his cell phone, yells, "I'm calling nine-one-one," as if it's necessary to announce it. The young woman takes out her own phone, holding it in front of her like a talisman warding off evil. Henrietta blinks in shock when she sees what is really happening: the young woman is filming the bleeding Senator.

"Stop that immediately," she snaps. The woman responds to her schoolmarm authority, shoving the phone back into her purse.

Henrietta puts one hand on the trunk of the tree to prevent an undignified and painful fall, leans over the dying man.

"Help is on its way."

He doesn't respond. She can't risk bending further, but she puts her hand on the side of his face, stroking it like a mother comforting a child. She looks at the wound once, then wishes she hadn't. There's so much blood. The front of his shirt is soaked in it, and his pants are wet through. Between his legs, the sidewalk is glistening crimson under the street lamp, a ripple pushing outward with every fresh gush of blood from the hole in his chest. The ripples are slowing.

He's saying something, Henrietta realises, and tilts her head so her ear is directly towards the man's mouth. It's just one word, the last word Robert Hanan will ever utter, and Henrietta Burton is the only person who hears it.

"Almost."

CHAPTER FIFTY-SEVEN

THE ANONYMOUS BLACK sedan pulls over half a mile before reaching Dulles Airport, stopping alongside a faded green Toyota behind a shuttered and dark insurance office. Tyson unscrews and replaces the number plates, tossing the old ones in the trunk alongside a shotgun and his sniper rifle. He unstraps his knife—still bloody—and drops it alongside everything else. Then he pulls out a canvas bag and unpacks its contents.

"Bluey. Your turn."

Jimmy joins him, shrugging off his jacket and holster and laying them alongside Tyson's weapons.

"They'll find something," says Blue. "A fingerprint, DNA. You're on record."

Tyson hands his companion a pile of new clothes. Canvas trousers, white shirt, a suede jacket. They dress quickly, throwing their old clothes in with the rest of their gear.

"By the time they find this, we'll have blown town, long gone."

He puts on a pair of wire-framed glasses and a purple beret. Blue stares.

"You look like a music producer who got trapped in the nineties. Or a movie director."

"Go ahead, laugh it up all you like," says Tyson, smoothing his headwear down, ignoring the fact Jimmy never laughs, "but this is subterfuge one-oh-one. Hiding in plain sight. What's anyone gonna see? A black guy in a purple beret. Maybe they'll notice the glasses. Nothing else, nada. I'm invisible, Bluey."

The Toyota's key is in a hollow plastic rock under the rear wheel. Tyson tosses it to Jimmy.

"Drop me at the Ramada, then go find some corporate hellhole of an airport hotel and have yourself a drink. You have a few hours to kill."

Blue turns the key. Puts the car into drive. Keeps his foot on the brake. Doesn't turn the headlamps on. Tyson swivels in his seat.

"You worried they gonna catch me, Bluey? That it?"

Blue doesn't answer.

"Roach has me covered. New ID in Chicago, then I'm leaving the country, taking off, not looking back. You sure you don't want half the money? It was the CIA's, so it's not like you're stealing it from anyone who needs it."

"Where will you go?"

"Someplace warm, I guess. Someplace quiet, no noise, not so many people. I got a lot to deal with, Bluey. Time I made a start. Never tried to live a regular life before. Might work. Don't think so, never really tried. Gotta try. For Kai, right? For Kai."

The car trickles forward. Tyson puts a hand on Jimmy's arm.

"What about you? You're young, Bluey. Still a kid. You got skills, sure, you're badass, a killer. That what you want? Is it worth it? You think? Gonna end up dead. Or gonna end up a crazy addict, talking to yourself, living like a bum. You can still walk away, make a choice, take a different path."

The atmosphere in the car changes so fast Tyson wonders if he's having a stroke. His skin prickles, the fine hairs on the back on the back of his neck peel away from his skin. His balls shrink to beads. He lifts his hand as the man beside him becomes still. Tyson is acutely aware that all his weapons are locked in the sedan's trunk.

Connor Tyson has met his share of killers, done enough of it himself. Some of them enjoyed their work, got a kick out of ending the life of a fellow human being. It's not business for them, it's their passion. If they weren't getting paid, they'd do it anyway. But this is something else. The rage in the huge man next to him goes so deep, there are no adequate words to describe it. He and the bald man with the dark wig might be on the same side, but right now he would give every cent of Castle's money to be out of this car and on a plane heading anywhere, as long as it's away from Jimmy Blue.

Blue flicks on the lights, and the Toyota accelerates out onto the highway. Tyson flashes a look at the driver. The moment has passed, the paralysing sense of danger has lifted as if he imagined it.

He doesn't ask any more questions.

———

Blue drinks in silence, sitting on a chair that looked comfortable but isn't. Bottled beer, bourbon chasers. A few night owls and a handful of coffee-slurping early-risers dot the hangar-like hotel lounge, which is broken into sections by rows of potted ferns as rumpled and tired as the guests.

With ninety minutes remaining before his flight to Los Angeles, he settles the tab and boards a shuttle bus for the airport. He uses the Tom Kincaid passport to go through security. He'll swap it out for Tom Lewis when he books his London flight at LAX.

Walking to his departure gate, Blue sees Tyson joining a line waiting to board a flight to O'Hare. He watches the purple beret until Tyson disappears through the gate. Then he follows the signs for gate C17, Los Angeles.

He'll be back in London tomorrow. Time to start the real work.

CHAPTER FIFTY-EIGHT

FOUR MONTHS later
London

Tom Lewis eats a bacon sandwich, punctuating each bite with a slurp of tea from a chipped mug. Every table behind the small cafe's steamed-up windows is occupied. The men; loud, quick to laugh, big, fast-talking, hair full of concrete dust, consume sandwiches, rolls, all-day breakfasts, and mugs of sweet tea as fast as the owner and her daughter can bring them. Some of the flirtatious comments border on being crude. Tom blushes, watches the television above the counter.

He's been with this crew eleven weeks, moving from job to job. This is the second site he's worked on, carrying bricks as the foundations of a big new house take shape. They're supervised by Werner, the boss, who hand-picked each of them. The pay is better than Tom is used to, and the men, although loud, rough, and plain-talking, treat him well. Rather than mocking him, they call Tom their mascot, says he brings them good luck. They praise his strength as he hefts stacks of bricks onto his hod.

"You a fan of the US political system, Tom?" Rocco, a small, sallow bricklayer whose precision and speed with a pointing trowel is legendary, points a fork-impaled sausage at the screen. Tom, who wasn't paying attention, focuses on it now. People in suits shaking hands, fireworks going off, streamers and balloons. A smiling man standing on a podium alongside an older woman, his arm around her shoulder.

"I mean, it's interesting up to a point, don't get me wrong." Rocco is still waving the sausage. "But—considering how America likes to boast about their bleedin' democracy to anyone who'll listen—their electoral college system leaves a lot to be desired, don't ya think?"

Tom squints at the small television. Not at the man and the woman. At the small group behind them, also smiling, also hugging, and shaking hands. One of them, a tall brown-haired woman in a dark suit, holds his attention, although he doesn't know why. He stares while the woman in the foreground waves her forward, hugs her, leans over to say something. The familiar woman steps back, folds her arms, and it's that gesture that convinces Tom he's met her, although it makes little sense. How could he know someone on television?

"So this is the new president, right, but he only needed to convince a few swing states to vote his way. A few swing states with more electoral college votes than other, bigger states. It all goes back to the confederacy, you know. Hardly democracy, is it? Eh, Tom? Hardly democracy, is it?"

Rocco often peppers his monologues with questions that require no response, but he pauses this time, putting the sausage in his mouth. Tom nods, not following at all.

"Mm."

"That's right, pal. You said it. Hit the nail on the head. You're quite the perspicacious observer of modern politics. That's why I like you."

"Mm," said Tom again. He remembers the woman standing, arms folded, as a door closed in front of her. Another fragment from the missing months in America.

Then a photograph of an old man fills the screen, and Tom wishes the volume was up, because he knows him too.

Rocco has almost finished chewing, He spits fragments of meat while he pokes his fork into a fried potato.

"And what about that geezer? You telling me some random loon knifed him, cos I ain't buying it. Murdered on the night they threw a party to celebrate his announcement as Grant's running mate? Coincidence? I don't think so. Five minutes poking around online, and you'll find plenty who say different. Some of them are conspiracy nutters, granted, but are you seriously saying some mentalist got Robert Hanan away from a swanky party, out into the street, and stuck a knife in him, all without the secret service even noticing he'd gone? Do me a favour. I reckon they did it themselves. Or the NSA, maybe the CIA. What do you think, Tom? Inside job?"

Tom picks up the other half of his sandwich. The food is tasty, he has a good job, the bedsit he's renting is warm and there's a skylight so he can lie in bed and look at the stars. He doesn't want to think about America, where he dreamed he was drowning, then woke up on an aeroplane circling Heathrow.

He lifts the sandwich to his mouth. Rocco puts a hand on his wrist.

"Better bring that back to the site with you, mate."

Tom looks around. The cafe is nearly empty, the bell over the door jangling as the last of the crew leaves.

Rocco stands, zips up his jacket. "Can't stay in here all day talking politics, Tom. Honestly, pal, once you get going, it's impossible to shut you up, ain't it?"

Tom follows Rocco out into the cold air. It's a ten-minute walk to the site just outside Elstree. His breath puffs out clouds of steam, and he keeps his eyes on the pavement under his boots, wary of icy patches. Although he doesn't want to remember, doesn't like the confusion that arises along with the dreamlike memories, he can't stop another face forming. Another woman, older, white hair cut very short. Pale grey eyes that see everything.

Kai. He liked her. They walked together. There's a calmness attached to those memories, a sense of grounding, and of peace.

She told him something important, or—rather—made something clear to him. Unlike many of his memories, this hasn't faded, although there are no details, nothing solid, or specific, to latch onto.

Tom is still thinking about it as he puts on his hard hat, loads the afternoon's first hod-full of bricks, carries it across the site to Barry and Rocco.

Kai had spoken about a choice. A choice Tom alone could make. That much he can remember. But nothing else. Whatever the choice was, he hopes it wasn't important, because it's gone.

ALSO BY IAN W. SAINSBURY

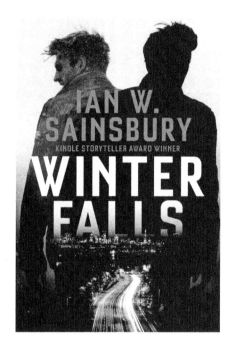

fusebooks.com/winterfalls

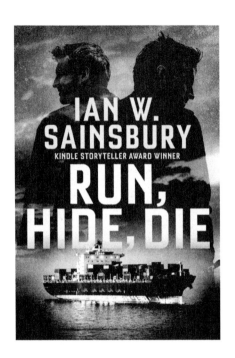

fusebooks.com/runhidedie

AUTHOR'S NOTE

I've loved telling the story of Tom Lewis's revenge. I've already written three Jimmy Blue novels. And I know there will be more to come.

Please leave a review if you can—it makes a big difference.

If you haven't signed up for your free Jimmy Blue story yet (and the occasional email from me), you can find it here:

fusebooks.com/ian

I have a website imaginatively named after myself, and I can be found in the usual social media places. I don't post photos of my dinner there, I promise.

Thanks for reading,

Ian

Norwich, 2021

Printed in Great Britain
by Amazon

17516991R00193